"WHEN A MAN KISSES YOU, DO YOU CONTINUE TO PRATTLE?"

"I haven't kissed enough men to know, only two—if you count the boy who dared to corner me when I was ten, but he went home with a bloody nose, though I wouldn't bloody *your* nose if you kissed me."

She fell silent and stared at his sensual mouth, craving his kiss. She closed her eyes to better savor the moment, the delectable impression of herself as a flower blooming under a scorching sun.

"Sarah," he whispered. "You're so tempting. And quiet now. Your unruly tongue appears to behave when I put my hands on you. Is it a momentary occurrence, or will it happen every time?"

"Why don't you kiss me and find out?"

HEART'S HONOR

SUSAN WELDON

AVON BOOKS ◆ NEW YORK

**To Donald Carey, a hero in every sense of the word.
Though you never say much,
all the women in your life love you dearly.
Thanks for always being there, Dad.**

HEART'S HONOR is an original publication of Avon Books. This work has never before appeared in book form. This work is a novel. Any similarity to actual persons or events is purely coincidental.

AVON BOOKS
A division of
The Hearst Corporation
1350 Avenue of the Americas
New York, New York 10019

First Avon Books Printing: October 1995

AVON TRADEMARK REG. U.S. PAT. OFF. AND IN OTHER COUNTRIES, MARCA REGISTRADA, HECHO EN U.S.A.

Printed in the U.S.A.

RA 10 9 8 7 6 5 4 3 2 1

Prologue

England, 1869

A heavy fog lay over the grove as Brendan Hammond, earl of Warwick, checked his dueling pistol. The damp morning air suited his morose mood. In a few minutes he might just be on his way to meet his Maker, he thought.

"It's not too late to call it off."

Brendan glanced at his second, John Wettersby, and replied, "It's a matter of honor, and the least I owe him."

"Lord Ashley's a dead shot." Wettersby sneezed, and promptly wiped his nose. "This damnable weather is bad for one's health. But then, one could say the same about challenging Ashley. His wife is a tasty morsel, though not worth forfeiting your life over."

"I didn't challenge Ashley. He challenged *me*." A church tower chimed the hour as a black curricle swung around the bend. Brendan watched the vehicle come to a standstill. "Would you have me labeled a coward?"

" 'Tis a devilish choice you have—coward or murderer. I'm glad it's not up to me. Shoot to kill, or say your prayers. Either way, you'll have to leave England."

1

Brendan scowled. "I'm not one for praying, not with my black soul. It'll be murder. I'll not stand target for any man."

Wettersby blew his nose. "I suppose it was bound to happen. You've cut a swath through the female population of London and come out unscathed until now. Pity Ashley chanced to come home early."

"Pity, indeed."

Brendan's attention drifted back to the vehicle, to the man dressed in black. Lord Ashley's reputation preceded him. And even through the dense fog, Brendan sensed the man's hostility. When another figure appeared beside Ashley, Brendan sucked in a harsh breath. Damn her. Leave it to Mariette to want to witness a duel. He wondered if she planned to shed a tear, and, if so, for whom.

Wettersby checked his watch, then followed Brendan's gaze. "He's taking his position. For God's sake, remember my words. The second you see the handkerchief drop, stand sideways. No sense giving him more to aim at than necessary."

Shifting the pistol to his right hand, Brendan squeezed the other man's shoulder. "I'll be leaving as soon as this travesty is finished. You've been a good friend, John." Brendan tucked an envelope into Wettersby's coat pocket. "If I die, follow the instructions in here."

"You're as good a shot as Ashley, and you have a distinct advantage. You're as cool-headed as they come." He dabbed at his nose again and sniffed. "He's still fuming and won't take the time to aim as he should."

The following minutes passed slowly. Brendan thought back on his life. Other than his vast wealth, he had nothing worthwhile to leave behind. He wished he had taken the time to marry and sire an heir. Had the occasion not been so somber, he would have laughed. It was better he'd remained single. If he survived this morning, he'd be called a murderer, and any family he might have had would have suffered consequences.

He spotted Lord Ashley holding his pistol ready. The silence became deafening. Then, taking Brendan off-guard, the handkerchief dropped. Ashley brought his arm up. Brendan reacted instinctively. Swinging sideways, he brought up his own arm and fired.

Seconds passed before Brendan realized he was unharmed. But Ashley seemed unbalanced; he staggered and dropped to his knees.

A piercing scream echoed in the grove. However, Mariette Ashley didn't do as Brendan expected. She ran to *him*, not her husband.

She threw her arms around Brendan's neck and sobbed freely. "You haven't killed him. He lives still. Shoot him again, oh, please."

Only then did Brendan notice the other vehicle parked to the side. The doctor. The small, gray-haired man hurried to Ashley and bent over him. Disgust coursed through Brendan. He pulled Mariette's arms from around his neck and shoved her aside. Breaking into a run, he reached the fallen man as the doctor came to his feet.

"He's gone," the doctor said. "Shot through the heart."

Someone grabbed Brendan's arm and clung to it.

"Brendan, did you hear? He's dead. We're free of him now."

Shaking his arm free, Brendan stared at the woman he'd called his lover for the past three months. She was a stranger, a coldhearted bitch. He pushed her forward so she had no choice but to see her husband's lifeless form on the ground. "Haven't you one tear to shed for him?"

She threw herself at Brendan again. "It's you I love. I did this for you, let it slip that I had a lover. And I knew you could not be bested in anything by the likes of him." She clutched at his lapels. "You can't leave me. Whatever shall I do?"

"I daresay you'll find someone to replace me soon enough."

Brendan lurched away and headed across the grove to his waiting carriage. His life as he'd known it had just come to an abrupt end. In the distance Mariette Ashley's wails reminded him of a screeching cat. Releasing a vile oath, he slid the pistol inside his waistcoat. He wouldn't miss her. But, bloody hell, he'd miss England.

Chapter 1

Missouri, 1870

Sarah Stevens stepped hesitantly onto the stone steps of the impressive, brick town house in Lafayette Square. Tall, wood-paneled doors loomed above her. She shouldn't have come, she thought. A girl from Georgia had no place in a big city like St. Louis.

But a sharp kick from inside her swollen belly reminded her of the reason she'd braved a thunderstorm to find the residence of Brendan Hammond.

Although the rain had dwindled to a fine mist, the damp, bracing air penetrated several layers of clothing, chilling her to the bone. She dropped her worn traveling bag, pulled her soggy shawl from her shoulders, and held it to cover her advanced pregnancy. Brendan would be surprised enough that she'd found him.

Fortifying herself with a deep breath, she knocked, but before she could rehearse what she planned to say, one of the massive doors swung open. A man with thinning gray hair and wearing an immaculate, long-tailed coat looked her up and down. She decided the starched white collar pinching the folds of his neck must be the cause of his pained expression.

He focused his aloof brown eyes over the top of her head. "If it's a handout you want, miss, kindly go to the back."

Sarah stiffened. Her situation might have been desperate, but she was no beggar. She stood straight, as her well-born mother had taught her, and said, "Sir, it's not charity I want. I've come to see Brendan Hammond. Is he at home?"

"Mr. Hammond did not mention he expected a young lady."

"He's *not* expectin' me. If you tell him Sarah Stevens is here—"

The door banged shut. Hugging her arms around herself, she shivered. If this was the hospitality to be found in a big city, she would take her father's farm any day. There, a visitor was welcomed and made to feel at home. When Brendan's horse had gone lame, her family had graciously taken him in. Heat climbed up her neck. *She* had done much more than welcome him. She'd given him her heart, her innocence, and a month from now she would give him a child.

A horrendous rattle came from nowhere and grew even louder. Sarah turned as a carriage careened down the street. The wheels cut through a wide puddle, soaking her with a sheet of water. Despair welled in her heart. Somehow she must see Brendan. How else could she make him accept responsibility for his child?

Brendan's hazel eyes and black hair came to her mind. He'd been so easy to like, with his friendly, coaxing manner, that she hadn't realized she was being beguiled until it was too late.

Sarah glanced down and frowned. She must look even worse now, with her hair and clothes dripping. She was tempted to put off their meeting until the morrow, but her funds were nearly gone and she had nowhere else to go. She considered the leaded-glass panels on either side of the entrance. This impressive house was nothing at all like her family's small farmhouse. Steeling herself, she took a deep breath and knocked on the door again.

She wasn't about to give the servant another chance to shut her out. The instant the door opened, she promptly wedged her traveling bag into the space. Taken off-guard, the man stepped back, and Sarah snatched her opportunity. She ducked under his arm and slipped inside.

"See here, miss, this is highly irregular!" The man seized her arm and ushered her toward the threshold. "I must insist that you remove yourself from these premises at once."

"Not before I speak to Mr. Hammond," she managed to say as she tried to wrench her arm from his grasp. Coated with mud, her heels skidded on the polished, inlaid wood of the floor. She braced a hand on the mahogany wainscoting on the lower, inside wall and caught her breath. "If you . . . will . . . just let me explain."

His fingers dug into her arm. Pain shot to Sarah's shoulder, refueling her strength. She pushed herself away from the wall, twisted around, and, not knowing what else to do, pinched his nose. The man released a snort that rivaled one from Wallace, her father's prize hog.

"I'm sorry," she said contritely, "but you left me no choice."

Sarah draped the shawl over her stomach again and inched along the elegant entrance hall, vaguely aware of the heavily patterned ox-blood wallpaper and a huge coat-tree with twisted branches. The grandfather clock in one corner chimed, giving her a start. The strong odor of furniture polish filled the air with the scent of turpentine, linseed oil, and vinegar.

"Stratford! What's that ungodly commotion?"

Sarah turned at the feminine voice and the rustle of skirts. A well-dressed woman of about fifty stood a few feet away. She bore a resemblance to Brendan, except for the streaks of gray at her temples. Many strands of pearls were wound around her neck, but it was the billowing, dark maroon silk dress that captured Sarah's attention. She longed to run her hands over the wondrous material.

Reclaiming his dignity, the servant tugged at his slightly crooked vest. "Begging your pardon, madam, but this young lady insists upon seeing Lord Warwick."

Her eyes as wide as saucers, Sarah gasped. *"Lord Warwick?* It's Brendan Hammond I asked for."

The lady favored Sarah with a sweet smile. "In England my nephew has the distinction of being a member of the peerage. I hope you won't hold Stratford's behavior against him. His devotion to duty is admirable, though oftentimes he oversteps his bounds." She looked Sarah over, then waved a bejeweled hand at the servant. "Have Mathilda serve tea in the study."

"But madam—"

"And don't dawdle!"

Giving a sniff, Stratford held his head high and slowly walked down the hall.

The minute he was out of sight, the lady said to Sarah, "And now, my dear, perhaps you'd like to explain how you know my nephew." She pushed open doors that slid back into the walls, swept into a paneled room filled with leather-bound books, and then pointed to the leather chair behind a mahogany desk. "Sit down, please. You look ready to collapse."

Sarah sank into the welcoming folds of the massive chair with a weary sigh. She waited while the lady closed the doors, before she spoke. "My name is Sarah Stevens, and I come from Georgia. My family lives on the outskirts of Atlanta." Clearing her dry throat, she weighed her words carefully. "Your nephew is . . . he's the . . . I met him and—"

"First things first," the older woman said. "I'm Mrs. Gertrude March Chauteaus.

Wouldn't you like to remove some of your wet things?"

Sarah clutched the shawl tightly against her.

Mrs. Chauteaus came around the desk and held out her hand. "You'll catch your death, and I'll feel responsible. You wouldn't want that, would you?"

"No, ma'am, but there's somethin' I must tell you."

"Nonsense, child. Nothing can be *that* urgent."

"Oh, but it is." Seeing Brendan's aunt meant business, Sarah lowered her eyes and surrendered the shawl.

"Saints above! Why, you're about to give birth."

"Not for another month," Sarah muttered. Color rode high on her cheeks. Her gaze still lowered, she told Mrs. Chauteaus how she'd met Brendan and been instantly caught under his spell. "I waited as long as I dared. I wasn't showin' then, but I knew I would soon. I couldn't allow my family to share my disgrace. I told them Brendan had written to me and wanted me to come to him so that we could marry. At first my plan was to live in some small town until the baby came, then find employment."

Sarah inhaled a fortifying breath before she rambled on in a faltering voice. "Mama and Papa were so understanding, but I suspect they realized they had no other choice. Papa hasn't much, but he insisted on givin' me money to see me through until I reached Brendan. But it's hard for a woman alone, especially in a town where you don't know anybody. I worried the baby would suffer, so I came here."

Sarah looked up. "I think Brendan should at least give his child his name. I don't ask anything for myself, Mrs. Chatoo."

A faint smile briefly played over the lady's mouth. "Call me Gertrude. It'll be easier." Reaching for a gleaming decanter, she sloshed brandy into a glass and drank it down. "Your parents won't worry that you've come to harm?"

"Mama has trained me to be self-reliant, and in some ways I'm too much like my father. If it weren't for the child, I'd manage somehow."

"I do believe you would," Gertrude said with a smile. "Are you absolutely positive the man's name was *Brendan* Hammond?"

"Yes, ma'am. He said he was from St. Louis. He bragged about his house. His willingness to give me the exact address convinced me he was sincere."

A soft knock on the door prevented Gertrude from replying. After a plump, cheery woman deposited a tray on the desk and swiftly left with the damp shawl, Gertrude filled a cup with tea. She laced it with brandy before she set it in front of Sarah. "Drink this. It may warm you up a bit."

Sarah never thought to argue. She sipped the strong brew, savoring the heat that warmed her from the inside out.

"Have you any proof of the man's identity?

A letter, perhaps? A token he might have given you?''

Sarah fumbled with the top button of her dress, then withdrew the chain that she wore over her heart. "He gave me this. He said it was old.''

Color fled Gertrude's face as she caught the gold locket in her hand. "*Old*," she repeated in a stilted voice. "I should say! That locket is a family heirloom. May I borrow it awhile? I promise to return it.''

Sarah unfastened the chain and handed it to Gertrude. Then, reaching into a hidden pocket in her skirt, she brought out a crumpled piece of paper. "I have a letter, too. Brendan left it for me. In it he says he loves me, two times, and apologizes for taking my innocence. He promises to return and marry me when he makes his fortune." Sarah swallowed and lifted her chin. "He also thanks me for a memorable interlude, stressing he'll always cherish the moments we shared. You can read it if you want.''

Her brows knitting together, Gertrude snatched the paper and quickly scanned it. Her face took on an ashen appearance.

"Can I see Brendan now?''

"Unfortunately, he's out for the afternoon.'' Gertrude turned the locket in her hand, finally closing her fingers over it. "You were truly innocent?''

As Sarah nodded again, she blushed to the roots of her hair. "Mama told me a man knows those things.''

"Describe him to me.''

Sarah grew extremely uncomfortable under Gertrude's piercing gaze but, suspecting the lady's motives, she complied with her wishes. "Dark hair and hazel eyes, like you. He was very handsome and personable and—"

"Persuasive?"

"Yes, ma'am."

"How old would you say he was?"

"About twenty-four or so, I'd guess." Gertrude's stricken look worried Sarah. "Is somethin' wrong?"

"And you're *absolutely* sure he gave you the name of *Brendan* Hammond?"

Startled by the woman's adamant tone, Sarah snapped, "I'm not lying!" Then, embarrassed by her harsh response, she said softly, "I know what I heard. Do you doubt me?"

A faint smile tugging at her mouth, Gertrude said, "My, my, beneath your bedraggled appearance, you do have gumption. You'll have need of it when I introduce you to my nephew."

"Introduce me? But I already know him."

"Of course you do, dear." Catching a fold of her magnificent dress, Gertrude marched to the door and pulled on a braided rope. "After you've eaten, bathed, and rested, you'll feel better. Then we'll see what's to be done about your unfortunate . . . situation."

Brendan Cyril Hammond alighted from his richly appointed carriage and strode to his Park Avenue residence. When the door opened at the precise moment of his arrival, he smiled his approval. Stratford always anticipated his needs. Brendan shrugged out of his coat, removed his hat and gloves, then handed them and his walking stick to the butler.

Chancing to look down, he scowled at the footprints marring the floor. "Would you care to explain why there is mud in the entry hall?"

Stratford averted his gaze. "'Twas the young lady, Your Grace."

"Young lady? I know of no woman here who would make an unannounced call."

"Precisely, sir. She was quite insistent."

"And don't call me Your Grace. We are no longer in England."

"I'm sorry, sir. It slips my mind."

Brendan narrowed his eyes on Stratford's pale face. "I gather you failed to discourage this woman?" Looking more closely at the man, he noticed something peculiar. "What the devil is wrong with your nose, man? It's as red as a cherry."

Stratford's complexion grew brighter. He held his head a degree higher. "As I said, sir, she was quite insistent. Your aunt may be able to shed more light on the matter. She is waiting to speak with you."

"My aunt? What the bloody hell has she to do with this?"

"Madam took the young lady into your study. Shortly thereafter, she invited her to remain."

Brendan raked his fingers through his hair. "Do you mean to tell me that this woman is still here?"

Stratford coughed, then said, "In the guest quarters. If you don't mind my saying so, sir, she was quite the worse for wear."

"Have this mess removed immediately." His jaw taut with annoyance, Brendan strode purposefully across the hall. He threw open the pocket doors so abruptly, they rattled in the walls.

His aunt, who had been sitting in a wing chair, quickly rose to fill a snifter with brandy and hold it out to him. "Finally. I was beginning to think you were going to make a day of it."

Brendan bit back a retort and calmly drew the doors closed before he went to her. He took the snifter. "It bodes ill that you wish to fortify me with liquor."

"I'm concerned with your health." She glanced at the front window. "Thank goodness it stopped raining before you came home. It stormed quite horribly earlier."

"The state of the weather is not my concern, madam. Stratford mentioned that you received a young woman."

"Ah, yes," Gertrude said, waving a hand airily. "Sarah Stevens."

Turning the snifter in his long fingers, Brendan went around the desk with the intention of sitting in his chair. The leather, however, was crusted with mud. "Bloody hell! She sat at my desk?"

"You needn't bellow. It was the safest spot. The poor thing was drenched."

Brendan withdrew a monogrammed linen

handkerchief from his pocket, snapped it open, and brushed the spot clean. Sitting, he placed the snifter on the desk and laced his fingers together on top of a stack of papers. "Perhaps you'd like to tell me more about this 'poor thing,' particularly why you welcomed her into my home."

Nonplussed by his disagreeable manner, Gertrude remarked, "When you hear her story, you'll understand why I felt obligated to take her in."

Brendan uncurled his fingers and drummed on the desk.

Gertrude reached for the decanter and spilled a liberal amount of brandy into a glass. "Drink your brandy. I've already had three myself."

Possessed by a formidable premonition that his well-ordered life was about to take a sharp turn, Brendan gulped down the entire contents of the snifter. The tidings his aunt seemed reluctant to deliver must have been grave if she sought to brace them both with drink.

"I thought to prepare you a bit first, but I see that prolonging the inevitable is having the opposite effect. Her name is Sarah Stevens, and she comes from Georgia." Gertrude paced to the window and back. "Dear me, this is difficult." She paced to the window again, then turned abruptly. "My guess is that she's eight months along. She claims that Brendan Hammond of St. Louis is the father."

Brendan sucked in a harsh breath. "Absurd! But I wouldn't have believed you could be duped so easily." Seconds later, he shot to his feet and crossed the room. "I'll set things straight."

Not allowing his aunt an opportunity to respond, he sent the doors banging into the walls again, stalked out of the room, and pounded up the stairs. Reaching the door to the guest room, he allowed himself several moments to master the anger surging in his veins. Before he'd left England there might have been cause to credit the girl's claim.

But not now. He'd lived chastely since his arrival in St. Louis a year before.

When he felt calm enough, he rapped on the door with his knuckles. Minutes passed, and he rapped again. He felt a vein in his neck throb. What did she think to gain by hiding from him? She must've known she'd have to face the man she'd accused of fathering her child. He tried the knob and found it unlocked. Stepping inside the dim interior, he saw the figure of a woman curled on the bed. He strode across the room and threw open the window hangings. Light fell over her face, but the girl did not awaken.

She wasn't what he'd expected. He swept his gaze over bare, delicate feet and one perfectly shaped calf. The seductive outline of a slender thigh and a gently rounded hip showed through a white cotton chemise. Her features were flawless—high cheekbones, a short, straight nose, a generous mouth, and long, dark lashes. Dark brown hair, damp and slightly curling, fanned out provocatively over her shoulder and the pillow.

Damn. She was a beauty.

He must have been insane to notice. Beneath the puritanical image he'd worked hard to project, he was still "Wicked Warwick," London's most notorious rake. Women had always been his downfall. He loved everything about them—their artful flirtations, their enchanting smell, and particularly the soft curves and valleys of their bodies.

Remembering his scandalous affair with Lady Ashley and his necessary parting from his homeland, Brendan scowled. A woman's wiles could lead a man to disaster, as he'd found out. The woman before him might have looked innocent and possessed the face of an angel, but apparently even she had the power to play hell with a man's life.

Purposely, he dropped his vision to her stomach. She hadn't lied about that, at least. She was near her time. He had hoped he'd find his aunt had been mistaken. No wonder she'd offered the chit sanctuary. His conscience would've prompted him to do likewise.

Brendan returned to the study, where he found Gertrude wringing her hands.

"Well?" she said.

He walked to the window to stare out at the gloomy day. "I see why you took her in, but just because she appears . . . innocent doesn't mean that she is. Looks can be deceiving."

"Is that *all* you have to say? Did you perchance speak with her?"

"She was asleep."

"She's pretty, isn't she?" Gertrude asked.

Brendan shrugged at the hint of suggestion in her tone. He had damned well noticed the girl's beauty, but he preferred to hide his weakness. Thus far he'd managed to convince his aunt that abandoning his life of excess had been an easy feat. If she had known of the difficulties facing him each day, she would have felt obligated to offer him advice.

Feeling a light touch on his arm, Brendan tensed. He raised an eyebrow as he glanced over his shoulder. "I'm not the father," he said simply.

Gertrude shook her head and smiled. "Even if I didn't know for a fact that you were here eight months ago, I wouldn't have believed you had fathered the girl's child."

He laid his hand over hers and patted it affectionately. "Considering my lurid past, your trust is admirable. On what do you base your conclusion?"

"For one thing, she's not the type of woman you usually prefer." She slipped her fingers from beneath his and patted his hand in turn. "But I should've said *preferred*. You've led an exemplary life since you arrived here. Despite your rather scandalous affairs in England, at least you never ruined an innocent, and you always treated your companions decently. Also, Miss Stevens described the man to me, and the age does not fit you. It does, however, fit your brother."

"Derek?"

His younger brother was a rascal, but he'd never resorted to malicious pranks before. De-

rek had always looked up to him, envying
Brendan's prowess with women and striving to
gain a reputation equal to Brendan's. It was inconceivable that Derek would do such mischief
to a brother he idolized.

"We have no proof," he said. "Why, the girl
could be a clever adventuress determined to
catch a rich husband."

"We have this," she said, holding the gold
chain out to him.

"Grandmother's locket? But I thought it
lost."

"It was. Now we know your brother had it.
Oh, Derek has outdone himself this time."

"Granted, my brother has always had a peculiar sense of humor—"

Gertrude gave an exasperated sigh.

"You disagree?" Brendan asked.

"I might have known you'd defend him. It'll
be interesting to see just how amused you are
when it comes time to tell the girl that the man
who seduced her is not the man she believes
him to be."

Brendan clenched his jaw. "I'd presumed *you*
had passed on that tidbit of information."

Gertrude left him and sat in the wing chair.
"I didn't have the heart. He left her a letter, and
I saw for myself, it's Derek's hand. It would be
best if you handled the deed. You're better
suited to these matters."

"Indeed?" His lips curled into a sardonic
grin. "I shall have the truth from her."

"Brendan, I must insist that you consider her
condition when you speak with her. For God's

sake, be gentle." Gertrude pressed her fingers
to her brow. "Bear in mind that she's most
likely an innocent pawn who's fallen victim to
your brother's charm. Why, he actually promised her marriage! Oh, how will we survive the
scandal if she sues for breach of promise? You
must do something, and very soon. If you find
Derek, perhaps he could be forced to marry the
girl."

Brendan strode to the door and jerked the
braided rope. "That may be a trifle difficult,
since I paid him a sizable stipend to stay away
from St. Louis." His aunt's surprised look
prompted him to explain. "*I* have reformed out
of necessity, but not my brother. I cannot very
well presume to lecture him on the evils of his
ways, when it's me he seeks to emulate. But I
thought it wise to guard my hard-earned reputation by assuring his silence. You know Derek cannot hold his tongue under certain
circumstances."

"He's been gone for some time. I'm sure his
funds must be nearly exhausted."

"I rather doubt it. I was especially generous."

"This is worse than I thought."

"Don't worry," Brendan advised. "Every
woman I've known has her price. If, as I suspect, Miss Stevens is just an imaginative
schemer, she'll settle for an exorbitant amount
and conveniently disappear."

Gertrude slowly rose. "You've become so
cynical, Brendan, but I suppose it's only natural. You're used to rich, aristocratic women
who use their wiles to get exactly what they

want. Unfortunately, what they wanted most was you in their bed! I fear you're in for quite a shock."

Mathilda answered Brendan's summons. Narrowing his eyes on his aunt, he requested that dinner be served in half an hour. After the maid left, he asked, "What do you mean?"

"I've always been a fair judge of character. Miss Stevens impressed me as exactly what she seems—a lovely, guileless girl whose only mistake was to succumb to a reckless charmer. You could prove me wrong, but my intuition tells me she won't take your money. And beware. She has a rare quality difficult to find these days—spirit. Have a mind to your manner, Brendan. Save your high-handedness for those women trained to defer to a man, because I suspect this one just might set you on your arrogant ear."

Sarah awoke slowly, unsure of her whereabouts. A moment passed before she remembered she was in Brendan's home. She pushed herself up and slipped her feet over the edge of the bed. *Heavens*, she thought, she felt as plump as the mattress. And about as energetic. But Brendan was surely home by now.

Hearing someone at her door, she admitted a maid who carried a tray laden with food. Sarah's mouth watered. To make her meager funds last, she'd lived on two meals a day for the past week.

"Mr. Hammond will see you in his study after you've eaten," the girl said.

Relieved, Sarah thanked her. She consumed everything on the tray, then felt even less lively. She glanced longingly at the four-poster bed. An image of Brendan flashed across her mind, fueling her with the strength to pull on her clothes. Though she dreaded the chore ahead, she knew she must demand that he fulfill his obligation.

Standing in front of the oval mirror in one corner, she frowned. Her best dress, which she'd sewn herself, was wrinkled, the sprigs of blue flowers slightly faded. She had done her best to alter it, but there hadn't been enough material in the bodice to let out. Goodness, her bosom was bundled so tightly, she couldn't take a deep breath. She tugged at the square neckline, then gave a frustrated moan. She looked awful, her stomach as round as a watermelon, her breasts resembling two ripe cantaloupes.

Someone was at her door again. Sarah's heart skipped a beat, but she found it was only Stratford. His nose remained a bit pink, reminding her of their earlier scuffle.

"The master of the house awaits your convenience," he said in a clipped tone. Considering Sarah with a disdainful look, he turned his back and walked down the hall. "Hurry, miss."

To think she'd been about to apologize for her behavior! Irritation coursed through her. Back in Georgia her family no longer had the means to hire servants, but had they still been so fortunate, she would have gladly fed *this* one to Wallace. Even Wallace, though, would probably have spit him out as too tart.

She carefully followed him down the magnificent curved staircase. Purposely she filled her mind with unimportant details, noticing smooth mahogany spindles and shiny balusters, and that the wide steps were covered with runners held secure with brass carpet rods. Her mother would have loved this house.

Waiting while the butler announced her, her gaze drifted to an ornate mirror mounted on a marble-topped base. This magnificent house brought back memories she'd thought long forgotten—of her pampered childhood on a prosperous plantation. But it wasn't the luxuries she missed. Her heart ached with loneliness to be held in her father's strong arms, where she'd always found comfort.

Stratford discreetly cleared his throat as he stood at the open doors, drawing Sarah from her musings. Clearly, he didn't approve of her. However, he could at least have made an effort to conceal his feelings. Catching a fold of her dress, she forced a smile and walked past him, but, thrown off balance by her cumbersome weight, she stumbled onto the toe of his shoe. His resounding yelp echoed into the room.

"Stratford!" came a deep, masculine voice. "What mischief are you up to now?"

The stiff-lipped servant pierced Sarah with a poisonous glare. "Nothing at all, sir."

"Well, then shut the blasted door and leave us alone."

"As you wish, sir."

Sarah inhaled and turned. The air rushed from her lungs. The man standing across the room resembled Brendan, but he was definitely not him!

Too astonished to speak, she forgot her manners and stared rudely, noting the differences and similarities between this man and the one she loved. He was taller and broader of shoulder, though his hair was the same shade of black. Gold speckled his penetrating hazel eyes. He looked extremely dignified in an expertly tailored black coat and starched white shirt devoid of frills. His stance, with his hands clasped behind his back and his feet widely spaced, impressed her as supremely confident.

Though older, he was much more striking.

"Are you Brendan's father?" she asked shyly.

"*Fa-ther?*" he sputtered. A muscle jumped in his finely molded jaw as his gaze turned angry. "I should say not!"

Chagrined that she'd made the wrong assumption, Sarah muttered, "It's just that you look somewhat like him. Naturally, I presumed you were a Hammond."

"For your information, Miss Stevens, I am a Hammond. *Brendan Hammond*, to be exact."

Chapter 2

"**Y**ou . . . *you* are Brendan Hammond?"
"Yes"

Brendan watched a myriad of emotions pass over the woman's expressive face—first shock, then hurt, and finally resignation. He hadn't intended to announce his identity right off, especially in view of her condition. Now, seeing the distress in her eyes, he forgot his ire.

"Will you accept my apology for speaking so bluntly?" She swayed slightly, alarming him. "Are you all right? Miss Stevens, you will kindly tell me if you plan to swoon."

"I most definitely am *not* going to swoon." Her voice faltered as she said, "I don't understand. Who was the man I met?"

Hard pressed not to glance at her blossoming waist, Brendan said softly, "My brother. Derek Miles Hammond."

Minutes ticked by, the only sound the splatter of rain against the windows. Despite her assurance to the contrary, Miss Stevens looked ready to drop into a faint. Feeling it wise to be prepared, Brendan moved toward her. Up close he saw that her eyes were a bewitching combination of gray and green. Even clouded with torment, they affected him. He wished he had the ability to read her mind, to know for sure whether she was truly upset—or just an accomplished actress.

"He lied to me," she said flatly. "He never intended to return, did he?"

"One is never sure with Derek, but I hesitate to second-guess him. He might have been sincere."

"Do you know where he is?"

"I do not," Brendan answered, omitting the fact that he'd paid his brother to disappear. "I haven't seen him for close to a year. It would be rather impossible to locate him before you—" Quickly, he changed course. "You would welcome this man knowing he pulled such a despicable ruse?"

"I'd like to hear his explanation. He's the father of my child. He must've had a reason for givin' me the wrong name. Perhaps he was in some sort of trouble."

He gave her a skeptical look.

She regarded him strangely. "You said he might have been sincere. A man with such a gentle nature cannot be so cruel. We should at least allow him an opportunity to explain. I hesitate to suggest such a thing, but perhaps he met with an accident. However, once your brother does learn of my situation, I have every confidence he'll want to marry me."

"I daresay."

It hadn't taken her long to broach the subject

of matrimony, Brendan thought. Judging by the lines of worry on her brow, she had no more faith in her words than he did. He crossed to his desk and propped a hip on the corner, folding his arms on his chest.

"What I meant was that your brother would want his child to have his name," she said in a softer voice.

"I feel I should mention that Derek has no money of his own. What he gets is by my good graces. At the moment, however, I am not disposed to generosity."

Her eyes narrowed, her lips pressing together in a fashion that made Brendan's stiff shirt collar feel too tight.

"If a wealthy husband is your true desire," he continued, "you should have come directly to me. I'm an earl, and sinfully rich to boot."

"Sinfully pompous is more like it," she muttered as she considered his Aubusson carpet.

Brendan stood up straight.

She boldly met his gaze. "I want nothing from you, *your Lordship*, though it's fortunate that you have so much money, since you are about as charmin' as Wallace."

Annoyed by the mocking inflection she used to address him, he snapped, "Who the devil is Wallace?"

"My father's prize hog," she said, a wry grin twisting her lips.

Brendan scowled. "My dear young woman, for a poor country girl, you are unfashionably direct."

"My family wasn't *always* poor," she

retorted, tilting her chin at a regal angle. "Before the War we lived on a grand plantation." A wistful note crept into her voice. "I was only nine when the unpleasantness began, but my memories are quite vivid."

He said nothing. Pride he understood only too well.

"I fell in love with your brother for himself, not because I thought he had money. *He* has a way about him that's hard to resist."

His aunt had been right. The girl had spirit and, to his annoyance, an infuriating lack of diplomacy. From what he'd seen thus far, Miss Stevens hadn't one biddable bone in her body. She was, in fact, the exact opposite of Florence Belmont, the demure young woman to whom he intended to propose. Why, then, did he find Miss Stevens infinitely more interesting?

Brendan stood. "If I've spoken out of turn, you have my sincere regrets. But I hope you don't mind if I reserve judgment." He pulled something from his pocket and held it out in his upturned palm. "He obviously wanted you to have this."

She stepped forward and gingerly lifted the gold chain and locket from his hand. "It's beautiful," she said, "but I cannot keep it, now that I know it's a family heirloom." She let it drop back into his palm. "Very few heirlooms remain in my family, but what we do have we cherish. We certainly wouldn't want them fallin' into undesirable hands."

Brendan bristled at her impertinence. Looking down at the top of her head, though, he was tempted to touch her hair. The wavy locks, which she'd attempted to confine with a blue ribbon, would feel like silk sliding through his fingers. She smelled faintly of soap, not heavily perfumed, like the women he knew in England. If she weren't burdened with child—

Damn. Why hadn't she taken the bloody locket?

Was it a clever stratagem to throw him off-guard, or a true indication of her character? Strangely, he wasn't sure which he preferred to believe. His aunt had been right about that, too. He *had* turned cynical.

He used a finger to tip up her chin. She looked startled by his move but stood still, gazing up at him with her lips slightly parted. The lines of her face bore a classic beauty. He couldn't doubt that at least one of her ancestors had aristocratic blood.

"I must commend Derek when I see him," he said, his tone unconsciously becoming low and persuasive. Without thinking, he said, "He has excellent taste in women. Not only are you lovely beyond words, your loyalty to my brother is admirable."

He brushed his knuckle along her exquisite jaw and felt her cheek grow warmer. Her reaction caught him unawares. Driven by long-ingrained habits, he inclined his head. Her eyes widened with surprise, looking more green now than gray. Startled, he pulled back abruptly when he realized how close he had come to kissing her. Damn. How easily he had lapsed into Wicked Warwick. But, he thought, his fumble might serve as a means to test her.

"Oh, no," she said breathlessly, shoving him away. "Whatever you have on your mind, sir, you are quite deluded. I've been taken in by one Hammond—I'll not be made a fool by another." She retreated a step, her mouth pulling into a frown. "That wasn't a very nice thing to do, Your Lordship."

Brendan arched a brow. In command of his senses again, he lied. "Unsporting, yes, but necessary."

"I declare, I do admire your maneuver, though. For a moment I actually thought you were bein' kind." She retreated another step. "Were you going to offer me money next?"

Brendan gave a long-suffering sigh. Miss Stevens acted so innocent and vulnerable, he decided it was certainly a ploy to deceive him. She was clever, all right, clever enough to advance to a more lucrative arrangement. She had to realize that, if Derek had truly intended to return to her, he would have done so long before this.

"How much do you have in mind, Miss Stevens?"

Her eyes narrowed. "You are insultin', sir."

Despite her stalwart manner, she appeared a bit weary. Was it another ploy to weaken his defenses? He watched her lay her hand over her cheek and inhale an irregular breath. Feeling a twinge of guilt, he gently gripped her arm, led her to the closest chair, and seated her.

"Thank you," she said sweetly. "I do feel a bit dizzy. It happens sometimes, so you mustn't blame yourself."

Brendan stiffened. "You don't say."

"I'm used to arrogant men who bluster about. My father has lost everything, yet he's every bit as imperious as you." She gazed up at him with a serene smile. "And I know it's difficult for you to accept that your brother has behaved dishonorably."

Brendan balled his fingers into fists. When he got his hands on his brother, he just might break his damn neck. She had the locket, which proved she'd at least met Derek, but he had to be certain. "Miss Stevens, if you feel up to it, might I ask you a few questions?"

"Why, certainly. Now that I'm off my feet, I feel much better."

"How did you happen to meet my brother? I wasn't aware he knew anyone in Georgia."

"He was traveling through, he said. He met up with a man who invited him to join him and a few of his friends in a game of billiards. He stayed several days at the man's home; then his horse came up lame near our farm."

"Why didn't he buy another horse?"

"Because my father didn't have one to spare. Well, actually, he did, but it was not as good quality as Derek's. Derek preferred to wait until his own healed."

Brendan clasped his hands behind his back and stared ahead. His brother had always had a fine head for horses, and wouldn't be caught riding an inferior mount. "How long did he remain?"

Sarah hesitated before she mumbled, "Two weeks."

"Two weeks? By God, he maneuvered fast!" He saw her face turn crimson and cursed his loose tongue. "Forgive me, Miss Stevens. I spoke without thinking."

"I reckon it was partly my fault." She lowered her head. "I loved him from the first instant. I had to remember to breathe, he was so handsome. And charming. The first time he kissed me, I lost my senses."

He couldn't explain why the thought of his brother and Miss Stevens being intimate bothered him. He closed his eyes, willing away the image, but the vision danced in the back of his mind. Derek kissing her, fondling her, making love to her. When he finally looked down at her, his gaze accidentally lighted on the tight bodice of her dress. He forced his mind back to the matter at hand.

"My brother has a scar from a childhood accident," he said suddenly. "I hesitate to ask such an indelicate question of a woman, but your answer will resolve my quandary."

Sarah bit her tongue, staying the retort that sprang to her lips. He had already made her speak rashly, and it was an unseemly trait she tried to govern. But this man would have tried the patience of a saint. She considered not giving him the information he wanted, then realized with a sinking heart that she had no choice.

"The scar is . . . on his right . . . *thigh!*"

Silence followed. Sarah tried to calm herself. Her voice had come out a squeak, except for the last part, but she realized her embarrassment would serve a purpose. Now he could no longer think her a liar. "Is there anything else you wish to know? Perhaps you'd like to hear more. Your brother is put together quite well, with broad shoulders and—"

"Enough!"

The earl's sour expression suggested he might have just eaten a lemon. Sarah couldn't help herself. Mimicking Stratford, she remarked, "As you wish, sir."

She watched his seductive lips press together. Brendan Hammond, though wickedly attractive, was entirely too inflexible—and haughty—to suit her tastes. He was a man who would quickly overwhelm a woman with a weak disposition. Thank goodness she had inherited her father's headstrong nature and her mother's wry sense of humor. Why, the earl's face would probably crack if he smiled, unlike Derek, who found amusement in simple things. Derek and she had much more in common.

Oh, how *could* he have seduced her if he'd had no intention of returning? But she wouldn't think of Derek's deceit now. She had the rest of her life to dwell on her mistake.

For the present she must deal with *him*, a man whose quiet authority gave her pause. She could tell Brendan Hammond was accustomed to giving orders and having them obeyed. Perhaps it would be wiser not to further antagonize him, as she was temporarily at his mercy.

"I'm sorry to be so much trouble." She noticed his fine, dark trousers fit his long legs superbly. He was an imposing man, actually. And he had a bewildering effect on her. Her stomach felt as if it were tied in knots. Deciding her reaction was merely due to worry over her circumstances, she added, "You must convey my gratitude to your aunt for her kindness."

"My aunt has a tender heart at times." He rubbed a hand over his jaw, then went to his desk, where he sat down. He propped his elbows on the chair arms, leaned back, and steepled his fingers together. "You'll remain here with us. I will, of course, attempt to locate my brother, but I rather doubt I'll have success. Out of necessity, you'll confine yourself to the house. It's fortunate that I've made do with a minimal staff. The fewer people who know of your . . . condition, the better."

"Confine myself to the house? That seems an extreme sentence, your Lordship."

"Sentence, Miss Stevens? I'm not a jailer."

"I appreciate your concern, and while I see the need for discretion, surely—"

"My dear young woman, you *will* abide by my wishes." He paused, tapping his fingers against one another. "Forgive me if I sound—"

"Overbearing?" Sarah supplied the word without thinking. The muscle ticking along his jaw betrayed his irritation, and Sarah softened her tone. "Truly, I meant no offense, your Lordship. It's just that I'm used to being out in the fresh air, and remainin' indoors for such a long time will be stressin' to my nerves."

"There's an informal garden behind the house. Will that suffice?"

"I suppose it must."

"And, Miss Stevens, you might as well address me as Brendan. Perhaps you can say it without inflection."

"Thank you, Brendan," she said pleasantly. "In that case, you must call me Sarah."

Never had she met a man who so thoroughly roused her temper. At the same time, though, she couldn't seem to look away from him. Gold sparks flashed in his hazel eyes when he issued his orders, making them the focal point of his face. Even a frown didn't detract from his handsomeness. She had the deranged notion that, were he to smile, he could have melted even the hardest heart. Except hers. If she were witless enough to fall in love again, Brendan Hammond would be the last man in the world she'd choose.

His steady gaze made her uneasy. Minutes ago he'd given her the impression that he meant to kiss her. Her face heated at the preposterous notion. A distressed look had crossed his face, almost as if he'd briefly lost his senses and was annoyed with himself for it.

She sensed he still doubted her and sought to take her measure. She knew she should have deferred to him, as her mother had always claimed was the proper deportment for a Southern woman. But something told her that this man, despite his obvious ire when she spoke her mind, would respect her less if she did. To her dismay, she found she did care what he thought of her. Uncomfortable with that realization, she glanced away to the rows of books behind him.

"While you are here, Sarah, if there is anything you need, Mathilda will be happy to see to it. Also, I'm positive my aunt will be only too glad to assist you. You've won her over."

But I haven't won you over, she thought. "You're gracious to consider my comfort, sir."

"Brendan."

Sarah awkwardly rose. Realizing he meant to do the same, she said, "Please don't trouble yourself, Brendan."

After he reseated himself, she went to the window, pushed aside the lacy white curtains, and gazed longingly at the park across the street. Despite the gloomy weather, the manicured gardens and abundant trees of all varieties, guarded by an elegant iron fence and gate, beckoned her. She missed Georgia, running barefoot across fallow fields and . . . There was no use dwelling on it. She couldn't go home with a child and no husband.

Her shoulders slumped. Derek had never intended to return or to marry her. He had used her. More than her embarrassment over her naïveté, his betrayal stung. But she had no choice now. For her child's sake, she would have to marry him and make the best of it.

"What will I do if Derek can't be found?" she asked herself, then wondered if she'd mistakenly spoken her thoughts aloud.

"I've been asking myself the same question."

Goodness, she *had* said it! Chagrined, she clamped her unruly mouth shut.

"Don't worry," he said, the compassionate tone of his voice surprising and confusing Sarah. "If I fail to arrive at a satisfactory solution, my aunt will no doubt have an opinion on the matter. Her tendency to meddle in affairs not her own is surprisingly indulged by her peers, by whom she is held in high regard."

Sarah took a deep breath. When had he left the desk and crossed the room? Without having to look, she sensed that he stood behind her. He exuded an energy that left the air around him charged.

"That's Lafayette Park you're looking at," he said. "There are walkways and pools, even a lake where ladies sometimes enjoy riding in the swan boats."

Although Sarah's mind registered his words, it lingered on his disturbing nearness.

"It's out of the question now, but one day you might want to stroll through it."

"Yes, I would," she muttered. Impossibly, he touched her hair, and his fingers brushed her neck. A disconcerting tingle raced down her spine. "Perhaps in . . . a . . . few months."

"Your ribbon was coming undone," he offered by way of an explanation.

Sarah instinctively reached over her shoulder to check the ribbon, but her hand encountered his. A shock wave rippled along her arm. Abruptly she jerked her hand away. It was ridiculous, she thought. He was Derek's brother, the one man she could never regard in a romantic way. Yet he sent her senses reeling with a mere brush of his fingers. When Derek had touched her, she'd felt warm and comforted. Why hadn't *he* caused her to experience these acute sensations? Bewildered, she slowly turned and faced Brendan.

His expression gave no clue to his thoughts. It occurred to her that he might be flirting with her again, but to what gain? She was as ripe as a June peach. Then sudden intuition ignited her anger. He thought her a Jezebel and sought to prove it. Had she been in his place, she might have thought the same. Rationalizing his motives, however, did not console her. She hadn't set out to seduce Derek. What had happened between them had just happened. She'd been weak, cast under the spell of a handsome, captivating man.

Some Prince Charming he'd turned out to be.

She searched Brendan's eyes, then wished she hadn't. His gaze never wavered, but hers did. She resented the fact that he could make her feel ashamed, and all reasoning fled. "Upon occasion, I've been accused of speakin' out of turn," she said.

A slight flush marked his cheeks. Abruptly, he lowered his hand. "I hadn't noticed," he remarked dryly.

"So . . . I hope you don't mind if I correct a misconception you apparently have about me."

"By all means."

The yellow lights sparking in his eyes as he folded his arms over his chest gave her a moment's pause. She considered the disapproving slant of his lips. Steeling herself, she continued, "You might as well understand right now that

I am not, nor will I ever be, agreeable to an unseemly alliance with you or any man. Furthermore—"

He held up a hand to silence her, but she could not stop now.

"Furthermore, I appreciate your takin' me in and tryin' to find your brother, but that doesn't give you the right to trifle with my emotions. I'm not the first woman to fall in love with the wrong man, and I certainly won't be the last."

"Sarah," he said quietly.

"If it makes you feel better to regard me as a trollop, kindly refrain from tryin' to lure me into a trap." She took a deep breath. "There, I've said what I wanted. Are you going to toss me out, your Lordship? Or are you man enough to accept a mere woman's criticism?"

Brendan bit back a smile. Sarah Stevens was certainly the most outspoken woman he'd ever met. She had no chance of winning a battle of words with him, yet she dared to give him a royal dressing down. It rankled that he'd had no ulterior motive when he'd adjusted her ribbon. He'd simply fallen prey to another moment of weakness. Her hair *had* felt like silk.

"I have no intention of *tossing you out*, Sarah," he said gently. "And I've suffered the sharp edge of a woman's tongue before and come away intact. I must say, you do baffle me. I was led to believe that Southern women were inclined to acquiesce to a male authority. Apparently I was misinformed. Were it not for your engaging accent, I'd think you'd been born in a different locale."

A light flush stained her cheeks.

"And rest assured that an 'unseemly alliance' is the furthest thing from my mind. I value an untarnished reputation." At least here in America, he thought. "Also, *trollop* is a rather harsh word."

She stared at him, allowing him his say. It was hard not to admire her courage in standing up to him, he thought. She had much to lose and nothing to gain by doing so—unless it was yet another ploy to throw him off-guard. Until he was certain, it would do him well to think before he acted. Presently, though, he'd reached an impasse.

"Are there any more like you back in Georgia?"

He watched her tilt her head at a regal angle again and almost lost the battle not to smile.

"I have two younger brothers," she said. "But I do have a female cousin. Lizzie and I are very much alike."

The prospect of two such women unsettled him. Then an image of Florence Belmont swept across the back of his mind. At least the young woman he planned to wed would never give him a moment's trouble. After all, he'd put much effort into choosing wisely. Florence was young, innocent, and reasonably appealing-looking. More important, she was properly biddable.

He met Sarah's gaze. She had the eyes of a sorceress, he mused, the combination of gray and green reminding him of looking through a mist at a lush forest. He must remember that his brother had already succumbed to her—and in record time. His aunt, too, had momentarily fallen under the girl's spell.

But if Miss Stevens thought to bewitch *him* as easily, she'd made a perilous miscalculation.

Chapter 3

~∽◯∽~

The next morning an incessant poking on his arm roused Brendan from a deep sleep. Dragging his eyes open a slit, he discovered Stratford peering at him. "What time is it?"

The older man retreated a step. "It's eight A.M., sir, precisely the hour that you requested I wake you."

Brendan ran his fingers over his stubbled jaw, then into his tousled hair. He must look like hell. He felt like hell. The restless night he'd spent before finally falling asleep close to dawn was not one he wanted to repeat. He pushed himself up in bed and stuffed his pillow behind his back.

Immediately, Stratford deposited a silver tray on his lap. "And what will you be wearing today, sir?"

Lifting a china cup to his mouth, Brendan took a swallow of black coffee before he responded, "Whatever you decide. It matters little."

Stratford's chin disappeared into the folds of

his neck as he studied Brendan with a peculiar look.

Brendan ignored him and continued to drink his coffee, though he knew his butler and acting valet would eventually break his silence. Since the older man had been in the Hammonds' employ for many years, he offered his advice frequently, whether it was appreciated or not. This morning, however, Brendan prayed the man would hold his tongue. He had a raging headache.

"Is my aunt about yet?"

"No, but the young lady is."

Miss Stevens was the one person he didn't want to see—not after being haunted by her face for most of the night. At one point he'd even felt remorse for thinking ill of her. The solace he'd found in a decanter of brandy had cured him, but he now wished he'd not indulged so freely.

"Where is she?"

"I'm not sure, sir, but I shall be happy to find out."

"No!" Brendan said, then regretted he'd spoken so loudly. Clamping a hand over his brow, he bit back an oath. "I just wanted—"

"—to avoid her, sir?"

"Exactly. You will assist me to that end, will you not?"

"Yes, sir."

"Also, I want you to *adamantly* instruct the others that the lady's presence is to remain a secret. They are to exclude her from their gossip or be dismissed without reference."

"As you wish, sir."

"What's the weather like? Any signs of rain?"

"To my knowledge it appears a fine day," Stratford replied as he dutifully laid out clean linen. "Will you be going to the races today, or to your gentleman's club?"

"Neither." Brendan's brows furrowed together at the thought of forgoing two of his more pleasurable pastimes. Instead he needed to hire a detective to locate his brother. "I'm tending to legal affairs."

"Very good, sir."

Stratford went to the armoire, and Brendan realized that by questioning him discreetly, the poor fellow had been attempting to figure out the correct attire for him that day.

Forty-five minutes later Brendan stood in the grand hall, where Stratford handed him his hat, gloves, and walking stick.

"Will you be late, sir? Madam will be asking."

Brendan smiled. "Of course she will. If all goes well, I'll join her for dinner." He turned to leave, then turned back, intending to request that their guest also be present. But a movement above him caught his eye. He glanced upward and groaned. He wouldn't escape undetected, after all.

"Good morning, Sarah," he called to the figure half visible at the top of the landing.

She stepped into full view and nodded.

"That will be all, Stratford," Brendan told his servant.

Walking to the bottom of the stairs, Brendan trained his vision on her. If he wasn't mistaken, her tense grip on the banister betrayed her anxiety. She had been caught spying on him. Else she was as reluctant to meet him as he was her. "Did you rest well?"

"Oh, yes," she said quickly. "Thank you for askin'."

He found her Southern accent alluring. Her hair hung loose, the dark waves forming a seductive frame for her face. Remembering the silky strands sliding through his fingers, he frowned.

"And you, Brendan, did you rest well?"

"I did, indeed," he lied. "I must go out for most of the day, but I anticipate your lovely company at dinner. You will most assuredly brighten our table."

She blinked; then, tilting her head, she regarded him with a queer look.

He supposed she thought his behavior odd, but complimenting women had always been second nature to him. Despite their differences and her increased size, she was pleasant to gaze upon. "Do I have two monstrous heads this morning? Perhaps a snake dangling from my nose?"

Her lips twitched before she pressed them together. "One very handsome head, but no snake."

"I'll have to remember to compliment you again, Sarah."

Relaxing her grip on the rail, she leaned forward. "You needn't go to such bother, your

Lordship. I've learned my lesson in that regard. I merely stated a fact, one I know you are all too aware of. It won't happen again."

"Oh?"

"Your brother filled my head with pretty words, and look what it got me. I suspect you, sir, would be even more adept at turning a woman's head."

"Indeed? You've flattered me again," he remarked, not attempting to disguise his amusement. "Do you think to fill *my* head with pretty words to gain my favor?"

"If that were my objective, I'd surely be slow-witted. Wallace would be easier to manipulate than you."

Before Brendan could say more, a spot of burgundy color to his left alerted him to his aunt's presence. Had she been there all along?

Sweeping an elegant but reluctant bow to Sarah, he set his smart bowler hat squarely on his head and settled it with a firm tap. Then, deciding his relative preferred not to reveal her presence, he tucked his walking stick under his arm and strode from the house.

Gertrude stepped into the hall with a wide grin. Judging from the intense glances she'd just seen pass between her nephew and their guest, a tumultuous storm was sure to ensue. Their encounter the previous evening must have been eventful, and she regretted she hadn't been there to witness it. But just as soon as Brendan returned, she intended to question him. Meanwhile, she meant to get what information she could from Sarah.

Watching the young woman cautiously descend the steps, she felt a moment's sympathy. Derek had done a foul deed when he'd compromised an innocent and gone on his merry way. It seemed futile to hope that Brendan could find his brother before the child came, but stranger things had happened. In the meantime, she was plagued by the lack of a solution to this situation.

Fate had intervened in all of their lives.

Sarah Stevens had touched a tender spot in her heart from the first instant, reminding her of the daughter taken by typhoid at the tender age of eight. The deep sorrow Gertrude kept buried in her heart had leaped to the surface. She knew firsthand to what lengths a woman would go to protect her child. Even if she had believed Sarah guilty of seeking a rich husband, she wouldn't have condemned her. However, she felt positive that such was not the case. Still, Sarah had been wronged and might sue for breach of promise, creating a scandal the city would never forget.

Sarah finally reached the bottom of the stairs. "You just missed your nephew, but I heard him tell Stratford to expect him for supper. Do you suppose he's gone in search of Derek?"

"I feel certain he has. Have you eaten?"

"Yes, ma'am."

"Good, because I want to speak with you, but not here."

"Brendan mentioned a garden in back. Could we go there?"

"A perfect choice," Gertrude said, locking arms with Sarah. "We'll have privacy and the benefit of a bit of sunshine."

The two women stepped outside, and Sarah sighed with pleasure.

"The spring flowers won't be up for a few weeks yet, but it's really quite lovely," Gertrude said. "Brendan's gardener has a knack for growing beautiful things." She followed Sarah's gaze along the cobbled path winding through a wide variety of expertly manicured shrubs. "Of course, it doesn't compare with the park, which you simply must visit."

"Brendan described the park to me, but it would be imprudent of me to be seen in public just now." Her mouth turned down. "I would so much like to see it. I'm used to bein' out of doors."

Gertrude sat on a wrought-iron bench that boasted a fresh coat of red paint. "Come, sit here, and tell me about your conversation with my nephew."

Sarah's mouth slid into a wry grin. "Conversation is a rather dull description of our meeting."

Gertrude waited until Sarah joined her before she said, "I thought as much. I hope he wasn't too beastly."

"I'm afraid my temper got the better of me, and I spoke rashly. Gracious, it's a wonder he decided to take me in at all."

Mastering a smile, Gertrude watched Sarah

look down and lace her fingers together on her stomach. "I know Brendan well, my dear, so you needn't cover for him. If he behaved like an arrogant ass, I hope you took him to task."

Sarah met Gertrude's eyes. "His behavior's only logical. You see, I understand his hesitation to believe Derek acted in an unprincipled manner. Being a gentleman of strict moral character, Brendan would naturally assume his brother possessed the same qualities."

Gertrude promptly coughed. She snatched a lace-trimmed handkerchief from her sleeve and pressed it over her mouth.

"Are you ill?" Sarah asked with concern.

Unable to respond, Gertrude shook her head. Hearing Sarah refer to Brendan as a paragon of virtue had nearly been her undoing. She still found it hard to accept that he had managed to reform. She wondered if Sarah would have been as generous in her praise if she'd known Brendan was known in England as Wicked Warwick.

Sarah started to rise. "Perhaps a drink of water will help."

"I'm all right now," Gertrude said, touching Sarah's arm. "I was just surprised to find such perception in one so young."

"Perception may not have played as great a part in my recognition as familiarity. Before the War, my father was the master of a prosperous plantation. He's still often quite arrogant, as my mother would readily confirm."

"And does he rule your mother with an iron hand?"

A wide grin captured Sarah's mouth. "He rules everyone *but* her. She patiently allows him to dictate orders, smilin' sweetly the whole while; then she does exactly as she pleases. My two younger brothers, though, are thoroughly terrified of our father."

"And what about you, Sarah? Do you quake in your father's presence also?"

"Heavens, no. Papa's really a lamb."

Gertrude's gaze followed Sarah's to a pretty brown bird perched on a tree limb. Curiosity got the better of her, inducing her to say, "It sounds as if you think Brendan is similar to your father."

"My goodness, that's not what I think at all. Brendan's the most—" She cast a glance at Gertrude, then continued. "You're undoubtedly aware that your nephew's incredibly . . . domineering. Forgive me for speaking bluntly, but I suspect you prefer honesty. He's not Derek."

"My, you *are* refreshing," Gertrude said. "Women normally fawn over Brendan, and, frankly, it has gotten a bit tedious. Why, in England—" Abruptly, she caught herself before she could give away her nephew's past. "He and Derek are alike in some ways, vastly different in others. Brendan is the more attractive, don't you agree?"

"Yes, I suppose he's handsome." Two bright dots of pink brightened Sarah's cheeks. "But I prefer that a man have an amiable personality and a gentle nature."

Gertrude hesitated a moment. "While I agree that Derek has always been favored with an affable manner, there are more important principles to be considered in judging a man's character."

Faint lines creased Sarah's brow. "Apparently so. It appears I'm a poor judge of men and gave my affection too quickly. You don't believe Derek was sincere, either, do you?"

"I won't lie to you, dear. While I love both of my nephews, I readily acknowledge their faults." She sighed, then put as much compassion as she could into her voice. "Knowing Derek as I do, I'd willingly wager he was in love with you at the time. Unfortunately, love's a fleeting emotion to some men."

"I've accepted that he must be a scoundrel. I should've seen past his allure."

"It's good that you no longer harbor any false illusions concerning Derek's intentions. I feel certain he didn't set out to wound you so deeply, and that he never gave a thought to creating a child. It's just that he . . . his dealings in the past have been with women of . . . women of indubitable sophistication."

"Goodness gracious, I *was* a dolt to take him seriously, when all along the attention he paid me was nothing more than a ruse to seduce me."

Gertrude felt the beginnings of a headache, and closed her eyes. "It pains me to have to ask you this, but you seem wise beyond your years, and I feel certain you'll understand my concern. Derek did approach the subject of marriage with you, and—"

"I want nothing from either you or Brendan," Sarah interjected. "I regret that Brendan seems to regard me as a Jezebel." Fine lines feathered across her brow as she frowned. "If I were concerned with wealth, I would've accepted Brendan's offer of money."

"Oh, dear me," muttered Gertrude. "I was worried you'd be hurt and angry enough to want to make Derek pay for his misconduct. Since he's not available, it seemed logical to assume you'd seek restitution from Brendan."

"My hurt has given way to anger, though I must accept part of the blame. Still, Derek is older and more experienced than I, and he should make amends." Sarah's complexion turned pink. "I should've been stronger. I don't know why I surrendered so easily."

"You mustn't blame yourself, Sarah. An innocent is never a match for a skilled rogue, and I do believe you were no match for my nephew. Derek, my dear, learned his devastating technique from a veritable master."

A notorious rake, who, to Gertrude's chagrin, just happened to be her favorite nephew.

Brendan departed the five-story brick building on the corner of Broadway and Chestnut Street, satisfied that he'd taken the proper measures to locate his brother. After making several inquiries, he felt confident that the telegram he'd wired to the Pinkerton Detective Agency in Chicago would accomplish his objective. He should have waited for a confirmation from the agency, but, since he'd supplied every possible detail regarding Derek, he felt positive they would take the case.

The streets bustled with activity at that hour, and a horsecar running on rails rushed past. Across the way, under the limbs of a tree, his driver and carriage waited with several others. Slipping his pocket watch from his vest, Brendan noted the hour. He was not anxious to return home too early. His aunt would no doubt question him regarding his plans for Miss Stevens, who presented a problem he hadn't yet resolved.

Unbidden, Sarah's enchanting eyes flashed across his mind. Brendan snapped his watch closed. She'd possessed his thoughts for most of the night; he refused to allow her to ruin his day, too. Then someone called his name. He looked to his left and smiled at two gentlemen friends with whom he frequently spent his leisure, visiting clubs, billiard parlors, and the races at Abbey Park.

"Hammond," the shorter of the two greeted him. "We're heading for a game of billiards." The man slid a newspaper under his arm as he checked the traffic on the thoroughfare. "I feel lucky today. Care to make a wager?"

Considering the man with a raised brow, Brendan gave him a confident grin. "Feeling lucky today, are you, Henry? I'd enjoy nothing better than trouncing you."

The other man broke into laughter and clapped Henry's back. "But he won't accept your wager, and him with estates in England

and investments that stagger one's imagination."

Brendan closed his eyes for a second to master the temptation at hand. Gaming had been another favorite pastime of his, and it was damned hard to say no. He'd thought living chastely would kill him, but he'd endured it this long. Bloody hell, if he could master his rapacious sexual appetite, turning down an invitation to gamble should be easy, he thought. "I wouldn't still have my holdings if I'd given in to either of you miscreants," he told the two men. "Can we not engage in a friendly game for the sake of sport? Charles? You're not afraid to take me on, are you?"

"I don't like the gleam in your eyes, Brendan, but I'll come and watch awhile." Then he glanced to both sides, leaned close, and in a conspiratorial whisper said, "Got plans to spend a few hours at the Temple. There's a luscious redhead I've been pleasuring who's pining for my company."

Brendan had heard about the Temple of Virtue often enough, but thus far he'd also tempered the temptation to visit that den of iniquity.

Charles nudged Brendan's arm with his elbow. "What'll it be?"

Brendan gritted his teeth and remembered his goal to refashion his life. He'd not been so enticed since he'd left England. "Sorry, old man," he told Charles, "but I fancy giving Henry a much-needed lesson."

Charles Beauclaire stroked his sandy-colored

handlebar mustache. "When you marry the Belmont girl, you'll have a change of heart."

"Now, Charles," Henry said with a shake of his head, "you were not to bring that up again. He's intent upon making a good match, and the Belmonts are well connected."

"Oh, I agree, the girl's sweet-natured. Brendan knows I'd never cast aspersions on her character. She'll make him a proper little wife. But he'll have to take his pleasures elsewhere. My own dear wife lays herself out like a beached fish, staring at the ceiling until I'm finished."

"Which should take all of thirty seconds, or so I've heard."

"Gentlemen, you're trying my patience," Brendan said. He held his mouth in a stern line. He knew the two men well enough to recognize a good-natured conspiracy to rouse his temper. It was damned difficult maintaining a puritanical image, and he suspected they'd somehow realized that he wasn't as morally righteous as he'd led them to believe. He couldn't afford a breath of scandal here, for fear someone would connect him with the wicked reputation he'd left behind in London. He didn't dare consider the repercussions to his life if word leaked of his dispatchment of Lord Ashley to his Maker.

"You might as well give it up, Charles," Henry advised, lowering his voice. "His problem won't be with the girl, but with her mother. That one has her eye on Brendan, herself."

Brendan felt as if he should defend Caroline Belmont, but he did not. He wouldn't be ma-

neuvered into a trap solely for his friends'
amusement, he thought, especially since they
spoke the truth. Mrs. Belmont was seductive,
beautiful, and blatantly lusty. She played hell
with his resolve every time he came within ten
feet of her. Worse, she readily recognized his
dilemma and tormented him until he thought
he'd go mad. It wouldn't have surprised him
to learn that she knew his desire far exceeded
hers, and that it took every ounce of his willpower to act indifferently toward her.

Within minutes, the two men had abandoned
their attempts to goad a reaction from Brendan,
and conversation turned to less-heated topics.
Eventually, they set off for the billiard parlor in
separate carriages for an afternoon of entertainment, which Brendan hoped would take his
thoughts from the problem preying on his
mind.

But four hours later, having played miserably
and suffered much teasing over it, he realized
he could neither ignore nor alter the path his
life now traveled. Sarah Stevens hadn't been
counted into his plans, but of one thing he was
certain.

The lady was trouble.

Sarah gracefully accepted Stratford's assistance, allowing him to seat her at one end of
the sprawling walnut dining table. Slipping off
her shoes, she settled more comfortably on the
high-backed, carved chair and propped her feet
on a low footstool tucked under the table. She
felt like a queen.

table linen elegantly edged with lace
been set with exquisite bone china and
splendid silver plate. Folding her hands in her
lap, she glanced to the top of the sideboard and
admired the carved wolf's head with fish-and-
fowl decoration. The room evoked warmth and
charm, making her feel at home, which an inner
voice reminded her she was not. Her arrogant
host might still toss her out. But contrary to his
words that morning, he had yet to return.

Sarah's stomach lurched at the thought of
eating at the same table with him. All night her
churning emotions had made it even more difficult to sleep than usual. By rights she should
have had her thoughts on Derek's perfidy and
her own foolish weakness. Brendan had probably devoted his day to instigating a search for
his brother—but to what possible end?

Yesterday she had come to this house with
the expectation of marrying Derek. Now she
dreaded the idea. His own family doubted his
sincerity. What happiness could she or her
child expect from a man who regarded her as
merely a flirtation?

Thank goodness Gertrude didn't seem to
hold her affair with Derek against her. Stratford
would probably never accept her, and neither
would the other servants. Sarah's thoughts
turned to Derek again. What if he came back
and denied ever having been to Georgia? Her
brows knitted together. Would anyone believe
her story if Derek claimed differently?

And what of Brendan? He must think her an
adventuress, yet just that morning he'd ex-

changed playful banter with her. Her gloomy mood lightened a bit. She had enjoyed those brief moments.

A sound from the hall startled Sarah to attention. Praying that it was Gertrude, she glanced at the door. Her breath caught in her throat. Her wish had not been granted, and the vision of her host in evening attire dashed any hope of digesting her meal. He looked magnificent, in a black coat with a starched white shirt emphasizing his good looks. He seemed to have grown even more attractive during their short separation.

A fluttering began in her chest, causing her further distress. Then his eyes briefly met hers before giving her a quick scrutiny. The flutter advanced to a hammering, which she decided an idiotic response, indeed.

"Sarah," he said, drawing out her name as he nodded.

Stratford scurried into the room and headed for a cabinet containing a selection of liquors.

"The sherry," Brendan decreed.

Brendan's British accent seemed more pronounced that evening. Refusing to look at him, Sarah studied the crystal wineglass while Stratford filled it. Under the table, her hands shook.

"Sarah."

Inhaling a breath, she reluctantly looked up and saw Brendan holding out his glass to offer a toast. When he inclined his head, bidding her to join him, she found herself woodenly obeying his command.

"To you, Sarah. May you get whoever, or whatever, your heart desires."

The clink of the glasses sounded loud in the silent room. Narrowing her eyes at him over the rim, she countered, "And if I don't know what that is?" *Or what you mean to imply?* she amended silently.

"Sarah, I might not have come to a final decision about you, but I know one thing. You are a very intelligent, clever woman."

"Why, thank you, Brendan. You certainly know how to flatter a woman."

He looked askance at her. "You're used to compliments from men?"

"Unlike men from other parts of the country, Southern men are known to lavish a woman with adulation. Even in his foulest mood, my father never forgets my mother is a lady."

"Exactly how many men have lavished you with adulation, other than Derek, of course?"

"You're direct, and your manner is contemptuous, sir! Is it your habit to insult women? If so, I see why you're unmarried."

The beginnings of a smile tugged at the corners of his mouth. "And, you, Sarah, have a reckless temper. I was merely engaging you in innocent conversation."

"You most certainly were not!" She set her glass soundly on the table, then groaned when sherry sloshed over the edge, spotting the table cover. "Oh, look what you've made me do."

"I? The stain is nothing, Sarah. I can afford to buy many more to replace it."

Sarah clamped her mouth shut. She knew he

thought her a Jezebel, but his blunt questioning had taken her off-guard. Someday, when he had accepted the truth about her, he'd regret his accusations. She'd make sure of it.

"If I have offended you, you have my regrets. I presumed you would expect me to question you."

"I'll not underestimate you in the future, your Lordship," she remarked quietly.

"A wise decision, Sarah."

Where was Gertrude?

As he set his glass beside his plate, Brendan probed her eyes. "I know you must be curious as to how I made out today, so I shan't hold you in suspense. I've hired a detective agency out of Chicago to find Derek. Just a few minutes ago I received a reply to my telegram, but the news is not encouraging. The agency feels positive it can locate him, but stressed that it may take some months."

Unsure whether she felt disappointment or relief, Sarah hid her reaction by sipping more sherry.

"I've already passed on this disheartening bit of news to my aunt, and she has assured me she will arrive at a resolution to your predicament."

"Thank you for goin' to so much trouble on my behalf," Sarah said. "I realize you must have many other pressing matters to see to."

"It was no trouble, and the least I can do." He pulled out his watch and checked it. "Where the devil is my aunt? Stratford! Go see what's keeping her."

"Right away, sir."

Feeling extremely uncomfortable, Sarah kept her eyes averted. She knew without looking that Brendan was watching her. Several minutes passed. Unable to bear his scrutiny a second longer, she boldly met his gaze. Dear Lord! Although he wasn't smiling, amusement danced in his eyes.

"My aunt warned me that you had spirit," he said, his voice actually friendly. "Most women wouldn't oppose me or speak to me with a barbed tongue."

Unsure how to respond, Sarah remained silent. She wasn't sure, but she thought the flash of gold light in his eyes represented a challenge.

"Come, Sarah. I know you have an opinion about my last remark."

"If you insist," she said hesitantly as she gathered her courage. "I think you intimidate women with your arrogant manner, obviously." The lights in his eyes twinkled even more. "My father tries to do the same with my mother."

"And?"

"He fails. She sees past his bluff."

He reached for his drink and took a swallow, giving her reason to believe she'd touched upon a truth she wouldn't have suspected. Sarah looked away and smiled. Was she right? Was his brusque manner a charade to hide a very human side of him?

"Your father has been lax in his duty," he said suddenly.

She slowly met his eyes again. "Should he

have beaten her until she recognized his supreme male authority, your Lordship?"

The glint in his eyes struck her as decidedly wicked. Sarah drew in a labored breath in anticipation of his response.

"That's not precisely how I'd handle the matter of insubordination. There are other, more pleasant ways to effectively silence a woman."

Sarah nearly choked, but covered her reaction with a cough. She studied him more closely. She saw the frown that he hid so quickly, and had the distinct impression he hadn't meant to say that. The temptation to tease was too great to resist. Adopting a serious tone, she asked, "Pleasant ways? What would they be?"

His eyes narrowed on her as his mouth slid into a grim line.

"You were referrin' to a kiss?" she supplied. "A man of such impeccable reputation could mean nothing more, right?"

"Sarah . . . you will kindly not pursue the matter."

Sarah bowed her head. "Yes, your Lordship."

A discreet glance confirmed her suspicion. He wore a scowl. Sarah touched a linen napkin to her lips. He was annoyed with himself, and she knew a smile on her part wouldn't be wise. As she refolded the linen, she noticed that, like the table cover, it was elegantly edged with lace. A dull tapping told her Brendan was now drumming his fingers on the table. Her father often did the same, and grew testy when his dinner wasn't served at the precise hour he desired.

Gertrude finally swept into the room, Stratford at her heels. She waved a hand at the servant. "Tell them to serve immediately, before my nephew mars the table."

Brendan promptly ceased drumming.

Sarah took the opportunity to admire the brass-and-crystal chandelier with etched-glass globes. No expense had been spared in selecting the house's appointments. To her left, crimson velvet draped the window and fell to the floor over white lace, then was looped back with gold tassels. The top of the window was crowned with gilded cornices, and a pedestal in front of it held a large potted fern.

Directly behind Brendan a group of family portraits in gold frames adorned embossed crimson wallpaper. A heavily bearded fellow with white hair stared at Sarah. The man's dour expression convinced her he must be one of Brendan's ancestors.

"That's Cyril Thadeous Hammond, Brendan's great-grandfather, the first Lord Warwick," Gertrude remarked. "Do you see the resemblance?"

"Definitely," Sarah agreed before she found Brendan frankly regarding her. She looked back at the portrait. "Were his eyes the same color also?"

"Yes. In his younger days, he was devilishly handsome—and had a scandalous reputation as a rakehell."

Brendan cleared his throat.

"But," Gertrude continued, "he shocked the peerage by becoming a model of virtue when he met and wed the right woman."

Hearing Brendan mutter an oath, Sarah watched him finish his sherry in two swallows. He then aimed his aunt a pointed look.

"Of course, the similarity ends there," Gertrude said. "Brendan is—"

"Miss Stevens has no interest in hearing ancient tales, madam," Brendan interrupted.

"Oh, but I do. My own great-grandfather—" Sarah stopped herself before she could reveal her ancestor's failings. Brendan thought little enough of her now. What would he think if he knew she was a descendant of a notable English lord who, after squandering away his wealth, turned pirate and became the scourge of eastern shipping lines!

"Do tell us more, Sarah," Gertrude bid.

Sarah was saved by the arrival of servants bearing trays of food. The sumptuous array gave off delectable aromas that would have tempted even a person of meager appetite, which, to her embarrassment, Sarah was not. When she finally finished eating and reached for her napkin, she chanced to look up. Her gaze collided with Brendan's. His mouth twitched, and she wondered if the emotion she read in his eyes could possibly be amusement. He must have thought her table manners appalling.

She had devoured everything in sight.

Her stomach felt weighted with lead. It shouldn't have mattered what he thought of her. But it did.

Chapter 4

Sarah paced the length of her room and stopped by the window. It was a beautiful spring day, and she was forbidden to enjoy it. She was permitted only to visit the private garden behind the house, but after a mere three days, she felt confined.

She closed her eyes, imagining her father's farm and the freedom she'd known in Georgia. If only she could go home. She missed Mama and Papa dreadfully, missed being taunted by her younger brothers. Heaven help her, she even missed Wallace.

She should've seen past Derek's facade to the man beneath. But when she felt a movement in her belly, she knew she wouldn't change things even if she could—the babe within her had come from one of their two nights of lovemaking, and she already loved her child desperately. But she had to face reality also. Brendan hadn't seen his brother for nearly a year. Derek might not ever come back.

Yet she dared not consider her future without him. Brendan had graciously taken her in, and she owed him a debt of gratitude for his kindness. But for how long could she expect him to behave so charitably?

Brendan Hammond was such a remarkable man. He was always dressed and groomed impeccably; his manners were faultless, his character irreproachable. The added bonus of wealth, title, and intelligence made him an exceptional man. That he was breathtakingly handsome seemed an overindulgence on the part of his Maker. Though she'd seen him only at dinner for the past three days, she'd grown fond of him. He wasn't quite the ogre she'd first thought.

She spared a smile. Just the night before, he had started to say something to her, then had shaken his head and begun a conversation with his aunt. This foible in his demeanor had struck Sarah as strange. She didn't know him well yet, but she found it endearing that he seemed at a loss for words in her presence.

Sarah left the window and paced the room again. She felt like a caged animal, a very round one. The child had grown heavy, and that day a dull ache had begun to throb in her lower back. Attributing her discomfort to inactivity, she continued walking. But it was no use. Her bedroom simply didn't provide enough space. And if she remained indoors a minute longer, she thought, she would lose her sanity.

Brendan had left early and, judging by his daily routine, would not return until late. Gertrude also had gone to visit a friend. No one knew Sarah in St. Louis. If she donned a large garment to hide her pregnancy, she might be able to slip unnoticed across the street. A few hours exploring Lafayette Park's lush grounds would surely cure her melancholy.

Peeking out her door, she searched the hall for any sign of servants. To her delight, she found the passage empty. Her plan had risks, but the idea of sneaking from the house offered a diversion she craved. After a thorough exploration of the upper floor, she held her breath and entered the room she believed to be the master chamber.

Though she knew it foolish to dally, curiosity got the better of her. The hunter-green silk damask with gold that covered the walls created a darkly dramatic atmosphere that suited Brendan. Rich velvets trimmed with wide panels of appliqué graced the windows. Preferring not to think of her host at repose in the nine-foot-long brass bed, she studied the old-rose rug covering the oiled wood floor.

She felt his presence, especially when she stood in front of the shaving stand in one corner. She touched a finger to the many implements—straight razor, strap, cup, brush, and soap—and felt an odd awareness. He might have appeared an inappropriate god, of sorts, but he was just a man—a man she couldn't seem to dismiss from her thoughts.

Sarah hurried to an oversized armoire against one wall. Fearing she'd lose her courage if she waited a second longer, she snatched an overcoat, ducked back into the hall, then tiptoed down the main staircase. Her heart was pounding when she reached the front door.

She quickly slipped on the coat, which, true to her expectations, dwarfed her small frame and hung nearly to her ankles. She stood still for a moment, inhaling the scent of the garment, an intoxicating scent that was Brendan's alone. A sound from somewhere in the house alerted her to the danger of her position. Moving quietly, she left the house.

Seeing no traffic or people on the thoroughfare, she crossed to the elegant iron fence that surrounded the park. The massive gate stood ajar, but at the exact moment when she passed through it, the rattle of carriage wheels warned of an approaching vehicle. A backward glance confirmed her fear. Brendan had come home early. Sarah slowly eased her way along the gate, then stepped first behind a wide marble gateway post and then behind a large tree.

She held her breath for as long as possible before she looked through the fence and saw Brendan alight from the carriage. She would wait until he'd gone inside before she ventured further into the park. Afterward, she'd simply sneak around the house, hide the coat, and enter from the rear. Everyone would assume she'd been in the private garden. Unfortunately Brendan was striding toward her, causing her heart to skip a beat.

Oh, dear God! Had he seen her?

She consoled herself with the thought that his intention to enter the park might have been just a coincidence—until he turned in her direction and she saw his furious scowl.

A chiding voice told her to confront him bravely. After all, he had no real power over her. He wasn't her husband or legal guardian, and he'd given his word that he wouldn't turn her out of his house, but he'd think her ungrateful for disobeying him. On the other hand, she thought, she might have been mistaken. On the chance that he hadn't seen her, she avoided the network of gravel walkways and slipped into a particularly dense growth of foliage.

A vein throbbed in Brendan's temple as he quickened his pace. Miss Stevens was surely the most irritating woman on the earth. He hadn't seen much of her lately, but the little witch still brought him problems. Sleep evaded him, worry having replaced his peace. His appetite had also waned, and the knowing looks his aunt gave him were beginning to annoy him. He had the distinct impression that she'd found a remedy for their predicament, but inexplicably, she'd chosen not to share it with him. Even Stratford had taken to watching him as if he were an egg ready to crack.

His inability to win at billiards was also causing him humiliation. And now, if his eyes weren't failing him, Sarah had not only dared defy his request that she not leave the house; she'd invaded his private domain and stolen his coat as well.

Perhaps he should've told her the city employed a rigid dress code to deter undesirables from loitering in the park. If he didn't intercept her, he knew that hired guards might even escort her to the Park Police Station, because they would think her odd for venturing out in such an inappropriate outfit, and would probably detain her. Brendan groaned in frustration. He couldn't allow her to suffer that indignity.

Where the devil had she gone?

And how had she managed to disappear so quickly? He remembered her saying she was used to being out of doors. In Georgia she had probably run free through the countryside, her skirts hitched to her knees.

He stalked along the main path, scouring the surrounding bushes and shrubs. Ten minutes passed before he spotted his prey, idly considering a bronze statue depicting a renowned senator in a Roman toga. His boots punished the gravel walkway as he lengthened his stride.

Twenty feet away from being apprehended, Sarah demonstrated her cunning. A quick turn of her head, a fleeting flash of startled gray-green eyes, and once again she vanished into the greenery. Why the devil was she running from him? He only wanted to protect her, see her safely back to the house, where no one would see her pregnant state.

He begrudgingly admired her adeptness. Even though she was heavy with child, he couldn't capture her. Unburdened, he was sure she could run like a doe. Determined to out-maneuver her, he adopted a slower pace and strolled further along the walkway. Sooner or later Sarah would show herself. But half an hour later, he was even more frustrated. He'd covered a good portion of the park, with no success.

Reaching into his pocket, he fingered the telegram he'd received from the Pinkerton detectives that afternoon. The agency hadn't been able to locate Derek. Time was running out, and he had to do something about Sarah soon. First, however, he must find the elusive little vixen.

Brendan closed his eyes and discovered sounds were more audible. Purposely he blocked out chirping birds and the chatter of two women close by but heard nothing to give away Sarah's position.

"Brendan Hammond!"

He glanced in the direction of the caller and cursed to himself. The women he'd heard, and whose voices he should have recognized, Caroline Belmont and her daughter, Florence, were headed straight for him. Damn. Sarah would be in a fine fix if Caroline spotted her now. Mrs. Belmont lived to spread rumors, and the town would feast on the tale of a pregnant young woman residing in the home of an unmarried man.

Brendan doffed his hat and swept them a gallant bow. "Ladies. What brings you to the park today?"

"Why, Brendan Hammond," crooned Caroline, "you know perfectly well we stroll the park each afternoon."

Brendan raised a brow as he watched the woman briskly ply an elaborate fan that matched her lavender dress and hat. Mrs. Bel-

mont looked ravishing, as usual, her pale gold
hair artfully arranged atop her head, her light
blue eyes taking in every aspect of his appearance.

"Do I?" he finally asked.

"Indeed, you do. I have mentioned it to you
several times."

"You look lovely today, Miss Belmont," he
said to the daughter. "Are you enjoying your
walk?"

In response, he received a timid, "Thank
you," and a curt nod. He'd never heard more
than a word or two from Florence but appreciated the young woman's retiring ways nonetheless. A furious blush spread over her fair
cheeks, reminding him of her innocence. Like
her mother, she had light hair and blue eyes,
and though tall she was slighter of figure.

Mrs. Belmont said something, but her words
escaped Brendan. Over her shoulder, he saw
Sarah disappear behind a bronze cast of George
Washington. It was a pity that Miss Stevens
was in a delicate state at the moment, or he
might have been tempted to turn her over his
knee.

"Whatever are you looking at?" Caroline
asked, her petulant tone gaining his attention.

"I don't believe it's a multi-legged bug on
your shoulder, after all," he replied with a hint
of a smile. "Just a speck of lint."

Florence squealed and hopped away, bump-
ing into Brendan, who smoothly stepped aside.

Caroline vigorously brushed her fan over her
shoulder as she danced in a circle.

Brendan grinned widely, but promptly pasted a distressed expression on his face and averted his gaze to the daughter. "I beg your pardon, Miss Belmont. I didn't mean to upset you."

Florence smiled sweetly.

Mrs. Belmont glanced around; then her perfectly shaped lips pursed as she pinned him with a venomous look.

Brendan wondered why today he felt no overwhelming desire to toss the lush woman on the ground and bury himself inside her. For months the sight of her had driven him crazy. For months her artful flirtation had severely strained his willpower. "No one saw you, madam."

She shot him another glare.

"Mother has promised to ride the swan boat with me," Florence said.

Surprised to hear a whole sentence from her, Brendan regarded Florence warmly. Here was a woman with whom a man could spend time and not suffer a moment's annoyance. He found her melodious voice calming and her serene manner appealing. "I hope you have an enjoyable afternoon, my dear."

Apparently recovered from her excitement, Mrs. Belmont spoke. "We would be pleased to have you join us. It's the least you can do, after nearly frightening us to death."

Out of the corner of his eye, Brendan detected a figure moving in the direction of the front gates. "I would like nothing better, ladies, but unfortunately there's a pressing matter I must see to." Bringing Caroline's hand to his mouth, he placed a leisurely kiss on her glove. His thumb slipped beyond the material and caressed the underside of her wrist. "Perhaps another time?"

Plying her fan again, Caroline boldly studied him from head to foot. "I will hold you to your word."

He released her hand and straightened abruptly. Bloody hell! What had he been thinking? It was bad enough to slip in Sarah's presence. Not long ago she'd been an innocent. But reverting to Wicked Warwick with a woman who knew the score had been a serious mistake. He'd given her the idea that he meant to pursue their attraction.

Brendan politely excused himself and set off at a swift pace in the opposite direction. Even if he had to sprout wings, he would not allow the cunning Miss Stevens to escape him again.

Sarah hurried toward the exit, shoving aside low hanging branches and detouring around bushes that blocked her path. She had seen her fill of Lafayette Park that day. Goodness, she felt like an outlaw with a bounty hunter hot on her trail. Brendan Hammond was certainly persistent. When he'd encountered the two women in the fancy dresses, she had hoped he'd forget about *her* and accompany them for a while.

Her outing had turned into a disaster. The excitement, too, had taken its toll. The idea of crawling into bed and sleeping the rest of the day—oh, for pity's sake. The sound of boots crunching on the gravel walkway behind her couldn't possibly have been his. He'd still been talking with the women when she'd decided to leave.

Sarah stopped and peeked around a tree. It *was* Brendan. He looked a formidable foe at that moment, his dark brows slashed together over narrowed eyes. She realized his determined stride would put him at her hiding spot in a matter of seconds. But suddenly she no longer cared.

When he came closer to her, she inhaled deeply, then called to him. He looked around before he left the walk to join her in the foliage.

"Miss Stevens," he said pleasantly, "I see you have discovered our park."

That he could speak in a civil tone when she knew he must be angry demonstrated a very strong will. Impressed and thankful that he was behaving civilly, she returned, "A very nice park, indeed."

Pressing his walking stick and gloves into her hand, he said, "Put these on."

Sarah never thought to disobey.

He closed the top buttons of the coat, his fingers brushing her neck, then adjusted the collar a bit higher. Tingles raced over her skin where he touched it. Next, he caught her hair in his fingers and twisted it atop her head. He held the mass with one hand as, meeting and holding her gaze, he transferred his hat from his head to hers. "The next time you feel like a stroll, let me know."

His gloves felt warm. His eyes picked up

lights from the sun dappling the ground. "You'd accompany me?"

Gripping her elbow, he escorted her into the open. Tipping up her chin with a finger, one side of his mouth lifted in a semblance of a smile. "Of course, Sarah. A few months from now, I'd be honored."

After checking the walk to make sure no one was coming, he said, "We are two gentlemen who happened to meet. Keep your head lowered and try to walk like a man, if you will."

Sarah giggled at the thought. "My skirt sticks out."

He glanced down, then frowned. "Only a few inches show. I suggest we not dawdle. My reputation will be a devilish mess, should anyone notice my walking companion."

"I'm sorry. I'll follow behind."

"Come, Sarah. We'll see this through together."

She was being escorted from a lovely park by a sinfully handsome earl, and she looked like a portly man who waddled like a duck! A portly man wearing a woman's dress. If her cousin Lizzie could have seen her, she'd have laughed herself sick.

The front door opened at the precise moment when they reached the house. Sarah returned Stratford's wide-eyed stare. The man looked as if he'd swallowed a mouse, but amazingly, he recovered in an instant. Brendan snatched the hat from her head, retrieved his walking stick, then pulled his gloves from her hands.

Betrayed by an unexpected wave of dizziness, Sarah gripped the closest object—Brendan's arm.

"Let me help," Brendan said softly, passing his belongings to Stratford. He deftly popped the buttons free and slid the coat from her shoulders, then handed it to his servant as well.

"Perhaps a cup of tea," Stratford volunteered.

"I think a rest is more in order," Brendan countered.

"Shall I fetch Mathilda, sir?"

"I'll see to Miss Stevens myself."

She must have been dreaming, Sarah mused, for she thought she detected concern in both gentlemen. Confused by Brendan's curious demeanor, Sarah studied his face. And found no clue to his thoughts.

He waited until Stratford retreated before he spoke to her. "I desire a word with you in private."

She watched him walk to the bottom of the staircase, where he patiently awaited her. Foreboding swept through her, leaving her knees wobbly. She had known better than to disobey his orders, yet she had done it anyway. Her mother always stood her ground with her overbearing father, but Brendan Hammond was another matter. He must have been angrier than she'd thought. He might have held his temper in the park only because he was waiting until they were alone to let her know his true feelings.

When he crossed his arms over his chest, he looked menacing, and Sarah faltered as she went near him. The child felt heavier, almost as if it had chosen that second to sink lower. An involuntary sigh escaped her. She reached out for the banister, but strong arms wound around her, sweeping her from her feet. Sarah's sigh became a gasp.

"Rest easy," he whispered, "you've just over-exerted yourself."

The walls and ceiling passed by in a rush as Brendan carried her up the curved stairs.

When he reached the top, he paused to re-settle her in his arms. Without so much as a glance at her, he headed for her room.

Weary from her afternoon, she surrendered to the temptation to rest her head against his chest, allowing her arms to slip around him. Hugging his solid body was a mistake. Her melancholia returned in full force. Having a child should have been a blessed event, a time of supreme joy for two people in love. She had no one to share special moments with, espe-cially the moments when the child moved in-side her.

And when the child came, who would share that glorious occasion with her?

For one crazy second she imagined Brendan holding a squirming infant in his arms, a beam-ing smile on his face. She must have been de-ranged.

"You'll have to open the door."

Brendan's deep tone brought Sarah back to reality. He stood in front of her room, question-ing her with a raised brow. Understanding, coupled with embarrassment, came to her.

Leaning forward slightly, she turned the knob, and he pushed the door open with his foot. Once inside, he gently laid her on the bed and backed away.

As he shut the door, he worked his shoulders up and down, bringing a flush to her face. Although he'd not shown any discomfort, she must have weighed a great deal. Then she realized what he had done—they were alone in her bedroom.

A laugh nearly escaped her. Propriety seemed a silly notion—her virtue was long gone.

"How are you feeling?" he asked.

Sarah sat up and eased her legs over the side of the mattress. "A bit tired, that's all."

Clasping his hands behind his back, he strode the length of the room and back, turning when he reached the spot directly in front of her. "Sarah, I expressly forbade you to leave the house."

His amiable tone failed to disguise his irritation, pricking Sarah's conscience. "The temptation was too great, and well, actually I—"

"Didn't think?"

"I did think. I thought you wouldn't come home for several hours."

"I'm sorry to have disappointed you, but I have news I wanted to discuss with my aunt."

"About Derek?"

His brows knitted together before he replied. "I received word from the detective agency that they haven't been able to locate my brother."

"Oh?"

Relief flooded Sarah, until she considered the ramifications of this turn of events.

"I'll speak with my aunt and let you know of our decision."

"*Your* decision?" She inhaled a deep breath to control the anger that had surged up suddenly. "I appreciate all you've done for me, but if you think to hide me away in the attic—"

"My aunt and I are only interested in helping you and your child."

"I know," she muttered. "But you can't understand what it's like to live differently than what you're used to. I feel trapped, kept in a cage."

A muscle ticked in his jaw. "It's only for a time. After the child comes, you'll be free to leave the house."

Having to look up at him proved a disadvantage, but one easily remedied. Sarah wiggled to the end of the mattress and, as gracefully as possible, came to her feet. He still stood above her, but she felt more on his level.

"You should rest, Sarah. You've had an eventful day."

"Do I look ill, sir?"

"Why, no . . . but you—you aren't yourself, and should have a care for the child."

"I don't think fresh air and exercise are grounds for concern. Nor is standing, so long as I don't overdo it."

He raised a brow but made no further comment, for which Sarah gave thanks. She grew uncomfortable. His presence in the close confines of her room played on her nerves.

"Promise me you won't try this again," he said.

Sarah laid a hand over her heart. "I promise I won't go to the park until after the baby comes."

"You underestimate me, Sarah." He tilted his head and studied her with a peculiar look in his eyes. "I was right. You're much too clever."

"Clever? What do you mean?"

He threw back his head and laughed. "You promised not to go to the park. When I find you next, strolling down the street, will you remind me that your promise included nothing about other destinations?"

Sarah bit her lip. She wasn't nearly as clever as he was, and she should've known he'd catch on. "The thought never entered my mind."

"Do you resort to subterfuge at home?"

She grinned. "Only with Papa. Mama is much too smart."

He raised a brow.

Quickly she amended her remark. "Not that I'm implyin' that my father is dull-witted. His finances might not be what they once were, but he tries to make up for it in other ways."

"No doubt by spoiling you."

"I'm his only daughter," she said indignantly.

"That explains much."

"I don't take your meanin'."

The lights appeared in his eyes again as his stance relaxed. "A man has every right to spoil his only daughter, especially if she's pretty and willful."

Sarah hesitated, unsure whether he was taunting her.

His eyes roamed her face overly long. "I would spoil you too, Sarah—" He stiffened as he cut off the rest of his sentence. "You must be a witch," he mumbled.

Brendan knew he was scowling. Bloody hell, he hadn't had much trouble maintaining his puritanical image until recently. He hadn't reverted to his former self as frequently as during the past three days—since the arrival of Miss Stevens.

He wanted to believe the worst of her. He didn't want to admire her spirit or find her amusing or feel compassion for her plight. Most likely she was playing him for a fool.

"Brendan, I . . . oh!"

He watched her stumble backward, pressing a hand to her distended belly. Assailed by a wave of panic, he gripped her shoulders and saw her seated on the bed. "What's wrong? Is the child coming?"

She looked at him with wonder in her eyes. "It turns now and again, and pokes me with an elbow or foot. It's quite wonderful." Taking his hand, she tugged it forward. "Do you want to feel it?"

He wanted to do no such thing. But the happiness he saw in her eyes prevented him from denying her. Resigning himself, he allowed her to splay his fingers over her abdomen, then move them until she was satisfied.

"It's not pokin' me right now. Wait a minute. Sit beside me, and you'll be more comfortable."

It was disconcerting, to say the least. A woman simply didn't invite a man to put his hand on her stomach. Heat crawled up his neck. There had been nothing sensual in her maneuver, yet he felt extremely ill at ease.

"Now, do you feel it?"

To Brendan's amazement, a small, sharp lump rose under his fingers. Too impressed to speak, he nodded.

"An elbow, I think," she said.

"I believe you're right, Sarah."

She smiled up at him, her eyes moist. Then, taking her hand from his, she lowered her gaze. "Please, forgive my impulsiveness. I—"

He touched her shoulder. "Don't apologize, Sarah. Thank you for sharing the special moment with me."

"I've been dyin' to share the baby's movements with someone, and I didn't think."

Good God, she'd be in the full throes of tears any second. He knew he'd take her in his arms to comfort her, and then his mind would be even more muddled. If she was an adventuress, she was devilishly good.

Leaving her staring after him, he rose and strode to the door.

Chapter 5

Gertrude left the dining room table, where she'd just finished eating alone. Her nephew's defection puzzled her. Stratford had acted peculiarly, avoiding conversation. Everyone, in fact, was behaving as if she'd come down with cholera.

"Stratford!"

She waited patiently, knowing the well-trained servant would appear with haste. When he presented himself, she bade him shut the doors. He performed the task, then positioned himself in front of her.

"You wished something, madam?"

"I wish to know what happened this afternoon during my absence."

"Madam?"

"Where is my nephew?"

"He has retired to the billiard room. He asked that he not be disturbed."

"I find that rather unusual considering he adamantly demands his dinner be served on time." She watched the man tug nervously on his waistcoat. Extracting information from him would be a tedious affair. "Do you not find it strange?"

"No, madam. It is not my place to question his Lordship's moods."

She circled the servant, aware that he followed her every movement. Picking a dead leaf from the potted fern in front of the window, she remarked, "What kind of mood would you say plagues him?"

Stratford sniffed.

Gertrude whirled around and crossed her arms at her waist. "I demand that you tell me what transpired in my absence."

"Very well, madam, since you insist. The young lady went out today. His Lordship returned early and, having apparently seen her, retrieved her from the park."

"Oh, dear. He must have been furious."

"He didn't seem so at first."

Gertrude waved a hand, prompting the man to continue.

"It was after he carried her upstairs." He fell silent, then continued. "It is my presumption that they must have had words. The young lady appears to have a mind of her own, and you know his Lordship does not brook—"

"I most certainly do. Thank you for your honesty."

Gertrude left the room immediately after Stratford, her skirt rustling in her haste. She considered speaking with Sarah, then changed her mind. Finding her nephew in the billiard room, bent over the table, she entered in time to see him send a ball flying across the table with such force it leaped over the edge and bounced off her foot.

Brendan straightened. "Forgive me. I didn't hear you come in. I haven't hurt your foot, have I?"

"Not a bit," she said, though the ball had landed smack on her corn. He'd been under a great deal of stress the past few days. Refashioning his life had been hard enough without the added burden of their guest, and she was determined to spare him at least this one trivial matter. More important issues were at stake. "I missed you at dinner."

He laid the stick on the table. "I wasn't hungry."

"Stratford told me what happened, so it's futile to hedge."

"Did he, indeed?" He rubbed his knuckles over his eyelids, then collapsed on a chair. "I chased the little witch through the park, and it was only by God's graces she wasn't seen by Caroline Belmont."

"You chased her? Brendan, she's hardly able to move faster than a man of your size."

He grunted as he reached for a nearby glass. "Speed isn't necessary when one has cunning. The lady knows her way around greenery."

Gertrude hid a smile at his sardonic tone. "I gather you drank your dinner?"

He held up the glass in a mock salute, then finished off its contents. Pulling a piece of paper from his pocket, he waved it in the air. "They haven't been able to locate my brother."

She had expected locating Derek would

prove a trial, but Brendan's tidings unsettled her. Wanting a distraction, she stooped to pick up the ball and set it on the table. There was a solution to their dilemma, if she could find the mettle to broach the delicate subject with her nephew. Brendan's somber disposition did not delude her. Deep down he knew what he must do.

Heaven help them all.

At a loss for where to look next, Sarah wandered through the rooms on the lower level. She owed Brendan yet another apology for having behaved so forwardly. His hasty departure from her room had been proof enough of his embarrassment. But she was unable to find him.

Spotting a hall she hadn't noticed before, she turned the corner. Her search had ended. Leaning slightly forward, his ear pressed to the door, Stratford earnestly eavesdropped on a conversation. Sarah slipped off her shoes and crept up behind him.

Brendan's and Gertrude's muffled voices came from within. Hearing her name mentioned, Sarah stepped closer. Stratford spun around, color flooding his pale cheeks. His eyes widened when he realized by whom he had been discovered.

He opened his mouth to utter something, but Sarah held a finger over her lips. "Don't offer an excuse," she whispered. "I've been frequently chastised for indulgin' my curiosity, and wouldn't think of exposing you." She heard her name mentioned again, deciding her course. "It'll be our secret." She flattened her ear to the door, then grinned when he joined her.

But Sarah's smile soon vanished. Not only were Brendan and Gertrude discussing her; they were determining her fate.

Stratford attempted to lead her away from the door. "Leave with me now, Miss Sarah. This isn't for your ears."

She mouthed an adamant, "No," and tugged him back. "I'll hear what they have to say about me."

Stratford rolled his eyes and reluctantly remained.

The conversation grew as heated as Sarah's own cheeks.

"I must speak with you now," Gertrude said. "A decision has to be made and acted upon."

Brendan looked up with a cynical grin. "I know."

"Are you going to send her away?"

"No!"

Brendan's swift, curt reply revealed much, prompting Gertrude to ask, "Do you have feelings for the girl?"

"Feelings? What are you getting at?"

"You at least like her, don't you?"

Brendan stood and stuffed the telegram back into his pocket. He strode across the room and stopped beside her. "Miss Stevens is undiplomatically vocal, stubborn, and proud, and hasn't a single biddable bone in her body. In short, she's totally unsuitable."

"Brendan, you haven't answered my question. I'm fully aware of her imperfections. She's exactly like me, yet you insisted that I live with you, despite the fact that I have two residences of my own."

"You have even more wealth than I, Aunt Gertrude, which allows you your eccentricities. You're also my relative, not my wife, and I've learned to tolerate your unseemly quirks."

Gertrude summoned her courage and asked, "Are you considering marrying her? 'Tis the thing to do, you know. Her child is, after all, a Hammond, and above all, Hammonds take care of their own."

The minute the words left her mouth, she knew she'd made a grave error, and that she'd touched the crux of his troubles. Even as a notorious rake, Brendan had always been venerable in his dealings—an honorable rogue. His face turned dark as a thundercloud.

"In case you've forgotten," he said in a lethally calm tone, "I have plans to offer for Florence Belmont."

Gripping his arm, she said, "I've kept silent for too long. Forgive me, but I must speak candidly. You need a woman with blood in her veins and the tenacity to stand up to you. Florence is a darling girl, but she won't make you happy, Brendan. She's entirely too docile for a man of your appetites."

"My appetites, madam? I daresay you're speaking out of turn."

"Because I'm a woman? Oh, do be reason-able. You, of all people, know I'm not the least bit decorous when we're alone."

"Very well, then, speak as you will, but my life's my own. I'll damned well not have it de-cided for me." He left her, returned to the bil-liard table, and picked up the stick. "We're not even sure of Sarah's character. Is it not bad enough that she would make my life a living hell? Must we gamble my fortune and good name as well?"

"What do you propose? Shall we wait indef-initely and have it known she bore Derek's bas-tard? That would do wonders for the Hammond name! Not to mention the effect it would have on an innocent who happens to be our own flesh and blood."

He slammed the stick down, muttering a vile oath. "Bloody hell, you're right, and there's not a thing I can do. I'm damned if I do, damned if I don't!"

Gertrude breathed a sigh of relief. She felt no guilt, knowing she had only maneuvered Bren-dan to a decision he would've come to on his own.

"Very well, I'll marry the chit. I knew all along it might come to this, but I'd hoped to persuade Derek to pay for his own blunder. She has no connections, and certainly no virtue left. Who knows how she'll be received, if in fact we pass her off. Have you given any thought as to how this marriage will be viewed? One simply doesn't acquire a wife and an offspring overnight."

Gertrude glanced at the door, sure she'd heard a sound a few seconds past. Footsteps faded away, and she decided it must have been a servant passing by. She looked at her nephew. "I've given it much thought and have concocted a credible story. There's bound to be gossip, but it'll die down in time. I shall personally see to it."

He raised a brow. "You were very sure of the outcome."

"I'm sure of you. You could do no less."

Brendan threw up his hands in defeat. "The sooner we arrange the marriage the better. If she's awake, send her to me."

Gertrude had an inkling that Brendan's outrage and ultimate capitulation camouflaged a truth about which even he had no knowledge. He'd always done as he wished, with no regard for anyone else's opinion, yet, for an unprincipled man, he lived by a high code of honor. She couldn't have made him marry Sarah.

He had, however, given in far too easily. Either he'd already resigned himself to the marriage or he had an ulterior motive.

Not until she reached her room did Sarah swipe at the dampness welling in her eyes. Brendan thought her totally unsuitable, among other things. She didn't know why, but his rejection hurt. Well, she wouldn't marry him if he were the last man on the earth!

Stratford arrived at her door, bearing her shoes. "His Lordship desires a word with you, Miss Sarah."

Sarah couldn't believe her ears. She detected no rebuke in his manner, and, incredibly, he offered her a sympathetic smile. "Thank you, Stratford. Kindly inform him that I'm too fatigued to honor his request."

Stratford's smile faded to a grimace.

Knowing that sending the servant to deliver such news would gain him a scolding, she relented. "Oh, very well, I might as well see him now."

He held out her shoes and waited while she put them on. Then, surprising her again, he offered his arm and led her down the stairs to the room she'd just left.

Outside the door, he said, "Do not hold his Lordship's words against him, Miss Sarah. He's exceedingly dissimilar from the image he portrays."

"I'll try," she returned, confused by the man's odd phrasing. She hadn't a clue to his meaning. She'd just begun to believe her first impression of Brendan Hammond had been wrong. After overhearing his conversation with his aunt, her opinion had changed.

"Come in, Sarah," Brendan said when she cracked open the door. "We have much to discuss."

Sarah indignantly held her head high and allowed him to escort her to a chair.

He dragged another close, then sat. "Sarah, I'll not waste time by 'hedging,' as my aunt phrases it. Time is the one thing you've run out of." He gently held her hand. "We'll wed at once."

She expected a proposal, not an abrupt command. Minutes ticked away as she worded a refusal in her mind. Her conscience took that moment to lecture that marriage to him would resolve her present problems and provide a name and security for her child.

And bind her to a man who regarded her as lacking the social graces necessary to his position.

He would forever hold her affair with Derek against her, and . . . She couldn't bear to think of the many ways in which Brendan could exact revenge for ruining his life.

Still, he was a principled man, unlike Derek, who—

"Sarah!"

"You are generous, sir, but unfortunately I must decline your offer."

She'd never thought to see him at a loss for a comeback, and found his look of astonishment a balm to her bruised ego.

"Why the hell not?" he eventually asked. "You have no other alternative."

"We're unsuited."

"Which has nothing to do with this," he said gently. "You must have a husband, and I'm volunteering. You and your child will want for nothing."

"I have a choice," she said indignantly, remembering his disparaging remarks about her to his aunt. Her child would be a constant reminder of her sin. She slowly rose, pulling her hand free. "I won't marry you, not in a thousand lifetimes."

"Sarah, you're acting irrationally. The child's a Hammond and deserves his birthright."

She marched to the door, but he appeared in front of her, blocking her way. "Nothing you can say or do will change my mind."

He raked his fingers through his hair, leaving it sticking out in places. "You refused my offer of money; now you're rejecting the only option to secure your future and your child's. Either you are demented or I've misjudged you. Which is it, Sarah?"

She returned his measuring stare briefly, then detoured around him. "Believe what you will. You have thus far."

Infuriating woman! Brendan went directly to his room.

He needed time to think. Sarah had stunned him by refusing his proposal, and he still found her action hard to accept. An adventuress would have welcomed the opportunity to become his wife.

Granted, his proposal had been curt, but their circumstances differed from the normal. They weren't romantically involved, or even in love. She couldn't expect him to go down on one knee and spout words of love.

She'd seemed almost incensed by his proposition, as if he'd insulted her. Did she think he wanted to abandon his own plans in order to assure her respectability, when a chance existed that Derek might be found in time? She'd released him from his obligation by refusing him, so why was he angry.

He had wrongly judged her. It was the only reason to explain her absurd reaction. She had no designs on his money or interest in gaining a rich husband, after all. And he couldn't stand by and allow her to destroy herself to preserve her dignity.

The lady was even more trouble than he'd imagined.

"Kindly allow me to wake his Lordship."

Sarah shook her head. She'd risen with the sun in order to flee without having to meet Brendan or Gertrude. She should have guessed that evading Stratford would prove impossible.

"But you cannot leave. What will become of you?"

"Don't worry. I'll send a wire to my father, and he'll see that someone meets me partway."

She pulled her shawl closer about her, shivering at the thought of having to deceive either of her parents. If she bought a wedding band, they'd naturally assume she'd married Derek. Then she'd say that they'd had a lover's spat.

"You're kind to worry about me, Stratford."

He glanced down the hall before he pulled something from his pocket and tucked it into her hand. "Allow me to offer some assistance, miss."

Sarah gripped the wad of money and regarded him with moist eyes. Now she wouldn't have to wire her father right away. "Thank you. I'll see that every cent is repaid."

Avoiding her gaze, Stratford sent for Brendan's carriage, then carried her bag out front.

"It's not too late to change your mind," he said as he handed her inside the vehicle.

"My mind's made up," she returned. "You'll see. Brendan will be relieved to find me gone. He can resume his life."

"I beg to differ, miss. He will have me served up on a silver platter."

Sarah smiled. "I believe I'll miss you, Stratford."

She waited while he gave instructions to the driver. Oddly, she felt sad at the prospect of leaving this house. It reminded her of the days when her father was wealthy. But it was only a structure, and the man who owned it could never bring her happiness. She'd brought Brendan enough trouble.

Even at this early hour the streets teemed with carriages, buggies and horses, and the larger omnibuses. Sarah occupied herself with seeing as much of the city as possible, surprised by the number of beer houses and saloons they passed. Every imaginable establishment lined the thoroughfares: fruit and cigar stores, bakeries, grocery and dry goods store, theaters, markets, churches, even a sturdy jail. All were constructed of brick, some with five stories.

On Fourth Street, she was captivated by the court house. Deciding it must be two hundred feet high, she admired the four massive circular galleries that rose to the cast-iron dome. Then she noticed the opera house. She imagined ladies in flowing gowns on the arms of dignified gentlemen crowding inside for an evening's entertainment and felt sad that she would never be one of them.

The levee bustled with activity; drays, wagons, and carriages rushed to and fro, and a multitude of men shoved one another in their haste to tend their business. Everywhere sacks, casks, boxes, barrels, and bulky pieces littered the paved slope along the river's edge. Steamboats were tied up at the wharf, with gangplanks run out for loading and unloading cargo. Above the wharves on a flat bench, gray and yellow structures gave off an offensive smell.

The carriage stopped just short of the structures, and the driver left Sarah and her bag in the only available vacant spot. As he prepared to depart, carefully retreating the way they'd come, she almost lost her courage and called him back. But there was no place to go, at least no place where she'd be welcomed and wanted. Except home.

She inquired after transportation, and found a spot on a steamboat scheduled to leave in three hours. With so many sights and sounds around her, she hoped the wait would pass quickly. Steamship whistles mingled with the cries of girls hawking apples and men selling cigars. The throng of men milling on the levee represented every level of society, from drunkards, pickpockets, and rowdies to distinguished gentlemen. But it was the homeless children scurrying about who brought sadness to Sarah's heart.

Had she been a fool to reject Brendan's proposal?

If her father didn't welcome her, her child might end up as one of these wretched souls. A young girl approached a steamboatman and lifted her shirt, gaining a few pennies. Aghast that the girl should have to earn a living in so shameful a fashion, Sarah quickly glanced in the opposite direction.

An hour later, she cursed her prideful nature. Her lower back ached something awful, and the offensive smell coming from a nearby building had soured her stomach. The prospect of traveling so far now seemed an irrational decision. She closed her eyes, praying for rescue from her impossible predicament. But even as she did so, she realized the futility of it.

Prince Charming didn't exist, especially in her case.

She grew so miserable, she made no attempt to hide her despair, and hid her face in her hands. The ache in her back subsided, then returned in full force. Merciful heavens, she'd have kissed the ground just to open her eyes and find Brendan Hammond in front of her.

"What do you mean, she's gone?"

Gertrude wrung her hands together and glanced at Stratford. "Tell him."

Brendan left his desk and approached his servant. Stratford stood very straight and looked discreetly ahead, convincing Brendan that he'd had a hand in Sarah's disappearance. "Out with it, man."

"Begging your pardon, sir, but I believe the young lady's destination is her home. Rather than remain with her, I gave the driver instructions to promptly return with the information of her whereabouts. Is that not what you would have done?"

"Where the hell is she?"

"The levee . . . sir," Stratford stuttered. "I'm sure by now she has secured passage on a ship."

Brendan growled low in his throat and held his hands at his sides. He wouldn't strangle the man, he decided, regardless of the provocation. "Why wasn't I awakened?"

"Sarah obviously wanted to leave without our knowing," Gertrude said.

"Preposterous. We've tried to help her." Stratford fidgeted, further arousing Brendan's suspicions. "If you know more about this, I advise you to speak up now."

"Miss Sarah overheard you and madam speaking in the billiard room." All traces of color drained from Stratford's face. "I was also present."

"Bloody hell!"

Gertrude slapped a hand over her mouth, muffling a gasp. "Brendan, you must do something. Sarah's in no shape to travel."

"I'm perfectly aware of that fact, madam," Brendan retorted, "though under other circumstances, I'd pit her against anyone." He turned to Stratford. "Have the gig brought around immediately. I'll drive myself."

When they were alone, Gertrude said, "After you find Sarah, take her to my hunting lodge. Reverend Gallsworthy's in my debt, and well he should be. I support his church in grand fashion. I'll send him to you. Perhaps it would be a good idea if Sarah stayed at the lodge for a decent interval after the birth. I'll see that the proper rumor is circulated."

"And what could that possibly be?"

"Trust me, Brendan. I'm an expert in matters of gossip. Everything will be in order when you return, and I'll explain."

"Assuming Sarah agrees," he muttered.

"If she rejected you last evening, it's no wonder, after she heard our conversation. And, knowing you, I suspect you issued an ultimatum in lieu of using your talents in the art of persuasion. You'll convince her otherwise, won't you?"

"Need you ask? I'm not a complete jackass."

Not wanting to waste another minute, Brendan set out for the levee, nearly running down two slower moving carriages in his haste. Images of Sarah assailed him. The amusement he'd experienced when he'd watched her devour her meal with unladylike zeal. The way her gray-green eyes flashed fire when he made her angry. Sarah, standing alone on a busy wharf, afraid, hurt.

She infuriated and exasperated him, yet she invaded his mind at every turn.

Now, because of her, his life was to veer from the path he'd chosen. But instead of wrath, guilt drove him.

What if he failed to find her?

Chapter 6

⌒⌒○○⌒⌒

Thousands of people clogged the levee, and someone might have recognized him, but fate had already graced him. He spotted Sarah almost immediately sitting on a crate in front of the buildings lining the ledge.

She looked a pitiful sight, her shoulders sagging, one hand held over her lower back. A steamboat whistle shrieked above the clamor of people, horses, and vehicles, but Sarah remained oblivious.

Cursing himself for a fool, Brendan parked his carriage a short distance to her right. How could he have thought her a scheming adventuress? He'd been told by more than one woman that he possessed a heart of stone. At that moment he could rightly have differed with them. That particular organ welled with compassion and the desire to pull Sarah into his arms and comfort her.

Lost in her own thoughts, she didn't hear him approach. "Sarah," he called softly, determined to deal with her in a gentle manner.

When she wearily looked up, her eyes appeared unfocused, then settled on him. A smile crept over her mouth. If he hadn't known better, he'd have sworn she was genuinely happy to see him.

"Brendan? Is it really you?"

"I've come to take you home."

She continued to regard him as if he were a phantom. "Sarah, are you all right?" He leaned forward, gripped her elbows, and eased her to her feet, catching her when she would have lost her balance. "You've sat in the sun too long. Come with me."

"I'm used to bein' out in the sun," she weakly protested.

"Of course you are, but you aren't to argue. There will be time for that later." Wrapping an arm around her, he led her to the carriage and lifted her to the seat. "Luck's with us. I don't believe anyone has recognized me."

Holding a hand to her forehead, she said, "It doesn't matter. When they learn of me, they'll spurn you soon enough."

He climbed in beside her and grabbed the reins. Guilt stabbed him again. "Sarah, you must forget what you overheard. Wealth and position have an advantage. Vicious prattle is easily crushed when one has the know-how and connections. My aunt has assured me she'll take care of everything. I've put my trust in her, and so should you."

She remained silent for a spell, until they'd traveled along several streets. "Where are we goin'?"

"My aunt owns a hunting lodge about five

miles out of town, left to her by her husband.
She's graciously offered us the use of it."

"But Brendan—"

"I hope you've seen the error of your thinking and have realized that we must wed immediately."

He glanced at her and noted her pursed lips.
Hell. It was bloody well difficult to remember
to phrase his words so they didn't come out a
command. He smiled to himself. He hadn't
learned much about her yet, but he knew she
didn't take well to being ordered about.
"Sarah," he said persuasively, "will you do me
the honor of becoming my wife?"

After a few minutes, she favored him with
another warm smile. "Yes. Thank you for
makin' such a sacrifice on my account."

"Don't make me out a martyr. If I didn't have
some feelings for you, I wouldn't be here right
now."

She said nothing for a moment. "I'll try not
to be a burden to you."

He nearly laughed at the absurdity of her
statement, but she sounded so sincere, he controlled himself. He didn't dare imagine their
life together. Despite her assurance, he doubted
Sarah could transform herself into a biddable
wife. Even if they managed to make a go of
their marriage, eventually Derek might return
and create a rift between them.

Half an hour later they reached the outskirts
of town and Gertrude's property. Brendan
turned down the narrow road leading to the
house. No one had used the lodge since An-

toine Chateaus had passed away five years earlier, but his aunt kept it up "just in case."

Upon catching sight of the house, Sarah exclaimed, "Oh, it's wonderful."

Brendan was used to grand residences, and didn't consider the simple wooden structure anything of the kind. Still, it afforded privacy, and the grounds were well kept. He wondered if the stable housed any animals or if they'd been sold off.

"Does Gertrude ever come here?"

"She says it reminds her too much of her husband, but she hasn't the heart to sell it."

Sarah's rapt attention and her overbright eyes told him she'd fallen in love with the place. He admitted it held a certain charm, especially the porch that wrapped around the front and sides.

He handed her down from the carriage, then took the lead to the front entrance. Several of the boards squeaked on the porch. Fearing they might be infirm, he directed Sarah around them. Her gait seemed slower that day, and her strained expression gave him reason to believe she suffered some discomfort. Glancing at her stomach, which he normally avoided doing, he thought the child rode decidedly lower than he remembered. An awful premonition struck him.

"Sarah, when's your time?"

"Not for several weeks, though I think the child has different plans."

Brendan choked on a cough. "You can't be serious. Have you any pain?"

"Just in my back, every so often."

"Is that significant?"

"I've never done this before, Brendan." A soft moan escaped her as she gripped his arm. "I . . . do, however, think . . . we should go inside . . . now!"

Brendan fumbled with the key, finally managing to turn it in the lock, then shoved open the door. Gently lifting Sarah, he carried her into the dim front room and deposited her in a leather chair. He spared a moment to look around and silently congratulated his aunt's choice of caretaker. The interior appeared as well maintained as the outside.

A quick tour of the house revealed a master chamber, with a smaller bedroom in the rear, a kitchen, and a stocked pantry. He fetched Sarah's bag from the carriage and placed it in the master chamber before he returned to the main room.

Her relaxed expression lessened his anxiety. "Are you feeling better?"

"Somewhat."

He headed for the door.

"You're not leavin'?"

At her worried tone, he glanced over his shoulder. "I must locate the caretaker and let him know of our presence. He might have a wife." Before he could say more, he heard the crunch of wheels out front. A tall, thin man dressed in black alighted from a buggy. "Sarah, the preacher's here."

"The preacher!"

"When my aunt makes arrangements, she acts with all due haste."

Sarah pushed herself to her feet. "Whatever will he think?"

"Gallsworthy has been paid well not to think. Don't concern yourself."

Sarah frowned. Although things were happening too fast, she had no thought of offering a protest. On the levee she'd wished for a prince to rescue her. Brendan Hammond might not have had all of the qualities she wanted in a man, but he was at least principled and an honorable man. He was also willing to relinquish whatever plans he might have had for his own life in order to marry her. She doubted she'd ever have the same starry-eyed feelings for him that she'd had for Derek, yet Brendan had earned her admiration.

Reverend Gallsworthy promptly stood them together, snapped open his prayer book, and began to recite the wedding vows. This wasn't the ceremony she'd always dreamed of, but Sarah consoled herself with the thought that she was fortunate to marry at all.

Midway through the ritual, the ache in her back advanced considerably, stabbing her so severely, she nearly cried out. Her knees went limp from the pressure. She reached toward Brendan, and he instantly wrapped his fingers around hers, while his other arm circled her waist. Grateful for his strong support, she met his gaze. His eyes burned with an intense emotion. The fine lines feathering across his brow confused her.

"Sarah, you must say your vow," he said.

The pain subsided, and she dutifully repeated the words after the clergyman, her voice dipping lower when she encountered the word *obey*. Brendan squeezed her fingers, confirming that her maneuver hadn't escaped his notice.

Reverend Gallsworthy produced a ring from his breast pocket and declared that Mrs. Chauteaus wished her nephew's wife to be wed with the cherished heirloom. Brendan reverently slipped the sparkling band on her finger.

Then they were man and wife.

"You may kiss the bride," the reverend said.

Oh, surely he wouldn't, Sarah thought.

Sarah tilted her head, wanting to see Brendan's expression. Her lips parted in surprise. He leaned down, amusement dancing in his eyes. His kiss astonished her. It made her envision the gentle stroke of an artist's brush on a valued canvas. Afterward, she touched her fingers to her tingling lips.

Efficient as ever, Brendan immediately took the man aside. Papers were signed, and Brendan scribbled a note that he asked the reverend to deliver to his aunt.

While Brendan saw the man to his vehicle, another intense pain struck Sarah. Feeling water course down her legs, she sucked in a breath. She grabbed the edge of a table to steady herself.

"Sarah. Is it coming?"

She hadn't heard Brendan come back. Unable to speak, she nodded.

"Bloody hell!" He rushed to her side. "The bedroom."

She started in that direction, while he followed close behind, mumbling unintelligible words. When they reached the doorway, he carefully lifted her in his arms and deposited her near the bed.

He turned down the covers and put her bag on a chair. Riffling through its contents, he found and whipped out a white cotton gown. He started to hand it to her, then, apparently reconsidering, laid it out on the sheet. "You'll have to get undressed."

"Not with you here," she said, her voice cracking.

"Sarah, we're man and wife now. If I fail to find help, you'll have to forgo your modesty anyway."

She indignantly lifted her chin. "What you say might be true, but until such time as I can't manage for myself, I insist that you wait outside."

He wiped his palms on his pants. "Very well. The caretaker must be on the grounds. I'll search for him."

"The caretaker? Wouldn't it be better to summon a doctor?"

"The caretaker is in my aunt's employ, and as such, is more trustworthy about not divulging the circumstances of our hasty marriage."

"Of course; you're right."

Only after she heard the front door shut did Sarah remove her clothes and don the nightgown. She was safely beneath the covers, in the throes of another ravishing pain, when she heard Brendan's knock. She wanted her mother. Or Clara, her nanny, who had remained with them after the War. Clara would know what to do. The pain finally subsided. What did a man know of birthing a baby? she asked herself. But Brendan wasn't just any man, a little voice told her. He was capable and confident, and he'd see her through this.

Not waiting for a response, Brendan burst into the room. "The bloody man has vanished! He'll pay with his hide when he finally shows himself."

"The poor fellow . . . is probably . . . tendin' his chores," Sarah managed to say.

He paced across the room and back, finally stopping beside her. "My education hasn't included the rudiments of childbirth. Sarah, I must locate a doctor."

"No. Please. You said the caretaker was more trustworthy. You've done enough for me already. I won't have everyone knowin' our marriage took place only hours before the baby came. Don't leave me here alone. I need you."

He mumbled beneath his breath again, lines of tension radiating from the corners of his eyes.

Thinking to ease his mind, she said, "Brendan, women have been havin' babies for thousands of years. We'll manage."

She watched him tap his fingers against his pants. She had never thought to see Brendan Hammond nervous, or even hesitant to cope with any situation.

"Leave it to a woman not to comprehend the seriousness of the crisis we face. How the bloody hell can you remain so calm?"

Sarah adjusted the dark blue counterpane so it was tighter under her chin. "Perhaps women are better equipped to deal with critical events than men." She grinned at his flabbergasted look. "When my youngest brother was born, my father was quite beside himself. My mother banished him from the house."

"Yet you will not allow *me* to leave long enough to summon assistance."

"That's different."

"How?"

"Because I want you here. I trust you and . . . " Sarah realized her words were true. If it had been Derek at her side, she wouldn't have been as calm. "Because I've no one else and—"

"Sarah," he said gently, "don't explain. I understand. I'll not leave you alone for a minute unless you desire it."

"Thank you, Brendan."

Twelve hours later Brendan stretched his shoulders and yawned. He'd sat in a chair beside Sarah's bed for so long, he felt part of it. The caretaker had finally shown up, but Brendan had sent him to retrieve his wife, who had gone to visit their daughter. The woman had given birth to six children, convincing him she had a wealth of experience.

The clock in the main room chimed twelve times. What was keeping the man? Obviously, Brendan thought, he should have inquired where the daughter was located. He needed to step outside for a moment to tend to nature's call. Since his discomfort was minor compared to Sarah's, he vowed to wait as long as he could. She'd taken to drifting to sleep between pains, but he knew she might awaken without warning. He'd given his word to remain, and he'd damn well keep it.

Studying her profile in the light from the sole lamp, he felt an overwhelming sense of helplessness. Regardless of his lack of knowledge regarding childbirth, he knew they hadn't much time. She would awaken within seconds. And suffer agony.

She looked so peaceful. And incredibly lovely, her hair spread over the pillow, her dark lashes brushing her cheeks. For the thousandth time he reviled his brother. Derek had done this to her, abandoned her to suffer alone. Well, not alone, he amended. He was at her side.

Sarah stirred, then abruptly awakened. Evidence of her struggle showed, her lips rolling together to keep from groaning. Groaning, hell. She probably wanted to scream down the roof.

"Sarah, it's all right. If it gets unbearable, go ahead and scream."

She adamantly shook her head.

Brendan sighed in exasperation. She had to be the most obstinate woman he'd ever known. And the bravest.

"Roll on your side, love. I have an idea that might ease your pain a bit." For once she obeyed instantly. Brendan slid onto the bed and began to massage her lower back, hoping his meager effort might lessen her pain. "Does this help?"

"Yes. Bren . . . dan, I feel so strange, as . . . if I need to push."

"For the love of God, wait. The caretaker's wife isn't here yet."

"Don't . . . know . . . if I can."

He felt her body tighten and cursed his inexperience in such matters. "We've no choice. You must allow me to look."

"No!"

"I've amassed a thorough knowledge of a woman's body, Sarah. Modesty be damned."

Her fingers clamped around his wrist, her nails biting into his flesh. "A few more minutes, please. She'll come."

"Five minutes, Sarah. No more."

The pain subsided, and she fell against him. Obeying an impulse, he brushed a lock of hair from her brow, then trailed his fingers over her cheek. Taking him off-guard, she turned her head and kissed his palm.

"You've been so kind to me, Brendan. I'm sorry to cause you—"

This time, she couldn't hold back. She screamed bloody hell. And he didn't know what to do, except hold her hand tightly. When she quieted, he dampened a rag and dabbed her forehead with it. Thinking to distract her, he said, "Tell me about your family. You said you have two younger brothers. What are they like?"

"Monsters." She paused and gave him a faint

smile. "Jonathan's fourteen, Tim thirteen. They constantly play tricks on me."

"I sincerely hope their capers aren't in Derek's league."

"Heavens, no. They hide my things, tie knots in my ribbons, and put frogs in my bed."

"Hmmm. When I was their age, my mind was on other pastimes. It wasn't frogs I—" Brendan shut his eyes. He'd done it again, nearly mentioned a particularly lurid escapade he'd had at age fifteen with the very seductive parlor maid. "Your mother. What's she like?"

"The most beautiful lady in all of the Atlanta area. My father was lucky to land her, or so she brags. She had suitors galore. I wish she were here with me."

The sadness in her voice made his heart ache. He held her much smaller hand in his. "Are you like her?"

"Very much," she said, her voice failing. "Mama's quite . . . outspoken . . . especially with Papa. But she knows precisely . . . when to humor him."

"Indeed? When is that?"

She attempted to laugh, but it came out a moan. "She says a vein in his throat becomes more prominent . . . tellin' her he'll soon spew more smoke than the . . . chimney."

Her nails bit into his hand. Sounds outside were heaven-sent. A stout, gray-haired woman appeared at his side as if in answer to a prayer.

"Out with you, young man. Leave a woman to a woman's work."

"Gladly, madam," Brendan returned. Leaning close to Sarah, he whispered, "Help is at hand. I'll be near. If you need me, just yell. I know you can do that."

She giggled and gripped his arm. "You'll truly be near?"

Pressing a kiss on her forehead, he squeezed her hand. "You have my word."

Now, when he was finally being dismissed, he didn't feel as relieved as he'd thought he would. Sarah and he had survived the past hours together. Never before had he felt as close to another person—or as inept. He stalked through the main room and outside, into a pitch-black night, where he found no tranquility. He tripped over a tree root, snagged his pants on a bush, and knocked his forehead on a low-hanging branch.

He would remember this night forever.

Sarah slowly opened her eyes, to find herself in strange surroundings. Her limbs felt weak, and she doubted she could lift a finger. She remembered the oddest things—the deep timbre of Brendan's voice offering words of encouragement, his gentle touch, his giving her sips of water. And pain. Blinding pain.

She was alone and empty. She glanced down and discovered her stomach was quite flat. Her heart lurched, then began to beat faster. Something had gone wrong; she just knew it. Then a sound drew her attention, and a woman with gray hair and twinkling blue eyes leaned over Sarah and placed something bundled in a blanket in her arms.

Sarah looked down at an extremely unhappy, tiny red face.

"Your daughter, Mrs. Hammond. She's a mite small but perfect."

A daughter.

"I'll call your husband now," the woman said, "before he wears a hole in the floor. My poor Amos has had the worst time keepin' him occupied." She shook her head as she started for the door. "Ain't nothing more bothersome than a new father."

Sarah continued to gaze at her daughter. Dark hair covered her small head, and when Sarah unwrapped the blanket partway, she saw that her hands were clenched in tiny fists. Tears stung Sarah's eyes. In the course of several hours she'd become a mother and a wife. Nothing would be the same anymore. This tiny being had changed her life. Hugging her close, she pressed her lips to a flower-soft cheek.

Several moments after the caretaker's wife had disappeared through the door, Brendan entered. A day's growth of whiskers gave him a roguish appearance. His wrinkled white shirt, with the sleeves rolled up to his elbows, stuck out of his black pants in several places. He'd discarded his cravat, and the opening of his shirt revealed a dark furring of hair. His hair fell over his brow in such disarray, Sarah decided he must have shoved his fingers through it many times.

He stood at the bottom of the bed. "Sarah, I've been worried. Mrs. Phelps refused to let me in."

"I'm sorry. Oh, Brendan, it's a girl. Come see your niece."

He came closer. "My daughter, Sarah. You must always remember and not slip, even when we are alone."

"Yes, of course. Do you want to see her?" She carefully extended the baby, wondering if he'd actually take her. Seconds ticked by. "She's so beautiful."

Just when she feared she might have expected too much of him, he leaned down and slipped his hands beneath the blanket. Straightening, he cradled the baby in his arms. Sarah held her breath as she watched a myriad of feelings show on his usually stern face—wonder, tenderness . . . Finally he looked at Sarah and broke into a wide grin.

The breath she'd been holding whooshed from her lungs. She'd once thought Brendan would look even more handsome if he smiled. She'd been right. She found it appropriate that the first smile he'd allowed her came from such a special moment.

"She is beautiful, Sarah. I believe she looks like you. Have you chosen a name?"

"No, I . . ." He seemed so honestly enchanted with her daughter, Sarah hesitated to swallow the lump that rose to her throat. "I haven't."

"It isn't imperative that we decide this minute." He gazed at the baby again and lightly touched a fingertip to her cheek. "I thought she'd be larger, but she looks healthy. Are you happy she's a girl?"

"Yes, are you?"

"It does present less of an obstacle."

"And if she'd been a boy, Brendan, would you still have claimed him as yours?" He pinned her with his gaze, and Sarah regretted her hasty question. Nonetheless, she wanted to know what he would have done.

"I married you. Does that not answer your question?"

Sarah lowered her eyes. Would she ever learn to guard her tongue?

"Yes, Sarah, I was prepared to declare a boy my son and heir. Are you satisfied?"

She responded with a barely audible, "Yes." Anxious to divert their conversation to a less volatile subject, she laid her hands on her abdomen. "I can see my toes at last."

"It must be a great relief to you."

Feeling extremely uncomfortable, she asked, "How long will we remain here?"

"Until you're strong enough to travel. When my aunt suggested this plan she obviously didn't figure the infant would arrive early."

"Several days should suffice, then."

"Several days? Sarah, my knowledge of these matters is limited, but even I know you'll have to lie abed much longer than that."

Sarah laughed softly. "You don't know me well enough, sir, if you believe such nonsense. I'll be up tomorrow."

Both of his eyebrows lifted in dismay. "Most assuredly, you will not."

She reached for the baby. Remembering how her mother handled her overbearing father,

Sarah gave him a sweet smile. "I'm lookin' forward to showin' her to Gertrude."

"My aunt will no doubt spoil the child rotten." He fell silent for several minutes, then confided, "She lost a daughter to cholera some years back, and though she never mentions it, I know she still pines for her. Rebecca Louise was only eight at the time."

Sarah hugged her precious bundle to her heart, stricken by this devastating news. "Gertrude must've suffered so. Do you think it would please her if we named the baby Rebecca?"

He considered, then aimed a smile at her. "Rebecca Louise Hammond. I believe my aunt will be *very* pleased. And Louise was my mother's name."

Giving in to a temptation, Sarah pushed herself upright and, sitting, placed the baby across her legs. As she began to unwrap the blanket, Brendan hesitantly sat on the edge of the mattress. "I've been dyin' to make sure she's perfect all over."

When Rebecca was naked, arms and legs flailing, she howled with indignation.

Brendan laughed. "She appears as modest as her mother. Should she turn such a bright red?"

Surprised by his show of amusement, Sarah glanced up at his face. She was seeing another side of Brendan, one she guessed he kept hidden from others. No trace of the arrogant, overbearing earl showed, and she marveled at her discovery. She'd thought him handsome before, but when he smiled and laughed, it warmed her heart. She could fall in love with this side of him, she thought.

"Sarah, she's eating her fist." He touched a finger to a tiny hand. "She must have an appetite rivaling her mother's."

"How indecorous of you to mention it," she remarked in a mocking tone.

"You were eating for two," he said quickly. "And I found it rather amusing."

She wrinkled her nose at him.

"You must be tired."

Deciding he'd suffered enough for mentioning her unladylike behavior during their first dinner together, she allowed him to change the subject. "I'm exhausted, but I want to hold Rebecca awhile longer." Remembering how he'd cared for her and tried to take her mind from her pain, she touched Brendan's cheek. "You were wonderful, and I—"

"There's no need to thank me, Sarah."

"Oh, but there is. You've accepted responsibility for us, even though we should be your brother's obligation."

Her attempt to soothe him had the opposite effect. His mouth slanted grimly, conveying displeasure. Was it the mention of Derek that had soured his mood?

Capturing her hand, he gave it a gentle squeeze. "I'll leave you to rest now."

Chapter 7

～～♡♡♡～～

Gertrude left an exclusive ladies' shop on Fourth Street. Despite her aching corn, which made walking difficult, she had thoroughly enjoyed her outing. She had charged a scandalous amount to Brendan for Sarah, and let drop select tidbits of gossip as well. By this time tomorrow every well-connected woman in town would know her nephew had not been an eligible bachelor all along. More important, all of them would sympathize with her feigned affront, which she'd gone to great measures to let known.

It simply wasn't appropriate to hide something as newsworthy as a marriage from one's aunt.

Spotting the very lady whose influence carried the most weight with the St. Louis aristocracy, Gertrude signaled the carriage driver to wait. When the woman came near, Gertrude greeted her warmly. "Why, Lilly Fromond, it's been ages since I've spoken with you."

"And, you, Gertrude, have been remiss in attending my recent socials."

The opening suited Gertrude, so she pulled a

121

face. "It's that naughty nephew of mine. He's treated me abominably, and I've been out of sorts."

"You don't mean that handsome devil Brendan?"

"The very same." She plucked a hanky from her reticule and dabbed a corner of one eye. "The rascal has behaved in a beastly fashion."

"Oh, my dear, you must tell me at once. Perhaps I might be of some assistance."

"Perhaps you might at that." Gertrude drew the woman aside and urgently whispered, "He's been married for nearly a year, and never saw fit to tell me."

Mrs. Fromond gave a horrified gasp.

"He said he was merely honoring a betrothment made when they were children. Sarah's family moved to America many years ago, so Brendan had nearly forgotten, until he received a letter reminding him of his obligation. That's why he came here, and all along I thought it was because he missed me so terribly. Since it wasn't a love match, and the girl chose to remain behind to care for her ailing mother, he thought it not worthy of mention." She leaned closer. "Can you imagine that?"

"Simply dreadful. Of course you must consider that he's a man, and men never put the same importance on such things as we." She laid a hand on Gertrude's shoulder, offering her comfort. "Why has he mentioned it now?"

"Because his wife has contacted him to let him know she's just borne his child. He's gone to see her and expects me to make all the preparations in his absence." She massaged the spot between her brows. "Sarah's from a distinguished family, but however am I to staunch the gossip that's sure to abound?"

Mrs. Fromond pressed Gertrude's shoulder. "Do not worry. When the girl's able to go out, I'll have a ball."

"Lilly, you're a godsend. I'll be eternally in your debt."

"Nonsense, Gertrude. Seeing the expression on Caroline Belmont's face will be worth it. She's been unbearable of late, putting on airs, and so positive Brendan was to propose to her Florence." She rolled her eyes, laughing daintily. "Anyone with any sense can see Florence isn't woman enough for that virile nephew of yours."

Gertrude shared the same opinion, but she was surprised by Lilly's remark. "You're very astute to notice."

"I admit I'm anxious to meet Brendan's wife." She used her gloved hand to cover a mischievous grin. "I always guessed him a randy devil. Are you positive it wasn't a love match? He must have wasted no time in fulfilling his husbandly duties."

"He said not, but Sarah sounds lovely," Gertrude remarked as she tucked her handkerchief back into her reticule. "He might be smitten and not even know it."

"Well, one thing is certain. He surrendered to her charms once, so he is sure to again. Oh, this is the best news. It has been dreadfully dull of late. A romance will liven up my next affair, especially since it involves Brendan. He's set so many female hearts aflutter, and now he's out of circulation. They will naturally be waiting in suspense to catch a glimpse of the one who's caught him." She paused to take a much-needed breath, then continued. "You simply must allow me the pleasure of telling Caroline. She snubbed me just last week, and after I'd already complimented her on her dress."

"Of course you may. I wasn't looking forward to the task, myself."

Unable to control herself, Gertrude wore a broad grin all the way home. She'd done her part. The rest remained in Brendan's capable hands.

Hearing the front door firmly shut, Sarah threw off the heavy counterpane and left her bed. Mrs. Phelps had turned out to be as demanding as Brendan, but the woman had finally left. During the five days since Rebecca's birth, either one or the other of them had been around when she'd thought to exercise her stiff muscles. Today, though, Brendan was still out on his daily ride—thank goodness. She was alone at last, and intended to make good use of the time.

After she had checked to make sure Rebecca slept soundly, Sarah walked into the main room, where box upon box cluttered the tables and chairs. Gertrude had certainly been busy, and must have spent a fortune. Packages had been arriving for two days.

Sarah took a minute to stretch, then indulged

in a thorough exploration of the lodge. It was wonderful to be so light-footed again, she mused, and despite the warnings from her overzealous care givers, she felt almost whole again.

The goods, however, drew her. Unable to stand the suspense a moment longer, she untied a bright yellow ribbon securing a box and peeked inside. The beautiful green hat adorned with ostrich feathers enchanted her. She'd never thought to own anything so frivolous again. Carefully lifting it from its container, she set it on her head and tied it in a large bow under her chin.

In another box, she found an assortment of undergarments, all trimmed with lace and looking very expensive. Holding a corset around her, she frowned. Though it would fit, it looked a torturous device. She hated being confined and had always disdained wearing restrictive garments, but she'd been naturally graced with a figure that allowed her the freedom to do so. Having borne a child, she realized, she'd probably have to conform and allow herself to be compressed into the ungodly contraption.

Dropping the corset, she pulled out a pretty chemise and marveled at its exquisite stitching and sheer material. It would feel feather-soft against her skin, unlike the rough cotton she was used to. Still holding the chemise, she used a finger to nudge the lid off another oblong package. Her mouth dropped open. The green silk dress was magnificent, of the finest quality and—

The front door abruptly swung open, and Brendan stood looking at her.

Sarah froze. His gaze collided with hers, and she wasn't sure whether her inability to move stemmed from the impact of his penetrating regard or from the sight of him. With the sky behind his back, a gentle breeze ruffling his hair, and a riding crop in his hand, he robbed her of her breath. His black pants disappeared into knee-high boots, and his white shirt was left open at his throat. The time he'd spent out of doors showed in his darker complexion, a fresh tint from today's ride staining his angled cheeks.

A gust of wind blew across the threshold, sending a leaf skittering along the floor.

"You're b-back," she stuttered. "I was just—"

A ghost of a smile played over his mouth. "Tallying your bounty?"

"You've been most generous, sir."

"Apparently so." He strode inside and calmly shut the door behind him. "You have my aunt to thank, as I most assuredly will when I receive the bills."

"She shouldn't have gone to such expense without speakin' to you first." Sarah glanced longingly at the dress, then back at him. Holding her head high, she said, "Return it all if you wish. I'm not accustomed to such finery and won't mind in the least."

"But *I* will mind, Sarah." He swept his arm in an arc. "As my wife, this is only a small portion of what will be yours. Besides, I want you to have anything you want."

"I've never had designs on your wealth."

"I know, Sarah. I judged you too harshly, and deeply regret any insult you may have taken."

His vision veered from her face and swept over her. Yellow sparks in his hazel eyes held her spellbound, and Sarah cursed her flaming cheeks. She shifted the chemise higher to block his view, then remembered it was an undergarment she held. She whipped it behind her.

His mouth slowly slid into a smile.

Unsure what action to take, she groaned and whipped the chemise back around.

"The hat's becoming on you and should look fetching with the green silk."

She imagined the sight she must make, clad in an oversized nightgown, her bare feet peeping from under the hem, and a hat boasting feathers perched on her head. "Turn your back, if you please, and allow me to make myself decent."

Still sporting a smile, he lazily walked around her and fingered the dress. "My aunt has excellent taste. The shade will bring out the green in your eyes."

"You've noted their color?" she asked, amazed that he'd paid any attention to her.

"I've *noted* everything about you, Sarah."

Her flush deepened.

"Do you know the color of *my* eyes?"

Hazel, a seductive combination of brown and gold, she thought. "I'm afraid I'm not as observant as you." He stood so near, she felt his presence and noticed he smelled of leather and fresh air. "Does it matter to you that I haven't looked as closely at you?"

He gave her a wide, knowing grin. "You shouldn't be on your feet this soon, Sarah. You might injure yourself."

He hadn't answered her question, which piqued her curiosity about how he did feel. "I'm young and in good health, Brendan. I can't remain in bed."

"I suppose you must be the judge of your capabilities."

Surprised by his capitulation, she glanced at him over her shoulder. "You're conceding the point?"

"Since it's impossible to watch you every hour of the day and night, I have little choice." He touched her hair. "I suspect you'll find a way to do as you wish anyway."

"Will you mind?" she asked.

He took the chemise from her and admired it for a second before he dropped it on one of the boxes. "It's bred into my nature to mind, Sarah. When a man is married to a desirable woman, he's naturally possessive of her."

Amazed by his remark, she said, "You find me desirable? I find that hard to believe."

When he tugged on the ribbon, untying the bow under her chin, Sarah's eyes rounded with disbelief. Slowly he lifted the hat and put it aside.

"Neither of us wanted this marriage, Sarah, but we're man and wife." He touched a finger to her chin, forcing her to meet his gaze. "And, yes, I find you desirable, even wearing that plain cotton gown." The corners of his mouth curved slightly. "The hat is an amusing touch."

"The hat? Are you in possession of your senses?"

"Perhaps not." He sighed and studied her mouth. "You've had a curious effect on me from the first, and the past few days haven't helped. I'd nearly perfected my facade, but I suspect that you, my dear, are going to be my downfall. I've never felt this close to a woman before. I've come to like you very much."

Sarah swayed, unable to deal with the conflicting emotions churning inside her. His fingers drifted across her cheek. An urgent howl from the bedroom startled Sarah, and she looked in that direction.

His hand abruptly dropped as he stepped back. "Rebecca's awake."

Brendan's withdrawal drew Sarah's attention back to him. "She's no doubt hungry, since she's slept so long."

"Then you must see to her immediately," he said rather stiffly, making her wonder at his change of mood. "I'll be returning to town tomorrow. My aunt thought it best if you remained here for several weeks. I'll send her to you if you wish."

Disappointment coursed through her. He'd been so kind and caring, she'd come to believe he might have grown fond of her. The conversation she'd overheard between him and his aunt sped through her mind. Of course he'd been kind. He'd married her to give Rebecca the Hammond name. He was too honorable to treat his wife otherwise. How could she have forgotten?

"That won't be necessary," she told him. "I'd like a little time to get to know Rebecca before . . . before returning."

Rebecca let out another cry, and Sarah rushed into the bedroom.

Brendan mastered a scowl and strode to the porch. He desperately needed a breath of fresh air. What in bloody hell had he been thinking? Living in such close quarters with Sarah had obviously gotten to him. To preserve what remained of his sanity he felt he must seek his own home, where the added buffer of his aunt and servants would hasten his return to sanity.

It had been the devil's own luck that he'd arrived at that precise moment, to encounter Sarah outside of her room. He had been caught off-guard at the sight of her in her nightgown, wearing a stylish hat, and he hadn't taken care to hide behind his prim facade. She'd looked delightfully appealing, innocent yet so very seductive; he'd instantly reverted to his wicked self. A year of playacting had gained him an untarnished reputation, but in his soul he remained the same man who had left England.

He should have known his reformation had been too easy. He'd always been able to dismiss any woman from his mind at will, for he'd never met one who could crawl under his skin. This was God's own punishment. Sarah was the woman he wanted most to resist, but she was the *one* woman who had the ability to possess his thoughts.

And she had belonged to Derek first!

He'd briefly forgotten that imperfection, until Rebecca had cried. The child was beautiful, and he already felt a great affection for her. The world would believe he had fathered her, and maybe in time he could forget that he hadn't.

He laughed aloud. His heart would probably always remind him of Sarah's sin, and, no matter how many lectures he gave himself, he would conjure up an image of them making love. Considering his lurid past, his inability to forgive Sarah for one indiscretion seemed hypocritical, but acknowledging his own defects of character didn't alter his feelings.

He'd wanted the woman he married to be innocent, his alone.

Damn his weak nature, he shouldn't have had sensuous thoughts about Sarah. But she also shouldn't have had the eyes of a seductress. He'd discovered her sweet and affectionate, not the coldhearted adventuress he'd first thought. She'd clung to him, kissed his palm, and made him realize he'd never before had a woman who wasn't a relative need him for anything besides sexual favors.

Sarah awoke the next morning with a start. She hadn't slept well, and neither had Rebecca. Suspecting she'd transferred her own restlessness to her daughter, Sarah felt a twinge of guilt. The poor little girl had suffered with colic all night. In the future, Sarah thought, she must learn to deal with her mixed feelings toward Brendan and somehow remain calm.

Finding the small drawer that had served as a cradle empty, Sarah's heart skipped a beat. She hurried to the main room and stopped cold.

A warm feeling swelled inside her at the tender scene she'd discovered. Sprawled in the red leather chair, his long legs extended in front of him, Brendan slept soundly. His head was cocked at an angle, and one arm dangled from the chair arm; the other was possessively locked around Rebecca. Four tiny fingers were wrapped around his large thumb. Rebecca's blanket was askew, as if she'd been held in many different positions, leaving one of her feet sticking out.

Sarah branded the image into her memory. She'd found Brendan a complicated, demanding man, though during their time at the lodge he'd allowed her a glimpse of another side of him. Perhaps she had judged *him* too harshly. Life with him would be difficult, but he would be a loving father to Rebecca.

She could at least attempt to be the wife he wanted, she thought. Lord help her, it wouldn't be easy.

She returned to her room to perform her morning ablutions while she had the opportunity. She knew Rebecca would awaken any minute, as would Brendan, and she wanted to feed her daughter and be dressed to see him off. She'd just finished when she heard Brendan stir and yawn loudly. A second later, she heard him speak in a low tone and knew Rebecca had also stirred.

She peeked into the main room and smiled. Brendan wore a somber expression as he untangled the blanket. Holding the baby against his chest, he spread the cover over her back. He'd just started to tuck it around her squirming body when she saw him frown. Quickly he held his charge away from him.

Seeing the wet spot on his shirt, Sarah covered her mouth to stifle a laugh. This also was an image she'd long remember.

Brendan started toward the bedroom, so Sarah donned a robe. He handed over Rebecca the minute he entered, and Sarah was hard put not to grin.

"One of the first things Rebecca will have to learn is the proper deportment when she's—"

Unable to contain her amusement a second longer, Sarah broke into unbridled laughter. Brendan's disconcerted expression added to her mirth, and some moments passed before she managed to say, "I hope you have another shirt."

His fingers deftly popping open his buttons, he grunted. "I daresay. Stratford sent me enough to last for a month."

Sarah's amusement faded as her gaze followed the course of his fingers. Dark hair swirled over the broad expanse of skin, diminishing into a line that disappeared beneath his belted trousers. She had seen her brothers barechested, and she'd even admired and touched Derek's chest, but she found the sight of Brendan's much more intriguing.

Apparently unaware of her regard, he pulled

the ends free of his pants and held the damp section away from his body. Then he looked at her.

Sarah gently laid her daughter on the bed. Rebecca's little fists waved in the air, and when one came in the vicinity of her mouth, she sucked it. Sarah self-consciously twisted her fingers into the folds of her robe. "You should've awakened me when you heard her."

"She was no trouble. I couldn't sleep, so we sat up awhile together." His eyes twinkled. "I believe a bath is in order."

Sarah studied the bedpost, determined not to look at his chest again. "I'll feed her first."

He chuckled. "I was referring to myself."

Unbidden, an image of him stripping out of his clothes and slipping naked into the sturdy brass tub she'd spotted in the back of the house shot through her mind. She sneaked a glimpse of him. She'd never leered at a man before. If he could have read her thoughts, he'd have thought her a Jezebel for sure. "How ... much time till you depart?" she asked.

Even if she returned weeks after he did, gossip would surely run rampant, with her the main topic. Brendan thought her socially inferior now. What if, upon her return, she disgraced them all? Sarah's insides churned. She would be expected to mingle with people as sophisticated as he was.

The sudden warmth of his hand on her shoulder caused Sarah to flinch. She was certain he meant his action to reassure her, and he could not have known that his touch sent a shiver down her spine. She held herself rigid to ward off the sensation.

Brendan withdrew his hand. "Don't worry. We'll succeed in this endeavor. There's nothing to it, actually."

There was a soothing quality to his deep voice, meant to cheer her. Unfortunately, her fears remained. He'd been wonderful to her. She'd simply die, she thought, if she disgraced him. "And if we don't—if someone happens upon the truth?"

"As I told you before, wealth and power do have an advantage. Trust me, Sarah. I vowed to protect you, and I will."

But Sarah's unease about returning to town continued to plague her.

Sarah fruitlessly struggled to fasten the back of her gown. She hadn't wanted to keep Brendan waiting, and had fed, bathed, and dressed Rebecca in record time. She wanted him to remember her in something other than an oversized nightgown. But she'd reached an impasse. Twisting her arms behind her in an attempt to reach the tiny hooks, she groaned. Either she couldn't wear the dress or she must seek assistance from the sole person at her disposal.

After a few minutes she went to the room in the rear of the house, but still she hesitated. Then, squaring her shoulders, she knocked on the door, which was slightly ajar.

"It's open, Sarah. You needn't ask permission to come in."

Barely through the entrance, Sarah halted. Brendan stood in front of an oval mirror hung over a small table, shaving. Her gaze lighted on his broad, bare back. "I thought you'd be ready." She swung around. "I'll wait outside."

"Sarah!"

She swung back around to find him wiping his face with a small towel.

"Unlike you, I haven't a modest bone in my body," he said with a twinkle of amusement in his eyes. "You came for a reason." His eyes swept over her. "Could it be that you need help with your hooks?"

Sarah swallowed and forced her vision to remain level with his face. "Yes, I've been tryin' to fasten them, but without any luck."

"Come here."

They walked toward each other. Brendan gripped her arms and turned her so that her back faced him. Beginning at the bottom, he deftly slipped the many hooks into the eyes. She felt his warm breath on her neck and the brush of his fingers through the thin chemise, and regretted that she'd left off the corset.

Upon reaching a point just above her waist, he tugged the ends of the material together. Flooded with embarrassment, Sarah sucked in a breath. Had she known the garment would fit so snugly, she thought, she definitely would have worn the corset. But the dress had looked large enough.

"It appears you have no more liking than I for a certain feminine vestment."

The air rushed from Sarah's lungs. "Oh? Pray

tell, what experience have you with feminine vestments?"

After a brief silence, he said, "Only that I prefer a woman feel soft—in case you were wondering."

His fingers moved upward, reaching her back.

"I wasn't wondering any such thing."

"I admit I find helping you enjoyable. It may be the only time you permit me such a luxury, since you'll have a servant to perform the task."

Unable to find the appropriate response to his surprising comment, she said nothing. He closed the last hook and moved away. She faced him.

His gaze swept over her again, leisurely taking in every aspect of her appearance. He gave a short nod. "Are you dressed to receive a suitor, Sarah?"

Sarah sucked in a breath at his remark, until she registered the slight hint of laughter in his voice. "Several," she countered. "Do you mind?"

He grinned. "You dressed for me, Sarah. We both know it."

"As you wish, your Lordship."

He grinned again. "Since we're trading favors, will you act as my valet?"

She watched in silence as he selected a crisp white shirt and pulled it on. His fingers moved with the same dexterity on the buttons as they had on her hooks, and she found herself staring again. He was the handsomest man she'd ever met, which, she was certain, accounted for her fascination with him. "What would you have me do?"

After he'd gone to the small table and splashed a fragrance on his face and neck, he dug in a large satchel, retrieved a stiff white, collar, and attached it to the shirt. Finding a fine, gray-and-black-striped cravat, he placed it about his neck. Then he positioned himself in front of her, lifting his chin. "I'm all thumbs. Stratford normally does this part."

He smelled delicious. More than delicious. The scent he wore was an evil potion. His finely chiseled jaw, smooth from his recent shave, gave him an elegant air.

Fingering the neat tie she'd fashioned, he gave another short nod. "You've done this before?"

"My mother's also all thumbs, and my father boasted that I made the best knot in all of Georgia."

A faraway look came into his eyes. "My parents have passed away, but I remember my mother shared your talent. Of course, I suspect my father stretched the truth just to have her fuss over him. I've found that Stratford ties a remarkable knot."

She glanced up at him. "Was your father a rakehell, too, like your grandfather?"

He raised a brow. "It's a family trait."

"Then I'm fortunate to have married you, aren't I?"

His mouth slanted into an unforgiving line before he replied. "In time you might not be of the same opinion, Sarah."

"I'll always be grateful to you—" A sound from out front drew Sarah's attention. "I think I hear the carriage."

Brendan hastened to don his dark gray waistcoat, which complemented his lighter gray trousers. He slipped an eye-catching, gold pocket watch in it, so that its chain dangled across the front, then slipped on his coat.

He looked so impressive, Sarah thought. Numerous women had most likely had their hearts set on marrying him. For the first time she wondered if he might have singled out one of them to court. In her wildest dreams she hadn't conceived that she'd end up wedded to such a man. An earl, no less. An honorable man, who had abandoned his own plans for his life to give her respectability.

"Sarah?"

She blinked twice.

"I neglected to tell you." He regarded her for a long moment. "When you pin on your hat, you'll look stunning in that outfit."

She looked him over.

"You're stunning now."

Capturing her hand, he bent her fingers over his and pressed his lips to her skin. How gallant he was. She would miss his presence terribly. But perhaps time away from him would help her to come to terms with her new station. Having Rebecca to herself would also help her to adjust to the changes in her life, she hoped.

After he kissed her forehead, he moved toward the door. "I'll pay my respects to Rebecca before I leave. I hope she'll mind her manners and not wet on me."

Sarah rolled her lips together. Brendan Hammond could be quite endearing, she thought. She would do well not to become too attached to him.

The weeks passed slowly, but Sarah cherished the time alone with her daughter. Not that she was really alone. Amos Phelps looked in on her constantly, and his wife also came every day, bearing food she swore was left over from their previous evening meal. While Sarah doubted she spoke the truth, she appreciated the older woman's attention. Brendan had most likely paid the couple well to tend her needs.

Rebecca flourished despite frequent bouts of colic. Sarah enjoyed the intimacy of nursing her daughter, but fretted because she knew she'd have to turn Rebecca over to a wet nurse very soon. The little girl had a voracious appetite and wasn't getting enough to eat. Constant worry that Rebecca wasn't getting enough milk only made the situation worse.

Sarah lifted Rebecca to her shoulder and began to rub her back as she'd been shown. Mrs. Phelps was surely a godsend. Her tips about caring for a baby always worked. Minutes later, Rebecca released a very loud burp.

"And what would his Lordship have to say about that?" Sarah asked the infant.

Rebecca bobbed her head, then sucked on Sarah's neck.

"Such unladylike behavior."

After her daughter had snuggled against her shoulder and drifted to sleep, Sarah's thoughts shifted to her return to town. The next day she would see Brendan again. Would he notice any change in her?

Had he missed her as much as she had missed him?

Sarah nearly laughed at her wayward musings. He'd probably been relieved to be free of the responsibility he'd so graciously taken on.

Chapter 8

From the moment she and Rebecca arrived home, the house was in a flurry of excitement. Exhausted from her travel, Sarah longed for the solitude and quiet of the hunting lodge. An undisturbed nap would have restored her vigor, but it seemed out of the question at that time.

Gertrude fairly glowed with enthusiasm, and refused to relinquish Rebecca to anyone else. Every servant in Brendan's employ vied for a chance to see *his* daughter, a fact that amazed Sarah. Gertrude's powers of persuasion must have been a gift from the Almighty, to have convinced them that Sarah and Brendan had been secretly married the entire time. Sarah supposed servants were frequently kept in the dark regarding their employers' private affairs, especially if an alleged friction existed between the employer and his wife. Stratford, of course, knew the truth but was playing along admirably—and pretending he had been a party to the deception.

Sarah decided that even if the other servants

had guessed that all was not as it appeared, they valued their positions more than they cared about spreading gossip. Brendan had been right. Wealth and high station did afford a person certain privileges.

"She's a darling, and will definitely be a hit in town," Gertrude said. "Shame she's too young to attend Lilly's ball."

Brendan rolled his eyes as he propped his hip on the corner of an overstuffed blue brocade chair in the parlor. "My aunt hasn't been idle in your absence, Sarah."

Sarah felt uncomfortable. Since the first moment of their reunion, Brendan had been looking at her differently. She unpinned her hat and handed it to Stratford. Glancing back at Brendan, she saw him quickly divert his attention to his aunt.

"When is the ball again?" he asked.

Gertrude clicked her tongue on the roof of her mouth. "I've told you several times, but as usual, you weren't listening."

Brendan laid his hand over his heart. "I beg your indulgence, madam."

Gertrude looked at Sarah. "The ball is in two weeks."

A rush of panic seized Sarah. She had thought there would be more time to prepare herself before she met Brendan's peers.

"Judging from Sarah's appearance," Gertrude continued, "two weeks will serve." She smiled at Sarah. "I just knew you'd look fabulous in that dress. Wait and see, Brendan; she'll

turn the head of every man present, and will
be the envy of all the women."

Sarah met Brendan's speculative gaze, noticing the upward slant of one dark eyebrow. She
doubted Gertrude's prediction would come
true but wished she could read his thoughts.
Did he agree, or was he worried that he'd be
laughed out of St. Louis society for marrying
beneath him?

"Oh, dear," Gertrude said. "Sarah, do you
dance?"

"Mama tried to teach me, but . . . I'm afraid I
had my mind on getting outside to follow Papa
around. I—"

"It's no bother." Gertrude waved a hand and
spoke to Brendan. "I wasn't sure, and so engaged Mr. Montand to instruct Sarah in the art
of dance. And I personally will see she's given
the proper know-how to maneuver anyone
who'll present a problem."

"If you're referring to Caroline Belmont, I believe Sarah's able to fend for herself."

Gertrude moved Rebecca to her shoulder.
"Just the same, I'll feel better if I give her a few
pointers. Caroline does put on a front with you,
but I've seen her at her best—or worst, I should
say."

Sarah blushed. She wasn't used to being spoken about as if she weren't in the room, even if
she was being complimented. Seeing that her
daughter had awakened, she extended her
arms to Gertrude, who reluctantly relinquished
the child.

But Brendan stepped forward with extended arms. "May I?"

Sarah placed the child in his arms. "Be forewarned," she said, "she's been dry for some time."

Brendan's mouth lifted in a rueful smile.

Sarah glanced at Gertrude. "Rebecca behaved most indiscreetly at the lodge."

Gertrude promptly grinned in appreciation. "My, my, you do have a way with women, Brendan."

Brendan ignored both Sarah and his aunt and rocked Rebecca in his arms. "Is the room ready?" he asked.

"My dear nephew, when I undertake a task I see it done in an efficient manner."

Brendan aimed Sarah a look that said, "I told you so."

"And the wet nurse? Has she arrived?"

"Brendan *Cyril* Hammond," Gertrude chided, "you have all the discretion of an ox."

Sarah flushed again. Apparently Mrs. Phelps had followed through and contacted Brendan with the suggestion to have another nurse Rebecca, as it would alleviate the child's stomach distress. Though grateful for the woman's concern, Sarah regretted the loss of her special moments with Rebecca.

However, having everyone know of her inadequacy hadn't been her intention. But she couldn't blame Brendan, she thought. He'd only acted in Rebecca's best interests and upon Mrs. Phelps's advice.

Passing Rebecca to Sarah, Brendan whispered, "You look wonderful. Forgive me for announcing your—"

"Say no more, please," she whispered back.

Gertrude shooed the servants from the room, then beckoned Sarah to accompany her upstairs. When they reached Sarah's former room, she paused in the hall. "Many years ago I also had to hand a child over to a wet nurse. It sorely grieved me, but I learned to accept the situation because my daughter no longer suffered from colic." She tenderly touched the baby's cheek. "It was so sweet of you and Brendan to name her after my Rebecca."

Sarah smiled.

Gertrude whipped her hanky from her sleeve and held it to her nose, her eyes moist. "Forgive me."

"Brendan told me about your loss, and I'm happy you're pleased."

Gaining control of her emotions, Gertrude sniffed and confided, "You'll find no fault with Marie. I chose her myself. The poor dear lost her own child very recently, and she has no one, not even a husband. She'll love Rebecca as her own."

Her throat thick with remorse, Sarah silently followed Gertrude into the room, which had been splendidly refurnished as a nursery during her absence. She'd been thinking of her own wants, and now gave thanks for her good fortune. Rebecca was alive, healthy and surrounded by people who would adore her. Yet it was with reluctance that she handed her daughter to the red-haired woman. Marie's drawn face was transformed at the first sight of Rebecca; her blue eyes filled with tears and tenderness. Unable to remain a second longer, Sarah rushed into the hall.

Gertrude immediately appeared at her side, locked arms with her, and proceeded to take her to the master chamber. Sarah uttered no protest at being escorted to Brendan's room. She understood the need to keep up appearances. She was his wife, and as such, was bound to fulfill her end of the arrangement.

But, Lord help her, she felt jittery all over.

Making herself useful, Gertrude turned down the bedcovers. "You look tired, and well you should be. A rest will cure what ails you. Did you like my hunting lodge?"

"It was very nice." Sarah sat on the side of the bed and popped off her shoes. "I'd very much like to go there again."

Gertrude motioned for her to stand, then unfastened the back of Sarah's dress. "I've no desire to see it again, so do consider it a wedding present."

"You're too gracious. Why don't you sell it if you feel so strongly?"

"Oh, my dear, I could never do that. My husband left his mark all over the place. But he'd have loved knowing I kept the lodge in the family."

Sarah removed the gown and pulled off several layers of petticoats. Wearing her pantalets and chemise, she crawled into the wide bed.

"Rest well," Gertrude said. "Everything will be fine, you'll see. I know Brendan's mule-headed and a bit haughty, but he's a man, and we must allow for that."

"He's been so good to me and Rebecca."

"You're just what he needs, if you want my opinion. He's become as stodgy as my own father. If anyone can stir some life into him, you're the one. It may, however, take a great deal of patience on your part, but I know you have the backbone to mold him into the man he's meant to be."

Sarah yawned and curled on her side. "Taming the devil seems an easier prospect."

Brendan prowled the house for hours. He read, he played billiards, he stared out the window. Nothing helped.

Sarah had looked ravishing, more beautiful than he could have imagined. The glow of motherhood had held him transfixed for several long moments.

He had anticipated her return but not his intense reaction to seeing her again. She'd worn the green dress with the matching hat. Rebecca, too, had grown prettier, and favored her mother even more now. Good Lord, they were sure to create a sensation.

He had held his feelings at bay for the past few weeks, unaccustomed to the closeness he and Sarah had shared at the lodge. Memories flooded his mind, some good, others troublesome, including the pain Sarah had suffered. The moment when he'd first held Rebecca had been so remarkable, it would remain with him

always. Maybe someday he'd hold his own
child in his arms.

Brendan sank down in a chair, then cursed
to find it a narrow wing chair his aunt had insisted he buy. Resting his elbows on the un-
obliging arms, he steepled his fingers under his
chin.

How the devil was he to survive sleeping in
the same bed with Sarah and not touching her?
And even when she was healed enough, would
she welcome him? She was grateful to him;
she'd made that plain enough. Bloody hell! He
didn't want just her gratitude. He'd missed her
company, having her depend on him.

His thoughts were definitely not those of
Wicked Warwick. He was used to depending
on others to perform tasks for *him.* He was used
to women who had no regard for his feelings,
who cared only about his proficiency in bed.
Unsure how to deal with Sarah, he decided it
would be best if he temporarily kept his distance.

Gertrude watched Brendan steal another
glance at his watch. Since Sarah had arrived a
week before, Gertrude had sensed the tension
between them. Brendan's restlessness told her
much. Until she was sure they'd settled into
their marriage, she had decided to postpone
moving back to her own house. Knowing her
nephew as she did, she felt her presence was
still needed.

Brendan rang for Stratford and ordered that
a brandy be brought to him in the parlor.

Finding she'd dropped a stitch in the sweater she was knitting for Rebecca, Gertrude devoted her attention to it for several minutes, then looked up to see him checking the time again. She grinned. She knew he was waiting until he was sure Sarah had fallen asleep before seeking his bed.

Adept at procuring tidbits of information from the servants, she had a fair idea of Brendan and Sarah's daily routine. Always managing to awaken before him, Sarah slipped from their room to spend several hours with Rebecca, returning to it only after Brendan had dressed and either gone downstairs or left the house. Brendan stayed out most of the day, into the evening some days, and occasionally missed dinner.

Brendan downed the contents of the glass, then released a weary sigh.

"Did you go to the races today?" Gertrude asked. Undeterred when he failed to respond, she repeated her question.

"Yes, I did. I have to do something with my time. Why?"

"I was just making conversation." She studied her last stitch. "You're wearing a track in the carpet, and the hour hasn't changed during the past five minutes, you know. And you might not have so much time on your hands if you devoted a few hours to your wife."

Abruptly he put away his watch.

"Lilly's ball is in a week."

"And?"

"In case you haven't noticed, your wife is

nearly recovered and will need an appropriate gown. I've made an appointment with Mr. Montand for tomorrow afternoon to give Sarah dancing instruction."

"Why tell *me* about the gown? Feminine apparel is your area of expertise, not mine."

Gertrude patiently laid aside her sewing. "Because you're wed to her, not I. And I don't know of a better way to staunch the wave of gossip abounding than to be seen in public. Sarah hasn't left the house and would enjoy an outing. She could benefit from your knowledge of what would be considered suitable to the occasion."

Brendan scowled. "I'm not a bloody fashion designer. I know only what I admire on a woman."

"Precisely. You know best what you wish her to be seen in."

His mouth curved into a cynical grin. "What I consider appealing on a woman isn't what I wish my wife to wear!"

"If you're afraid other men will leer at her, it makes no difference what she wears. Dress Sarah in a flour sack and men will still find her desirable." She rose and tucked her knitting under her arm. "Would you have the other women snicker behind her back?"

"Of course not. That's why you're the perfect choice to accompany her. Your taste is flawless."

"Flattery will not gain my favor, Brendan. I'm otherwise engaged."

He considered her for a moment. "With whom, may I ask?"

"It's not your affair, but Mr. Montand has asked me to stroll in the park."

He gave her a faint smile. "It's time you kept company with a man, though I wonder that you would pick a mere dance instructor."

"My husband was a fur trapper, and our family looked down on him for years. When he amassed a fortune, they changed their tune fast enough. Unlike some, I don't believe a prestigious name necessarily denotes strength of character." She raised her chin. "I happen to like Mr. Montand and won't be dictated to."

To Gertrude's chagrin, Brendan clapped his hands and laughed.

"Spoken like a true Hammond," he said.

Fire licked her cheeks; she hadn't meant to divulge so much. But, frankly, she mused, she didn't care what anyone thought, even her nephew. Mr. Montand was devilishly handsome and debonair, and he made her feel young again.

His aunt's behavior intrigued Brendan. She was an attractive woman. Her interest in a man, any man, delighted him. Mr. Montand, if not wealthy or connected, was popular with the St. Louis society crowd and was morally principled, which was more than he could say for himself. If their association developed into a love match, Gertrude might become preoccupied enough to stop meddling in his own affairs.

"You don't approve of Mr. Montand?" she asked.

"You have my blessing." He resisted the temptation to check his watch again and strode to the door. "If you'll excuse me, I'll retire now."

"As will I."

Brendan stepped aside, allowing her to exit first.

She stopped and gave him a peck on the cheek. Then, a smile hovering on her lips, she patted his waistcoat. "Sarah is surely asleep by now, so you needn't delay any longer."

Having successfully needled him, she proceeded upstairs, leaving a frowning Brendan behind.

It was bloody well difficult to gain a measure of privacy in this house!

He'd thought his maneuvers a clever ruse, yet his aunt had seen through him. Sleeping in the same bed with Sarah had become a torturous undertaking, one he doubted he could endure for much longer. Adding to his misery, his presence didn't seem to bother his wife, who slept soundly each night.

Not so he. Brendan lay awake for hours on end, smelling her sweet fragrance, achingly aware of her soft, warm curves just inches away. At least once a night she rolled over, smack up against him, requiring him to gently nudge her back to her own side of the bed. It was hell. Tonight would be no different. He wondered how long a man could spend his nights painfully aroused and still retain his sanity.

Thank God Sarah rose first, though sometimes during the early-morning hours he lay throbbing and wretched, gazing with longing at a seductive bare calf or thigh that had come uncovered.

When he did sleep, he dreamed—of Sarah. Most recently he'd dreamed of Sarah as he imagined she'd been in Georgia, running through the countryside, her skirts hitched to her knees. He saw himself chasing her, catching tantalizing glimpses of her shapely legs, lured by her unbound hair shimmering in the sunlight. When he finally overtook her, they tumbled to the sweet-smelling grass, and her sultry laugh floated away with the breeze. He pinned her to the ground. She wiggled beneath him, bringing him agony, but there was no reason to hold back—she was his alone. He thrust into her welcoming, hot body and shuddered with ecstacy.

Fire raced to Brendan's loins, and he hardened with blinding desire.

Bloody hell!

Banishing the torrid image from his mind, he stalked up the stairs. Sarah must have cast an evil spell on him to stir a demon deep in his soul.

Brendan entered the master chamber quietly. Upon hearing Sarah's steady breathing, he undressed and pulled on the nightshirt he'd borrowed from Stratford. He mumbled an oath as he slipped into bed. Normally he slept naked, but out of necessity, he'd made this concession. Suddenly feeling contrary, he yanked off the nightshirt and tossed it across the room. He stretched out on his back with his hands tucked under his head.

Damn, Sarah smelled sweet, like soap and lavender. She sighed and moved, and her backside rubbed against his hip. Her warm body inspired sensuous images in his mind. If he rolled on his side he could—

He inhaled a tortured breath. He had survived thus far, and refused to weaken now. Besides, he wanted more from her than a quick release for his lust.

Within minutes, the pattern of her breathing changed, warning him she no longer slept soundly. He dared not move, or he knew he'd face a problem he had avoided—that of being in the same bed with a woman who fired his passions, and having to exchange words with her.

He wondered if she realized her hip pressed his, and if she did, whether the intimate contact sparked any response in her. Considering her fiery temper, he presumed she might possess a passionate nature as well. Love and passion hadn't counted into his plans when he'd married Sarah.

Sarah lay very still, waiting for Brendan to roll on his side. In the spot where their bodies touched, her skin felt warm. She sensed that he was awake. So why hadn't he moved?

Normally she didn't hear him come to bed, though that night something had pulled her from sleep. He seemed restless, and the air fairly crackled between them. She wondered how many hours remained until daylight. Thus far she'd managed to avoid the need to meet or speak to him when in the privacy of their bedroom, but she knew she was only putting off the inevitable. That he seemed of a similar mind had worked to her advantage.

A prickly sensation danced over every square inch of her skin. She had never felt such unnerving sensations, and she didn't know how to deal with them.

Forcing out a yawn, she stretched. Her maneuver temporarily gained her a scant inch of space but resulted in an even more upsetting outcome. Because the mattress dipped lower on his side, she now rolled closer to him. She heard a sound and realized he'd clicked his tongue against the roof of his mouth. Good Lord, he must have been just as unsettled by their familiar contact as she was.

Well, he could have remedied the situation, too. According to her calculations, his large frame extended past the middle section of the bed—into her allotted area!

Could he be trespassing into her space intentionally? she wondered. Whenever they'd chanced to meet during the past week, he'd acted strangely. She'd thought she read desire in his eyes, but since her experience was limited, she wasn't sure.

The idea of making love with Brendan intrigued her. He professed himself a morally principled man, yet she sensed he would be a skilled lover. And he'd claimed a thorough knowledge of a woman's body. Precisely how had he gained experience in such matters without compromising his morals?

That night, however, she craved only his affection—to be held in his strong arms. What would he do if she happened to move closer?

Finally, torn with curiosity and a need she didn't understand, she produced another yawn and rolled in his direction. Her leg came up against his, and her arm flopped over onto his chest. She had expected her head to rest against his shoulder or arm but discovered with dismay that her face had collided with his bare, hot chest. Her breath lodged in her throat. Wasn't he wearing anything at all?

Then she noticed that he not only also held his breath; his entire body had gone rigid. And well he should have been uncomfortable, for daring to retire in his altogether. She ordered herself to return to her side of the bed. Unfortunately, her senses reeled out of control, rendering her unable to fulfill that command. He smelled and felt so masculine, so familiar, she felt as if she would never want to move. She had vowed to guard her heart in the future. How quickly she had forgotten.

But this man was her husband, a little voice said. A man she found entirely too captivating. A man to whom she also owed a tremendous debt.

Avoiding him had shown her how lonely she'd been. Suddenly he expelled his breath, and his muscles relaxed. When his arm settled

around her, pinning her tightly against him,
Sarah gasped. Her hand jerked, and slid lower
on his chest. Finding it on his abdomen, she
thought to recoil but found herself trapped by
his strong embrace.

The pressure of his hold gradually lessened.
Before she had registered the change, his hand
had boldly roamed over her hip, then down her
leg to her knee. His fingers worked the material
of her prim cotton gown upward, slowly baring
her thigh. Too shocked to protest, she trembled
in silence. When he swept the gown to her hip
and splayed his fingers over her stomach, she
released a squeak. She felt branded.

"Sarah, you're driving me mad."

Sarah released a quivery sigh and grabbed
his wrist. The low, seductive timbre of his voice
betrayed his aroused state. She wasn't ready to
become intimate with him yet. She attempted
to fling his arm away but she found he was
much too strong.

"Are you having second thoughts? I'm aching for you."

"Please . . . I just wanted you to hold me."

He released her immediately. Her embarrassment acute, she remarked, "Forgive me, please.
I know you expect more from me, but I—"

"Sarah, please don't."

She rolled to her back, putting a little distance between them. Seizing the sheet, she
snapped it over her, tucking it securely under
her chin. A wife was supposed to see to her
husband's needs. She'd already failed him.

After a long silence, the bed creaked. His arm

came around her, his long, warm length pressing along the entire side of her. His lips touched her throat, then her neck under her ear. "Let me hold you."

She lay still, absorbing his heat. It felt so good, having him this close. Turning, she lay her head on his arm. "Are you positive you don't mind?"

"Positive."

"You're naked," she said suddenly.

"As the day I was born. Does it disturb you?"

"Well . . . won't you take a chill?"

He chuckled. "I should say not. It's devilishly hot."

"I'm very comfortable. Is the temperature different on your side of the bed?"

His chuckle turned into a laugh. "It's a veritable inferno."

Sarah fell silent. She knew he was still aroused; the hard ridge burning against her leg was proof. His willingness to forgo making love touched her heart. He was so different from the man she'd believed him to be. In the past, she would have sworn that he'd be the kind of man who would demand his husbandly rights.

"If you're truly miserable, you can *do it*."

"Do it?" He snuggled closer. "I'll make love to you when *you* claim you're in an inferno, not before."

"But I don't usually mind the heat," she returned, a trace of her amusement in her tone. Heavens, her face was surely beet red, she thought, but thank goodness he didn't know that. "Summers in Georgia are extremely hot."

He didn't answer for several minutes. "You tempt me to prove you wrong, Sarah. I'd wager you just haven't been exposed to the right source of heat."

Sarah smiled at his display of male ego. "I've spent many hours outside—without benefit of a hat. Do you claim to be more potent than the sun?"

"In time you'll have your answer."

"Perhaps you've also spent many hours outside without a hat."

He groaned. "Go to sleep, Sarah."

"I'm not sleepy." She laid her hand over his cheek and felt a day's growth of whiskers. "Will you hold me like this every night if I wish?"

"Is it your wont to have a raving lunatic for a husband?"

"No, your Lordship."

He seized her hand and held it between them. "Bloody hell, Sarah, you'd torment the devil. And I thought I had forbidden you to address me as your Lordship."

Barely able to hold back a laugh, she managed to say, "I believe it was more of a request."

"I'm making it a formal command."

"As you wish."

She heard him sigh. He said nothing more. Content, Sarah soon fell into a deep sleep, snuggled in his arms.

*   *   *

Brendan dismissed Stratford the next morning, then stood for a moment, looking about. Nothing was the same anymore. He saw Sarah's presence everywhere. Her toilet articles, clothes, and scent had changed his bedroom from a private retreat into a chamber of torture.

And from all indications, his torture had only begun.

He wondered how long he could master his desires. The hours he'd spent simply holding her had severely taxed his stamina. Despite his lack of sleep, he admitted he'd found the night rewarding in a way he'd never before known. Sarah was so soft and comforting, he looked forward to repeating the experience.

He went into the hall, intending to go downstairs. Instead, he found himself outside of the nursery, listening to Sarah hum a soft lullaby. A smile touched his lips at the slightly off-key sound. His wife wasn't musically inclined, and he suspected it wouldn't be the only area in which she lacked talent.

Tiptoeing to the doorway, he saw her sitting next to the window in the ornate rocking chair his aunt had procured. His breath caught at the tender scene. Still wearing her shapeless nightgown, Sarah looked enchanting. Her loosely braided hair was untidy, and love and tenderness showed in her expression as she gazed upon her child. Rebecca basked in her mother's affection, making small cooing sounds. Embarrassed to have intruded on the private moment, he retreated a step, then turned back.

A lone tear trailed down Sarah's cheek. Then

another. Her lullaby became sobs, confusing
and alarming him. He'd thought her happy. He
strode across the room and laid his hand on her
shoulder.

She glanced up, a faint tinge of pink staining
her damp cheeks. "Brendan—" She inhaled a
shaky breath. "What are you doin' here?"

"I wanted to apologize."

She blinked, questioning him with wide eyes.

"For last night. I should have realized it was
too soon, that you wouldn't want to . . . that
you . . . bloody hell!" He frowned before he
continued, "I'm not used to having a woman
in my bed every night, and—"

Sarah sniffed as she held up a hand. "I
wasn't crying over that."

"Well, I'm pleased to hear it." He locked his
hands together behind his back. "Might I inquire as to what has you in such a state?"

Gazing down at Rebecca, she surrendered to
another bout of tears. "She's . . . just . . . so . . .
beautiful."

Brendan mumbled under his breath, "Indeed, she is." He knew he would never understand a woman's penchant to cry over
something that pleased her. Resting his hand
on her shoulder again, he said, "I'll wait downstairs."

She tilted her head to glance at his hand.
"Wait for what?"

"Why, for you, of course."

"Me? Are we goin' out?"

"My aunt failed to tell you?" He sighed. "I
can see that she has. Mrs. Fromond's ball is

nearly upon us. We must acquire an appropriate gown for you.''

He watched Sarah chew on her bottom lip.

''It's not my idea, but my aunt's. Being seen
together is sure to generate favorable gossip.''

Her eyes briefly narrowed on him. ''It's kind
of you to go to so much bother, Brendan, but
I'm able to purchase a dress on my own.''

''I think not, Sarah.''

Sarah looked down, humiliated. She knew it
was ridiculous to feel hurt because he wanted
to accompany her only to make sure she didn't
disgrace him. ''I hope you don't mind if I reserve the right to choose the color.''

''Choose anything your heart desires, Sarah,
so long as it's fitting to the occasion, outra-
geously expensive, and tastefully modest.''

''I'll try not to disappoint you.''

Brendan regarded her warily. ''You do realize that I have the final say about which garment we select.''

''Why, yes, of course.''

When he strode from the room, she broke
into a smile. She'd been dreading her first outing as his wife, but now she looked forward to
it.

Chapter 9

Sarah's enthusiasm lasted until the carriage stopped in front of a row of fashionable ladies' shops on Fourth Street.

"They call this section Verandah Row," Brendan remarked.

The sounds of rumbling streetcars and neighing horses echoed on the street, and stylish patrons swarmed in front of the airy establishments.

Brendan alighted first, then handed her down to the walk. After giving instructions to the driver, he gallantly offered her his arm. Holding her head high, Sarah allowed Brendan to lead her. They strolled along the walk a short distance until, having decided which shop would best serve their needs, he had escorted her to a distinctive-looking shop.

Although she felt people staring, Sarah pretended not to notice. A bejeweled matron, whose fleshy neck encroached upon her vast bosom, left the store, blocking the narrow entrance. Brendan touched the brim of his hat. He ushered Sarah back, unobtrusively allowing enough space to accommodate the woman's girth.

164

The lady's gaze returned to Brendan twice. Directing Sarah through the door, he flashed the pink-faced woman a devastating smile.

Amused despite her jittery nerves, Sarah continued inside. Her husband had left the woman flustered and at a loss.

The shop was smaller inside than Sarah would have expected, but the decor was distinctly feminine. Frilly curtains graced the windows, and dainty chairs upholstered in reds and pinks were set in select locations. Bolts of material stood everywhere. A petite woman introduced herself as Mrs. Germaine.

Brendan reciprocated, then fell silent for a moment. "We have need of a ball gown," he finally stated, his British accent pronounced. "My wife will also require the necessary . . . trappings."

Sarah had expected him to be uncomfortable. Most men would have felt ill at ease when forced to enter a female's domain. Once again, though, Brendan had surprised her. He was in total command even surrounded by feminine frills.

"But of course," the store owner replied. "You are no doubt attending the Fromond ball?"

Brendan scanned the shop, his vision lighting on a gown hanging on a far wall. "Have you better to offer than that? Price is no object."

Sarah couldn't believe her ears. She thought the gown lovely.

"Ah, you are one of impeccable taste, Mr. Hammond." She briskly headed for a door to the rear of the shop. "Please come with me, Mrs. Hammond."

Sarah touched Brendan's sleeve, whispering, "You shouldn't have told her price is no object. Why, she's sure to up the price, and there's no need to pay an exorbitant amount on my account."

He looked at her with a bemused expression. "My dear wife, I am very rich."

"You won't be for very long if this is how you conduct your affairs."

Moving behind her, he ushered her forward. "Don't interfere, Sarah. I know what I'm about."

Sarah made a face as he swept her into the back room, where the dressmaker waited by a small, round platform in front of a wide mirror. At her urging, Sarah lifted the hem of her blue silk morning dress with white spot pattern and stepped up onto the platform. Seeing her reflection, she decided she liked the dress after all. She'd thought the apron front made her look bulky since her stomach was not as flat as before.

"If you'll be so kind as to wait in the front, sir, I'll call you when your wife's ready," the woman said before she scurried away.

Brendan hesitated, then turned on his heel and retired to the front of the shop.

Sarah was considering the black and blue banding on her skirt when Brendan's image appeared in the mirror. He stood over a delicate, pink-fringed chair, holding up his coattails.

"But I thought . . . You're goin' to remain here?"

"I'll explain later," he returned, his curt tone brooking no argument.

The frilly seat looked too fragile to hold his weight. Sarah refused to smile, even when his muttered oath reached her ears.

Mrs. Germaine returned. Nonplussed by Brendan's presence, she draped several gowns over a chair, then joined Sarah on the platform. "We will have to remove your outer garments, Mrs. Hammond."

Sarah looked askance at the woman. "Precisely how many?"

"Down to your unmentionables."

Closing her eyes, Sarah fought the rise of color that began climbing up her neck. By asking such a naïve question, she'd demonstrated her inexperience. Also, the woman had presumed she'd feel no embarrassment at disrobing in front of Brendan. She cast him a glance. He winked at her.

"Don't mind my wife," he said, his eyes twinkling with mischief. "She's overly modest."

Sarah swallowed her dismay and allowed the woman to release the hooks down the front of her dress. Stepping out of its folds, she felt Brendan's intense regard. She refused to allow her embarrassment to show. Thank goodness she'd worn the despised corset today, she thought, though she wondered if she might have been covered better if she hadn't. One glimpse of herself confirmed her suspicion. The short corset compressed her waist but thrust her bosom upward, granting Brendan an eyeful. Glancing to the side, she noted that he no longer seemed amused.

"We'll have no trouble at all, sir," the woman exclaimed. "She's made to wear Worth. It just so happens I have three to chose from."

"By all means, get on with it, madam."

"Oh, I have the perfect one to go with her coloring." Mrs. Germaine selected a gown and displayed it to Sarah.

Banishing all other thoughts from her mind, Sarah concentrated on fitting into the sumptuous gown of light gray shot with green silk threads, trying to pretend Brendan wasn't present. She adored the dress. The material was as gossamer as a butterfly's wings, the color meant for her. In her dreams she'd worn wondrous dresses and danced the night away at a lavish ball in the arms of a dashing prince, but she'd never believed her dreams could come true.

Once the dress was fastened, Sarah whirled around, delighted with the style and feel of the spectacular creation, which draped up and back to an elaborate bustle form, then fell in graceful folds to a long train that swept the floor.

"It won't do!"

Shocked by the intensity of his tone, Sarah faced Brendan. "You can't be serious."

A dark eyebrow winged upward.

"But Brendan, it's gorgeous."

Sarah saw a muscle tick in his cheek. She shouldn't have contradicted him, she realized. She might have lacked actual experience in social matters, but even she knew the gown was perfect. Remembering that Mrs. Germaine was listening to their conversation, she phrased her argument differently. "Darling, you said I could choose the color. What don't you like about it?"

"The neckline, Sarah." His gaze slid lower and lingered overly long. "It's entirely too revealing."

Sarah tucked her chin flat against her chest to see for herself. And saw his point. Her bosom swelled over the gown's curving lines. She'd been so entranced with the material and spectacular train that she hadn't taken note of the scandalous cleavage. As she tilted her head, her eyes met his. The sparks of gold glittering in the hazel depths gave him a wolfish appearance; she believed he might devour her without further provocation.

It was definitely not a look she would have expected from a man of strict moral character. Were she to have met him as a stranger, she might have thought him a threat to a woman's virtue—a man skilled in the art of seducing a woman.

Like Derek, only ten times more irresistible and dangerous.

She'd never worn such a daring dress and normally would have agreed with Brendan's assessment. But the way he fixed his eyes on her made her tingle all over. No one had ever looked at her quite the same way. She liked having him devour her with his gaze.

He motioned to Mrs. Germaine. "Try another."

It was a command, not a request. Disappointment coursed through Sarah.

Perched on the flimsy ruffled chair, Brendan managed not to scowl as he endured the torment of having to watch Sarah disrobe and then try on two more dresses. If three of his aunt's cronies hadn't entered the shop and tittered behind their hands as they gaped at him, he wouldn't have put himself at such a disadvantage. But the women were sure to rush from the shop with news of his and Sarah's outing. He'd given them something juicy to gossip about. Soon everyone in town would know he was so enamored of his wife that he'd allowed her to drag him into a woman's dress shop.

Sarah attempted to hide her disappointment, but whenever their gazes met, the daggers she shot him were plainly evident. However, his reasons for rejecting the first gown were his own. Fortunately, he'd disguised the most blatant reason by placing his hat on his lap.

The material of the dress had been created by Satan to hurtle a man down a path of destruction. The tight bodice emphasized Sarah's waist, drawing attention to her full breasts—a lush display sure to inflame *any* man, even one well past his prime. Brendan still suffered the painful dilemma of an untimely arousal. God help him if he needed to stand before he'd mastered his desire, he thought.

Though it had been unfair to deny her the dress, he must preserve what remained of his sanity. Just as his aunt had predicted, Sarah would be envied by every woman at the ball, and every man would fall under her spell the moment they arrived. While he intended Sarah be a hit, he preferred not to present a breath-taking temptress! He knew only too well the course a man's thoughts ran when in the vicinity of an irresistible siren. He was a prime example.

He wanted to drag her into his arms, kiss her senseless, then spend hours making love to her.

Brendan shook his head, hoping to clear his drugged mind. The third dress would suit his purpose, he decided, despite his aversion to its proper neckline, torrent of ridiculous ruffles, and pleats and bows descending from below the waist to the train. He despised ruffles and bows.

As if she'd read his mind, Sarah gave him a long, patient look. Turning to the shop owner, she said, "May I please have a private word with my husband?"

Brendan waited until the woman had disappeared into the front room before he left the miserable chair. "Sarah, I know you want the other dress, but I've decided we should take this one."

"But I don't like this dress." She jammed her hands on her hips, green lights flashing in her remarkable eyes. "Why didn't you just come without me?"

He threw his hat and gloves on the chair and approached the platform. Because she stood higher than usual, they were eye to eye. "I thought you might enjoy trying on dresses, as I'm told most women do." He let his gaze leisurely roam over her. Even in a garment he thought dowdy, she set his pulse pounding. "I'd hoped you would trust my judgment."

She plucked at the ruffle adorning the neckline. "If this is what pleases you, then you—" Quickly, she bit her lip.

"Do go on, Sarah, though lower your voice," he said through clenched teeth.

Laying her hand over her middle, she inhaled a breath. The barely perceptible narrowing of her eyes warned of disagreement. But her response surprised him.

"You've been kind to accompany me here, when I know you feel out of place. I'll wear the dress if you really like it."

He hated the damnable dress. He stared into her eyes and fell prey to their seductive allure. He saw himself wandering through a hazy forest where he was destined to lose his way.

"I declare, you rob me of thought when you look at me like that! Do you do it intentionally?"

He nodded.

She plucked at the hideous ruffle again. "The dress is awful, Brendan, and you know it."

He averted his gaze, breaking the spell she'd cast over him. "Sarah, I don't want you to make a spectacle of yourself. Is it your desire to have every male present lust after you?"

To his amazement, her lips slowly slid into a knowing smile. "Are you includin' yourself?"

"Myself most of all. Would you have me drooling over your lush bosom?"

"I believe I'd like that, very much." Her eyes grew wide, betraying her chagrin over her quick reply. "May I put on the other dress, please? Perhaps if you see it again, you might change your mind."

Brendan arched a brow as he grinned. "By Jove, you're obstinate. Very well. But hurry, Sarah, because I want to take you to the Planter's House afterward."

"Turn your back, please."

"Sarah, be reasonable." He glanced toward the front room to assure them that no one was near. "Soon I hope to dispel every trace of modesty you possess."

Sarah's cheeks turned pink as she twirled her finger, prompting him to face the opposite direction.

Brendan complied with a sigh.

Minutes passed. The rustling sounds fueled Brendan's imagination. When Sarah softly called his name, he steeled himself and turned around. And regretted his foolhardy concession. Sarah looked even more desirable in the damnable gown than before. Mrs. Germaine hadn't been available to fasten the hooks, so Sarah held the garment together behind her. The action forced her breasts upward even more, displaying a tantalizing view indeed.

"You like it," she said, her cheeks deepening to a fetching shade of crimson as a result of his open regard.

"What I find astounding is that so modest a

woman is willing to flaunt her—'' Hurt flashed in her eyes, and he instantly damned his rash comment. "Sarah, I do like the gown. Too much." He went to her. Fingering the shimmering material, his mouth lifted in a sardonic grin. "Far too much." Acting on impulse, he wrapped his fingers around her upper arms. "You may have it," he said, pulling her close, "if you dare."

"Brendan," she said breathlessly.

"You may have the gown, provided you're prepared to suffer whatever . . . *consequences* . . . might arise."

Damning himself for his weakness, he reverted to Wicked Warwick and pressed his lips to her enticing cleavage. She sucked in a harsh breath and trembled, encouraging him to trail hot kisses all the way to her throat.

"Brendan Hammond," she said weakly. She tilted forward. "Goodness, you . . . my knees are bucklin'."

Mrs. Germaine's voice intruded. He lurched away from Sarah. If the woman hadn't chosen that moment to return, he would have been kissing his provocative wife with all his pent-up passion.

Sarah suffered as well. On wobbly legs she presented her back. When her gaze met his in the mirror, he watched her swallow, then study the floor.

Fishing his card from a fine leather case he kept in an inside pocket of his coat, he told the woman, "We'll take this one, after all. Kindly have it delivered."

"Oh, very good, sir. You've made a wise selection."

"I rather doubt that," he grumbled. "But since my wife has her heart set on it, I cannot deny her. I'll wait in front while you see to the rest."

Brendan escaped before either woman could utter a word. Upon reaching the outer room, he gave thanks when he found it empty. He desperately needed time to master the urgent craving drumming in his loins.

Sarah stared in awe at the limestone front of the Planter's House. A full four stories high, with a partial fifth floor, it filled the entire block on Fourth Street. When Brendan took her inside, she feared her neck would become permanently crooked from her attempts to see everything. They climbed one of the beautiful staircases that spiraled upward in four complete revolutions, and he paused to smile at her on the second floor.

"Would you like to see the grand ballroom?"

"Oh, yes," she said, too excited to hide her pleasure. Since they'd left the dress shop, his manner had seemed less strained. She was, in fact, enjoying his company tremendously. "Is that where Mrs. Fromond's havin' her ball?"

Brendan nodded and led her to a set of massive doors, where he pushed one slightly open. Sarah peeked inside, to find a social function was being held. She only had time to notice that the orchestra platform, decorated in striking detail, rose more than eight feet above the floor.

Peering over her head, Brendan whispered, "The decorations were copied from the temple of Erechtheus in Athens."

His breath brushed her temple, stirring a strand of her hair. Her skin still felt hot where he'd pressed his lips. Sarah made to retreat but encountered a rock solid body. His arm stole around her waist. She gasped on a breath as tingles raced to her toes.

"Sarah," he said, his voice deep and beckoning, "you'll be more beautiful than any woman here."

She turned and found no space between their bodies. He still held the door with one hand, her with the other. Speechless from his flirtatious manner, she gazed at the chiseled lines of his face. She was growing attached to him. She even thought him irresistible when he scowled.

What was happening to her? In the dress shop he'd made her quiver all over. She'd never felt like that before, as if someone had heated her blood over a hot flame. Derek had done much more and not caused her to melt.

Unsure how to deal with these unsettling sensations, she said, "Someone will see us."

"Let them. We're married, or have you forgotten?" He jerked her tightly against him. "If I kissed you in front of all these people, no one would think anything of it."

She pushed against his chest. "Except that perhaps you're bold and impulsive, which frankly, I think impossible. You're a man who controls his impulses."

He chuckled and pressed his lips to her temple. "You're right, Sarah. I've always controlled my impulses when I wanted, but you tempt me to act impetuously."

Her heart skipped a beat. She surely felt a physical attraction to him because he was handsome, accomplished, and he'd been kind to her, she thought.

Lies. It was something more, a deeper emotion, which frightened and thrilled her.

She wanted him to kiss her.

Unbidden, her arms slipped up around his neck, her lips parting in invitation.

With a low groan, he pulled her into the hall, closing the door. Not bothering to see if they were alone, he clasped her tightly against him again. His eyes were blazing with desire.

Sarah's breath caught. "Are you goin' to kiss me?"

"You sorely tempt me to do just that."

"But I'm not doin' anything."

He laughed and cupped her chin with his fingers. "Sarah, you play hell with a man's resolve. Your lips are begging to be kissed. You enchant me."

A soft gasp escaped her. "You give me too much credit, your Lordship. I don't know how to enchant a man."

"Precisely. Your innocence is a powerful weapon."

"But I'm not—"

He awkwardly maneuvered free of her. "Bloody hell! You've robbed me of my senses."

"I didn't mean to," she said. She watched him glance down the hall. She'd just told him a fib. It thrilled her to think she could rob him of his senses.

"I want to show you one of the dining rooms."

Sarah fussed with her reticule in an attempt to calm her raging emotions. He'd had every intention of kissing her; she just knew it. Judging by the slight tint staining his cheeks, he still wanted to. What must he think of her? she wondered. She'd flirted with him in the hall of a very public place like some hussy.

He circled her shoulders with his arm. "The fault is mine solely, Sarah. Let me show you the hotel's dining room. The appointments are extraordinary."

Brendan was being gallant again.

Sarah shoved the thought aside and allowed him to lead her. She admired the luxurious carpets, costly paintings, and the exquisite china and cutlery, which Brendan said had been made in England and bore the hotel's initials. Once they were seated in the center of the dining room, she occupied herself by stealing glimpses of other patrons, especially the stylish women.

Their waiter returned for the third time, but Sarah could not bring herself to eat a meal. Her stomach churned from Brendan's disturbing behavior.

Brendan ordered Planter's Punch for her, brandy for himself. Dismissing the waiter, he tapped his fingers on the table cover.

"You must be famished," she said. "You

needn't go without just because I'm not hungry."

"Sarah, if I wanted to eat, I would. I prefer the brandy."

"Oh." She noticed a woman at a nearby table boldly staring at Brendan. "Do you come here often?"

"Upon occasion. Are you suitably impressed?"

"Yes, I think the hotel's grand." Seeming oblivious to his surroundings, his gaze wandered over her face. She felt as if she'd swallowed a rock. "I imagine . . . there . . . are many rooms," she stammered.

"A hundred and fifty. And this is only one of two dining rooms. Sarah, you look pale. If you feel unwell, we can leave."

Out of the corner of her eye, she saw that the woman was still staring at Brendan. "I'm fine," she said. "But an extremely attractive woman with blond hair is borin' a hole in your back. Can't you feel it?"

"Is she alone, or with a man?"

"Her companion's a younger woman; they look related."

His mouth was set in a somber line as he removed his gloves. Capturing Sarah's hand, he tugged her glove off also, then covered her fingers with his. She sensed every eye in the place upon them. Surely his daring action was a breach of etiquette. The rock in Sarah's stomach turned into a butterfly, harassing her. His thumb grazed back and forth over her skin.

"Ignore her, Sarah. She's not someone you should know."

"*You* must know the woman well to guess her identity without so much as one look at her."

Tiny lines feathered from the corners of his eyes as he frowned. "Not in the way you think."

Sarah tried to pull back her hand, but he tightened his grip. "If you mean familiarly, I don't think that at all."

"Indeed? Why not?"

"Brendan, you told me yourself that you're morally principled."

His hold relaxed again as his thumb stroked the sensitive underside of her wrist. Captivated by the stimulating sensations he evoked, Sarah discovered his fingers were long and graceful for a man. He kindled a spark in her just by caressing her wrist, but, she thought, if he were to touch her more intimately . . . The image of a flaming torch being put to a field of dry hay burst through her mind. Wildfire racing across a field, setting the hay ablaze, leaving it devastated.

"Caroline Belmont is an acquaintance, nothing more," he said.

"Tell *her* that. Gracious, she's eating you alive with her eyes."

His grin came slowly, holding Sarah spellbound. She hadn't noticed it before, but his teeth were as impeccable as everything else about him.

"She might find me bloody well bland. Rest

assured; she'll spit me out straightaway."

Sarah smiled in response. "I believe you underestimate yourself, sir. Bland's too mild a description."

He leaned forward. "What word would *you* use, Sarah?"

"Spicy." His eyes twinkled with amusement, tempting her to add, "Definitely spicy, though I think she's decided you aren't on her menu, after all."

"Should I look?"

"I wouldn't, if I were you. Now she's aimin' you a poisonous look."

The waiter appeared, requiring Brendan to straighten so the server could place their drinks on the table. Sarah tasted her punch, watching Brendan over the rim of the glass.

He savored his brandy, swirling it around before he swallowed half of it. Then, pulling out his watch, he checked the time.

"Are we late?" she asked. She didn't want their outing to end.

"Not late, but we should be on our way soon if you're to meet my aunt. We have nearly accomplished our objectives."

"Thank you."

He looked surprised. "For what, Sarah?"

"For allowin' me the dress, for bringing me here, and for—"

He leaned forward. "I don't want your gratitude, Sarah."

"What, then?"

A devilish grin captured his mouth. "A dangerous question for a woman to ask. Do you really want to know?''

She toyed with her napkin, avoiding meeting his heated gaze. His ability to flirt with a woman far surpassed Derek's. She'd succumbed too easily once already. Surely he couldn't still be testing her. "I'm not sure. It's been a special day. Am I not allowed to be grateful?''

"You're too easily pleased," he remarked. "You must learn to be more demanding. My position allows me to give you anything you desire.''

Sarah felt her mood dip. Earlier, he'd mentioned that they'd nearly accomplished an objective. Could his ardent attentions have been merely a ruse? "My desires are simple, Brendan. No amount of money can fulfill them.''

"Explain.''

"I'd rather not.''

"Ah, I must guess, is that it?''

"No. But one day I hope you learn what's important to me, and become of the same mind." Sarah noticed a movement in their direction and realized the blond woman was headed their way. "She's comin' to see you.''

Brendan downed his brandy, his brows knitting together. Caroline Belmont's potent perfume arrived at their table before her. Sarah thought the fragrance overpowering and wondered if it appealed to her husband.

Brendan rose to greet the woman. Before he could introduce Sarah, Mrs. Belmont began to chatter.

"Brendan Hammond, you certainly know how to set the town on its ear. Everyone's talking about you and this so-called marriage of yours." She leaned toward him, artfully batting her lashes. "I knew you weren't as righteous as you'd led me to believe. And you've proved me right. Why, it's positively indecent to be seen in public with a paramour while your devoted wife is still recovering from childbirth. My—"

"Caroline," Brendan warned, his eyes narrowing to slits.

Undeterred, she continued. "My Florence is devastated. She was sure you meant to propose." She brazenly flicked her gaze over him. "But this arrangement may prove more interesting."

"Caroline! Cease talking this instant!" He jerked a chair out from the table, then issued a calm but decisive order no one of sound mind would have disregarded. "Sit down. You're creating an exhibition no one will soon forget."

Pursing her reddened lips, the woman flounced her blue silk skirt and obeyed.

Sarah toyed with her glass with shaky fingers. So . . . she had been right. Brendan had chosen a woman to court—a very young one, if Mrs. Belmont were to be believed. Judging by Brendan's haggard expression, the woman spoke the truth. Guilt assailed her. If she hadn't happened into his life, he would have married well, and to a woman he must have wanted.

"I daresay you jump to conclusions quickly," Brendan stated, a vein throbbing in his neck.

"For your information, Sarah *is* my wife, not a paramour!"

Caroline's mouth dropped open as she snapped her head to the side to stare at Sarah. "Impossible. She wouldn't be out this soon, and look so—"

"I assure you I speak the truth. Sarah's an exceptional young woman, as you will undoubtedly learn."

At Brendan's encouraging nod, Sarah said, "It's a pleasure to meet you, Mrs. Belmont. Brendan has spoken kindly of you."

The woman extended a limp hand, which Sarah gripped and gave a mighty shake. Mrs. Belmont grabbed hold of the table to keep from falling from her seat.

Brendan overcame a sudden urge to laugh. Women didn't normally get the best of Caroline Belmont, and Sarah had done it innocently. Deploying the pretense of adjusting her chair closer to the table, Caroline righted herself. Disaster was sure to strike if he didn't take matters in hand. He clicked his fingers at the waiter, then stated, "I'm sorry, but we must depart. Sarah has an engagement this afternoon."

Caroline took his cue and came to her feet. "I shall see you both at Lilly's ball." She gave him a pointed look. "You have been invited, haven't you?"

He inclined his head in response.

Brendan eyed the calculated swing of the woman's hips as she returned to her table. Caroline was going to be a thorn in his side, not to mention an obstacle to his plans.

Chapter 10

Brendan settled into the soft folds of his favorite leather chair in the study, a copy of the *Journal of Speculative Philosophy* in his hands and a pair of rimmed spectacles on his nose. Every woman in his household except the nursemaid had vacated his home—Gertrude and Sarah to Mr. Montand's dance studio, Mathilda on an errand, and the cook to replenish her food stock. He anticipated a few hours of undisturbed quiet, during which he fully intended to subdue his unmanageable lust for Sarah.

When he heard a light knock on the pocket doors not five minutes later, he snapped, "Come!"

Marie stuck her head inside.

"Come in," he said in a more amicable manner, snatching off his spectacles.

"I'm sorry to bother you, sir, but I have to go out for a while. Rebecca needs a few things."

"Can't it wait?"

"No, sir." She wrung her hands together as she kept her vision lowered. "I won't be long.

185

I've put Rebecca down for her nap. She won't be no trouble, and will sleep till I return."

"Very well, you may go."

Brendan returned to reading his journal. Five minutes passed before another knock sounded. Giving a sigh of frustration, he jerked off his spectacles again. When Stratford entered, Brendan tilted his head in inquiry.

"I'm sorry to disturb you, sir, but I thought you might like a spot of tea."

"You realize, of course, that there's no one to prepare it."

"Indeed, I do, sir. It is rather peaceful, is it not? I took it upon myself to prepare the tea."

"Thank you, Stratford. Tea will be fine."

"Very good, sir."

The servant promptly carried in a silver tray and set it on the small table beside Brendan's chair. After he'd poured a cup, he straightened. "Will there be anything else, sir?"

"Thank you, no. I just want to read my journal. Don't interrupt me again unless the house is on fire!"

Stratford slipped silently from the room. Brendan took a sip of tea, then once again lifted his journal. He'd read two paragraphs when he heard yet another knock. "Bloody hell!"

Stratford cautiously peered into the room.

"What the devil do you want now?"

"Sir . . . Miss Rebecca is wailing like a banshee."

"Damn." Brendan stood and laid his paper and spectacles on his desk. "Have you gone to see what ails her?"

"Goodness, no." The man's eyes widened with dismay. "Begging your pardon, sir, but I've no experience with young children."

"Well, that makes two of us." Brendan strode into the hall. "Come along, man."

"Sir, I—"

"Stratford," Brendan said with a growl as he took the stairs two at a time, "I might need your assistance."

Muttering beneath his breath, the servant followed. Upon reaching the second floor, Brendan picked up his pace. Rebecca's howls of indignation echoed from the nursery. He reached the cradle in record time and gazed down at the small, irate person.

"The little miss has an excellent set of lungs," Stratford remarked from behind him.

"I daresay." Uncovering the infant, Brendan scooped her into his arms. As if on cue, Rebecca ceased bawling and hiccuped. "There, now," he crooned. "Someone has arrived, though I doubt we're who you intended. What's troubling you, sweet?"

"Perhaps she just wants to be held," Stratford volunteered. "I've heard that is oftentimes the case."

An awful aroma assaulted Brendan's senses, causing him to turn his head. "What's that ungodly stench?"

Stratford backed away. "I think the little miss has fouled her drawers, sir."

Holding the baby away from his chest, Brendan searched his coat for any sign of an indiscretion. Out of the corner of his eye, he saw

Stratford inch toward the exit. "Don't think to leave!"

"But, sir, I must get you a clean coat."

Brendan gave the servant a wry grin. "To hell with the coat. I'll probably need an entire wardrobe. You will, however, remain." He held out Rebecca. "Take her while I see what must be done."

"Oh, sir, surely you jest."

"Surely I do not!"

Stratford reluctantly took possession of Rebecca, who released a howl. Holding her awkwardly clear of his person, he wrinkled his nose.

Brendan tore off his coat and waistcoat, then his tie. Rolling up his shirt sleeves, he surveyed the room. "What do you suppose they use to . . . to bathe her?"

"I wouldn't know, sir. Might I suggest a washcloth?"

Taking Rebecca from Stratford, Brendan turned her over and noticed the dark stain on the rear of her otherwise pristine dress. "Get something to cover the bed, and be fast about it."

The servant vanished for several minutes. When he returned, gasping for breath, he spread a fresh sheet over the counterpane on the bed. "This should suffice."

"I sincerely pray it does." Gently Brendan positioned the infant on the cover, then, hands on his hips, considered his alternatives. "I think it best if I procure the necessary objects while you undress her."

Stratford choked. "*Your Grace*, it would not be proper."

Brendan pierced the servant with a steely glare. "Let me rephrase that, Stratford. I order you to undress Rebecca."

"I respectfully decline, sir."

Brendan turned to Rebecca, his expression somber. "I shan't forget this, Stratford."

"Yes, sir," the older man said quietly.

Removing a garment from so small an individual required extreme care. Brendan devoted his full attention to the task. His large hands dwarfed the baby's tiny limbs, so he took special pains not to pull or tug too hard. He'd never conceived of undressing an infant and marveled that her skin felt like velvet. When he finally eased the material over Rebecca's head, baring her to the air, another furious howl filled the room.

"She's overly modest," he explained to Stratford.

Unsure what to do with the soiled garment, he hurtled it across the room, where it landed clear of the rug, on the polished wood floor. "In the future, I want it understood that there's to be at least *one* female in the house at all times."

"As you wish, sir."

"Find me fresh drawers and a wet cloth—several, by the looks of it."

Without hesitation, Stratford rushed to do Brendan's bidding and returned out of breath again. After he hung the cloths on the bed rail, he searched the chest of drawers for clean linen. Approaching the bed, he pressed the linen over his nose and watched in horror as Brendan released the safety pin securing the diaper in place.

To Brendan's chagrin, Rebecca cried louder, her thrashing legs hindering him. He stuck the pin in the sheet a safe distance away and deftly unwrapped her. Once he'd secured her ankles with one hand, he cleaned Rebecca's squirming bottom. Pulling the fouled diaper clear of her, he carefully tucked it into a ball before he offered it to a pale-faced Stratford.

"If anyone learns of this, I'll personally hold you responsible. Do I make myself clear?"

"My lips are sealed, sir," the servant vowed as he eyed the diaper. "What would you have me do?"

"Dispose of it."

Stratford handed him the fresh linen. Judiciously taking possession of the diaper, he promptly clamped his fingers on his nose and moved out of Brendan's line of vision.

Hearing the window slam open, Brendan turned in time to see the servant lean out and drop his burden to the garden below. "Stratford! That's not precisely what I meant."

Stratford looked aghast. "Surely you did not intend that I carry it through the house?"

Biting back a grin, Brendan folded the clean linen to form a triangle and slid it under Rebecca. "You will, of course, see it properly dispensed with."

"I had every such intention. I shall instruct the gardener to bury it within the hour."

"You *are* a genius, Stratford, but I'd find another remedy for the dress."

"Oh, good Lord."

"Stratford?"

"Nothing, sir."

Brendan held the three ends together over Rebecca's belly. Gritting his teeth, he sent the pin through the cloth only to find it firmly imbedded in his thumb. Reciting a litany of curses, he jerked the point of the pin free and completed his chore. To his credit, Stratford handed over a clean gown before Brendan thought to ask for one.

More confident now, Brendan made short work of redressing Rebecca. Afterward, he stood back with a confident grin.

"Well done, sir," Stratford said, admiration in his tone.

Quiet now, Rebecca seemed content to suck on a finger. Brendan took the opportunity to wash his hands and redress himself, leaving off his tie. Then, finding a crocheted blanket, he wrapped it around Rebecca and settled her in the crook of his arm. She stared at him with wide blue eyes. "She's a beauty. She has Sarah's mouth, and her hair's already beginning to show a tendency to curl."

The older man moved closer, his mouth breaking into a rare smile. "I believe you are right, sir."

Brendan touched her fist and chuckled when five little fingers latched onto his thumb. "Do you think I should put her back in the cradle?"

"She appears wide awake," Stratford said.

"Perhaps she might like to read with me awhile." Feeling Stratford's gaze, Brendan noted surprise in the man's eyes. "It seems a shame to leave her here alone since her mood's improved. Why the devil are you staring at me like that? Have I grown another nose?"

Taken back, Stratford tugged on his waistcoat. "I beg your pardon, sir. It's just that you are behaving out of character."

Brendan smiled as he headed for the door, the child still in his arms. "So I am."

Gertrude briskly fanned her cheeks as she glanced across the carriage. Sarah's behavior had been eccentric the entire afternoon, particularly during her dance instruction. If she hadn't known better, Gertrude would have believed Sarah felt ill. Poor Mr. Montand had gotten his toes tramped on dozens of times, while his student's attention had continued to drift. Though curious to learn what had transpired between Brendan and Sarah that morning, she'd somehow refrained from asking.

Her own morning had been wonderful, and her mind kept going over her walk with the dance instructor. Mr. Montand had been so charming and witty, she'd felt years younger, and she looked forward to seeing him again. Being present for Sarah's instruction had been an enlightening experience. She had known of Mr. Montand's intelligence, exemplary manners, and charisma, but she hadn't imagined he could be so patient.

In her mind substituting herself for Sarah in

his capable arms, Gertrude's face grew even hotter. She worked her fan faster. It simply wouldn't do to arrive at the house in such a state. Brendan would guess the reason, then question her. She preferred to keep her romantic musings to herself for the present.

The carriage door swung open, alerting her that she hadn't noticed they'd arrived. Nudging Sarah, who also seemed preoccupied, Gertrude alighted and headed for the entrance. They didn't speak until they'd reached the second story where Marie anxiously awaited them.

Sarah instantly regained her senses, asking, "Is something wrong?"

The woman hesitated, running her hands down her brown, pleated skirt. "His Lordship let me go out, but when I got back Miss Rebecca wasn't in her bed."

Sarah's eyes grew large as she started down the hall, but Gertrude caught her arm. "Wait," the older woman said, "I'm positive Marie knows more."

"Yes, ma'am," Marie confirmed. Lowering her voice, she confided, "*He* has her."

"Brendan?" Sarah asked.

"I looked through the doors'n there they sat—him readin' his paper out loud, and Miss Rebecca on his lap." She leaned closer. "I didn't go in."

Gertrude smiled. "Well, if that doesn't beat all. I have to see this with my own eyes."

She was halfway down the stairs before she looked over her shoulder to find Sarah following her. She stopped just short of the doors and, laying a finger over her mouth, peeked through the narrow opening. Unable to believe her eyes, she stepped away to allow Sarah to take her place.

Sarah pulled Gertrude aside. She'd just opened her mouth to whisper something, but Brendan cleared his throat. Startled, both women abruptly turned.

"Have neither of you nothing better to do than spy on me and titter outside my door?"

"We weren't titterin', and we most certainly weren't spyin' on you," Sarah answered. "I just wanted to . . . borrow a piece of paper."

"Paper?"

"Yes, paper. I haven't written my parents since our marriage."

"By all means," he said, allowing her room to pass.

Sarah gave her hat and gloves to Gertrude, then proceeded into the study.

Hard put not to grin, Gertrude said, "And I've come for Rebecca."

As he handed over the now-sleeping child, Brendan's reproving look convinced Gertrude that he didn't believe either excuse. She'd thought Sarah's retort brilliant, and couldn't pass up a chance to needle him. "I must say, you do surprise me, *Cyril*. It appears you've already made a conquest."

As Gertrude would have expected, Brendan's mouth tightened. "I've expressly forbidden you to address me by that odious name."

"Yes, you have," she returned with a laugh. "I don't know why it slipped out. You have made me curious. Whatever possessed you to play the doting father?"

"Suffice it to say that I happen to enjoy women, particularly those of such a tender age. They don't continually harp."

Sarah stepped back into the doorway and kissed her daughter's cheek, preventing Gertrude from pursuing the matter. Brendan relinquished the baby.

Following his wife into the study, Brendan shut the doors soundly behind him.

Sarah went to the desk, where she awaited Brendan. Lying had its own retribution, she thought. In this case, perhaps it would serve to make her tend to a chore she'd been putting off. Her parents must have been worried about her. But how was she to explain all that had happened since she'd left home?

Brendan motioned for her to be seated in his overly large chair. Rounding the desk, he took paper from a middle drawer and laid it in front of her.

"You'll find anything else you might need within reach."

Sarah briefly closed her eyes, inhaling his enticing scent. His nearness threw her mind into a spin, jumbling her thoughts. Thank goodness he had chosen not to linger over her, and instead had seated himself in a chair next to a window.

She dipped his pen in ink and wrote a salutation. Pausing, she attempted to find the right way to tell her parents of her marriage and child. But words failed her.

Minutes passed, and Sarah looked up. Brendan held a journal a foot from his face, his eyes pinched half closed in concentration. Though she thought it an uncomfortable position in which to read, she remained silent. She forced herself to write a first sentence, informing her parents of her address and her marriage. She released a sigh, her shoulders slumping with despair.

"Tell them the truth, Sarah. They won't hold what happened against you."

"How can you say that? You don't even know them."

"I know you, Sarah. Thus I have every confidence in your family." He lowered his journal. "If you fabricate a story, it'll backfire one day. And you'll hurt them more." He studied her face, as if searching for some truth. "Or are you ashamed to admit you've married me and not my brother?"

"How can you suggest such a thing? Even if you weren't morally principled and infinitely more steadfast, they wouldn't find fault with you." A sly smile captured her mouth. "I myself haven't found a single one."

"Is it so important to you that I'm . . . morally principled?"

"I do admire you for it. Why do you ask?"

"I've known men of scandalous reputation who have changed. Would you regard them as less admirable for seeing the error of their ways and having the strength to reform?"

She considered a moment. "It wouldn't be

fair to hold a person's past against him if he's truly repented.''

He nodded, apparently satisfied with her answer.

She contemplated her letter again. Postponing her chore wouldn't gain her peace of mind, she realized, so she took Brendan's advice and simply related the events as they'd happened. When she finished, she felt a rush of relief. Her family might have been disappointed in her, but she hadn't lied or withheld one item of truth. Perhaps the news of their granddaughter would soften their reaction to her letter.

Sarah blew puffs of air on the ink, her gaze once more roving to Brendan. She noticed the spectacles on the small table and bit her lip as she realized that her arrogant earl couldn't read without assistance. And he was vain, to boot. A little voice cautioned her to keep silent. She didn't listen to it.

"You'll ruin your eyesight," she said.

The journal crinkled as his arms fell to his lap. "I beg your pardon?"

"I said you'll ruin your eyesight by readin' without your glasses."

He glanced at the table, his composure a bit ruffled. "I had hoped you wouldn't notice."

"I'm quite observant."

"I daresay. A proper wife would've contrived not to notice, much less remark upon, her husband's imperfection."

"Many people can't read print up close."

He stared at her, reproach in his eyes.

"Personally, I don't regard such a minor thing as an imperfection."

Sarah folded her letter, and tucked it into an envelope. Writing her parents' address, she smiled. She found his annoyance with his infirmity not only amusing but endearing as well.

The scene she'd witnessed when she'd spied through the door played in her mind. Brendan possessed a tender side he preferred to hide. She realized that she could easily fall helplessly in love with him.

When she chanced a look in his direction, she noted the spectacles were now perched on his fine nose. Goodness, his handsomeness wasn't compromised one iota, she thought, though she doubted she could have convinced him of her discovery. He was, after all, a male—an extremely stubborn one.

"How did your dance instruction go?" he asked suddenly.

"I'm afraid you'll find I have no talent to speak of."

"You've had but one lesson, Sarah."

"You don't understand. I'm not musically inclined. You've married a completely unaccomplished woman, though I hope you aren't *too* disappointed."

"You've already demonstrated one talent, and you do it superbly."

"Really? And what might that be?"

"You're able to fashion a knot in a man's tie."

Pleasure rippled through her. He seemed determined to pamper her ego.

"A change of partner might help you master

your dancing. I've found that I'm not as accomplished with some women as with others."

"Oh? And have you danced with many women?" He raised a brow, and she knew she'd asked a foolish question. "Forgive my stupidity. Naturally, when a man reaches *your* age, he's danced with an abundance of women."

"Indeed," he said with an edge in his voice, "a man of my *advanced* years has. Precisely how old do you think I am?"

Sarah fidgeted in her seat. Her rash tongue had roused his ire, reminding him of their first encounter, when she'd thought him Derek's father. "I'm not sure. Why don't you tell me?"

"That would be too easy, my dear. Guess."

"One hundred and two."

"Clever. Thirty-two is closer to the truth."

"As old as that." Sarah clamped a hand over her mouth. Leaving her chair, she walked slowly around the desk and leaned against it, her hands behind her. She gripped the edge of the wood. "I don't know how that popped out. Thirty-two isn't so old. Why, my father—"

His hazel eyes riveted her, as the fingers of his right hand drummed the chair arm.

"Can we change the subject?" she implored.

His fingers continued to abuse the chair arm. His gaze, however, became more intense, burning through the material of her dress and heating her skin as it slowly traveled the length of her. Dear Lord, when he looked at her like that she could actually feel her blood move through her veins.

"So," he said, "you have no talents."

His deep tone further unnerved her. "Well, I do have one talent that can't be disputed. I've made a beautiful baby."

Removing his spectacles, he laid them and his journal on the table. Then, bracing his elbows on the chair, he steepled his fingers together. "I look forward to testing my own abilities. What do you think, Sarah? Will I sire handsome sons?"

Sarah attempted to swallow but discovered her mouth was dry. She imagined making love with him and then bearing his son. She didn't love him.

Or did she?

Could she find such prospects thrilling if all she felt was desire? The emotions swirling within her were so different from what she'd felt for Derek.

Not wanting Brendan to know the course her mind was wandering along, she dared to adopt a teasing manner. "You'd no doubt excel at sirin' handsome sons. For a man in his dotage, you're exceptionally preserved."

To Sarah's relief, he smiled. Encouraged by his improved mood, she ventured closer, stopping when she stood within inches of him. "Brendan, I truly meant no insult. I don't regard you as ancient. You're the perfect age for a man. It's just that sometimes I've no control over my tongue and—"

"I'll have to cure you of speaking out of turn?"

"You can try, but I think you'll likely not

win. I can't help the way I am. You'd be wise to learn to tolerate my—" The remainder of Sarah's words lodged in her throat as Brendan pulled her onto his lap.

Cupping her face in his hands, he gave her a melting look. "When a man kisses you, do you continue to prattle?"

"I haven't kissed enough men to know, only two—if you count the boy who dared to corner me when I was ten, but he went home with a bloody nose, though I wouldn't bloody *your* nose if you kissed me."

She fell silent and stared at his sensual mouth, craving his kiss. She wondered if it would surpass the luscious sensations she experienced every time he touched her. His fingers trailed along her cheeks, pausing when they reached her shoulders. She closed her eyes to better savor the moment, the delectable impression of herself as a flower blooming under a scorching sun.

"Sarah," he whispered. "You're so tempting. And quiet now. Your unruly tongue appears to behave when I put my hands on you. Is it a momentary occurrence, or will it happen every time?"

"Why don't you kiss me and find out?"

Chapter 11

Brendan's brows shot upward. Embarrassed, Sarah started to slide from his lap, but his arm clamped around her, holding her in place.

"You're a continual surprise, Sarah."

She was a surprise? He'd pulled her onto *his* lap.

Gold lights danced in his eyes as he considered her mouth. Goose flesh rose all over her body. Relaxing against his arm, she inhaled deeply. Then, acting upon a wild impulse, she brushed her lips over his. The brief, light contact left her heart thumping.

Fine lines creased his brow. "Sarah . . . "

Growing bolder, she slid her arms over his shoulders. He was so handsome, so appealing, so very masculine. But it wasn't passion alone she wanted from him. Lord help her, she longed for a deeper commitment. Warmth and laughter, a sharing of minds.

To be loved by him.

The realization stunned her. Throwing caution to the wind, she brushed her fingers along his hairline, detouring under his ears, until, reaching his shirt, she opened several buttons and wound a dark curl around one finger. "You aren't wearin' your tie."

"No," he answered in a much lower tone. "I am not." He resettled himself in the chair, his mouth slanting in a grave line. "Stratford will be announcing dinner any minute."

Sarah sighed, her hands dropping to his waistcoat. Fingering a button, she sought a way out of her predicament. He obviously didn't want to kiss her but was too much of a gentleman to say so. He might have had another motive for pulling her onto his lap, she mused, though what that was she couldn't fathom.

"Well . . . I'm not hungry, but you must be," she said.

Resettling himself again, he mumbled beneath his breath, "Sarah, you're a bloody temptress."

She blinked, confused by his erratic behavior.

"I'm hungry, all right," he admitted as he leaned forward. He bent her back over the chair arm, his breath caressing her mouth. "For you, Sarah. Tempting the devil is dangerous. The devil will most assuredly devour you."

He allowed her no opportunity to prepare herself. His mouth swooped over hers. His lips were gentle and searching, sending her mind into a spin. He fulfilled every dream she'd ever had, especially those of the Prince Charming who visited her in the night to sweep her into his strong arms and carry her off to paradise. She moaned softly in her throat, dizzy from the pleasant sensations fluttering over her skin. He must have cared a little to kiss her so sweetly.

Sarah ran her fingers through his hair as she pressed more tightly against his chest. Hearing a similar moan from him, she grew more confident. She began to kiss him back, her lips moving on his with an instinct she hadn't known she possessed.

Good Lord, Derek had never made her feel this alive.

A low, agonized groan came from deep in his chest as his tongue slipped inside her mouth. Sarah gasped. Taking advantage of her surprise, he thoroughly devoured her, filling her with a sweet, hot languor. She melted against him and duplicated his movements. She felt as if she were caught in raging rapids, being swirled around and around. He groaned once more and held her so tightly, she thought she'd swoon from the blood rushing to her head.

Brendan slowly broke off their kiss. When Sarah could focus on him, she noticed that molten gold overshadowed the hazel color of his eyes. His heavy breathing hinted that he shared the tumult roiling deep within her. But once again, he allowed her no time to gather her thoughts.

His mouth reclaimed hers. Now, though, there was no gentle stroking, but rather an urgent yearning, a yearning she shared totally. She didn't need to put forth any effort, for he was a veritable master in the art of kissing. Blood pounded through her veins, igniting an inferno deep in her abdomen. His free hand moved around her waist, inching higher, then sneaked over her breast.

The intensity of his kiss lessened, allowing him to whisper against her mouth, "For shame, Sarah. You've neglected to wear your corset again."

She gasped, and found him quick to seize the advantage once more. His tongue dove past her lips. He'd compared himself to the devil, and he proficiently demonstrated what he'd meant. His movements compared with making love, thrusting and retreating, invading and conquering. Although she was tempted to duplicate his sensuous maneuvers, her entire being was erupting with unfamiliar feelings. She was satisfied to allow him to exhibit his skill.

Heavens! She'd given herself to a boy, when she'd always craved a *man*. *This* man.

The next instant, he dragged himself free of her. His eyes were wild, his nostrils flaring, as if a demon possessed him. Tugging his arm from beneath her, he gripped her waist and unsteadily came to his feet, bringing her with him. Barely able to stand, Sarah sidestepped to regain her balance. She'd brazenly thrown herself at him, and now she feared that he must really think her a Jezebel.

Sarah's gaze flashed below his waist to the very visible hard ridge outlined by his trousers. Heat surged in a very private place. Her cheeks felt aflame, and she suspected they'd turned a bright crimson. Quickly, she stared at the rows of bookcases behind him. An instant later, she found herself in his arms, being carried up the stairs.

Inside the bedroom he resettled her in his arms, gazing into her eyes with a curious expression. The instant his head began to lower, she jerked instinctively, and he paused to aim a devastating smile at her.

"I've been accused of many things, Sarah, but not of biting—leastwise not in the last quarter of a century."

She tried to imagine him as a child. He always behaved with such dignity, the picture of him sinking his teeth into someone refused to form. "Were you very precocious?"

"Very. My nanny at the time swore I was Satan's spawn."

Sarah giggled. "I find that hard to believe."

His head slowly approached, curing her of her amusement. But his lips merely brushed across hers before he slowly lowered her to her feet. Sarah's heart drummed at a furious pace.

As she watched him stride to the bureau, she availed herself of the pleasure of letting her eyes roam over him, admiring the impressive width of his shoulders, and his trim waist. She'd never looked at length at a man's backside before, but even that part of his anatomy was sculptured perfectly.

Sarah nervously wet her lips. She had craved this moment. Why did she feel so jittery?

Because she loved him, her mind supplied. Because her experience was comprised of two brief encounters with, God help her, his brother. And because, despite his self-proclaimed untarnished reputation, she knew Brendan would be adept at lovemaking.

He threw back the bedcovers, leaving them orderly.

She sucked in an uneven breath.

Standing sideways, he removed his shoes. His profile struck her as grand. She wanted to swallow, but her throat refused to cooperate. Before she could manage another attempt, he walked toward her.

"Are you always so precise?" she asked, her voice breaking.

"I want no distractions." Slipping his hands around her waist, he stepped close and nibbled on her ear. "You drive me mad, Sarah. Once I touch you, my sanity will leave me, and there will be no opportunity to tend to the minor details."

His tongue laved the area below her ear as his fingers worked deftly behind her, unhooking her dress. She still held her arms at her sides. The most delightful sensations danced over her skin from his ardent attention, causing her to tilt her head to better accommodate him. She could barely speak but thought she must summon the presence of mind to do so.

"I hesitate to interrupt you."

"Then don't," he said against her neck.

"You've forgotten to lock the door," she reminded him quietly.

His shoulders dropped in frustration. "Bloody hell."

His departure from her left her with a sinking feeling, as if her legs had lost substance and were refusing to support her weight.

"Now, where was I?" he asked upon his return. Slipping his arms around her waist again, he kissed her nose. "I hope you haven't grown cold in my absence."

The remaining hooks sprang free to the sound of his chuckle, sending a luscious shiver down Sarah's spine. "Your touch is exceptionally potent, your Lordship."

His mouth curved up on one side as he studied her. "Are you positive you want me to continue?"

Sarah took matters into her own hands and popped open the rest of the buttons on his shirt. Then, tugging the material out of his trousers and over his shoulders, she drank her fill of his chest. A quivery sigh escaped her.

"You may look to your heart's content, Sarah. As I told you at the lodge, I haven't a modest bone in my body." He wiggled his arms so that the shirt fell to the floor. Catching hold of her hands, he flattened them over his heart. "You may touch as well. But, I warn you, I intend to do the same to you."

Her knees nearly buckled at the thought. Heat swept along her nerve endings, pooling low in her abdomen.

"Before I've finished, your modesty will be thoroughly compromised."

"Threats, sir?"

She stirred herself to explore the very masculine territory she'd exposed. Grazing with her fingertips over the contoured lines of his

shoulders, she felt the hard ridges and inden-
tations of his chest and sides.

He held his breath for the duration of her
exploration, expelling it when she reached the
area just above his trousers. "My own rather
unscrupulous modesty will be breached,
should you venture any lower."

"Is that an invitation?"

"I daresay it is. Are you up to it?"

"You'll think me a Jezebel."

"Perhaps," he whispered with a bemused
smile. "On the other hand, I just might welcome a forward move."

An image of Florence Belmont glimmered in
Sarah's mind. Would he have expected the
same of her, a very properly brought up innocent? As for Sarah, she was finding him to be
far more fascinating than she'd imagined. "You
jest."

He shook his head, his smile turning sardonic. "Beneath my puritanical image beats a
very human heart, Sarah. Did you think I was
carved of stone?"

She trailed her fingers over his abdomen, and
he flinched and drew in a breath. "I've never
known stone to feel so warm. It's just that
you've impressed me as—"

"Good God, Sarah. You weren't going to refer to me as stuffy."

Sarah bit her lip.

"Anyone who knew me before I came to St.
Louis would gainsay your theory."

"I'm sorry if I've wounded your ego."

He closed his eyes for several seconds before

pulling her tightly against him. Easing her gown down to her elbows, he placed a searing kiss on her shoulder. "There are things about me you don't know."

Fearing he meant to ruin the moment, she flung her arms around his middle and hugged him to her. His back felt as warm as his abdomen, and she traced the indentation of his spine.

"Bloody hell, Sarah. When you touch me you sear my skin."

She leaned closer, kissing the side of his neck.

He reached behind him and seized her wrists. Compelling her to put her arms at her sides, he made short work of shoving her gown free. It puddled around her feet with a soft whoosh. He tugged at a stubborn tie at her waist, cursing when the thing wouldn't come undone. "I find a woman's petticoats a trying affair."

"Let me," she offered, amused by his ineptitude. Within moments, two petticoats joined the gown.

"Leave the last."

She glanced up, into narrowed hazel eyes that looked aflame with gold, and couldn't still her racing heart. He didn't resemble the arrogant, masterful lord now. Passion blazed not only in his eyes, but in his pained expression and in the trembling that rocked his body.

He opened the ribbon at the neckline of her chemise, and skillfully flicked open the lace-trimmed undergarment. A wicked smile possessed his mouth as he dipped a finger into the valley between her breasts. The breath Sarah had been holding exploded from her.

"Sit on the bed for me, Sarah. I want to indulge a fantasy that's plagued me the entire afternoon. But first—"

His hands disappeared under her petticoat, and before she could blink, her drawers lay in a heap at her ankles. "Mercy!"

"Your pact with the devil precludes mercy. Now, if you please, to the bed. My fantasy grows impatient."

So he fell prey to fantasies also, she mused. She wouldn't have thought it of him. Curious and overheated, she obeyed his request. Her eyes opened wide when he knelt before her and removed her shoes.

"I could've done that," she protested weakly, anticipation sending a wave of dizziness over her. His hands slid up the back of her legs and stopped when they reached her knees. Sarah rolled her lips together to stifle a gasp.

She leaned forward and ran her fingers through his hair, leaving it falling forward in disarray. He looked even more handsome, unabashedly grinning like a dissolute pirate intent upon stealing her virtue, if she'd had any left to claim.

"You're proven my undoing," he said. "I'm hard put to temper my— Suffice it to say, it's been a very long time, and I was never one to deny my—" His expression turned grim as he sought one of her garters and eased a stocking down her leg. "This is what I've wanted to do."

Sarah leaned back, bracing her hands on the

bed, too enthralled to move or utter a word. The sensations he awakened in her held her spellbound, tuned to his touch. He whipped the stocking free of her foot, then performed the same act with the other leg.

He looked up. His gaze collided with hers, and she would have sworn fire leaped between them. She went weak all over, sinking back onto her elbows because the muscles in her arms turned to water.

"I've only just begun, Sarah. You've sought to seduce me. Now I'll demonstrate my own technique of seduction."

Despite his warning, Sarah was unprepared when he pushed up the hem of her petticoat and skimmed with his lips along the inner side of her knee. She moaned softly. His skilled mouth roamed at will, advancing upward, until it ceased its electrifying progression inches short of her throbbing center. Her inner thigh felt scorched.

"Glory be!"

He laughed roughly, sounding more in pain than amused. "I pray you offer the same exclamation when we've arrived at the culmination."

Sarah sucked in a breath, desperate to gain enough air to enable her to speak. "If I didn't know better, I'd think you have done this many times," she managed to say. "Or are you genuinely a devil."

"Are you pleased?"

"I'm delirious!"

"Good. I'm beyond reason, and will have this through."

Returning fervently to his chore, he reenacted the same flaming ritual with her other leg. When he finally lifted his head, Sarah felt as if he'd trickled hot honey all over her body. Summoning her strength, she wiggled further into the middle of the bed.

He pushed to his feet, his eyes smoldering with passion. "There's no escape," he said.

"I've asked for none," she returned with more assurance than she possessed. "I think I've wanted you to make love to me from the first minute I saw you."

He laughed as he began to unfasten his trousers. "You think? If my recollection serves me well, you thought me in my dotage."

The impious look in his eyes, the nimble movement of his fingers as they progressed along the front opening of his pants, mesmerized her. Her stomach knotted when he stood dauntlessly naked before her. "I declare!" she exclaimed, gaining a wide grin from him. "You're definitely not elderly."

"Untie the ribbon on your petticoat."

Though she was boldly ogling him, no power on earth could have stopped her. Her quick affair with Derek hadn't prepared her for the spectacular sight of Brendan blatantly, powerfully aroused.

"Sarah, the ribbon," he reminded her as he dug one knee into the mattress and wrapped his fingers around her ankle. He dragged her closer.

"You said I can look all I want," she countered weakly. Heat seeped through her veins.

He laughed again, obviously enjoying her ardent perusal. "Touching's more to my liking."

He crawled forward and impatiently tore at the ribbon until it came free. Inching the petticoat over her hips, his amusement faded to rapt contemplation.

Sarah squirmed, overheated and breathless with anticipation. None of her dreams had hinted at the delirium she was experiencing. She hoped her heart could bear the strain, because she feared the human body wasn't intended to withstand such an emotionally wracking and physically demanding onslaught.

Her petticoat went flying. He fell over her, cradling her face in his hands. "It's my desire to spend the remainder of the day and the entire night loving you, Sarah."

He burned hot and hard against her thigh. He made her insensible, longing to have him inside her, as close as two people could come. Impatient to know him intimately, she wiggled again until she was in position to circle her legs around him. Her accomplishment incited an anguished groan from him that echoed her own.

"Sarah! That was a reckless deed."

He lay throbbing against her, his body tense. Even in her inexperience, she knew he was striving to master his desire. And though she was eager to see what exquisite torture he would subject her to next, she feared she'd perish if he prolonged her agony.

"Reckless. But so very, very nice." She lifted her hips, crushing herself against him, letting her body tell him how much she hungered for him.

"You're a natural-born sorceress."

"Only with you."

His hands covered her breasts, his mouth finally claiming hers. She wanted to lie still to savor the blistering excitement tearing through her, but he pressed her into the mattress as his tongue invaded her mouth. He vanquished any thought of lying motionless. Her reaction was spontaneous. Her hips rose against his, beseeching, yearning for him to extinguish the fire he'd ignited. She wanted to absorb him into her and never release him.

Sarah grazed over his back with her fingers, then moved down to his buttocks. His kiss deepened. She wondered if he intended to devour her, but couldn't have roused a protest if it had been his goal. Digging her nails into his skin, she released a long, wracking moan and kissed him back. He endured for several seconds before he gently retreated.

Gripping his shoulders, she attempted to pull him close again but discovered his movement meant only a detour to another more devastating attack upon her senses. In the same manner that he'd laved her ear, his tongue sampled first one of her breasts, then the other. He swept a circular course, working his way inward, leaving Sarah writhing, her moans at a fever pitch. When she thought she could stand it no more, he advanced his beguiling assault and nibbled on one nipple. Sarah sucked in a breath and rose against him again, but this time he mumbled an oath and shoved his hands under her bottom and plunged inside of her.

"Glory be!"

She experienced no pain, as she had with Derek the first time. Instead waves of desire radiated from her innermost regions and shuddered through her. She wanted their burning union to go on forever even if it meant the excruciating tension gripping her would remain as well. But Brendan decided their course by instigating a series of daring movements that sent her mind and body reeling. She gouged her nails into his back as she convulsed in an ecstatic spasm that rivaled an explosion of dynamite.

She felt his warmth explode inside her and contracted her muscles in the hope that she was heightening his pleasure. He fell, spent, atop her, his harsh, hot breath scorching her neck.

"Bloody hell, Sarah." His tone was low and tortured.

Sarah grinned and hugged him close. "That was *bloody* marvelous, your Lordship," she said in a hoarse whisper, fondly mocking his speech. "You've left me as limp as a wilted flower."

Amusement and desire laced his voice. "A rose minus her thorns?"

"More like a dandelion," she countered.

He tenderly kissed her lips, grazing back and forth with his tongue. Then, meeting her gaze in the dim light, he gave her a wry smile. "The dandelion and the prize hog. What was his name?"

"Wallace."

Sarah swallowed her amusement, amazed that he could joke about the unfair comparison she'd made during their first meeting. Had Brendan changed, or had she learned to see past his image of perfection? But perhaps he'd always been this different, likeable person inside.

Her face expressionless, she remarked, "My father puts a high value on that irascible, demandin' boar. Wallace is the best stud in the county."

"Might I construe that as a roundabout compliment?"

"I daresay," she returned.

"Mocking me won't get you on my better side, Sarah."

"Oh, there's a better side than the one you just demonstrated?"

The corners of his mouth twitched as he brushed tendrils of hair from her still-flushed face.

"I daresay," she answered for him, grinning when he rolled his eyes.

"You please me greatly, Sarah," he said gently. "Though the circumstances of our meeting and subsequent marriage weren't ideal, I deem you a prize of which I'm unworthy." He kissed her forehead before he rolled to his side. "If you wish to freshen up, do so quickly. I'll look elsewhere."

Sarah felt the loss of his bodily contact

keenly, but she appreciated his consideration. She performed her ablutions hastily while she considered his remark. How could he think himself unworthy of her? She'd found him lacking in no area other than in occasionally being high-handed. His behavior that day made that minor flaw seem unimportant.

Glancing at the bed she saw that he lay on his back, studying the ceiling. The light cast shadows over half of his face. His expression looked somber, and she wondered at his thoughts. He'd said she pleased him greatly. Regretting that he might have been referring only to their fevered joining, she opened a drawer in the bureau and dug through the assortment of pretty gowns Gertrude had bought for her.

"Cover yourself if you wish, but it'll be a waste of precious time."

Sarah paused to peek over her shoulder, and found Brendan's heated gaze considering her. "You said you wouldn't look."

"And I honored my word."

Light was reflected in his hazel eyes as they leisurely traveled the length of her bare body. Sarah grew warm all over again. "You aren't honorin' it now."

"'Twas only given for a few minutes. I'd hoped you had grown less modest." He tossed back the covers, confirming he had no such reserve.

"Good heavens! You want to do it again?"

Deep, masculine laughter filled the room. "It *is* entirely possible, you know."

"I know no such thing." Snatching the gown on top of the pile, she held it in front of her and approached the bed. Unable to compel herself to look elsewhere, she admired his engorged manhood. When he laughed again, heat flooded her cheeks. Forcing her gaze back to his face, she stammered, "I . . . you're brazenly conceited to exhibit yourself so shamelessly."

In response, he seized a handful of the gown and flung it out of sight. "Come back to bed, Sarah," he said softly.

"It appears I've little choice in the matter," she muttered, disguising her pleasure and amusement. "I've unleashed an insatiable monster."

"Devilishly ravenous."

Sarah crawled across the bed and fell atop him. "Tonight has altered my perception of you, Brendan Hammond." He splayed his hands on her bottom, forcing her belly tightly against his powerful erection. "You don't feel one bit elderly."

He chuckled as he reversed their position. "How does *this* feel?"

"Won-der-ful," she said when he came inside her.

He loved her to distraction with painstaking thoroughness, rendering her incapable of thought or speech. *Wonderful* seemed an inadequate word, she thought during the seconds following their blinding consummation. His tenderness, the way his mouth and hands had cherished her, his anguished moans during their lovemaking, had left her with a heavy feeling. He'd doused the burning ache he alone could ignite in her body, taking her to heaven in the process, but what of her heart?

He hadn't said he loved her.

Already she wanted more.

Tucking the covers over them both, he snuggled against her, his arm possessively binding her to him. "I was right about you from the start, Sarah. You're a scheming seductress bent on draining me dry."

Sarah tensed.

"You've drained every last vestige of my strength and, though I'd very much like to make love to you again, I require a few hours rest."

She slowly relaxed, relieved he hadn't said what she'd feared, that her wanton response to him had convinced him she was a loose woman after his wealth. "It must be due to your advanced years," she taunted, poking him in his ribs.

He seized her hand and brought it to his lips. "A proper wife—"

"—wouldn't mention her husband's infirmity," she finished for him.

"A proper wife," he continued in a sterner voice, "is obedient, deferential, and minds her tongue at all times."

"Wasn't I obedient just a few minutes ago, sir?"

"You were a siren."

"Didn't I defer to your demands and wishes?"

"Most passionately."

Slipping her hand free, she eased her leg over his, bringing them closer. She kissed his neck, prolonging the pleasure for several long minutes, using her tongue to provoke his capitulation.

"Sarah," he whispered hoarsely, "you'll leave a mark, and I'll have a devil of a time explaining it."

Against his skin, she muttered, "You'll just have to say that your wife feasted upon you."

Dragging her on top of him, he growled deep in his throat. "And so you shall."

Chapter 12

Brendan awoke slowly the following morning, replete and sluggish after a memorable night. A contented smile hovered about his mouth as he remembered the three explosive times he and Sarah had made love.

Bringing a lock of her hair to his cheek, he gazed at her. In repose, she was even lovelier. Her dark, wavy hair curled over the pillow. Long, dark lashes brushed her cheeks. The bedcovers had become tangled toward morning and lay haphazardly across her hips, exposing more than they hid.

He trailed a finger over her shoulder, then down her side. His wife had turned out to be a wildly passionate and sweetly loving woman, and he yearned to repeat the fervent hours they'd spent. But, he thought, Sarah wasn't long recovered from Rebecca's birth and might suffer some aftereffect, should he become too greedy.

He crossed his arms over his chest and contented himself with gazing at her. A startling fact struck him. He'd wanted her from the first, even when he'd wrongly judged her of foully scheming to deceive him. He'd found her beautiful and desirable though she was carrying his brother's child. Clamping his lips together, he pushed the thought of Derek from his mind. His brother was an obstacle he'd somehow managed to overcome, and he damn well intended that it would remain that way.

"You look as mad as a scalded cat," a sleepy voice remarked.

Brendan blinked. "I'm just angry that it's already morning."

Suddenly aware of the view she unconsciously afforded him, Sarah drew the sheet up under her arm, tucking it in to cover her breasts. "I suppose there's no need to ask what shameless deed you were up to a few minutes ago."

He gave her a wicked grin. "I found the scenery breathtaking."

Her cheeks turned a charming shade of pink as she pushed herself into a sitting position. "What time is it?"

"Nearly ten."

"Good Lord! Mathilda and Stratford must be in a tizzy, and Rebecca will be takin' her mornin' nap any minute. And Gertrude . . . Whatever will they think?"

Unable to contain his amusement, Brendan laughed softly. "I rather imagine they've assumed I've overslept because my extremely passionate, demanding wife whiled away the night ravishing my body."

Sarah's cheeks burned a bright crimson. "Oh,

surely not. Have you heard any of them
knock?"

"At least ten times," he said with mock sincerity.

Snapping the covers free, Sarah leaped from
the bed and dashed to the bureau, where she
grabbed clean underclothes. "You should've
awakened me. How could you have let me
sleep so long? I'll never be able to face them.
Why, we've even missed breakfast, and I'm
hungry enough to eat a cow."

He watched her toss a chemise on the bed
rail, then frantically pull on her drawers, thoroughly enjoying the provocative sight of her
dancing breasts. "I daresay I'm having my
breakfast right now."

After she'd ineptly tied the ribbon and
quickly donned the chemise, she heaved a
breath and glanced at him. "How can you lie
there and grin like the fox who's just swallowed
every chicken in the hen house?"

"I only devoured one," he countered with a
lazy grin. "But it was so plump and juicy, it
spoiled my appetite for meager fare."

Her eyes narrowed on him as her hands went
to her hips. "I'll have you know I'm nearly the
same size as before." She looked down and
pressed her hands over her stomach. "Do you
really think I'm plump?"

"You're perfect."

"Then why did you—" Seconds passed before her expression softened. "You were
teasin'?"

He nodded. "Is it so surprising?"

She nodded. "You're very different from the arrogant earl I met when I arrived." She closed the distance between them and sat beside him. "I didn't like you very much then."

"Your opinion has changed?"

"Drastically. When you smile, you melt my heart."

"I'll have to remember to smile often."

She touched his cheek, her gaze turning tender, and Brendan marveled that so innocent a gesture could affect him so deeply.

"Smile at me too often, your Lordship, and— Oh, good heavens."

Concerned by her abrupt change of tone, he caught her hand. "What is it?"

Her eyes large, she asked, "Is it possible that you've given me another child?"

"I should hope not!"

Her eyes widened more.

Noticing her hurt look, he rephrased his words to more adequately explain his feelings. "I'd rather not burden you unnecessarily."

Her hurt look remained.

"Do you think you might have conceived? I admit it was the furthest thing from my mind at the time."

"It only took twice with Rebecca. Last night . . . You were much more . . . amorous than—"

He released her hand.

"Forgive me," she said contritely. A long moment passed. "I take that back."

His gaze flashed to her.

"I can't always remember not to mention

him. And I would never compare you with anyone.'' She lowered her head. ''Truly, there's nothing to compare. The short time I spent with your brother is a vague memory, vastly different from what we shared. At least from what *I* shared with you. However, your perception of last night might clash with mine.''

''The fault lies with me, Sarah, not you. In time I'll not react so boorishly when you slip and mention Derek's name. He is, after all, my brother.''

''You still hold it against me.''

''Not in my heart,'' he explained with sudden insight. ''My rather uncharitable mind, however, rashly puts words in my mouth.''

''Should I stuff a gag in your mouth?''

Brendan bit back a smile. ''A suggestion worthy of consideration. Perhaps a dash of compassion might suffice. I'm my own worst enemy, at times.''

She trailed a finger over his hand, drawing a line up his arm. ''If you can forgive my . . . imprudence, I can certainly tolerate your occasional lapses.''

He covered her hand with his, preventing her from continuing her intoxicating exploration of his arm. Their time at the lodge swept across the back of his mind. She'd suffered such pain giving birth to Rebecca, he remembered, he couldn't bear the thought of her suffering again too soon. While he hadn't given the matter any thought during the past evening, in the future he would.

Had she conceived? Running his fingers

through her hair, he imagined Sarah holding another child in her arms. A boy. His son. The image brought a lump to his throat, shaking his control. Her arms slipped around his neck.

Good God, when had he stumbled and lost his heart?

Pulling her arms from around him, he met her adoring gaze. He should confess, he knew. She had a right to be told of his past, of the countless women with whom he'd shared a bed. But he was afraid Sarah wouldn't look at him with such devotion if she knew him for the hypocrite he'd become. Eventually she'd find out. At the moment she felt gratitude. Until he was sure of her love, he mused, he was just selfish enough to accept a reprieve and amass so many memorable moments with her that she'd have no choice but to forgive him.

By then maybe she would even be carrying his child.

"You look so glum," she said.

"I suppose that's preferable to stuffy."

"Indeed, it is. Whatever were you thinkin'?"

Lowering his head, he kissed a path from her throat to her breasts.

Sarah sighed. She considered him with an odd expression, leaving him confused about what she was thinking.

"Sarah, I must ask you to tell me when your next monthly arrives."

She drew back, her mouth sliding into a bleak line.

"It's necessary. I'll take every precaution to

assure that I don't impregnate you, though I can't guarantee it won't happen."

Leaping to her feet, she cast him a wounded look, but a second later he wondered if he'd imagined her reaction. She hurried across the room, where she pulled the corded rope. "I'd best hurry if I want to see Rebecca before Marie puts her down for her mornin' nap."

Not wanting to be caught in his altogether in front of the female servant, Brendan muttered a curse and left the bed. Sarah hadn't replied to his request, and she'd put him in the awkward situation of having to make himself decent in a scant amount of time. "You might've waited until I'd shaved and gotten on my pants."

A slight smile touched her lips. "Have you suddenly grown modest, your Lordship?"

Dragging on his trousers, Brendan aimed her a sardonic grin. "Don't count yourself protected. Should I decide to discipline you, Sarah, all I need do is dismiss Mathilda upon her arrival."

Her smile intact, Sarah collected her petticoats and gown from the floor. She shook out the gown before she gently draped it over the end of the bed. "I declare, I'm simply quakin' with fright."

About to fasten his trousers, Brendan hesitated at her insolent taunt. A retiring wife was said to be a man's solace, but he was finding a feisty woman infinitely more exciting. His recently cooled ardor flickered to life. "I prefer you quaking with desire."

Sarah tossed her hair over her shoulder as she turned away from him. Brendan hastened to fasten the waist of his trousers. She looked enticing in her frilly drawers, her perfectly rounded backside luring his gaze. When she bent over to pick up her corset, he cursed and tore his vision from her.

"You were quakin' also, your Lordship," she casually remarked. "And groanin', and—"

"Sarah! You are to use my name when you address me."

"Yes, Brendan," she said with appropriate meekness.

With purpose in his step, Brendan strode around the bed, seized Sarah's arm, and pulled her against him. Finding a wide grin on her face, he released a frustrated sigh. "Do you prefer that I personally silence you with a kiss?"

She visibly melted, leaning into him, her arms curling over his shoulders. "If that's your wish."

Brendan stiffened in response, desperately attempting to master the desire still simmering in his blood. "Bloody hell, Sarah, we spent most of the past night making love and still you make me hunger for more."

"You're a lusty devil, your Lordship."

He had just angled his head to ravish her with a kiss when a distinctly masculine knock jarred him to his senses. Stratford had the worst timing.

Sarah shoved herself away from him, her eyes wide with indignation. "Oh, it isn't Mathilda at all!" She began a frantic search for her robe, and managed to tie the sash before Brendan reached the door. Heaving a breath, she frowned when she noticed his bemused expression. "You could've warned me that Stratford would probably come first."

Brendan lifted a brow as he admitted the older man. "I had no way of knowing."

She gave him a skeptical look then, and squaring her shoulders, nodded a greeting to Stratford before she exited the room.

"I beg your pardon, sir," Stratford said. "I expected you to be alone."

"Sarah will want to spend a while with Rebecca."

"Very good, sir."

He watched the servant cross to the large armoire.

"What will you be wearing today, sir?"

"Anything. I believe I'll remain at home."

His head turned slightly, Stratford regarded him askance.

Brendan went to his shaving stand. "Is it not normal for a newly wedded man to want to keep his wife company?"

"Indubitably."

Brendan cast him a glance and noticed Stratford had moved closer. In his upturned palm rested several hairpins. To Brendan's consternation, heat crawled up his neck. "Sarah must have dropped them in my study."

"My opinion precisely, sir. I concluded that she would not like to misplace them."

"No, she wouldn't," Brendan agreed as he deposited the items on the bureau.

Inclining his head, Stratford cleared his throat. "Sir, would you care for an ointment?"

"An ointment?" Brendan repeated, dumbfounded. "What the devil for?"

Stratford looked uncomfortable as he withdrew clean linen from the bureau. "For your back, sir."

Brendan froze, closing his eyes. Memory of lovemaking with Sarah swept across his mind; her nails had raked his skin as she cried out in ecstasy. The heat staining his neck now flooded his cheeks.

Brendan began to soap his face, hoping it covered his uncommon embarrassment. He was a man of notorious fame, yet a single night in Sarah's arms had left him acutely flustered. He'd never before experienced such profound feelings for and physical fulfillment with a woman.

Good God, he had actually made love, not just gratified his lust.

The realization left him confused. "Kindly do not pursue the matter!"

"As you wish, Your Grace."

Brendan slammed a fist on the stand, sending several articles to the floor. "Can no one address me in the manner I request?"

"Sir?"

"Never mind." Brendan lathered his face, ignoring Stratford as he replaced the fallen articles on the stand. "You will, of course, forget having found Sarah's pins in the study, and won't mention—"

"Sir! My lips are sealed, as always." Stratford

laid out attire, then produced a wet towel so that Brendan could wipe his face. "Might I be so bold as to say I am pleased to see that your marriage is obviously a triumph?"

Brendan snatched the towel. "You *bloody well* may not!"

"Very good, sir."

"You may take your leave—before I'm tempted to choke you. I'll dress myself."

"As you wish," the older man replied, looking pale. Reaching the door, he hesitated.

"What is it now, Stratford?" Brendan asked in a softer tone, regretting his fit of temper.

"Will you be wanting something to eat?"

"A capital idea. I'm hungry enough to eat a cow."

Stratford blinked. Then, shaking his head, he tugged on his waistcoat and left.

Worry over the approaching ball stretched Sarah's nerves taut. She hadn't fared any better during her dancing lessons, which convinced her she had the grace of a yard animal. She felt positive that learning to dance was a lost cause and that she would surely disgrace Brendan.

When she managed to push that worry from her mind, other concerns arose. She had persuaded Brendan to purchase the shimmering dress and now regretted that he'd given in. The idea of any man but him ogling her bosom made her stomach churn, leaving her with a nauseous feeling. And she knew she'd be entirely too noticeable if she tripped her dance partner and caused him to lose his footing.

Everyone would jeer, and she'd want to die.

Seated at the dining room table, Sarah raised the dainty china cup in front of her and sipped her hot tea. She must control her raging emotions, she thought. Only one day remained until the ball. Somehow she must gain more confidence.

At that moment her most pressing problem surfaced in her mind. Brendan himself. Making love with him was wonderful. He'd fulfilled her expectations and more. She'd fallen in love with him. Although he'd said and done all the right things, he hadn't yet said he loved her.

Sarah glanced up and smiled. Brendan stood in the doorway.

"Good morning, Sarah." As he crossed the room, gold lights sparked in his hazel eyes. Stopping by her chair, he leaned down and gave her a leisurely kiss. "You look radiant. Dare I hope I'm the cause?"

"You know you are."

He seated himself. "Have you mastered your dancing? The ball's tomorrow, you know."

He *would* inquire about that particular worry, she thought. "My fears were unwarranted, after all. I'm doin' quite well," she fibbed.

Stratford entered and refilled Sarah's cup, then poured a cup for Brendan. "Do you wish your breakfast now, sir?"

Glancing at her, Brendan declined.

Sarah bit her lip. Her husband was so observant, he must have guessed how her worries plagued her.

Despite her apprehension about attending

the ball, she'd always dreamed of such a glorious occasion. The thought of arriving with a handsome, enviable escort sent a thrill coursing through her. Every woman was sure to envy her and pine because no man present could compare with Brendan.

"Brendan . . . if you prefer, go to the ball without me. I'm sure no one will care, and, frankly, I'll be happy to stay home."

"Absurd. I daresay that would set tongues wagging."

"But, Brendan, I—"

"I understand your misgivings, Sarah." He gave her an encouraging smile, one that reached his eyes, causing crinkles to fan out from the corners. "I look forward to the ball, myself."

"You do?"

"I want to see your eyes sparkle. You'll be the most beautiful woman there, and I'll have the honor of claiming you as mine."

He had shocked her. Brendan watched Sarah closely, spotting the conflicting emotions that showed on her expressive face. At least he could relieve some of Sarah's anxiety over Mrs. Fromond's ball, he figured.

"Sarah, I want you to enjoy your first ball. Will you save all of your dances for me?"

Her response was easy to read. Pleasure and panic. Her lashes brushing her cheeks, she said softly, "Of course."

"Sarah, are you positive you've mastered your dancing?"

Her eyes flashed to his. "I might've exaggerated just a bit."

Brendan rose and came around the table, extending a hand. "Come with me."

Allowing him to steer her into the hall, she asked, "Where are you takin' me?"

"To the billiard room. It has sufficient space." When they met Mathilda in the hall, Brendan instructed her to send Stratford to him. Once inside the room, he ushered Sarah to a chair. "I should've thought of this before."

Stratford appeared, and Brendan bade him take a position at one end of the billiard table.

"Sir, might I inquire as to your intentions?"

"Lift your end and help me move the blasted thing out of the way."

His tongue ticking against the roof of his mouth, the servant gripped the edge of the table. At Brendan's signal, he attempted to hoist the massive piece of furniture. Brendan moved his end two feet, but Stratford grunted from the exertion. Guessing the older man wouldn't be of any help, Brendan shooed him away.

"Thank you, sir. It *is* much heavier than I expected. Do you not think you should hire men to—"

Lifting Stratford's end, Brendan silenced him with a look.

"Begging your pardon, sir, but is there a reason you are straining yourself?"

Brendan heaved a breath, then skidded the table two more feet. "Yes . . . I want to assist Sarah with her dance lessons. Have you an objection?"

"Certainly not, sir."

"Good," Brendan said as he dusted off his hands, "because it'll be your job to supply us with music."

Stratford's eyes bulged as he stiffened. "Music? Sir, might I remind you that there are no musicians available?"

Crossing the room, Brendan held out a hand to Sarah. "Improvise, Stratford."

Sarah came to her feet. Brendan led her into the middle of the open space he'd provided. Standing opposite her, he took her hand, noticing that her dove gray dress brought out the gray in her eyes. A white, delicately pleated yoke emphasized her fair skin, and the exquisite cameo pinned at her neck added just the right touch. He recognized the pin as his mother's, and made a mental note to thank his aunt for having had the foresight to present it to Sarah. He should have thought of it himself.

He smiled at her. A faint flush colored her cheeks, pleasing him. She was easily moved, and reacted to him with the slightest provocation. They had been made for each other, he thought. Whenever they came close, sparks flew. He felt like a schoolboy about to take a girl in his arms for the first time.

"Brendan, I did lie to you before." She glanced at his feet. "I hope your boots are constructed well, for your toes are sure to suffer."

"We'll see." He tugged on her hand, drawing her nearer. "I think you might be surprised at the difference a new partner makes."

She laughed softly. "I hope you're right."

Wrapping his arm around her waist, he felt her tremble. "Are you as jittery when Mr. Montand gives you lessons?"

She shook her head; then, gazing past his arm, she whispered, "Stratford looks like he has swallowed a mouse."

Brendan bit back a grin. "Stratford, you may begin."

"Sir?"

"Sing, or hum, if you prefer. Make it a waltz. Chopin, if you please."

Silence reigned, during which time Sarah giggled. When Stratford had cleared his throat four times, she pulled her hand from Brendan's and clamped it over her mouth. The older man began to hum a distinctly sour tune that Brendan could not in good conscience have credited to the distinguished composer.

Brendan looked over his shoulder, narrowing his eyes on the ashen-faced servant. "My good man, you have all the musical expertise of a screech owl."

"Yes, sir," Stratford agreed, hanging his head low.

"Leave at once."

"Very good, sir."

Brendan waited until Sarah and he were alone before he surrendered to laughter. Several minutes passed before either regained control. Brendan acknowledged a difference in himself. He tried to recall the last time he'd allowed himself to find amusement in anything. More important, he'd never before laughed with a woman, only with his men friends.

With a finger under Sarah's chin, he raised her face to caress it with his gaze. She was sweet and soft. He wanted her love. He read invitation and reservation in her eyes. Her eyes. They mesmerized him, lured him into forest-green depths where a gray haze beckoned, an enchanting haven where, he thought, a man could lose his sanity. And his soul.

He kissed her forehead, fighting the desire to send her pins flying and tangle his fingers in her hair. Did Sarah love him? But how could she? He wasn't a lovable man, at least in his opinion.

"Brendan . . ."

"Hush, Sarah."

He'd become inflexible, overbearing, and, though he found the word intolerable, stuffy. He didn't mind being overbearing. Hell, most men were. They were born to lead, to protect, and to provide. In England, as Wicked War-wick, he had led a scandalous life, though he'd never really enjoyed himself, except for physi-cal pleasure. Bedding a woman for her beauty, breeding, and hot-blooded nature had come naturally to him.

Pulling his thoughts back to the present, he laid his hand under Sarah's and held her in the position for dancing. There had to be more than what he'd known in the past. God help him, deep down he realized he wanted more.

Gaining control of his meandering thoughts, he asked, "Can you close your eyes and imag-ine we're in a grand ballroom and there's an orchestra playing music?"

"I doubt it. More than likely I'll hear Wallace snortin' in his pen."

Brendan smiled and held her closer, inhaling her fresh scent. He found it more provocative than the liberal dousing of costly perfume used by his past lovers.

"Mr. Montand doesn't hold me this close."

"I should hope not. I'll hum a little of my favorite waltz, just to give you the idea of the melody. All you need do is follow my lead."

Brendan hummed as he began to move, but halted when his partner stumbled over his foot. Noticing that her fingers gripped his and that she held herself rigid against him, he allowed several inches of space between them.

"Are you as stiff with Mr. Montand, Sarah?"

"Not quite. Oh, it's impossible. Even with Mr. Montand I'm fumble-footed. Brendan, I'll never learn."

"Look into my eyes, Sarah, and forget everything else. Pretend your feet are wings. Lean against me and allow me to guide you. Once you feel the movements, you'll see what I mean."

He pulled her close again. "Put your hand higher on my arm."

"Like this?" she asked as she draped her arm over his, her hand resting on his shoulder. "It seems impossible. How is either of us to move?"

Having Sarah in his arms sapped his strength and sent fire racing to his loins. "The idea is to become one, and dance as such." He began to hum again. Slowly, he swept her forward, keeping his steps simple. "There. You're following without tripping."

"Yes," she said breathlessly. "But it's unsettling, bein' so close. You have a magnificent voice. Can you sing as well as you hum?"

"I do everything well, my dear." He held her even closer. "Is it my voice that unsettles you? Or perhaps you know of my desire to take you here and now."

She stomped on his foot and clung to his shoulder. "Oh, you made me lose my concentration."

Brendan chuckled. "Perhaps it would be best if we forgo conversation," he suggested. Lord, he wanted to kiss her. The warmth of her skin penetrated layers of clothing, searing his hand. He imagined pressing her this close, having her bare flesh against his. "Sarah, I must insist that you wear your corset when you attend the ball."

"Oh, I will," she said hurriedly, "else my bosom—"

"Yes?"

"I think you know what I mean."

"Indeed, I do." He sucked in a much needed breath. "Shall we try it again? Concentrate and cease talking."

"As you wish, your Lordship."

"Sarah."

As he began to move, he heard a faint giggle.

"Sarah! You're trying my patience."

"I'm sorry. I remembered Stratford's pitiful attempts at humming, then his sour expression. It reminded me of the way he looked at me the first day when he opened the door."

An image of the servant's red nose popped into Brendan's mind. "What, precisely, did you do to the unfortunate fellow? His nose resembled a cherry."

"He was bein' so rude, I pinched it."

Wearing a wide grin, Brendan swept Sarah into a circle, advancing the length of the floor and back. "We've managed the room."

Sarah's eyes sparkled. "Let's do it again. Oh, you *are* the devil. You made me forget what I was doin'."

"At your service, madam."

Brendan spun Sarah around and around, stopping when she squealed with happiness. It took little to please her, he mused. And, apparently, himself as well. He felt lighthearted.

The tantalizing feel of her pressing closer against him, scorching the length of him, taunted him to make good on his threat. But he'd already been too greedy. Releasing her, he bent into a perfect bow.

"You should have no reservations about the ball, Sarah." He straightened, smiling down at her. "You've been taught by a master, if I do say so myself."

She returned his smile. "Your lack of confidence is endearing, sir."

To his amazement, he was becoming used to Sarah's wont to mock him. Bringing her hand to his mouth, he gallantly placed a kiss above her knuckles. "Until later, madam. I eagerly await holding you in my arms again."

"You're incorrigible, sir," she said with a provocative grin.

Brushing his lips over hers, he whispered, "You're right, Sarah. I daresay parts of me are extremely uncontrollable and ponderous at the moment."

"Brendan Hammond! You have a wicked mind."

Sarah's innocent remark came so close to the truth, he flinched. He was wicked to his core. God help him when she discovered the truth.

Chapter 13

Wearing her robe over a luscious new chemise, Sarah impatiently sat still while Mathilda arranged her hair. The silk chemise felt sinfully sensuous against her skin—almost as sinful as Brendan's touch.

Her stomach lurched again, as it did every time her thoughts drifted to her husband. Her mind returned to him too often, especially since she'd begun to dress for the ball. Because he required less time to prepare himself, or so he'd stated, he'd dressed first. The glimpse she'd stolen of him when he'd gone downstairs had robbed her of her breath. His intoxicating scent lingered in the room still. When she closed her eyes and inhaled deeply, she felt dizzy.

It had to be a dream, one that her cousin Lizzie would have envied to her dying day. If only Lizzie were there, she thought longingly. They'd laugh and chatter, and Lizzie would express wonder over Sarah's good fortune. Later, Lizzie would want to know every detail of the night's happenings.

Mathilda finished. Holding a mirror before

Sarah, she said, "Have a look, ma'am, and see what you think."

"Goodness," Sarah exclaimed as she examined the lush, artfully arranged rolls, interwoven with delicate pearls. On each side of her face, tendrils of hair brushed her cheeks, ending just below her ears. "You've outdone yourself."

"His Lordship will think you're a goddess."

Sarah smiled as she patted the woman's hand.

Mathilda bustled about, collecting the rest of Sarah's apparel. Handing over a pair of delectably soft stockings, her plump cheeks dimpled. "When he gets a look at these, his collar's sure to wilt."

A furious blush covered Sarah's cheeks. She remembered how he'd removed her stockings before they'd first made love. Would he do the same thing that night?

Mathilda pushed two strands of gray hair back into the bun at her nape. Her blue eyes twinkling with merriment, she knelt before Sarah to help her don the stockings. She adjusted one lace-trimmed white silk garter midway up Sarah's leg and was reaching for the other garter when they heard someone clear his throat. Both women glanced up.

Mathilda immediately rose, bobbing her head. "We aren't done yet, sir."

"My aunt's in need of your assistance. Kindly spare her a few minutes. I want a word with my wife. You may return in, say, ten minutes."

"Yes, sir."

Brendan asked, "Are you excited, Sarah?"

She eyed him suspiciously. "I feel like a moth flutterin' around a lit lamp." His laugh was low and seductive, fueling Sarah's unease. "Did you forget somethin'?"

She raked her gaze over him, seeking his reason for returning before she'd sent word that she was presentable. No, she thought, she saw nothing missing from his person, not so much as a hair out of place. Formal evening attire lent him a dashing, sophisticated air. His immaculate white shirt and collar, which stuck up in points, boasted an extra allotment of starch. He was the most imposing man she'd ever seen.

"I declare, you look magnificent," she muttered. "Will all the men there be this handsome?"

"I should hope not."

Sarah lowered her head and grinned.

"I thought you would be ... well ... further advanced in your—" He came closer and stopped in front of her. "I hope I didn't embarrass you."

Staring at the high sheen on his shoes, she grinned again. "It seems it's you who are the most embarrassed."

Brendan dropped to one knee, the second garter dangling from his finger. "Not only have I no modesty; I'm never embarrassed."

He eased the garter over her ankle, then slowly, provocatively slid it over her calf.

Sarah sucked in a harsh breath but released it just as quickly. "You're even more wicked than I thought."

Her mind mushy from the feel of his fingers

brushing her leg, she wiggled in an attempt to dispel the wretchedly impious uproar his touch had inspired in an unmentionable spot.

"Bren-dan. Please, I'm nervous enough."

His fingers inched higher, tantalizing her; then all of a sudden they seductively gripped her leg.

"Your thigh feels like hot silk, Sarah."

Sarah trembled. Brendan's bold remark made tempestuous images flash across her mind—his hands exploring her entire body, setting her aflame, his lips following in their wake. "What are your motives, your Lordship?"

He stood abruptly, his hands on her arms lifting her with him. He dragged her smack against him. "Sarah, tonight will be hell. Hours of torture until I have you all to myself again. You've bedeviled me."

His hot breath warmed her face. "I . . ." Good Lord, she'd almost said that she loved him. "You've bedeviled me too. I don't deserve your kindnesses." She caressed his cheeks. "You're too nice to me."

"Dammit, Sarah, I don't want gratitude or your thinking I'm *nice*. I've never been regarded as nice."

He had spat out the words. Desire glimmered in his hazel eyes as they devoured her, confusing her. "What do you want, then? Tell me."

He released her. The muscle ticking in his jaw told her he couldn't or wouldn't answer.

He took a small, ornate gold box from inside of his elegant black long-tailed coat. After he flicked open the lid, he held the box out to

Sarah. "They were my mother's. There are many more, but I hesitate to overwhelm you."

"It's too late for that," Sarah said in disbelief. "My own mother once owned several pearl necklaces, but she donated them to the Southern cause." A smile of pure pleasure graced her face. "I'll be honored to wear them."

"The jewels are yours by right, Sarah. You needn't return them."

She turned around and held the ends of the necklace out to him. When his fingers grazed her neck, she felt warm inside. She tilted her head to gaze at him over her shoulder and found his expression strained.

"Sir, your aunt's ready."

"Thank you, Mathilda," Brendan responded. "You may resume helping my wife."

He exited swiftly, without another word, leaving Sarah to stare after him in wonder. She heard voices in the hall, and wasn't surprised when Gertrude swept into the room.

"You aren't ready yet. And here I thought I was taking unduly long. I see Brendan has given you his mother's pearls. That was remarkably brilliant of him."

Sarah fingered the necklace, praying the tumult roiling through her veins was going unnoticed. "Yes, he surprised me. Sometimes I don't understand him."

"Only sometimes?" Gertrude asked, rolling her eyes. Gertrude's simple green silk gown made her hazel eyes pick up green lights.

Sarah unbuttoned her robe and handed it to

Mathilda. She admitted, "I don't know what he wants of me sometimes."

"I presume you're asking me for advice?"

Sarah nodded.

"Let me consider for a moment."

Realizing that Gertrude wanted to wait until the servant was out of earshot, Sarah didn't pursue the matter until Mathilda had pronounced her ready.

"Isn't she gorgeous?" the woman asked Gertrude, who wore a sly smile as she considered Sarah's gown.

"Positively ravishing. Tonight should prove *very* interesting. You may tell my nephew that we'll be down shortly." When Sarah and she were alone, Gertrude continued. "My advice to you, dear, is to follow your heart."

"My heart hasn't been a reliable organ in the past."

"Your heart wasn't involved in your affair with Derek. He used his charm to seduce an innocent, which in my estimation, relieves you of blame. You merely *thought* you loved him." She fell silent, withdrawing a small vial from her reticule. "I suspect you've recently learned the difference between love and lust."

A secret smile played over Sarah's mouth.

"Really, dear, you must learn to control your expressions. You give entirely too much away."

Aghast that Gertrude had apparently read her mind, Sarah frowned.

"So you've fallen in love with Brendan. Or is it lust that has brought color to your cheeks?"

"He most certainly knows how to . . . excite a

woman," Sarah admitted with a bitter laugh. "I fear I've fallen in love with him. If only . . ."

"He's besotted with you," Gertrude confided, handing Sarah the small vial.

Sarah stared in bewilderment at Gertrude. Then, accepting the offering, she shook her head.

"You doubt me?"

"Brendan might be attracted to me, but it's probably because I'm the only female available. He's too honorable to seek a mistress."

"Rubbish!"

Sarah gaped at Brendan's aunt.

"Mark my words, he's in love with you. His damn masculine pride has him acting the fool."

Averting her gaze, Sarah said, "You probably know Brendan better than anyone, but in this case you're wrong. He can never let himself love me. His pride won't let him."

"You know?"

"Of course. I'd have to be utterly stupid *not* to know. He's an earl, and I'm—well, not his social equal."

"A minor inconvenience, I assure you. Time's on your side. Time and my wealth of experience in dealing with men. Now you have in your hand my most powerful weapon."

Confused, Sarah fell silent.

"French perfume. Very expensive, and certain to bring a man to his swift and irrevocable downfall."

"I've never used perfume before."

"I've been considering moving back to my own home, but I haven't wanted to leave you

completely at the mercy of my nephew. Listen
well, Sarah. If you want to make him admit his
feelings, you must see to it that he falls so under your spell that he can think of nothing
else."

"You mean seduce him?"

"What else?" Gertrude took possession of the
vial, popped out the stopper, then dabbed a liberal amount under both of Sarah's ears. With
another sly grin, she also placed a dot in Sarah's cleavage. "There! That should do it. His
downfall is inevitable."

Sarah's brows furrowed together. "But we've
already—what I mean is—"

"I should've known. He's been in the best
mood of late. I fear, though, that if you want
him to admit he loves you, you must pry it out
of him. Oh, I'm so pleased. Fate threw him together with the one woman meant to tame his
wicked heart."

"Wicked?" Sarah repeated. "Oh, you're
wrong. He may be many things, but he's above
reproach."

A look of concern passed over Gertrude's features before she continued. "Trust me, unless
you want him to remain tight-lipped. Once you
have him panting for you, do not, under *any*
circumstances, relent. At least promise me
you'll give my suggestion a try."

"I have nothing to lose, do I?"

"Exactly, dear. Nothing to lose, and *everything* to gain."

*   *   *

Brendan tapped his foot, glowering at the winding staircase for the tenth time. Snatching his pocket watch, he checked the hour.

Standing beside him in the hall, Stratford also glanced upward. "Sir, Mathilda said they were both ready. Do you wish me to go up and ascertain what the delay means?"

Just as he was about to respond, Brendan heard the rustle of skirts above them. He nudged the older man, then looked up in time to see his aunt come down the stairs, followed by Sarah. He held his breath, awaiting a full view of his wife. As he had anticipated, when Sarah stepped off the bottom step and his aunt moved aside, he felt as if he'd been felled by an ax.

Bloody hell. Words couldn't describe Sarah in that spectacular gown, with his mother's pearls against her fair skin. The end of the necklace lay between her breasts, drawing his attention to the tantalizing display. He wondered if the pearls had picked up heat from her, and if they were warm to the touch.

Flustered to realize he'd allowed his vision to linger overly long on her sumptuous bosom, he cleared his throat. "Ladies. I'm in awe of your beauty."

His aunt nodded her acceptance of his compliment. Lowering her lashes, Sarah fiddled with one of her gloves.

"Both madams look divine," Stratford spouted.

"Why, thank you, Stratford," Gertrude said. Sarah aimed him a sweet smile, then smoothed a hand over her other elbow-length glove.

"The carriage is waiting," Brendan remarked. "Are you going with us, Aunt Gertrude, or have you other plans?"

A light flush stained her cheeks. "Mr. Montand has asked me to accompany him. I hope you don't mind."

"I'll miss your company." His vision veered to Sarah. "But I'm positive I'll not be lonely."

Brendan followed his wife from the house, into the carriage.

"What the devil are you wearing?" he asked after several torturous minutes.

Flouncing her skirt so it flared over his feet, Sarah's eyes flashed to his. "What do you mean?"

"I wasn't aware that you wore perfume."

"Oh," she replied, her hand going to a spot beneath her right ear. "Do you like it?"

Brendan scowled. "It's positively indecent."

"Does it disturb you?"

Her coy question deepened his scowl. "It does."

He watched her hand detour lower and press over her cleavage, and knew she'd placed the devastating scent there as well. His mouth quirked up on one side. He saw his aunt's hand in Sarah's flirtatious manner. "Did my aunt lend you the fragrance?"

"Why, yes. She's very generous."

"I daresay." Brendan threw open the window beside him. Seeing Sarah touch her hair, he reconsidered and slammed it shut.

"Are you feelin' out of sorts?" she asked.

"Why do you ask?"

"You seem perturbed, and I thought you might be sufferin' from some malady."

"Did my aunt also influence your behavior, Sarah?"

"Heavens, no." She folded her hands primly on her lap.

In the close confines of the carriage the scent of the potent perfume grew overpowering, heightening Brendan's awareness of Sarah. He jabbed a finger between his stiff collar and throat and stretched his neck. To no avail. He knew his death from suffocation or sexual frustration was imminent.

"Sarah, you needn't wear the perfume again in order to arouse me."

"Yes, your Lordship. Your aunt thought you'd like it, but apparently she was mistaken."

Brendan muttered an oath. "I prefer you the way you are, Sarah."

Tilting her head lower, she briefly considered him from beneath her lashes before she gazed out the window.

His body temperature seemed to rise several degrees. He'd been seduced by women proficient in the art, but not one had had the power to plunder his senses like Sarah.

He desired her more than he would have believed possible.

Sarah slid her tongue over her lips, still staring out at the passing scenery. The innocent gesture sent fire racing to Brendan's loins. He wondered what held her interest, or if she merely sought to give him time to regain his senses. Absurd! She seemed determined to excite him beyond endurance and purposely not grant him a reprieve.

Brendan inhaled a breath, then closed his eyes against the heady fragrance permeating the carriage. Against Sarah. How the devil was he to exit in front of the Planter's House in an obvious state of arousal?

"Oh, look," Sarah exclaimed. "There are dozens of carriages, and so many people goin' in."

Christ! They'd arrived.

"And there's Gertrude and that sweet Mr. Montand." Seconds passed. "I hadn't noticed before, but he's certainly solicitous of her. Goodness, the way he's inclinin' his head makes me think he's smitten."

Brendan smiled at Sarah's exuberance. He intended to see that she enjoyed herself that evening. Even if it meant he must claim every dance, she'd not languish on the sidelines. Three hours later, he nearly laughed at his unwarranted concern. Ironically, he found himself the one languishing at the edge of the dance floor. That it was by choice didn't improve his humor.

Sarah had been a hit from the first moment. Lilly Fromond had seen to that, introducing her to everyone, monopolizing Sarah's time, and, to his eternal annoyance, seeing that her dance card was filled. Thus far, Sarah had been squired around the floor by every man capable of breath and movement. Except *him*.

Someone touched his arm. Brendan turned

and acknowledged Caroline Belmont's presence with a nod.

"All the women are simply beside themselves over your wife," she said as she followed his gaze to the couple waltzing past them. "Everyone is speculating on why you haven't danced with her even once."

When the pressure of her fingers increased, he glanced down at his arm, then at her, reprimanding her daring act. "Where's your husband?" he asked coolly.

Caroline snapped open a frilly fan and set it moving in front of her face. "Mr. Belmont has availed himself of your wife's charming company three times, but at the moment I haven't the faintest notion of where he could be. Were you a gentleman, you'd ask me to dance."

Brendan arched a brow at her forwardness, then dismissed his irritation. Caroline was exactly the type of woman he'd always found exciting—obtrusively voluptuous, overtly passionate, and his for the asking. She'd made that clear enough from the start. It had taken some months to convince himself he could actually live a chaste life with so great a temptation close at hand. Now he felt confident that he'd made the right choice.

Seeing Caroline's eyes settle on a particular couple, he glanced at the dance floor and discovered the source of her interest. Charles Beauclaire swept past with the most beautiful woman present securely in his arms. Sarah. A grimace pulled Brendan's mouth into an unfriendly line. Charles, while his friend, was a confirmed womanizer, not a man Brendan would have liked his wife to spend any time with.

Sarah's cheeks were pink from exertion, her eyes glowing as they darted from couple to couple. Was she searching for *him?* Perhaps he'd chosen the wrong course. Should he have asked other women to waltz?

To his consternation, he felt no compunction to share his favors with anyone else. He was jealous, he admitted, though no lecture he gave himself could alter his disposition. He'd never suffered jealousy before, and reviled himself for succumbing to the detestable emotion.

"Brendan Hammond," Caroline said peevishly, tapping his arm with her fan. "Are you going to ask me to dance or not? Your own wife has abandoned you and amused herself the entire evening."

His jaw taut, Brendan executed an elegant bow. "Let it not be said that I neglected to behave with gentlemanly aplomb."

The moment he took Caroline into his arms, he knew he'd made a mistake. Although he intentionally held her as far away as possible, she adeptly wiggled closer, brushing against him. Concerned with the whereabouts of his wife, he swept his gaze over the couples crowding the floor. The waltz had nearly ended when, finally, he spotted Charles's blond head.

He spun Caroline around and propelled her in the direction he wanted to go. What the devil had Charles just said to Sarah to make her laugh? Remembering his friend's predilection to frequent the Temple of Virtue on Green Street, Brendan sent Charles a withering glare.

As if he sensed Brendan's animosity, Beauclaire sharply met Brendan's gaze, brandishing a satisfied grin while he held Sarah closer. Brendan's glare became more hostile.

Looking from one to the other, Sarah hastily attempted to move away from her partner but accomplished the opposite. She must have gotten her feet tangled with those of her partner, Brendan mused, because Charles performed a series of undignified hops before he managed to regain his rhythm.

Mr. Montand, with Gertrude as his partner, passed between Brendan and Charles. Brendan noted that his aunt seemed oblivious to the tension in the air. Several acquaintances took the opportunity to taunt Charles about his failed grace on the dance floor.

Brendan slowed his pace and remained a distance away, following Sarah's movements. Had she trod on the feet of every other man she'd danced with? Or had only Charles commanded that distinction? Somehow he knew the truth. Each of her partners had suffered equally. But due to the tremendous turnout, her lack of expertise wouldn't have been obvious to anyone else.

When the waltz finally ended he felt a bump against his knee and realized his own partner had deliberately knocked against him. "Forgive my inattentiveness," he said with mock sincerity. He quickly scanned the room and found a means of escape. "I see your daughter over

there. She looks decidedly down in the mouth.
I feel obligated to rescue her."

Brendan congratulated himself. The exchange
of partners worked smoothly; Caroline did not
dare protest.

Several minutes later, he was glad that he'd
invited Florence to dance. Though he hadn't let
his intentions be known to her, he *had* considered offering for her. Caroline's mention in the
dining room of her daughter's disappointment
over his marriage caused him a moment's regret. He hadn't intended to wound Florence.

Light as a butterfly in his arms, Miss Belmont
was an exquisite dancer. Her head lowered, she
had yet to meet his eyes or speak a word.

"Have you been well, Miss Belmont?" he
asked in an attempt at conversation.

"Yes," she timidly said.

"Did you enjoy the swan boats?"

She gave him a curt nod.

Casting about for another question, he realized he had no idea what interested her. "With
what do you amuse yourself?"

She blinked, her pale blue eyes finally lifting
to his. Just as quickly, she stared at his coat
lapel. "I do not take your meaning."

"What do you do all day?" he asked to clar-
ify the question.

"I like my needlework."

A thrilling pastime, he mused. He conjured
an image of Sarah sedately sitting, satisfied to
repeatedly jab a needle in and out of fabric.
Brendan smiled, knowing full well that his wife
would never be content with such a tedious

pastime. "I imagine you're quite proficient at your needlework."

He received another curt nod.

Not a single spark passed between him and Florence. Brendan knew a moment of disgust with himself. He performed a series of difficult turns, admiring her tremendously when she anticipated his every move. Stealing a closer glimpse of her, he observed the many ruffles and bows on her pristine white dress. Good God, she looked young; a veritable infant, compared with Sarah.

How could he have imagined sharing his life with a virginal, lifeless child who left him cold? She was sweet-natured, and a perfect choice for some *other* man. He tried to envision making love with her. She would never have thought to deny him his conjugal rights. She would have obeyed him in all things, behaving with proper deference to his authority. The image took root in his mind of her chaste white body under his, her expression frightened as she perfunctorily accepted his invasion.

No passion.

No emotion.

A loveless union he would have come to abhor.

He should have kissed her at least once to be sure. But he knew that, were he to have embraced Florence, he would have remained detached. Hell. Once again, his aunt had been right. Marriage to Miss Belmont would have left him miserable, unfulfilled, and unsatisfied. Before long he would have found himself fre-

quenting dens of iniquity with Charles Beauclaire.

The dance ended. Bringing Florence's hand
to his mouth, he nonchalantly placed a light
kiss on her glove. "It's been a pleasure, my
dear."

Determination coursed through him. He intended to find his elusive wife and claim at
least one dance before the night was through.
He turned and nearly knocked over his aunt,
who laid a hand over her heart at his sudden
move.

"Madam," he said solemnly, "I request the
honor of this waltz. You have avoided me the
entire evening. I hope you haven't sat out many
dances."

"Rogue," she replied as she allowed him to
lead her onto the floor. "You know perfectly
well that I've not missed a waltz."

"Yes, I know. It warms my heart to see you
enjoying yourself at long last. Where's your
earnest admirer? Have you tired him out?"

"Henri has gone to fetch me a glass of punch.
In case you hadn't noticed, your wife looked
thirsty a few minutes ago. Though you needn't
worry that she's suffered for lack of your company. That handsome, debonair Mr. Beauclaire
has already seen to Sarah's needs."

"What?" Brendan abruptly asked.

"You heard me. Sarah's danced more than
once with him. If you don't soon come to your
senses and dance with her yourself, I believe
I'll cut you from my will."

"I have every such intention," he countered.

"As for your will, be assured that I care naught. Derek, however, might become your puppet for considerably less."

She aimed him a smug smile. "No doubt you're right. However, it wouldn't give me the same pleasure as having you beg my favor."

Brendan chuckled. "You wish for the impossible." A moment passed, during which he registered an amusing fact. "The fragrance you're wearing is very seductive, don't you think? And remotely familiar. Has your Mr. Montand responded as you intended?"

"He has, indeed. But what of you, Brendan? Does it affect a man of your tastes?"

As he glanced over her head, his eyes happened to light on Sarah. "I find it quite captivating, damn you."

Gertrude's laughter brought his attention back to her. "You've spotted Sarah. I suggest you leave me for her, but before you do, it would better serve your interests if you removed that furious scowl from your face."

Coming to a halt at the edge of the crowd, Brendan handed his aunt over to her eager escort. "Drink your punch, madam." In a lower voice, he added, "And mind your own business. I'm off to acquaint Sarah with the proper manner in which to discharge her wifely duty."

Brendan left his aunt with a startled expression on her face. Resolution in his stride, he cut a swath through the center of the room.

Chapter 14

"**H**e looks as if he wants to hang me."
Sarah handed her empty glass to her most recent dance partner. "Really, Mr. Beauclaire, I doubt my husband has any such intention."

He threw a worried glance over his shoulder, his attractive, sandy-colored handlebar mustache dipping over his frown. "Good God, I don't see him now."

Sarah refused to look for herself. The last time she'd searched the room for Brendan, she'd found him in the arms of Caroline Belmont. Then he'd gone on to the woman's daughter. Sarah hadn't been able to help herself. She'd stared long and hard at the woman Brendan might have chosen to wed, and found her mood deteriorating.

The girl was tall, slim, blond, and delicately pretty, nothing at all like herself. She took note of the qualities Brendan admired in the young woman. Miss Belmont oozed refinement and breeding. More important, Sarah suspected the girl could be easily manipulated. Remembering the conversation she'd overheard between Brendan and his aunt, she decided that particular quality would most appeal to her husband.

"Do you see him?" Beauclaire asked, drawing Sarah from her troubled contemplations.

Her gaze froze on the tall, distinctive man cutting through the crowd, headed straight for her. "Actually, I do. He's comin' up behind you."

Beauclaire jerked in response and nearly dropped one glass. "Thank you for the pleasure of your company," he said in a rush. "Please excuse me, but I've no wish to part with my head."

"But you said you and Brendan were friends. He'll want to greet you."

"My dear lady, I doubt—"

"Beauclaire!"

Charles lurched away from Sarah. Holding both glasses in one hand, he offered the other in friendship to Brendan.

Brendan clasped the man's fingers in a vise. "Leaving so soon? You must allow me to thank you for amusing my wife."

Although Brendan's words came out sounding cordial, Sarah noticed the barely perceptible edge of sarcasm in his tone. Gertrude had been shrewd to encourage her to honor all the requests on her dance card in order to irritate Brendan. Just as Gertrude had predicted, Brendan seemed provoked enough to behave in a possessive manner.

"I'm late for another engagement," Beauclaire muttered.

"You don't say," Brendan crooned, raising a brow. "I'm surprised that you've not seen to it already." Releasing the man's hand, he gave him a mirthless smile. "Give my regards to your wife."

Charles Beauclaire's face went white.

Brendan turned to Sarah. "Have you a space on your card for your husband, or must I await the decline from one of your endless sea of admirers?"

Sarah swallowed her amusement. Checking her card, she forced her voice to sound solemn. "Your name isn't here, save for the last."

His mouth twitched on one side as he narrowed his eyes on her. "That's too damn bad." Snatching her card, he tossed it over his shoulder. "Now you have no choice but to spend the remainder of the evening with me."

Sarah leaned forward, urgently whispering, "Can you do that? Isn't it a violation of some rule?"

Wrapping his arm around her waist, he eased her into his arms. "I make my own rules when it suits me."

"Obviously." A fresh-faced young man approached, and stopped when he found Sarah otherwise engaged. "I believe this must be *his* dance."

"Sorry, chap," Brendan told the young man, "my wife has lost her card. Hence, I've laid my claim to her."

Deferring to the commanding tone of Brendan's voice, the man retreated. The orchestra began a romantic waltz. Seeing Brendan's sat-

isfied nod, she knew he'd had a hand in its selection.

Sarah concentrated on following Brendan's
lead and congratulated herself when she managed to avoid treading on his shoes. He appeared content not to engage her in
conversation. Halfway through the next arrangement, Sarah applauded Brendan's adeptness on the dance floor. She no longer needed
to mind the direction of her feet, for movement
came instinctively. She released a small sigh
and inched a bit closer, her arm stretching over
his shoulder. She could have remained in his
arms forever.

He leaned away briefly, locking his gaze with
hers. Amusement twinkled in his eyes, now
glinting gold lights. She anticipated a remark,
but without warning, he swept her into a complicated series of steps that brought them to the
center of the floor.

His vision never left hers. He held her entranced, even when he lowered her into a reckless dip, bending her low over his arm. The
slight curve of his mouth gave her to believe
he was pleased with her newly acquired grace.
Lifting her back into his embrace, he held her
much closer than before.

This was what he'd meant by moving as
though they were one, she mused. Thought fled
from her mind as he whirled her around and
around, the magnificent train of her dress
sweeping the floor in a circle. A flashing
glimpse of the immediate area showed no other
people nearby. Sarah realized that she and

Brendan were dancing all alone, with an audience on the sidelines.

"You're the belle of the ball, Sarah," he whispered, his voice so low and sensuous, it caressed her. "And you were right to maneuver me into buying that dress. It's devilishly spectacular on you."

Sarah missed a step at his words, but Brendan merely chuckled and gently lifted her, expertly covering her fumble. She was supposed to be seducing *him*, not the other way around.

"I did *not* maneuver you, sir."

He chuckled again.

Lights from hundreds of candles perched in elaborate gold candlesticks placed about the massive ballroom gave off a romantic glow. It afforded an appropriate background that reminded Sarah of glittering stars as Brendan continued to whirl her in a giant circle across the gleaming floor.

He could have been a prince, she thought. Prince Charming of her dreams. But even her dreams hadn't done justice to this reality.

Tonight would remain in her heart forever.

Gertrude gently swayed in time to the music as she watched her nephew squire his wife around the floor. What a vision they made. Brendan looked so handsome, his polished air commanding attention, while Sarah fairly sparkled. Gertrude could remember no occasion when the St. Louis society had quit the floor in order to gape at a couple. And *gape* aptly described their profound regard. Why, Caroline

Belmont's mouth hung open so far, she might have lured a bat into its vast cavern.

"*Très magnifique.*"

Gertrude smiled at Henri Montand and caught the wink he sent her. "If you're referring to Sarah, I quite agree. I believe your instruction has paid off."

He laughed softly. "It's your nephew who is due the credit, madame."

"They *are* wonderful together, aren't they?" Gertrude said. "Everyone's enraptured."

"I beg to differ. That one," he said, indicating Caroline Belmont with his eyes, "wishes him malice."

Gertrude followed his gaze. "Dear me, but you're right. She looks positively green with envy."

"*Oui,* I see *envie,* but there is more to it. This woman is a *fille de joie,* yes?"

He'd proclaimed Caroline Belmont a harlot, and he was a superb judge of character. Glancing again at the woman, Gertrude felt her facial muscles grow taut with strain. Caroline had the look of rejection about her. Surely she'd not set her sights on enticing Brendan to her bed.

Within seconds, Caroline's expression had become triumphant.

"*Mon Dieu!*" Henri exclaimed. "She has just thought of a way to cause trouble."

Clapping her hand over her heart, Gertrude's opinion mirrored that of her perceptive escort. Caroline could not have suspected Brendan of any foul deeds. He'd lived with discretion since he had left England. An awful premonition sent a chill down Gertrude's spine.

The woman had somehow learned of Brendan's scandal and planned to use her knowledge to exact revenge for his rejection.

Sarah felt a moment of melancholy. Brendan and she were no longer alone on the dance floor. He'd slowed his pace, making her wonder if he, too, regretted the end of such a glorious night. She gazed up at him. In the dim light, he looked even more handsome.

Meeting her eyes, he smiled. "Have you enjoyed your first ball?"

"Oh, yes . . . especially the last part," she said.

"Dare I presume you refer to me?"

Her gaze dropped to his mouth. "You're a far better dancer than any of my other partners."

Catching a movement out of the corner of one eye, she noticed Gertrude waving a hand. Satisfied that she had Sarah's attention, Gertrude laid her head against Mr. Montand's chest as they danced.

"What has captured your attention, Sarah?"

She flashed her vision back to Brendan. "I just spotted your aunt." Understanding came to Sarah. Gertrude had been reminding her that she should have been attempting to seduce Brendan. "How long until we must leave?"

"This is the last dance."

The news inspired her to make good use of the remaining time. Duplicating Gertrude's move, Sarah slipped her hand from his and pressed her palm flat against his broad chest. Taking her cue, he wrapped his free arm around her as well. Warmth coursed through her. She laid her head on his shirtfront and inhaled his scent.

Brendan stiffened. "Tell me Mr. Montand hasn't taught you *this* move."

"He certainly has not. Why? Do you mind?"

"Actually, no. I'm merely curious about your motives."

Sarah grinned. Brendan was entirely too astute to be tricked by a woman. Persistence, however, was a virtue she possessed in quantity. Gathering her courage, she lowered her voice and said, "I like bein' in your arms. You make me feel warm and safe and . . . and—"

"And what, Sarah?"

"You make me tingle all the way to my toes," she admitted hesitantly. "You make me feel things I've never felt before."

Undeterred by his silence, she nestled closer. In response, he stiffened again. Dared she believe her nearness accounted for his reaction? When *he* missed a step, she decided she might have just been given her answer.

Was passion enough? she asked herself. She loved him. And he was her husband. If Gertrude was right, all she needed to do was coax him to say the words she most wanted to hear.

But if she couldn't have his love, she decided she'd take his passion and revel in it.

"Sarah."

The orchestra had stopped playing, and cou-

ples were leaving the dance floor. How could
she have not noticed?

As Brendan escorted her to the carriage, Sarah's mind worked feverishly. She knew she had
no experience in maneuvering a man, so she
would have to rely on her instincts. Brendan
was a challenge; he was well versed in the art
of seduction, and would recognize an obvious
ploy. But what other kind was there? The beginnings of a headache furrowed her brow. It
made little difference if he knew her intentions.

Inside the carriage, she waited until they
turned down the first street before she put her
plan into action. Though it was dark inside the
vehicle, slivers of moonlight played over his
face, betraying that he was scrutinizing her.
Surely he was aware that she was studying him
also. Why didn't he say something?

Acting on impulse, she suddenly rose and
squeezed onto the seat beside him, offering as
an excuse, "I should've brought my wrap. The
air's a bit chilly."

His arm immediately came around her shoulders. "Are you warmer now?" he asked, a distinct trace of amusement in his voice.

"Yes, thank you."

Stretching out one arm, she slipped free the
tiny pearl button at the top of her elbow-high
glove and leisurely peeled the soft material to
her wrist. Achingly aware of his intense scrutiny, she tugged each finger free before flinging
the glove to the opposite seat. As she duplicated the process with her other hand, she ca-

sually remarked, "I've been wantin' to do this all night."

Brendan remained silent, so she allowed her head to rest against the side of his chest. After a moment, she leaned across him, her hand lighting on his thigh, and looked out the small window. "The moon's full tonight. Have you noticed?"

He cleared his throat, twice.

She withdrew to her former position, her fingers sliding further up his leg as she did so. She glanced up at his face and saw the slight upward curve of his mouth. Heat seeped through his elegant trousers, warming her hand. For a man who apparently performed no physical labor, he possessed an extremely sound limb.

Seconds passed while she listened to the crunching sounds of the carriage wheels on the road and the squeak of the vehicle as it bounced over an occasional rut. Brendan's labored breathing also filled the interior.

Unable to think of a more audacious deed than laying her hand on his leg, she resorted to verbal suggestion. "Goodness, you *are* put together well. Why, your leg's as rigid as iron."

He groaned low in his throat before he mumbled something unintelligible.

"I'm sorry, I didn't understand you."

Lightning quick, Brendan's fingers clamped over her hand and lifted it, holding it between their bodies. Bending slightly, his eyes locked on hers. "My words weren't meant for your delicate ears."

Sarah's breath caught. A tedious moment followed, during which she attempted in vain to still her racing heart. "My ears aren't delicate."

"What game are you playing, Sarah?"

"Game? As I live and breathe."

"Since you mentioned it, your breathing is rather irregular."

She tugged on her hand, but he held it tightly. "I . . . I'm still a bit chilly, that's all."

"You feel very warm to me." He brought her hand lower, pressing her palm over the front of his trousers. "I'm willing to wager that your little pastime has you just as overheated as I."

Judging by the hot, turgid rise burning beneath the material of his trousers, her plan had worked on both of them. Breathless from the torrid thoughts welling up in her mind, she indignantly proclaimed, "I was merely attemptin' to entice you."

"And so you have." Sliding her hand back and forth along the pulsing hardness, he laughed low in his throat, but it came out a strangled sound. "I was planning to do the same, but I found it more amusing to see how far you intended to go."

"You might've said so," she squeaked out. "Heavens, you're so hot and—"

The carriage stopped abruptly. Close behind another did likewise. Sarah promptly pulled on her hand, but Brendan refused to release her. "We've arrived. And it appears your aunt and Mr. Montand are right behind us." Still he kept her trapped. "Brendan Hammond! We'll be caught in a highly unseemly—"

"Unseemly? I think not, Sarah. We're man and wife."

"Oh, you're unconscionable."

Grinning broadly, he released her hand.

"How are you goin' to leave the carriage with your pants poppin' out?" she whispered.

Brendan broke into a pained laugh. "Very carefully. You go ahead."

Not waiting for assistance, Sarah hopped to the ground. As she walked toward the front entrance, she heard the faint muttering of a foul oath from inside the carriage.

Stratford immediately admitted Sarah, then continued to stand at his station, awaiting the arrival of Brendan and his aunt.

"Good evening," Sarah greeted him.

The sleepy-eyed servant whispered, "How was your evening, madam?"

"We had a marvelous time." A glance outside showed that Brendan discreetly stood sideways, speaking with Mr. Montand. Sarah managed to control the smile hovering on her lips. "Will you inform Brendan that I've gone to check on Rebecca?"

"I will with pleasure."

Sarah lifted her skirt and skipped up the stairs. She wondered if her cheeks looked as hot as they felt. She was immensely pleased with herself, even if her plan had almost backfired. Brendan had responded to her blatant, if somewhat awkward, attempts to arouse him. Unfortunately, she'd misjudged her timing.

If she'd waited until they were home, Brendan's mood might have grown even more heated. But, knowing him, it would only take a matter of minutes to revive his passions.

A half hour later, Sarah paced the bedroom. What was keeping him?

She had been afraid that his peers would find her socially inferior, but they had greeted her warmly and even seemed to like her. She also wasn't the type of woman Brendan might have wanted, demure and innocent, like Florence Belmont. Yet she and Brendan were wed. And if he didn't regard her as proper enough to be the mother of his children, he had little choice. Unless he planned to spend the remainder of his life downstairs, the probability existed that she'd bear him an heir.

Most important, she'd fallen in love with him. The emotions she suffered were surely love, she thought. She longed to be close to him, to share his life, and to have his children. Derek's image had completely faded from her mind. The romantic interludes they'd shared also seemed a vague memory.

Mathilda came, offering her assistance. After Sarah had inquired after Gertrude, she sent the maid to bed. Thank goodness Brendan's aunt had retired, she thought. Gertrude had probably sought her own room without speaking to Sarah in order to allow her nephew and his wife time alone.

Sarah crossed the room again, stopping in front of Brendan's shaving stand. She gazed fondly at the many objects precisely placed.

Finally, with determination in her step, she left the bedroom and hurried downstairs. Her courage waned when she reached the door to his study, staying her from entering.

Brendan scowled into his snifter of fine brandy, bemoaning his still-sober state. Releasing a vile oath, he squeezed the snifter with such force, the glass shattered in his hand. That night he'd come to a shocking realization. He loved his wife.

He looked up and found Sarah standing a few feet away.

Concern showed in the gray-green depths of her eyes as she came to him. "Have you a handkerchief?" she asked so calmly that he flinched.

Fishing in his trouser pocket, he produced the linen, then patiently watched her turn over his hand and search for an injury from the broken glass.

"You've made a fine mess, your Lordship. That stain won't come out of your pants, you know. And you might've cut yourself severely and left me a grieving widow."

He glanced down at the long wet spot marking the length of one thigh, dismissing it with a shrug. "I have plenty more. Besides, you would've been a very rich widow."

Snapping the handkerchief open, she fell to her knees and dabbed at the stain. "Were you unfortunate enough to be poor, you wouldn't regard your clothes with such abandon. And I've no wish to wear black."

Her ministrations sent fire to his loins, preventing him from responding. She still wore the damnable gown that ravished his senses. Kneeling before him, she granted him a spectacular view, which, to his frustration, he enjoyed tremendously. A gentleman would have looked away. Wicked Warwick, however, would not. Her movements caused the pearls to perform a seductive dance over her voluptuous cleavage, which drove him mad.

He gripped her wrists and hauled her to her feet. "You're not my servant, Sarah."

She lowered her lashes.

He slid his hands up her arms but stopped short of encountering the bare skin of her shoulders. "Do you care for me just a little?"

She looked up at him, her eyes glittering with unshed tears. Lowering her head again, she fell silent for a second. "More than a little. I know I'm not what you want, not like Miss Belmont."

He tipped her face up. "Had I married Florence, I would've been miserable."

"And what have you gained by marryin' me?"

"How can you ask that?"

"But I'm nothing like her, not cultured and meek."

His mouth lifted at the corners as his gaze roamed over her. "You have other, more redeeming qualities."

Giving in to a temptation that had plagued him the entire evening, he slipped his fingers under the necklace and trailed them along its length. Her skin had indeed given warmth to the pearls. His knuckles brushed the tantalizing hollow between her breasts, making his breath turn shallow.

"Such . . . as?"

He grinned. "I presume you want to know every aspect of why I find you irresistible?"

"Yes!" she said with a toss of her head.

His grin deepened. "I daresay you're devilishly breathtaking, intolerably outspoken, a seductive witch who sears my soul at every given opportunity. Furthermore, you tempt my wrath repeatedly by—"

"Please, say no more. You've hit upon enough of my flaws." Her delectable mouth fell into a pout. "If you still wish to marry Miss Belmont, you can divorce me."

"Marry Florence? I think not."

"But you—"

"I want you, Sarah."

She slipped free of him and crossed to his liquor cabinet, where she withdrew a snifter and filled it with a generous amount of brandy. He raised a brow when she downed half of the liquid without batting an eye. "And where did you learn to do that?"

"My father, though financially strapped, somehow always managed to procure his spirits, though this tastes decidedly stronger than *his* brandy." She indulged in another unladylike swallow, darting her tongue over her lips afterward. With a challenge in her eyes, she added, "He enjoys tipping a glass quite often, and sometimes forgets to relock the drawer."

"Uh-huh. Another disagreeable habit you have, my dear. That brandy, by the way, was given to me by your ardent admirer, Charles Beauclaire, for Christmas. I wouldn't drink any more if I were you."

"You said that you want me," she reminded, her cheeks growing pink. "You must've been referrin' to physical wants."

Brendan cleared his throat. "You intend to speak bluntly?"

"Well, it's fairly obvious"—she swallowed the remainder of her drink before she continued—"that you're easily aroused."

Unable to hide his astonishment, Brendan's eyes widened. He considered her a moment, then sent her a reproachful glance.

"I suppose I've really spoken out of turn this time," she muttered with a hiccup. She plunked the glass on his desk. "But who's countin'?"

Brendan mastered a smile. He should have been affronted by her behavior, but he wasn't. She was beautiful and saucy—and tipsy, by the looks of it. And more woman than he deserved. He watched, amused, as she came back around the desk, tripping on her skirt. She muttered quietly and lifted her hem, alleviating the problem. Amazingly, she walked a straight line toward him.

"Madam, you're disgracefully intoxicated."

"I most certainly am not." A sly grin slid over her mouth. "But I do feel fortified enough to continue our discussion."

"I daresay you must. Shall I see you to our bed?"

She stood straighter. "There's something I want to know first."

"Ask me anything."

"I . . . I was wonderin'." She took a deep breath. "I was wonderin' if you . . ."

She wove her fingers into her hair, loosening several rolls and sending tiny pearls scattering on the floor.

"Come here." When she did as he bade, he began to pull the remaining pins from her hair. "You've ruined Mathilda's expert handiwork, and I thought it fetching."

"The pins were stickin' me." She fell silent, closing her eyes. "It feels so good when you touch me, like a feather ticklin' my skin. And then I get warm all over. No one has ever made me feel such startlin' sensations."

Dropping a handful of pins into his pocket, he considered her dreamy expression. "Not even Derek?"

"Never Derek. It was pleasant when he touched me, but nowhere near the same."

Brendan froze.

Sarah opened her eyes, gazing at him with undisguised adoration. He'd never thought to have a woman look at him as if he were a god, of sorts. "Sarah, are you trying to ask me if I love you?"

"Yes."

He threaded his fingers through her mane of silky hair, draping it over her shoulders. "I do love you." Pulling her against him, he leaned low and pressed his lips to her throat. "I love you very much. But what of you? I know you're grateful to me, but—"

"Oh, Brendan, I love you, too—something awful."

He drew her arms over his shoulders, requiring her to stand on her toes. "Show me."

His laugh was deep and husky, a true indication of his flaming desire for her. The gray in her eyes faded to a smoky green, her lips parting. She laid her palm against his cheek and stroked him, and his laugh turned into a groan. No woman had ever caressed him so gently, or with such true affection.

Then she slowly loosened his tie. Pulling it free, she dropped it on the floor. One by one, she pushed buttons through the holes, opening his shirt. Her lips met his chest, branding him. And he was lost. Cupping her chin with a hand, he forced her to meet his gaze.

"Don't kiss me yet. Wait until we're upstairs."

"I won't," he whispered.

Pulsing with a desire so fierce no power on earth could have arrested it, he swept her into his arms and strode with purpose up the winding staircase.

Chapter 15

Sarah stretched and yawned, still drowsy from sleep. She'd had the most exquisite dream, one in which she'd attended a lavish ball and danced in the arms of a prince. Brendan. Afterward, he'd loved her for most of the night, professing his devotion to her time and again.

Blinking open her eyes, her mouth slowly slid into a smile. It hadn't been a dream.

She rolled on her side. Brendan slept soundly. Her smile widened. He also snored. She wondered if Prince Charming fell prey to such a human failing. But Brendan was very human, not a fictional character.

He loved her.

Sarah's heart swelled with happiness. Using a fingernail, she traced a line down the center of his chest. Then, leaning over him, she kissed the underside of his chin. He mumbled her name in his sleep and eased an arm around her.

Using her nail again, she drew a line down his nose to his top lip. When that didn't wake him, she crawled over him and kissed his eyelids.

Mumbling an unintelligible sentence, his eyes focused on her. Before she realized his intention, he had flipped her over and covered her body with his. "I've married an insatiable siren."

"Disappointed?"

He gave her a quick kiss. "No. I adore you."

Her heart swelled once more. "Tell me you love me."

He grinned. "I love you."

She ran her hands over his jaw. "You're as prickly as a rose bush."

He groaned. "Could you compare me with a cactus next time? 'Twould seem more masculine than a rosebush."

"As you wish, your Lordship," she said with an impish grin.

He flopped over onto his side and gathered her in his arms. "You've a devilish tendency to taunt me, Sarah."

"I'm sorry, your Lordship."

Another groan filled the room. "Did you truly enjoy yourself last evening?"

"Oh, yes." She sighed with pleasure. "All my life I've dreamed of goin' to a ball. But you made it special."

"I did nothing save give you a dancing lesson." He glanced at his pocket watch on the table beside the bed. "Goodness, it's only seven. You have me up early."

"I wanted you to myself for a while. Do you mind?"

He touched her chin with a finger. "I'm glad

you thought of it. Did you rise so early back in Georgia?''

"With the sun, at least after the War. Before that, I was allowed to do as I wanted, and had servants to fulfill my every wish.''

"Slaves, you mean?''

Sarah nodded. "I was just a child then. After the War, everything changed, though several of our people chose to remain. Clara, for one. I always loved her more than the others. She was a nanny to me.''

"How did your family adjust to the change in your lives?''

Glancing at the ceiling, she spoke wistfully. "It was hard, very hard. Not for me, particularly. Children adapt more easily. But my parents suffered the most. Mama was used to grand things. Her family had always been wealthy. It made me sad to see her wearin' her once-beautiful gowns until they were faded with age. Papa took it especially hard. Our house was as fine as this one but the Yankees burned it to the ground.''

"He never rebuilt it?''

"There wasn't any money left. I know it grieved him, too, because my grandfather had built Whisperin' Oaks. Papa had promised always to guard it from harm.''

"Is your grandfather still alive?''

"Heavens, no. He succumbed shortly after the conflict began.''

Brendan tried to hold his voice even as he questioned Sarah, so as not to deepen the melancholy he sensed in her. So many people had suffered during that time. "How did your father survive?"

A faint smile flickered over her lips. "Papa never gives up. He built another house close by, though it wasn't nearly as grand or large. Just a farm, was all it turned out to be. But we were happy enough. Mama even learned to cook—with Clara's tutoring, of course."

Brendan bit back a grin. "And did you learn, also?"

"Good Lord, no. I nearly burned down the house, and Papa forbade me to go near the stove."

Thinking to save the details of what he knew he'd find amusing for another time, Brendan asked, "Was your father a good planter?"

"The best in the area. He still is, in fact. Out of necessity, his harvest is small. He hasn't enough money to pay many field hands."

Brendan filed the information away for future use. "Tell me about your grandfather. Where did the fellow find the capital to build Whispering Oaks?"

Sarah's eyes grew large, piquing Brendan's curiosity.

"I suspect a dark secret. Am I right?"

"You don't want to know," she said.

"But I do."

She hesitated, squinting at him. "All right, I'll tell you if you promise not to think too harshly of him."

"You have my word."

"Grandpa's wealth came from an unseemly

source." She released a breath before she continued. "The sea."

"He was a sea captain?"

"Not precisely. He was . . . a pirate. A long time ago Black Hawk was the scourge of the eastern shippin' lines."

Caught by surprise, Brendan fell speechless.

"You see, he fell on hard times in England and couldn't pay his debts." Her voice lowered to a whisper. "Grandpapa was an inveterate gambler, and he wagered more than he had. His property was seized, and he was forced to flee."

"And what was the name of this illustrious gentleman?"

"Montagu Kent."

"Montagu Kent! By God, Sarah, he was a bloody duke!"

"You knew him?"

"I know of him. Who hasn't heard the tales of his escapades?" Brendan stared at Sarah for a long moment. "A story circulated that five years after his disappearance, he returned to England and abducted the woman he loved, Lady Sarah Wellsborough. I don't suppose she happened to be your grandmother?"

"Why, yes. I'm named after her."

Brendan threw back his head and laughed.

"Do you find my ancestors that amusin'?" she asked indignantly.

"Forgive me," he managed to say. "Sarah . . . your lineage. By God, you've aristocratic English blood in your veins."

Sarah shrugged. "In this country such things

don't count for much. I'm just Sarah Stevens. My family keeps that part of our history a secret. Grandpapa, after all, gained a scandalous reputation, one he preferred to hide after he retired from the sea. He was always afraid someone would learn he was Black Hawk."

"Indeed, a secret better kept hidden. What of your grandmother? Does she still live?"

"She returned to England after Grandpa passed on. Sometimes I wish—"

Bringing Sarah's hand to his mouth, he pressed his lips to her palm. "You have only to wish, Sarah, and I'll see it granted. Within a year, you'll see her again."

"Oh, Brendan," she said as she threw her arms around his neck. "You're entirely too good to me."

Warmth flooded through him. "Absurd. I've enough money for two lifetimes. What good is all my wealth if I can't use it to make the woman I love happy? Sarah. Don't weep. Bloody hell!"

Gertrude touched a pale pink rose. Bending to sniff of its fragrance, her mind drifted to Mr. Montand. Her lips tingled with remembrance of the kiss he'd given her during their carriage ride home. It had been years since she'd felt so foolish or so alive.

She hadn't meant to lose herself so completely, but when his mouth had moved over hers with such shocking abandon, her inhibitions had flown out the window.

She straightened and watched a small brown

bird lift its wings and sail over the top of the house. French endearments had flowed from Henri's lips as his kisses had strayed down her throat to the edge of her gown. Laying a hand over her bosom, she inhaled an unsteady breath. She stood there, in the private garden, pining over a man like some silly debutante.

She'd been waiting for hours to speak with Brendan. Her nephew, however, had yet to leave his chamber, thank goodness. She hoped he'd spent the night embracing his wife, and perhaps even confessing his love. If so, she could return to her own house. It was rather difficult to encourage an ardent suitor when one was constantly surrounded by family and servants.

Hearing the crunch of shoes on the walkway behind her, she turned to find Brendan. He sipped from a cup of coffee as he approached.

"Stratford must've relayed my message," she said by way of greeting.

"Actually, he didn't. You wanted a word with me?"

"Since last evening, but I didn't want to interfere with . . . I hope you and Sarah—"

"Good Lord, it's inconceivable that one could keep a secret in this house."

"So your night did go well. Did you perchance tell her you loved her?" Noticing two bright dots of color on his cheeks, Gertrude covered her amusement by studying a deep red rose. "You needn't answer. It's fairly obvious that you did."

"Madam, you overstep your bounds."

"Prying into your affairs wasn't my intention. The reason I wanted to speak to you was to warn you about Caroline Belmont."

A long moment passed before he asked, "What about her?"

"I have a nagging feeling she's found out about your past. Otherwise she's devised some indecorous scheme to cause you trouble."

"Your imagination's running wild."

"Be that as it may, I'm not alone in my thinking. Henri came to the conclusion first, and I've found him an estimable source of—"

"Gossip?"

"For a man, he's most unusual," Gertrude explained. "I trust his opinion implicitly. I myself saw the look on her face when she was watching you and Sarah dance. There's no doubt in my mind that Caroline had an ulterior motive in pressing her daughter's suit."

Brendan spoke nonchalantly as he finished his coffee. "I've been aware of her attraction to me from the first. She's an extremely seductive woman married to an older, inattentive man. Naturally, she's apt to fantasize occasionally. I see no harm in it, and have feigned disinterest during each of our meetings."

Gertrude lifted a brow. "*Feigned* disinterest? Surely you never considered a liaison with her."

Snapping off the very red rose Gertrude had been eyeing, he handed her his cup, then worked the stem of the flower through the small buttonhole in his lapel. "You have a short memory, madam. When I first came here, I found it extremely difficult to overpower my sexual yearnings, especially since I'd never refused a willing woman before. Caroline tempted me greatly."

"But you obviously found the strength to resist her?"

"To my amazement, yes."

"Then you're to be admired."

Brendan made a face, obviously uncomfortable with her compliment.

"And that's why we must do all in our power to guard your commendable reformation."

Fine lines gathered at the corners of his eyes, betraying his feelings.

"Do you regret not having told Sarah about your past?"

"You know me too well. As if it isn't bad enough that my life's a lie, Sarah looks up to me as a paragon of virtue. I'm trapped in a web of my own making."

"I beg to differ," Gertrude said compassionately. "You may regard your life as a lie, but I don't. It would only be a lie if you were falsely maintaining a principled mien. You've truly mended your ways."

"I daresay I'm a candidate for sainthood!" he said dryly. "I've deceived my wife and haven't the courage to enlighten her. Making matters worse, I had the gall to condemn her for succumbing to my brother, when I've tumbled half the female population of England."

Gertrude smothered a grin. "You exaggerate. So you've gained a bit of experience. That's only natural for a virile man, and doesn't make you an unconscionable fiend. Sarah loves you for the man you are now."

"A hypocritical liar?"

"You're considering confessing?"

"I almost unburdened my conscience last night, but somehow I lost my train of thought."

Handing back the cup, she straightened his slightly askew tie. "I cannot advise you in that delicate matter. You'll have to come to your own decision and suffer the consequences. Bear in mind that, if what I suspect is true, Caroline Belmont might very well relieve you of the problem."

"It wouldn't be to her advantage," Brendan muttered, his brows knitting together. "She wouldn't want it known that she'd pursued a match between a known scoundrel and her daughter."

"You may have a point, though you should consider a woman's vanity. You and Sarah made a spectacular sight at the ball, and I heard whispers of how much in love you appeared. Caroline just might be vindictive enough to endanger her own reputation in order to get even."

"I need time to think. Sarah's bound to be hurt by the news. I hesitate to ruin our happiness."

"I know," she returned, patting his shoulder. "You realize, of course, that prolonging your confession will also make her all the more angry."

He gave her a rueful grin. "She'll serve me

my head on a silver salver, and I'll deserve it."

Gertrude gave his stiff collar a tug, sliding it higher on his neck. "If you do decide to go out, it would behoove you to take special pains to hide your love bite."

Brendan clicked his tongue and stiffened, dots of color appearing on his cheeks again. Not wanting him to see her smile, Gertrude ducked past him and went inside. When she reached the formal hall, she clapped a hand over her heart. "Egad! It's *you!*"

Derek Miles Hammond removed his hat and shoved it at Stratford. Then, approaching his aunt, he bent to kiss her cheek. "Is that any kind of greeting, when I've come such a long way just to see you?"

Gertrude allowed him to kiss her. "You spout rubbish, as usual. The parlor, right now, young man. I'll have a private word with you before you upset your brother."

After Derek had moseyed into the room, she said to Stratford, "I beseech you to keep Derek's arrival from Brendan for the moment."

"Madam, I am relieved. I do not wish to be the bearer of such tidings."

Gertrude fortified herself with a deep breath and followed Derek. Her younger nephew's sudden appearance was sure to cause discord in the household. But, she thought, if she maneuvered him just right, perhaps he might be persuaded to postpone his visit for a reasonable length of time.

"I would've preferred Brendan's study," Derek remarked as he picked up a priceless figurine from a small mahogany table.

Gertrude hurried across the room and retrieved the figurine. "No doubt you wish to sample your brother's supply of liquor."

Giving her a knowing grin, he sauntered to the opposite wall and studied a portrait of his father. "My brother takes after him more every day, don't you agree?"

Gertrude gently replaced the art object. She whirled around, folding her hands at her waist. The rascal was up to no good, she thought. "Why are you here? Brendan said he'd paid you to avoid St. Louis."

"You wound me, Aunt Gertrude. Can't I come for a visit without your thinking the worst of me? Didn't you miss me?"

"I always miss you after you've gone. Your timing, however, is abominable."

"Why?" He slowly turned, his eyes searching her face. "Has something happened that I should know about?"

"Many things have happened," she replied. "But you may rest assured that your brother remains in good health."

"I never thought otherwise."

Gertrude harrumphed. "Naturally, you're pleased." She watched him closely, noting the barely perceptible tightening of his mouth. She had never treated him so rudely before. Determined not to weaken, she declared, "Brendan has taken a wife."

His lips parted with surprise before he clamped them together. "I presume it was to keep up his righteous appearance. Don't tell me he's managed to act the model of virtue all this time."

"Your brother has truly changed. One would think you'd be pleased that he's mastered his baser instincts."

Derek laughed and plopped down on the settee, crossing one leg over the other. "I suspect you're hinting that I should follow his example. Don't tell me he's actually in love with this woman."

"I believe he is." She paced the room and back. "If you've come for money, I've a suggestion you might want to consider."

"Again, you wound me."

Gertrude harrumphed again. Nothing *she* could say would wound the rascal, she was certain. The only person capable of such a feat was Brendan. She consoled herself with the thought that she acted as much in Derek's behalf as Brendan's. "How much would it take for you to absent yourself for another six months?"

Derek crossed his arms over his chest and dispassionately stared at her for several moments. "Are you offering me money from your own coffers?"

She stopped in front of him. "I am. You realize, of course, that I'm worth more even than Brendan." The way he continued to study her made Gertrude uneasy. She suspected that, despite his indolent manner, he could be quite ruthless. Why had she never realized it before? "You would have to give me your word. Also, you must never mention this conversation to your brother.''

Derek stood abruptly. ''Your offer and distinct hostility intrigue me. But more than your generous proposition, your nervous behavior advises me not to act rashly.''

''My nervous behavior?'' she muttered, taken aback. ''Are you implying I have something to hide?''

''You've been wringing your hands together for the past five minutes.'' He aimed a predatory grin at her. ''I, however, know you well. You aren't given easily to anxiety. I believe I'll remain awhile and see if I can unearth why you want me gone badly enough to finance me.''

Furious and dismayed, Gertrude held her arms at her sides. Derek not only resembled Brendan; he'd inherited his intelligence . . . and shrewdness. What had happened to the amiable nephew she remembered? Maybe she should have checked her anger and deployed a sweeter approach. Despite Derek's penchant for causing trouble, she was genuinely fond of him.

''Very well, do as you wish, but you're mistaken if you think to get anything more out of Brendan. He has a family to consider now.''

''Family? Has he put his child in her this soon?''

Gertrude released a sigh of exasperation. She hadn't meant to let that tidbit of information loose, but Derek would have found out soon enough anyway. ''He has a daughter. Rebecca Louise Hammond.''

''Impossible.''

"Oh, it's not only possible; it's true. Now do you see why I thought to buy your capitulation? If you have any regard for your brother, you'll accept my offer and leave him in peace. The girl doesn't know yet of his past affairs. He should be allowed to enlighten her when he feels the time's right."

"I see. You think it necessary to buy my silence." Derek strode to the window and pushed aside the lace curtains. He stared out, deep in concentration.

Gertrude found she was wringing her hands again and, annoyed with herself, pressed her arms to her sides. Seconds ticked by like hours. A breeze outside forced a tree branch against the window. The scraping sound grated on her nerves. Finally, unable to stand the suspense a minute longer, she demanded, "Well, what will it be?"

He turned and gave her a devastating smile. He'd just opened his mouth to speak when the pocket doors flew open.

Brendan strode into the room and froze. "*Bloody hell!*" Pinning his irate gaze on his brother, he demanded, "What the devil are *you* doing in my home?" He drew in a harsh breath and faced Gertrude. "I thought I heard voices a few minutes ago. When Stratford assured me I was hearing things, I knew there was a conspiracy."

Undaunted by his brother's unfriendly greeting, Derek came forward, offering his hand. "Marriage not agreeing with you, old man?"

Brendan abruptly banged the doors shut,

then glared at Derek. "She told you?"

Gertrude meekly explained, "Merely that you'd wed and have a daughter."

Derek withdrew his hand. "You look well," he said to Brendan in a pleasant tone. "She must be a hell of a woman to have snared *you*. I admit I'm flabbergasted. I never thought you'd pull it off."

"Pull what off?" Brendan snapped, still narrowing his eyes on his brother.

"Your reformation. You were serious, after all."

"I'm sorry to disappoint you, but I didn't stumble even once."

"Can't say your defection pleases me," Derek said. "I always thought you a rather dashing rogue."

Brendan's silence hinted at much, Gertrude mused. Wanting to instigate a temporary standoff between her nephews, she ventured, "Brendan is still dashing."

When Brendan sent her a reproachful look, she quietly took a seat in a brocade wing chair. Unless he meant to remove her by force, she wasn't about to leave them alone. God only knew what would happen.

"I look forward to meeting the woman who caught you," Derek said. "She must be something special."

"I daresay," Brendan retorted as he stuffed his hands in his trouser pockets.

"Well, where is she? Call her down and introduce me. It's not every day that a man acquires a sister."

Ignoring his brother's request, Brendan asked, "Why are you here?"

"I have a little problem." Derek glanced over his shoulder at his aunt, then lowered his voice to a whisper. "Do you suppose we might talk in private?"

"You most certainly may not!" Gertrude chimed in. "I don't trust either of you not to resort to fisticuffs."

Derek looked incredulous. "My dear aunt, what an unseemly suggestion. Why would we want to strike each other?"

"You'll know soon enough."

Brendan shot her a warning glance. "I'll handle this matter, madam, if you'll kindly remove yourself to the dining area." He gave her a coaxing smile. "If you'll occupy my wife for a time, I'll be eternally grateful."

Catching his meaning, though still not pleased with the arrangement, Gertrude abided by his wishes.

"So you hesitate to introduce me to your lady," Derek remarked when they were alone. "Do you regard me as a threat?"

Brendan scowled as he walked further into the room. What a disastrous turn of events. He hadn't expected Derek to reappear so soon and was at a loss as how to handle this delicate situation. Upon seeing his brother, his first impulse had been to sock him in the jaw for stealing Sarah's innocence. But violence wouldn't have changed anything.

"This is rich," Derek said with a sneer. "Wicked Warwick has become so besotted with a woman, he seeks to hide her from his own brother. Rest easy, old chap. Though I've done my best to emulate your prowess with women, I regret I haven't quite mastered your expert technique."

Brendan balled his right hand into a fist but quickly grabbed hold of it with the other. The image of Derek kissing and fondling Sarah sped through his mind. He saw their naked bodies entwined, Derek mindlessly thrusting into her. Heaving a breath, he forced his voice to sound calm. "Tales of your escapades have preceded you. It was decidedly unsporting of you to use my name for your nefarious purposes."

Derek chuckled. "I thought it awfully clever, myself. However did you find me out?"

Brendan gritted his teeth before he could respond. "I only know of one instance. Were there others?"

"Three, actually." After a brief silence, Derek asked, "How, precisely, did you learn of it? Were you contacted?"

"You could say that." Brendan rubbed his knuckles, attempting to contain a sudden rush of fury. He'd intended to prolong his brother's suffering, but changed his mind. "One of your conquests showed up at my door."

"Which one? The blonde or the redhead? I doubt it was the brunette."

"Have you forgotten their names so soon?"

"Your list far exceeds mine. Can you recite their names at whim?"

"*My* conquests were well versed in the art of

seduction and knew the rules of the game," Brendan spat out. "Whereas you've stooped low enough to compromise innocents."

Another brief silence fell. "Only the brunette was innocent, but she was sweet as a Georgia peach. I couldn't resist her. Afterward, I did feel sorry for using the charms I'd learned from you."

"Did you, indeed? Did you also regret promising marriage? You didn't learn *that* from me."

"It was unsporting of *her* to tell you." Derek released a weary sigh. "She didn't seem the vengeful type. I almost returned for her—until I came to my senses. I've no intention of hitching myself to one woman, when there are so many more to enjoy. And that I *did* learn from you. I suppose she was surprised to find you're Brendan Hammond, not me?"

"*Surprised* is putting it mildly."

He was tempted to tell him of Sarah's condition when she'd arrived but decided otherwise. He wasn't ready yet to let his brother know that he'd fathered Rebecca.

Rebecca was his now, not Derek's!

"Eventually, however, I was able to pacify her."

"You bought her off?"

Brendan's lips tightened to a formidable line as he faced his brother. "Unlike you, she adamantly refused my offer of money."

Derek lifted a brow. "Did she? Maybe I should reconsider and marry her, after all."

"You forfeited your chance when you seduced her, then abandoned her to suffer the consequences alone," Brendan stated, his tone as sardonic as he could make it. "Her name, by the way, is Sarah. She's off limits to you now; that is, if you value your life."

"I never would have believed it!"

Brendan clenched his fists at his sides.

"You married Sarah Stevens?" Derek burst into laughter. After a few moments, he controlled himself enough to say, "Pardon my amusement. It's just that you've astounded me. Who would've thought that the most infamous rake in all of England would take one of his younger brother's castoffs to wife."

His vision blurred by a red haze, Brendan sent his fist flying, soundly clipping Derek's finely molded jaw.

Chapter 16

◦─◦◯◯◦─◦

"**A**nother cup of tea, Stratford, if you please."

Sarah laid aside her napkin and regarded Gertrude with a critical eye. Brendan's aunt had already had her cup refilled three times in the past five minutes.

"I'm unbearably thirsty," Gertrude offered by way of explanation.

Sarah smiled slyly. "Else you're tryin' to detain me for some reason. Drink any more and you'll surely float from the room."

Stratford arrived with an ornate silver pot, ready to replenish Gertrude's tea. She held up a hand to stay him. "Never mind. Sarah's on to us."

"A most unfortunate turn of events, madam." He faced Sarah with a grimace. "We were under orders from his Lordship."

"I presumed as much," Sarah said. "Now, if either of you cares to explain, I'm listening."

"Derek's returned," Gertrude confessed bluntly.

Sarah's breath lodged in her throat.

"I wanted to remain with them, but Brendan ordered me to occupy you, most likely to spare you a confrontation before he'd brought Derek up-to-date."

"Heavens, this is unexpected."

"To us all."

Sarah glanced toward the door. "Was it wise to leave them alone together?"

Before Gertrude had given any indication that she might rise, Stratford had pulled out her chair at the precise moment when she rose, impressing Sarah. "Brendan has had enough time. Someone should have a look."

Sarah stood also. "I'll go."

Gertrude marched into the hall. "I do hope Derek has minded his tongue. Since Brendan's . . . arrival from England, Derek has developed a nasty habit of baiting him."

Catching up with Brendan's aunt, Sarah said, "I wish he'd waited a bit longer to come. Brendan and I have just—Oh, Derek's goin' to ruin everything."

"He may or he may not. He was bound to come back, and it's probably better to have it over with." She stopped outside the parlor and held Sarah's hand. "You would've dreaded this moment whenever it came."

An ominous thump from inside the room was heard. Sarah stared at the closed doors while she imagined the action to match the sound.

A body hitting the floor!

With a gasp, she burst into the parlor, then

stopped so suddenly, Gertrude plowed into her back.

Sarah felt she couldn't believe her eyes. Brendan stood over his brother, his right hand still balled into a fist, his dark brows furrowed together. He wore a murderous scowl.

Gertrude stood frozen a few feet away, as Sarah crouched down and nudged Derek. Leaning closer, Sarah touched Derek's neck and sighed with relief when she felt blood pulse through a vein.

How could she have given herself to this man?

Derek was handsome, but he could never have compared to his brother. She felt nothing for him now but concern for his welfare. His complexion had turned pale, and a wide red mark covered his chin.

"Is he alive?" Gertrude asked in a shaken voice.

Sarah nodded.

Out of the corner of one eye, Sarah saw Brendan move away, then return. Quick as a flash, water splashed over Derek's face.

"That should bring him around."

The cryptic tone of Brendan's voice made Sarah wonder if he felt any remorse at all for having punched his brother senseless.

Derek sprang to alertness, shaking his head and sending droplets of water in all directions. His hand immediately went to his jaw as his eyes darted back and forth between the people towering above him, and finally settled on Brendan.

"You pack quite a wallop, old man." His vision detoured to Brendan's hand. "Should I bother to get up, or just stay where I am and save myself a broken jaw?"

When Brendan didn't answer, Sarah glanced up and found him studying her. He looked a formidable foe, and she understood Derek's hesitation to rise.

"Thank God you've suffered no permanent damage," Gertrude said. She turned toward the hall. "I'll leave you to settle your differences in private."

Feeling a touch on her hand, Sarah diverted her attention to Derek, who had the audacity to grin at her as he squeezed her fingers familiarly.

"You're more breathtaking than I remembered," he said. "I suppose you also want to bash me for not coming back."

Sarah snapped her hand free and pushed herself to her feet. "I have no feelings at all for you, sir, though I owe you a great debt for your ill treatment. Thanks to you, I happened upon your brother and discovered the true meaning of love."

"*Love*, is it?" Derek said as he stood and dusted off his black frock coat.

"Yes," Sarah responded. "I've come to love him deeply."

"Of course you would," he countered, deftly moving out of Brendan's reach. "He has much to offer."

Seeing her husband move forward slightly, Sarah stepped in front of him. "*Brendan* is a

man of honor, and above reproach. He offered
me a home and respectability and a name—"

Derek's gaze swung to Brendan before it returned to Sarah. He laughed softly. "Who am I
to malign my sainted brother?"

Brendan's fingers gripped Sarah's upper
arms. Guessing his intention to move her aside,
she pivoted and caressed his hand. Tension had
pulled his face into a grimace, but her touch
softened his expression. "Might I speak with
Derek alone?"

He looked as if he wanted to object, but went
rigid instead. His hazel eyes searched her face.
She saw no sign of the gold lights that flashed
at times. If only Derek hadn't chosen this day,
even this month, to return.

"Very well," Brendan said, "if it's your
wish." Casting Derek a hostile glance, he strode
from the room.

Sarah's shoulders slumped. Maybe she
should have allowed Brendan to deal with his
brother, but she didn't dare chance a repeat of
what had just happened. She wanted no man
fighting over her. The slam of the front door
jarred the outer wall, rattling the window.
Sarah ran to the window and watched Brendan
stalk across the street to Lafayette Park. Relieved to find he hadn't gone far, she turned
and discovered Derek standing within inches of
her.

His resemblance to Brendan caught her off-
guard for a moment, until she focused on the
differences that set them apart. Derek lacked
Brendan's height and breadth of shoulders; and

his features, though striking, stirred no emotion in her. Even his hazel eyes seemed less appealing, not dazzling, like Brendan's.

"I owe you an apology, Sarah," he said.

The sincerity she detected in his voice astounded her.

"I did care for you."

"At the moment, you mean."

"I see you're much wiser than when I met you." He touched her hair, until she slapped away his hand. "Ah, the little farm girl has learned her lesson. Being the wife of an earl is much more advantageous than a roll in the hay with a penniless—"

A sharp crack echoed in the room.

"My apologies again. I deserved to be slapped. But you should've done it sooner—when I first kissed you."

"I was beguiled then."

"But no longer? Is my brother truly that much more accomplished in bed?"

Sarah's hand tingled with the need to slap him again, but she refused to allow herself to slip a second time. She'd reacted instinctively, without thought. Keeping her voice much calmer than she felt, she held her chin high and retorted, "He makes my blood sing through my veins."

Derek grinned. "You *have* changed, Sarah. I like you even more. I know you don't believe me, but I do truly regret my behavior. And I'm gratified that you've found happiness. You *are* happy?"

"Deliriously."

Derek broke into laughter, and several moments passed before he remarked, "I've emulated him all of my life, you know."

"You're nothing at all like Brendan."

Derek shook his head. "Brendan has always been my idol—until he offered me money to leave St. Louis so I wouldn't disgrace him with his peers."

Although his words had sounded detached, Sarah glimpsed sadness pass over his features. "Why did you feel it necessary to deceive me by usin' Brendan's name?"

He wandered away from her. "You've grown inquisitive, also."

His attempt to dodge her question, combined with his maneuver to hide his expression from her, confirmed Sarah's suspicions. Brendan's rejection had wounded Derek deeply, though she doubted questioning him further would prompt him to admit it. She watched him work his jaw, then grimace. "I'm sorry I slapped you," she offered, feeling pity for him.

He turned abruptly. "You had every justification, as did Brendan. I provoked him, too."

Confused by his words, she simply stared at him.

"I should've stayed away."

"Your return was inevitable," she said calmly. "Perhaps it was for the best. There are things we must resolve."

"My aunt said you have a child."

His sudden remark brought a gasp from Sarah. He came closer, his gaze locking with hers so gravely that her heart lurched with dread.

"I don't believe for one moment that you went to my brother's bed that quickly." He tilted his head, his eyes exploring her face for her reaction. "Brendan has always had a way with women, but you're different. The only other conclusion I can reach is that the child's mine."

"No!" Sarah cried as she fled toward the door.

"Sarah, please don't upset yourself so. Come back."

The tender tone of his voice partly soothed her panic. Though wary, she slowly returned to him. Holding her head lowered, she fought to calm her raging emotions. She'd intended to tell him about Rebecca, but not until she'd prepared herself to deal with him, should he have sought to claim her daughter.

"Sarah, I've no means to care for a daughter."

She looked up. His smile, the tenderness she read in his eyes, convinced her that he meant no malice toward Rebecca, at least. She was shocked, but strangely, she also resented his cavalier attitude.

"That's why you came looking for me, wasn't it? Because I'd left you pregnant?"

Sarah nodded. "But I thought I loved you, too, and wanted— You'd promised to come back and marry me."

"I knew I hadn't judged you wrong," he said,

more to himself than to her. "You must really think me a cad."

Sarah didn't respond for several seconds. "It wasn't necessary to make promises you didn't mean to keep. I'd never met anyone like you, and most likely would've still succumbed to your charm. You see, I thought you were the Prince Charming of whom I'd always dreamed."

He laughed and ran a hand through his hair. "It's ironic, isn't it? Because of me you met your true prince."

"Yes!" Feeling a twinge of guilt for replying so adamantly, she lowered her gaze. "Brendan's the man I've always wanted. But you shouldn't feel slighted."

He laughed again. "Lady, I'm used to it. My brother always comes out on top, while I'm left to envy him."

"Derek, I—"

"Don't feel sorry for me. It's time I accepted responsibility for something. Fate, however, has served me with a punishment worthy of my crime. I can never claim my daughter as my own or I'll ruin her."

"You mean to keep silent?" she asked incredulously.

He ran his fingers through his hair another time, deep furrows creasing his brow. His troubled expression reminded Sarah of Brendan. "I've no alternative. Besides, what would I do with her? The only woman I've ever considered marrying is my brother's wife."

"You leave me speechless."

A sound out front drew his attention, and he peeked out around the edge of the curtain as if he expected someone. Looking relieved, he offered her a faint smile. "It's just a neighbor. Now, unless you've deceived me and you're not as happy with my princely brother as you claim, I'd like to see my daughter."

"You must remember that she's your niece. Give me your word."

Offering his arm, his mouth slid into a smile. "You would accept *my* word still?"

"If it's sincerely given."

"Damn, Sarah. I was a fool to let you go. Upon my honor, however much of it I have, I'll do my daughter no harm."

Sarah slipped her arm through his and led him upstairs, where they found Rebecca peacefully sleeping. Sarah lingered by the door while Derek tiptoed to the cradle. She should have felt some emotion, she thought. The father of her child was seeing his daughter for the first time. In her heart, though, Brendan was Rebecca's father.

To his credit, Derek appeared extremely moved as he very tenderly smoothed his palm over the baby's dark hair. He closed his eyes briefly, his features contorting into a pained grimace. Sarah's stoic facade cracked. She laid the back of her hand over her mouth to stifle any sound she might make and looked away.

Derek did possess a heart, after all. Within minutes, however, he swiftly passed by her, exiting the room without a word. Sarah inhaled a deep breath. He'd given his word, and for some inexplicable reason she trusted him to keep it. It appeared that sin did have its own retribution, at least for him.

But what of her? She'd sinned also, and had ended up gloriously happy with Brendan. Would fate exact retribution from her yet?

Worried because Brendan hadn't returned to the house, Sarah walked briskly through the massive gates of Lafayette Park. The park was lovely that day, with sunlight dappling through the trees and birds chirping, but she had no mind to appreciate either. She'd searched several paths before she spotted him standing alongside a lake.

Her throat grew thick. He looked so bereft as he stared across the water, absently watching a couple enjoy a ride in a swan boat. The man's laughter drifted to Sarah, increasing her melancholy. She yearned to hear Brendan laugh again in just such a manner.

She watched him for several minutes more. With his hands clasped behind him and his spine set in a rigid line, he appeared as unapproachable as when she'd first met him.

Now, because of Derek's untimely arrival, Brendan had been reminded even more strongly of her transgression.

Approaching him, she laid her hand on his shoulder. "Are you all right?"

"I'm fine. Are you?"

"As well as can be expected. I hope you know my reasons for wantin' to see Derek alone weren't of a romantic nature."

The sunlight reflecting from the water pierced Brendan's eyes, but he held his unfocused vision on the ripples. He felt temporarily numb. "Sarah, I no longer care if you've been with my brother one or a thousand times."

Blast Derek. He'd picked a devilish time to reappear.

"Let's walk awhile," he said as he tucked Sarah's arm through his.

They walked along the path surrounding the lake. Sarah slipped her arm free and stood looking across the water. Brendan gazed in the opposite direction. When, a few minutes later, he looked back at Sarah, he found her crouched near the water's edge. His mood lifted at the sight of her. Mindless of her costly green day gown, she was attempting to lure a stout duck closer. Tension drained from Brendan as he trod silently in her direction. His taut mouth moved into an appreciative smile when, despite the fact that she held nothing edible in her hand, the duck waddled right up to her.

Standing several feet behind her, he nearly laughed aloud when she impulsively reached out to pet the animal and it honked in protest and awkwardly trotted away.

"Next time bring a treat, and he'll eat from your hand."

Sarah started at his unexpected remark. Losing her balance, she tumbled to her backside with an undignified display of petticoats. "Brendan Hammond, you shouldn't sneak up on a person like that!"

Before she could rise, he sat down next to

her, crossing his legs. "You have a way with animals."

She nodded and arranged her skirt to cover her legs.

"Do you miss Georgia very much?"

Meeting his expectant gaze, she regarded him solemnly. "Sometimes."

"Do you want to go back?"

Her eyes widened. "Only with you. A visit now and again would suffice. I do miss my family, and I'd like them to know Rebecca."

"And me?"

She touched a finger to his chin. "Especially you."

Capturing her hand, he turned it over and pressed his lips to her palm. "You've neglected to wear your gloves, madam, and will cause a scandal should anyone learn of your breach of etiquette."

"Goodness, I never thought. I was too concerned with—"

"—Finding your husband?" he finished for her.

She nodded again, flushing when his lips advanced over her wrist to her elbow.

"Your eyes are flashing different shades of green, Sarah. Is that significant?"

Lowering her voice and projecting a distinctly British accent, she answered, "I daresay it is."

Heat crawled through Brendan's veins at the seductive look she gave him. "You tempt me to investigate."

"But naturally, you cannot." Wrinkling a

brow, she dared him with a wink. "We're in the open, and someone might see us."

"Hell, Sarah." His swift movement brought a squeal of surprise from her. Not caring who saw then, he pulled her down beside him in the sweet-smelling grass. "You rob me of my sanity."

"Brendan! Let me up. Have you lost your mind?"

Cradling her face in his hands, he stared deep into the gray-green depths of her eyes. "My mind and my heart."

She covered his hands with hers, her eyes growing moist. "Do you really mean it? You're not just sayin' that because . . . he came back?"

"Yes, I mean it. You can say Derek's name. And *later* you can tell me what transpired after I left."

"Nothing transpired, Brendan. Nothing will, ever again."

He brushed his lips over hers, wanting to kiss her senseless, as he had the night before. "Don't speak of it now. I have other designs on you."

"Designs? Such scandalous behavior will surely leave your reputation in tatters." She attempted to glance around, but he held her face, so she could not. "Oh, you're shameless, sir. I hope no one is watchin'."

"You're as shameless as I, Sarah," he told her with a grin. "A woman worthy of a man of my so-called appetites. But I'll not have anyone speak ill of you." Coming to his feet, he pulled her up with him. "There's an alternative, if you're game."

She flounced her skirt, removing loose blades of grass. "That depends on which appetite you're referrin' to." She slowly looked up, her gaze roaming over him. "I've already eaten. Of course, if it's something else you have on your mind . . ."

She could be a witch when she wanted, he thought. He wanted her there and then. To be buried inside of her and know she was *his*. To have her know that she belonged to him and erase memories of anything that had come before he had claimed her.

Pulling Sarah to his side so that her skirt provided some cover for his conspicuous excitement, he said with a growl, "Indeed, madam, it's something else I have on my mind, as you will soon find out."

"Where are you takin' me?" she asked when he steered her in a direct path toward the gates.

"To the hunting lodge. It's the only place where we can be alone. Do you mind?"

"How can you ask?" She waited patiently while he spoke with Stratford, then summoned the closed carriage to be brought around. As he ushered her inside, she inquired, "This sudden desire to hunt—do you intend to make a meal of your prey after you've brought it down?"

Brendan waited until the carriage had moved out of sight of the house before he seized Sarah's waist and sat her on his lap. He bound his arms around her, smiling at her startled expression. "But I've already brought down my delectable prey."

Sarah wiggled into a more comfortable position, her cheeks growing pink. Hugging her arms around his neck, she brushed her lips over his in the same manner that he'd done earlier. "Did you tell anyone of our outing, so they won't worry?"

"I did," he replied as he pressed his lips over hers in a more urgent manner.

"Did you tell the driver to hurry?" she asked when he lifted his head a fraction.

"I expressed that it was a matter of the utmost urgency."

He kissed her again, leisurely tasting her, until she moaned softly and melted against him, stoking the fire that already blazed in his loins. He felt he couldn't get enough of her. Moving his hands over her dress, he reached her breasts. With a groan of protest, he broke away long enough to mutter, "Damn, Sarah, you're wearing your corset today."

Her laugher filled the carriage as she nibbled on his lips, coaxing him to kiss her again. "I'm afraid you'll have to wait a bit longer. It's impossible to do any more until we arrive anyhow."

"Oh, but you're wrong." Deftly, he lifted her, his voice coming out strained. "Help me out. Swing your leg over mine."

Sarah gasped, then giggled when she realized his intention. Perched on his lap, straddling him, her eyes glinted with mischief while he fumbled beneath her skirt.

In the middle of unbuttoning his trousers, he paused. "You should be shocked, not amused, Sarah. Why aren't you?"

She grinned. "I imagine I'll be *quite* shocked when you accomplish your daring objective."

He fumbled for several seconds more, growing impatient with the obstacle of her layers of clothes but burning to bury himself inside of her while enough time remained. When, finally, he was free, he slid his hands up the inside of her thighs and smiled at her sharp intake of breath. "I do approve of female unmentionables. They allow a man easy access to his heart's desire."

"The openin' in my drawers wasn't intended for—Heavens!"

"You're so wet and hot," he said, his voice coming out a hoarse whisper, "I can't wait. You're mine, and I want you to remember that always."

The carriage hit a rut in the road, knocking Sarah's head against the ceiling. Brendan simultaneously cursed and groaned from the pleasure and pain. Not allowing him time to recover enough to ask if she'd hurt herself, Sarah lifted herself up slightly and came back down upon him, impaling herself on his throbbing manhood. The carriage hit yet another rut, forcing him deeper inside. He mumbled another curse. "Move carefully," he grated out, "or you'll injure yourself."

Her cheeks deepened into a vivid shade of crimson as she regarded him from beneath her lowered lashes. "It's not injury I'm sufferin'. How ingenious . . . of you . . . to think of doin' it here." She slid up and down on him. "Why, you're as stiff as a flagpole, your Lordship."

Brendan groaned. "I won't be for long if you move like that again."

She sat very still, caressing his cheeks. "It's just as much fun when I don't move. I love havin' you inside me. It makes me feel that I possess a part of you. Mine alone."

Brendan shut his eyes and savored the exquisite moment. She possessed more than a part of him. She possessed his soul. He wished they could remain joined forever. Her mouth met his suddenly, her lips slanting over his persuasively. He clamped her tightly against him. He invaded her with his tongue and kissed her ravenously, demonstrating the sensuous movements another more demanding part of him craved. Her velvety sheath tightened in response.

Passion took control of his mind and body. He gripped her hips and plunged upward, again and again, until she writhed in ecstasy. She imitated him, driving downward to meet his thrusts, sending them both to a violent finale.

"I saw fireworks," she said breathlessly.

"I did, too."

"I don't want to let you go."

"You don't have to," he said, his voice a raspy whisper.

This time he loved her more thoroughly. In the back of his mind he knew time was his enemy, but he didn't care.

The carriage stopped suddenly, and Brendan held Sarah tightly to keep her from sliding backward. Moving as quickly as possible under the circumstances, he shoved her onto the opposite seat and flipped her skirt into place. Refastening his buttons took a dexterity he lacked at that moment, but he forced his fingers to obey his mental commands. Sarah's giggle hindered his efforts.

"Hush, Sarah, or we'll be found out." The driver chose that second to fling open the door and lend an arm to her. "Bloody hell!"

Sarah walked several feet away from the carriage and inquired after the driver's well-being to allow Brendan extra minutes to make himself decent. When he appeared at her side, she nearly sighed with relief that the awkward moment had passed. Brendan put his arm around her shoulders, slipped a key into her hand, and steered her toward the front porch.

His voice was strained. "Go directly to the bedroom and strip yourself naked."

Grateful she faced the opposite direction, so the driver couldn't witness her expression, she whispered back, "Insatiable scoundrel!"

"I'll be along directly, madam," he replied in a normal tone, giving her an unabashed grin before he assumed a strictly businesslike demeanor and returned to issue further instructions to the man.

Sarah never thought to disobey his shameless order. The passionate minutes they'd shared in the carriage had merely whetted her appetite for him. The house appeared empty, but she called out just to be sure. She hurried into the bedroom, where she found to her dismay that she couldn't do as he'd asked. Her dress hooked behind her, presenting an obstacle he hadn't considered. She removed everything she could, and was unpinning her hair when he strode through the door.

His gaze flashed over her, then slid to the pile of underclothes littering a nearby chair. "In the future, you're forbidden to purchase any gown that doesn't fasten in front."

"Yes, your Lordship," she said with extreme deference. "Should I inform the seamstress of the reason for your request?"

"You may not." He spun her around and made short work of releasing the tiny hooks, then swept her hair off one shoulder. Tasting the tender spot at the juncture of her neck and shoulder, he slipped his hands inside the dress. "The driver won't come back for two hours, and I gave the caretaker enough chores to occupy him for the rest of the day." He wanted to spend some time with this woman he loved, holding her, loving her. He wanted to forget the world outside of their embrace . . . and the past he was suddenly afraid might come back to haunt them.

Sarah wiggled, and the dress dropped to her waist. A delicious shiver traveled down her spine from the kisses he placed on her neck. Within seconds her corset had fallen between them. "One day I'm goin' to ask you how you learned to so thoroughly distract a woman that she isn't aware she's bein' disrobed until it's too late."

His lips ceased laving her neck. Slowly, he came in front of her. Tipping up her chin with a finger, he gazed at her. "Before we leave, there's something I must tell you."

His gaze, tender and somber at the same time, distressed her, but she chose to ignore her misgivings. Sensing he planned to reveal something she didn't want to hear, she plucked the somewhat smashed red rose from his lapel. She pressed it to her nose and inhaled its sweet fragrance before he tossed the flower to join her underclothes.

He swept her dress to her feet, removed her chemise, then gazed at her from her head to her toes and back.

Sarah's breath caught from the yellow sparks glinting in his eyes. "It's not fair. You're still dressed."

"A fact that's causing me misery. I'll have to instruct my tailor to allow more room in a certain area to accommodate my lust for you."

Sarah dropped her vision to his trousers and grew warm all over. A slow, appreciative grin captured her mouth. "I've married a veritable—"

"—Stud?" he supplied.

Laughing at his brazen interruption, she shoved his coat off his shoulders, then pulled open his tie. "I'm not certain . . . yet. When I get that far, I'll let you know."

He seized her hands and moved them lower. "I prefer that you decide *now*."

"As you wish, Your Grace," she said in a perfect imitation of Stratford. With more precision than she would have imagined herself capable of, she had his pants open and pooled at his feet. Sarah tapped a finger on her chin as she pretended to consider. "Your shirttail's in the way, but I'd say the word definitely applies."

Two swift movements and the remainder of his clothing hit the floor. Giving a growl of impatience, he swept her into his arms and strode to the bed.

Sarah stretched and yawned. She felt drowsier than a lazy cat—an extremely satiated feline. Two and a half tantalizing hours had passed. Brendan had donned his shirt and trousers and gone to let the driver know they would require even more time before they returned home.

He came through the door and sat next to her on the bed. Pulling down the sheet, he fondled her breast, then playfully nipped at it with his teeth. "We've made love for two hours, and I still want you."

She touched his hair. "I must be a Jezebel. I want you, too."

"I've never been accused of gluttony before," he admitted as he put the sheet back in place. "I believe I'm actually grateful to Derek. If he'd behaved honorably, I never would have met you. And I would've turned into one of those frustrated, lifeless men I've always scorned."

She smiled at him. "You're far from lifeless."

He smiled back, lifting a brow. "I'm pleased to hear you say it." Giving her a leisurely kiss, he released a gratified moan. Against her mouth, he mumbled, "I can even sympathize with Beauclaire. His wife, you see—"

"Should you be tellin' me this?"

"Probably not. I daresay it's not the gentlemanly thing to do." He sat back and caught a strand of her hair in his hand. "I feel fortunate, and can't help wanting to brag about it."

Sarah's heart swelled with happiness. Struck by an unsettling thought, she stared at him. "But, naturally, you won't. Goodness, you aren't thinkin' of braggin' to your male friends about how wanton I am."

"Positively not! Let them think I'm like them, sexually deprived."

A horrified look crossed her face. "Do you think I'm normal?"

"How the devil would I know? I've only had—" Who's to say what's normal? I happen to adore you the way you are." Straightening, he shoved his arms into the garment, then sat unmoving for a long minute. "Sarah, I've never *loved* a woman before."

She gripped his arm. "I've never loved before, either. With Derek it was only infatuation."

He angled his head, both brows raised.

"Well, even you have to admit he's handsome. Why, he strongly resembles you. And he can be utterly charmin' when he has a mind. Once I met you, though, I knew he was a poor imitation of the man of whom I had always dreamed." Noticing the fine lines forming on his brow, she reminded him, "You said I could mention him."

"It's all right. How did your talk go?"

"Much better than I imagined. He knows

about Rebecca and has promised to keep silent."

Brendan's mouth quirked up on one side, doubt clouding his eyes.

"He's given his word," she said.

"Derek?"

"Oh, heavens! Do you think he means to break it?"

"On the contrary. I've never known him to give his word before."

Sarah clamped her hand over her heart, profoundly relieved. "You had me worried."

"Did you tell him, or did he guess?"

"He's quite clever. He knew right off. He said he had no way to care for a daughter, which I suppose is true enough," she said, leaving out Derek's comments regarding her.

"I sense that you've forgiven him."

Brendan's intense regard prompted Sarah to reveal more than she'd intended. "Derek admitted he's always idolized you. While he didn't actually put it in words, I believe you hurt him deeply when you gave him money to leave St. Louis."

Lines furrowed across Brendan's brow again. "I never thought he'd take offense. We've never minced words, and he, of all people, should have realized it wasn't personal." He fell silent, slowly shaking his head. "I suppose you want me to believe he used my name in retaliation for my inadvertent slight?"

Sarah nodded.

"Absurd. I've never known him to be thin-skinned."

"I admit, it's no excuse for his churlish actions, but perhaps you might speak with him. He did express remorse for the way he treated me. His punishment will be endless, seeing his daughter grow up as yours. It might have a sobering affect on him, make him want to emulate his venerable brother."

Brendan frowned. "I'll consider your suggestion, though I can't promise anything. And don't refer to me as venerable."

Crawling to her knees behind him, Sarah wrapped her arms around his shoulders and kissed his cheek. "Whyever not? You've barely a fault, and that's one of the many reasons I fell in love with you. Derek has so little, but we have everything."

He inclined his head, his shoulders dropping slightly.

"You said earlier that you wanted to tell me something." She splayed her fingers over his chest, her mouth retreating to his ear. "We should go back soon."

Capping her hands with his, he leaned his head out of her reach. "Kissing my ear muddles my mind, Sarah."

"I'll remember that. So . . . what's this matter you wish to speak of that you seem to be putting off? Have you some deep, dark secret—a foul discrepancy in your character?"

He sat straighter, sucking in a harsh breath. "Quite foul, my dear." He brought her hand to his mouth and pressed a kiss above her knuckles.

Sarah pulled her hand free. She gripped his

chin and turned his head. Trembling from a dire premonition that the secret he wanted to reveal might change everything, she slanted her mouth over his. Although he resisted for a moment, she put all of her love into her kiss, and sighed into his mouth when she felt him surrender.

Brendan twisted, wrapping his arm around her waist and sliding her around him, onto his lap. He took control of the kiss.

Smashed tightly against his chest, with his tongue ravishing her mouth, Sarah quickly expelled every other thought except the delirious heat he alone could ignite in her body.

Chapter 17

~~~~~~OOO~~~~~~

Sarah reached the front hall and met Stratford just as she finished tugging on her gloves.

"The carriage is waiting, madam."

"Thank you, Stratford. You may tell the driver I'll be there in a few minutes. Is Brendan still in his study?"

"Yes, madam."

"For pity's sake, must you address me so formally?"

Stratford's chin blended in with the folds of his neck as he peered at her with censure in his eyes.

Remembering their first meeting, she held back a smile. Though she would never feel comfortable with the polite deference with which he now treated her, she knew she'd simply have to accustom herself to it.

The house seemed so quiet. A week had passed, during which Gertrude had moved back to her own home, taking Derek with her. Although her presence was sorely missed, Sarah knew that both she and Brendan owed his aunt a great debt for allowing them this time alone.

She found Brendan absorbed in reading a journal, his spectacles perched on his aristocratic nose. The past week sped through her mind—outings during the days, luncheon at Planter's House, afternoons at Abbey Race Track, and walks in the park. They were becoming a regular sight about town. People still tended to whisper behind their hands upon occasion, but Sarah no longer minded.

She loved the nights best. Hours of passion, being held in Brendan's strong arms while he whispered endearments, made her long for the end of each day. She wished their idyllic interlude could go on forever. But she sensed it would not.

Brendan hadn't seen fit to speak with Derek, who, to Sarah's amazement, had kept his distance.

Brendan must have sensed her presence, for he looked up, then quickly removed his spectacles. "You're ravishing."

Sarah grinned. No matter how many times she assured him that glasses didn't deter from his handsomeness, his male vanity took over.

As if he'd read her mind, he said, "I can't see you unless I take them off."

So much for her presumption, she thought. "Thank you for your kind praise, sir."

"You're going out to purchase more bounty and leave me penniless, I presume?"

"Indeed, your Lordship," she countered as she rounded his desk. She brushed a strand of dark hair from his brow. "It's a glorious day, and since you prefer to spend it reading your stuffy old papers, I thought to amuse myself."

Gold lights flickered in his eyes. He fingered the black braiding on the bodice of her blue morning dress, his voice dipping sensuously low. "With slight provocation, I might be persuaded to amuse you myself."

"Brendan Hammond, you spent half the night amusin' me." Considering his sly smile, she asked, "What precisely does an earl usually do all day?"

"Do?"

Sarah nodded.

"Madam, I do whatever pleases me. Just overseeing my vast wealth occupies much of my time. And there are my homes in England—"

"You have homes in England still?"

"An estate in the country and a town dwelling in London. Are you suitably impressed, Sarah?"

"Will you take me to see them one day?"

"I rather look forward to it. Naturally, we have to plan our excursion well in advance and take care that nature doesn't interfere."

"Nature?"

His hand dropped to press over her abdomen. "I won't put you at risk, should you conceive."

Sarah's eyes widened in disbelief. "But I thought you didn't want a child."

"Of course I want a child. Several, in fact, if you'd be so obliging, but I prefer to allow you enough time to recover from Rebecca's birth. You'll kindly space them at two-year intervals."

"As you wish." Sarah's mouth slid into a wide grin. The touch of male arrogance that he'd never be able to master had become dear to her. Her heart swelled with love. He had only been concerned for her welfare. She touched his cheek. "I expect that you'll devote much of your time to this endeavor?"

"I've already devoted too much time, love, and will have to be more careful in the future. As much as I long for you to bear my own heir, I favor having you to myself for a while still. Our darling Rebecca will have to suffice for now."

Sarah heard a muffled sound through the doors. "Stratford has cleared his throat to remind me the carriage is waitin'." She reluctantly retreated a step, wondering if she dared suggest that Brendan alter his intentions for the day. She said, "You can't put off speakin' with your brother indefinitely. Derek hasn't intruded durin' the past week, and Gertrude has hinted to me that he desperately wants a word with you."

"No doubt he's in need of more funds."

"Your aunt also told me that she offered to finance him but he refused her."

"Did he, indeed? I daresay he must be in some other sort of bind, then." Brendan frowned. "I suppose you're right, and I should see him at once."

"I won't be unduly long," she hinted. "If you leave now, we might both arrive back with time to spare before dinner." She strolled toward the door, then glanced at him over her shoulder with what she hoped was a provocative look. "If your meeting with Derek doesn't go well, I'll find some way to cheer you."

His frown slid into a sumptuous grin that melted her insides. Before surrendering to the desire glittering in his eyes, she hurried outside.

Sarah's excursion to explore the ladies' shops downtown turned out a rare treat. She had expected Brendan to protest and insist she be properly escorted, but he hadn't. Exiting the fourth establishment, having succumbed to the lure of Brendan's abundant wealth, she didn't feel one twinge of guilt. She'd purchased bounty not only for herself but for Rebecca and Brendan as well. As she glanced up and down the street, she sighed. Brendan's carriage crept a bit closer, with Tibbs, the driver, conspicuously averting his gaze.

She hadn't been alone at all. Acting in Brendan's stead, Stratford had seen that the driver kept an eye on her. Having enjoyed herself too much to mind, she continued down the street but slowed her pace when she noticed a man departing what appeared to be a beerhouse. He turned in her direction.

She waved, and Derek strode toward her. He tipped his hat gallantly and greeted her with a warm smile.

"Good heavens," she said, "you shouldn't be here."

"And where should I be?"

Sarah smelled the slight odor of spirits on his breath. That and the devilish glint in his eyes told her how he'd been spending his time. "At your aunt's house. Brendan has probably been waitin' to speak with you for some time."

"Rest easy, dear heart. Impatient as my brother is, he's probably already gone home in a snit. I'll just come along with you. It's important that I see him immediately."

Sarah considered it and shook her head. "I don't think that's a good idea. He might jump to the wrong conclusion."

"We've only met by accident. Are you afraid he'll think we spent the morning together in an unseemly fashion?"

"No, I feel certain he'll accept my explanation."

"But there's always the possibility that he won't?"

Sarah lifted her chin a fraction as she narrowed her eyes on him. "Brendan trusts me. He knows I'd never engage in an unbefitting manner with you ever again. Besides, I encouraged him to visit you."

"Then you have nothing to worry about." He linked arms with her. Inclining his head, he whispered, "But should you grow weary of his dictatorial ways, you can always come to me."

Sarah jerked her arm free, incensed by his suggestion.

Derek's handsome mouth slanted into a wry grin. "You've grown much wiser than I thought, Sarah, but not wise enough. Brendan's all but given you permission to seek your pleasure where you want. My offer still stands."

Seething with fury, Sarah's hand itched with the need to slap him. But she wasn't going to cause a scandal on the street just to indulge her anger. "Brendan has done no such thing!"

"He has. A man of his kind doesn't trust his wife."

Sarah silently fumed.

Derek was a striking man. She noticed women of every age openly regarding him. Dear heavens, gossip was sure to abound, she thought. Most likely none of Brendan's peers had met his brother, and would think the worst. They were nearing the carriage when Sarah heard a familiar voice call out her name.

Caroline Belmont pushed through a throng of people, holding her hat in place, several deep rose plumes jiggling from her hasty movements. "I hadn't thought to see you out without your husband," she said by way of greeting. "How is it that Brendan isn't with you?"

Sarah smiled at the woman. "He was tendin' to his business affairs."

Mrs. Belmont turned her gaze to Derek. "You simply must introduce me to your handsome escort. I haven't had the pleasure."

Before Sarah could perform the introduction, Derek swept off his hat and executed a lavish bow. "Derek Miles Hammond at your service."

Sarah watched the couple with interest, fascinated by the manner in which Mrs. Belmont batted her long lashes while she fingered the white lace adorning the deep V of her rose silk gown. Derek also seemed entranced by the artful flirtation, and couldn't seem to draw his gaze from the woman's lush bosom.

"Brendan has done St. Louis society a disservice by keeping you hidden. Have you just arrived?"

"I've been here a week. Had I realized the town possessed such an exquisite woman, I would've make myself known sooner." He brought her hand to his mouth and, beaming her a smile, pressed his lips to the bare skin above the edge of her glove. "Sarah has been remiss in her manners and not told me your name."

"Caroline Belmont."

The woman fairly melted from Derek's ardent attention. Sarah could not resist interjecting, "I *have* been remiss in not telling you *Mrs.* Belmont's name."

Mention of Caroline's married state didn't faze Derek, who continued to dazzle her with his abundant charm. But Sarah felt she couldn't fault any woman for falling for his technique, when she herself had been so easily led astray. She had to admit he possessed the same debonair traits as Brendan, and was nearly as handsome. He looked splendid, in a dark morning coat with gray striped trousers, his cravat tied in a flawless knot. Uncomfortable, feeling like a third wheel, Sarah glanced in the opposite direction.

"Oh, you *are* a scoundrel, sir," Mrs. Belmont gushed as she wiggled her hand free. "I see you take after your jaded brother. Have you a reputation to equal that of Wicked Warwick? Or

have you many more women to conquer before
you can claim such a distinction?"

Gaping, Sarah snapped her gaze back to the
woman.

"My dear lady," Derek said with a distinct
edge to his voice, "such indiscriminate divulging of unproven hearsay is extremely unwise."

"My source is most reliable," Mrs. Belmont
retorted. She slanted Sarah a vindictive look.
"My sister-in-law recently visited London. She
had the distinction of meeting Lady Mariette
Ashley, who told her in the strictest confidence
that she'd enjoyed a long, passionate affair with
the earl of Warwick—Brendan Hammond, to
be exact—before he left London for St. Louis.
She also said that he'd been known about town
as Wicked Warwick, a title he had earned
throughout the years by his vast number of
conquests."

Feeling as if a sharp spike had just been
driven through her heart, Sarah sucked in a
harsh breath. The woman had delivered her
discourse with such assurance and venomous
intent, Sarah knew she spoke the truth. Dizziness assailed her. She jammed two fingers
against her forehead and prayed for strength.
Seconds later, she met the woman's gaze
squarely. "My husband will surely not appreciate the fact that you're spreadin' vile rumors
behind his back, Mrs. Belmont."

The woman swallowed, then gave Sarah a
predatory grin. "I merely speak the truth. A
gentleman of such notorious fame must know
that a reputation so widespread as his will

eventually follow him. I do, however, regret that I have been the bearer of such ill tidings. I hope my impromptu slip of tongue hasn't tarnished Brendan in your eyes."

"I'm well aware of my husband's past and don't hold it against him. As you must be aware, he's gained an untarnished standing here."

Caroline's mouth puckered. "Brendan might have convinced everyone otherwise, but I know the full truth. I suppose you're also aware that he killed Lady Ashley's poor husband in a duel. *That* is the reason he left England."

Sarah felt faint. Brendan had killed a man over the man's wife. Derek's eyes, wide and full of dismay, searched Sarah's face. She studiously ignored him. Colors swam before her eyes. She took a deep breath and glared at Caroline. "Brendan has told me everything! If you value your own standing, I advise you not to tell anyone else what you know."

Mrs. Belmont didn't reply for several moments. Her rouged lips pursed together, giving Sarah the impression that she didn't appreciate having been foiled. If she perished in the attempt, Sarah vowed, she wouldn't allow the woman to learn just how much hurt her callous words had caused.

Brendan had been known as Wicked Warwick in London. That title alone betrayed his past. Dear Lord, he must've been an even greater scoundrel than Derek. Worse, he'd not owned up to the fact, and had paraded himself as a man of impeccable character. *And he'd murdered a man in a duel!*

A deep, cutting pain coiled around her heart.

She felt Derek's hand at her elbow. Though she found his touch repugnant, she lacked the strength to pull away.

"It's been a pleasure to make your acquaintance," Derek told Mrs. Belmont. Lowering his voice to a more intimate tone, he added, "We will meet again. Very soon, I promise you."

Sarah nearly choked. Whatever pastime Derek had planned for Mrs. Belmont, she didn't want to know about it. Forcing her words to sound sincere, she said good-bye to the woman and allowed Derek to steer her to the carriage. Once inside, she stared with unseeing eyes out the window, her lips trembling from the truths she'd learned about Brendan.

Why hadn't he confessed?

Thinking back, she realized he'd come close to telling her several times, but he'd stopped and let her believe in him—honor him—love him for a man he'd never been.

"Sarah?"

Sarah's gaze slowly slid to Derek. "It was the truth, wasn't it? Brendan's whole existence is a lie."

"Yes."

The tears Sarah had been holding at bay flooded her eyes. Burying her face in her hands, she sobbed freely. When Derek laid his hand on her shoulder, she jerked away. "Don't touch me. You and your brother are just alike. Procurers of women's hearts."

Sniffling, she dug in her reticule and found she'd forgotten her handkerchief. A second later Derek waved his own in front of her nose. She snatched it and dabbed at her tears. "I'll never forgive him."

"When you come to your senses, you'll forgive him. Now, blow your red little nose and prepare yourself. You've only a few minutes before we're home."

Sarah did as he suggested, then tucked his handkerchief in her reticule. Upon reaching the front door, she halted abruptly.

Derek nonchalantly adjusted the cuffs of his coat. "You're making too much of it, Sarah. Remember, you were mine first and can be again. I haven't as much money as my brother, but I promise you I'll—"

Sarah swung her arm, intending to give him the slap he deserved. However, despite his appearance of nonchalance, he reacted much too fast. To her horror, she found herself bound in arms that felt like steel. "Release me this instant!"

"Oh, no. I'm not about to be slapped a second time."

"You mangy toad!"

He crushed her against him, his head lowering. Unable to move, Sarah considered her alternatives. His mouth approached. She allowed him to kiss her, then bit his bottom lip. Derek instantly released her.

She glared at him, her stomach roiling. "Don't touch me again!"

Not wanting to be in the presence of any man

at that moment, she dashed across the street to the park.

Brendan released the curtain and, scowling, left the window. Retreating to his desk, he poured a liberal portion of bourbon into a glass and drank it down. His recently banked annoyance at having gone to his aunt's house to find Derek gone, returned and swiftly advanced to rage. Sarah and Derek must have met in town.

The sight of Sarah in Derek's arms filled his mind.

But rather than jump to conclusions and wrongly accuse her, he decided to temper his rage until she explained it.

He filled his glass and emptied it as quickly as he had the other. Then, clenching his hands into fists, he sucked in a breath.

Gossip had begun to die down. He didn't want anyone spreading tales about Sarah, and he feared that Sarah's being seen with Derek also might promote suspicions about Rebecca. It would be best, he mused, if people believed that Derek and Sarah had recently met.

Jealousy churned his insides.

Sarah loved *him*, a little voice in his head reminded him.

Derek entered the room and headed straight for the liquor cabinet. "Sarah went to the park."

Brendan's scowl deepened at the curt announcement. "I'm aware of that fact. Dare I ask the reason?"

Having helped himself to Brendan's liquor, Derek faced his brother. "I wouldn't know."

Steepling his fingers in front of him, Brendan saw through his brother's feigned innocence. "Something must have happened to upset her."

"It's not of my doing," Derek remarked with a shrug. "This time it's you who must suffer the blame—you and Caroline Belmont."

Brendan's heart slammed against his ribs.

"I never said a word; nor did I intend to. But Mrs. Belmont had no such qualms. She filled Sarah in, enjoying every second of it. She took special delight in revealing why you murdered Ashley."

"That viper-tongued bitch!" Closing his eyes, Brendan shoved his fingers through his hair. He thoroughly reviled himself for his deception. He had wanted to spare Sarah for as long as possible and had probably hurt her more than necessary.

"Though you needn't worry that knowledge of your past will spread further. Sarah was magnificent, quite the little actress. She pretended she knew everything, and gave the woman an implied warning. I also intend to meet Mrs. Belmont again, and will personally see her vicious tongue silenced."

"I'm fully capable of handling Caroline Belmont."

"Indeed, you are. However, in this case, you can turn the odious deed over to me. I'm prepared to give her what she wants, whereas you aren't."

Brendan shook his head. The day had begun pleasantly and developed into a catastrophe. "You're welcome to her. But lay a hand on

Sarah again and I'll be guilty of murder in this country as well."

"Lay a hand on Sarah?" Derek said incredulously.

"I saw you out the window."

"I must say, you're awfully calm, old man."

Brendan shot his brother a venomous look. "Trust me, I'm not. I want to hear Sarah's side before I let loose of my temper." He glanced at the window. "I should seek her out now and—"

"I advise against it. Sarah's in a stew right now. Give her some time, or she might lop off your head." Derek took a seat at Brendan's desk, crossing his feet on its edge. "Besides, I need a favor, or quite likely my neck will be lengthened considerably."

Despite Derek's easygoing manner, Brendan detected a rare, underlying uneasiness in his brother. And, though Derek hadn't exposed any vulnerability, Sarah might have been right. Reconsidering the stipend he'd paid Derek to avoid the St. Louis area, Brendan decided he'd been thinking only of himself, not the insult his actions had implied.

"What's the nature of your problem? If you need more money, I'm sure—"

Derek held up a hand. "My problem isn't financial. Rather, it's an altercation with a Southern gentleman who took exception to the terms of a wager—after the fact."

Anticipating a long story, Brendan sat on the corner of his desk. "Go on."

"It happened in New Orleans during a sup-

posedly friendly game of billiards. I had the
devil's own luck and trounced the fellow four
times. Unfortunately, he was a wretched loser
and wanted to up the stakes. An all-or-nothing
sort of thing. Needless to say, my winnings
were extraordinary."

Brendan hesitated before he asked, "What
did he put up against your winnings?"

"His house and the land it sat on."

"He must've been confident."

"Oh, he was. I soon realized that he'd been
playing me false and was more accomplished
at the game than he'd let on."

"I presume he took you?"

Derek shook his head and smiled ironically.
"I found a way to distract him. His wife, a very
beautiful lady with the most remarkable green
eyes, had been silently watching from a corner.
Those sultry eyes hadn't missed a move I made.
I returned her avid interest whenever I could,
and was rewarded. Philippe LaFleur, I found,
proved susceptible to my ploy, and his play became so inferior that I was the victor."

"I fail to see your problem."

"I'm getting to it," Derek said. "LaFleur attempted to renege on our deal, offering me another piece of land. When I refused, he became
quite desperate. As you know, I loathe being
tied down to one place. What would I do with
his house and lands, no matter how grand they
were? I offered him an alternate payment."

"What did you ask for?"

"The favor of his wife's company for one
night."

Leaping to his feet, Brendan pinned his gaze on his brother.

"Before you say anything, let me explain. Nothing happened. To my amazement, LaFleur agreed to the terms, even the stipulation that he leave the premises and not return until morning."

"She must've been a goddamn goddess!" Brendan exclaimed.

Derek smiled. "She was. I had every intention of claiming my winnings, until we were alone. I'll spare you the minor details. We hadn't advanced past a kiss when I discovered a startling fact. This woman, whom I desired enough to forfeit LaFleur's holdings, was a gentle flower." Derek's feet slammed to the floor as he sat up straight. "The bastard beat her regularly. And it wasn't the first time he'd used her to pay off his losses. But I should've guessed when he insisted she liked to watch him play."

Derek rose and paced the room. "I wanted to kill him with my bare hands, but, of course, he'd left the house. We talked all night, that's all. In the morning, LaFleur came home. That's when I made a fatal error."

Brendan sucked in a much-needed breath in anticipation of the dire outcome.

"He knew nothing had happened. By God, he knew. Maybe it was the way she cringed when he looked at her. Before I could utter a word, tell him I considered the wager paid, the bastard struck her full in the face." Derek paused, his features contorting with pain. "She went down hard on the floor. I was sure he'd killed her."

Catching his arm, Brendan hauled Derek in front of him. "Was she dead?"

"No, but I didn't know it at the time. I've never felt such rage before. I grabbed his shirt-front and clipped him one on his jaw, and from then on it's all a haze in my mind. We fought for some time. I got in the last punch. LaFleur reeled back and fell, hitting his head against the fireplace. Good God, he bled like a stuck pig! I didn't mean to kill him, though he sure as hell had every intention of killing me. It was just like your run-in with Ashley."

"Were there any witnesses? The wife?"

"She came to a few minutes later and started to scream. Servants rushed in. I thought it best to vacate the premises." Gripping Brendan's arm, Derek hung his head. "LaFleur has a very influential brother. He's hired men to hunt me down and bring me back to hang."

"Did you explain to the law what had happened?"

"Hell, no. If I'd showed my face, I'd have been dead by now. They weren't interested in hearing it was an accident. They were out for blood—my blood." He returned to the desk and reached for the decanter of bourbon with shaky hands. "You're my only chance, the only one with enough money and prestige to see I get a fair trail. If LaFleur's henchmen catch up with me first, I'll pay with my life. But either way, I'm damned tired of hiding. Today was the first I've dared venture out."

"You should've come to me sooner."

Derek glanced up. "You'll help me?"

"I daresay I have friends who are more influential than this LaFleur. I'll have the matter straightened out with all due haste. Afterward, I want you on the first ship to England."

"England? But I don't want to go—"

Cutting off the rest of Derek's protest, Brendan strode with purpose from the room.

Chapter 18

Brendan found Sarah within minutes, sitting on a stone bench beneath a statue. She looked so forlorn, he hesitated to approach her, but he knew he could not delay the inevitable confrontation any longer. He advanced toward her.

Sarah's reaction was swift. Reminding him of a startled bird, she sprang to her feet and fled down the path.

With a curse on his lips, Brendan set off after her. Sarah was no longer burdened with child, and, as he'd once speculated, he soon lost sight of her. He came to a halt in front of a fountain and stared at several brown birds bathing in the glistening water. He felt he couldn't blame her for wanting to avoid him.

After a few moments, he grew impatient and called to her. Receiving no response, he detoured through the thick foliage, pushing branches out of his way, sure she'd chosen to hide in the greenery. A soft gasp to his right exposed her hiding place.

"Sarah," he whispered. "I know you're there.

Come out." When he received no answer, he spoke louder. "You can't elude me indefinitely, or is it your wish to confront me within earshot of others?"

She appeared suddenly, giving him a start. "You lied to me, let me think you were above reproach, when all along you were even more unscrupulous than Derek."

He had no counterattack to her softly uttered accusation. "I have no defense, except to stress that my affairs were with women of experience." Seconds passed. "You said once that you'd not hold a man's past against him if he'd truly repented."

"You could have told me."

"You held me in such high regard, I recoiled at the thought of disillusioning you. If you recall, you said you admired me for my righteous ways." He inched closer. "Can't you still admire me for the man I've become?"

"You lied to me." She stepped back, maintaining a distance between them. "I fell in love with you under false pretenses."

"Sarah," he said, his tone patient, "come home with me now. I'm sorry."

She adamantly shook her head.

Taking matters into his own hands, Brendan made his move. He lunged forward, gripped her arms, and pulled her into his arms. Prepared for a struggle, he clamped her in his embrace. But Sarah offered no resistance. Raising a brow, he studied her taut mouth.

"I haven't time for this nonsense, Sarah. You will cease immediately."

She broke into a bitter laugh. "Orders, your Lordship? Will you command me to love you, too?"

"If it's your wish to be commanded, so be it."

He slanted his lips over hers. Deploying all of his skills, he delved inside her mouth with his tongue in a searing kiss that left him throbbing and more desperate than ever to gain her forgiveness. Sarah moaned deep in her throat as she leaned against him and surrendered to his passionate embrace. He released his hold on her, and much to his relief, she remained in his arms willingly.

Several heart-pounding minutes later, she tore her mouth from his and shoved him away. "I won't let you seduce me at your whim. How . . . many . . . women have you kissed the way you kiss me?"

"I daresay hundreds, at the very least," he remarked cryptically.

"I should've known," she countered. "You claimed a reputation above reproach, yet you're utterly proficient at lovemaking. Such proficiency does come from experience, doesn't it?"

"But I never kissed any of them as I do you." He released a tortured sigh and brushed his fingers over her cheek. "Sarah, none of them matter. That is all in the past."

Tears glittered in her eyes as she turned from him.

"Sarah, I was at the window when you returned," he said solemnly.

Slowly, she faced him. "Appearances can be deceivin'."

"How well I know that. Why don't you explain what happened, why you kissed Derek."

"He kissed me, and I bit his lip and left."

Brendan clenched his jaw. So his brother had thought to win Sarah back. Judging by her manner, Sarah had resisted. But what about next time? Did she still harbor any feelings toward Derek?

"In case you're wonderin'," she said coolly, "I feel nothing for him now."

Relief swept through him. When she turned away again, he struggled to find words to repair the rift between them.

Sarah sedately headed back to the path, a slight droop to her shoulders. He watched her until she had vanished from sight. He'd allow her time to come to terms with the truths she'd learned about him, he decided.

But what if she never forgave him? his mind asked.

Bloody hell!

Gertrude touched an elegantly embroidered napkin to her lips and glanced across the large front room of their hostess, Mrs. Balfour. Spotting Brendan, she noted his bored expression. The dinner party to which they'd all been invited had turned out to be a tedious affair.

"I'll relieve you of your plate, *chérie*," Henri whispered, his warm breath brushing her ear. The most delightful shiver traveled down her spine. "When we return to your house, I shall relieve you of your inhibitions, as well."

Gertrude lowered her lashes and savored the husky quality of his voice, pleased that tonight at last he intended to further their courtship. She was more than ready. His nearness alone excited her in ways she'd never before known.

Their fingers met when he took her plate to hand it to a passing servant. Gertrude awarded him an encouraging smile. "I do believe I'm taking a headache. I'll express my regrets to Mrs. Balfour while you summon your driver."

Henri's dark eyes moved over her face with tender regard. "Ah, *mal de tête*. You are in luck." He leaned close. "I have the perfect cure for such a *maladie*."

A furious blush suffused Gertrude's cheeks. "Allow me to tell my nephew that we are leaving."

Gertrude inhaled a breath and walked toward Brendan. She saw him cast a wretched look in Sarah's direction. Sarah, however, seemed not to notice as she listened attentively while their hostess regaled her with a story.

Derek materialized out of a group of gentlemen, blocking Gertrude's path. "I suspect you wish to inform Brendan of your impending departure," he said. "I'll relay your message, if you wish." His eyes sparkled with mischief. "Your ardent suitor's chomping at the bit, madam. In case you were wondering, I plan to return rather late."

"I don't know what you mean to imply, young man," Gertrude spouted indignantly.

Derek gave her a devil-may-care smile. "I think you do."

"If you're so clever, why don't you do something to repair your brother's marriage." She searched the room again and nodded in Brendan's direction. "He's quite miserable, and so is Sarah. I have it on good authority that they've barely spoken for three days."

"Stratford, no doubt?"

Gertrude stiffened. "He's as concerned as I. Can't you speak with Sarah and soften her up a bit?"

"I've done my best, but she refuses to listen to anything I have to say. My guess is that you'll have more luck."

"I don't want to meddle in their business."

Derek cleared his throat. "Yet you expect me to?"

"You owe your brother a great deal for all he's doing in your behalf to clear your name. He's spent many hours and an outlandish amount of money hiring men to go to New Orleans and bribe the truth from LaFleur's manservant. Once the trial's over, you'll be free. I do hope you've learned a good lesson from this, and won't indulge in another of your malicious escapades."

"Until then all I need worry about is Rupert LaFleur. He still believes I murdered his brother."

"Put your faith in Brendan. All will be well."

"Your Mr. Montand is pacing the corridor. I'll do what I can to bring Sarah around, though

I suspect my efforts will be fruitless. Should I
fail, the chore will fall to you."

Gertrude caught his arm. "Who is it you're
seeing tonight?"

He lifted a dark brow, reminding her of Brendan. "Caroline Belmont. Surely you have no
objection. She's far from innocent."

"But she's married."

"So were Brendan's paramours."

"I'm sure your brother would object to your
choice of women."

Derek smiled. "He already knows. In fact,
I'm doing him a favor by seeing the lady."

"Rubbish!"

Derek adjusted his cuffs and glanced across
the room. "My dear aunt, you worry too much.
I'm precisely what the lady wants and deserves. Let me handle her in my own way."

After she had promised to drop by Brendan's
house the following day, Gertrude shook her
head and left her nephew. She had more important matters to attend to than his love life.
Furrowing her brow to pretend a headache, she
went to bid good night to her hostess.

Sarah pretended interest in the idle chatter of
two of St. Louis's most socially prominent
ladies. Her thoughts, however, were on Brendan. Her heart ached, and no lecture she'd
given herself could alleviate her hurt.

She had to restrain herself from searching for
his handsome visage in the crowded room. She
knew that if she found him with another
woman, she'd want to die. The oddest sensa-

tion fluttered over her skin, compelling her to find the source of her disquiet. She swung her gaze to her left—and found Brendan conspicuously watching her.

Her stomach tightened. Dear God, even knowing of his scandalous past, she was irrevocably drawn to him. Telling herself it was merely a physical attraction she felt, she tore her vision from him and found Derek standing in front of her. The two ladies greeted him before turning toward a matronly woman sporting a lavish assortment of jewels.

"Are you enjoying the party, dear heart?" Derek asked her.

"Actually, no," Sarah returned, then lowered her voice to a whisper. "I'm bored to tears."

"Aunt Gertrude has made me promise to convince you to see reason concerning my brother. I see by your set mouth that nothing I say will sway you."

"A very wise deduction," she returned.

"I liked you much better as a naïve farm girl, Sarah."

"I imagine you did. But you might as well move on to another more advantageous conquest. I'm married to Brendan, and won't ever consort with you again."

"Grant me a small amount of intelligence, Sarah."

"So you've already found someone."

"You sound surprised. Hammond men have been known to tire quickly of women."

His words brought an unwilling frown to Sarah's face.

"But I'm sure that's not the case with my brother," Derek continued in a more pleasant tone. "Brendan loves you. If you're as smart as I believe you are, you'll not hold his past against him. It's over and done with, my dear. Now, having done my duty, I beg your leave."

Sarah watched him tour the edge of the room and stop when he encountered Caroline Belmont. Disgusted that he'd want to align himself with the woman, she spun around. And collided with a large male body. Brendan's.

His fingers circled her arms, steadying her. His lazy grin confided his pleasure at her unexpected turn. "I daresay I'm ready to quit this travesty of a gathering."

"I am also," she said quietly, avoiding his gaze.

Within minutes, they were ensconced in the carriage, on their way home. The silence stretched endlessly, marred only by the crunch of the wheels on the road, grating on Sarah's nerves. She'd thought of him as her perfect Prince Charming and discovered him fallible. Had she expected too much?

Brendan had forgiven her affair with Derek.

Thank goodness he'd ceased his attempts to persuade her to forgive his wicked past. She'd needed the past few days to realize how much she still loved him.

His leg bumped hers, stirring heat in her body. Unbidden, their fiery coupling on the way to the lodge invaded her mind and sent a tremble racing to her toes.

"Are you cold, Sarah?" he asked.

Feverish was more like it, she thought. She burned for his touch, to have him whisper endearments in her ear as he caressed her all over. She'd missed him terribly. "I'm very warm."

Then the carriage halted in front of their house. Tibbs opened the door. Sarah allowed the servant to help her to the ground, then quickly escaped into the house and sought the safety of their bedroom.

Attired in her nightclothes, she dismissed Mathilda and headed for Rebecca's room. She desperately needed to hold her precious daughter. But when she tiptoed to the cradle, a sliver of light from the hall revealed a tall figure looming by the window.

Holding the baby in his arms, Brendan slowly walked toward her. His eyes looked dark and unfathomable, his mouth downcast. He kissed Rebecca's forehead before he gently placed the blanketed bundle in Sarah's arms.

Sarah's heart ached. He was such a good father to her daughter.

She remained in the nursery for half an hour. Finally, she crept back to her own room. She must tell Brendan that she was ready to forgive him, she thought. Dropping her robe on the rail, she slipped into bed. He hadn't made a move to touch her in the past three days.

His warmth invaded the entire bed. She'd accustomed herself to lying near the edge of the mattress to allow a wide berth between them. That night, however, she acutely felt the loss of his affection.

Sarah curled into a ball on her side. Minutes

passed. She'd just rolled over to tell him of her change of heart, but she found his large body filling the middle of the bed.

"Sarah . . ."

Reaching out to him, she slid close against him.

His arm came around her, urging her even more tightly against his body. "Does this mean you've forgiven me?"

"I was such a fool. What you did was long ago."

He eagerly kissed her cheeks, forehead, and nose, and eventually her lips. "It's been the longest three days of my life, Sarah. Promise me you'll never hate me again."

"I never hated you."

His hands touched her all over, stoking a fire that blazed out of control. His lips roamed at will and incited her until she begged him to stop. When she could no longer bear the exquisite agony, his hot body covered hers and loved her until her moans echoed from the walls.

He was inside her again, filling her completely, his whispered endearments making her whole and mending her heart. Her nails clawed his back, and she felt him flinch before he drove into her in frenzied abandon. She convulsed, fearing she'd shatter from the intensity of her release. But he remained hard, throbbing within her until she once again writhed beneath him.

His mouth claimed hers with a desperation he hadn't shown before, clearly demonstrating the depths of his love. Her body arched against his to draw him even further inside as her arms wrapped around his neck. She returned his kiss with a matching desperation, determined to show him how much she regretted her recent behavior.

When he finally lay beside her, spent, his breathing as erratic as hers, he said, "I feel as ancient as time. You've stolen my stamina."

"I shouldn't have married a man in his dotage." She slipped her leg over his and lay half across him. "Will you recover?"

"I daresay—in a month I should be ready to take you on again."

"A month?" She caressed his chest, venturing across his abdomen, but he caught her hand before she could reach any lower.

"A week, then."

"That's entirely too long," she protested. Finding his chest close at hand, she laved a trail down the center with her tongue.

"Bloody hell, you seek to hurry me to an untimely demise."

"That's not my intention, your Lordship; I merely mean to atone for taking so long to come to my senses."

He chuckled. "Consider your punishment served. Tomorrow, however, I may demand a more stringent restitution."

Sarah crooned and nipped at his belly, receiving a mumbled oath from her victim. "I'm your obedient servant, my lord. Will you be very demandin'?"

"I should say." Seizing her quickly, he flattened her atop him. "Will you dutifully submit?"

"Most dutifully, sir."

"Damn, Sarah, you tempt me to make love to you again before morning."

"Then I think you should."

Morning came too soon. Wondering what had awakened her, Sarah peered over her shoulder and saw that Brendan had already risen. She watched him pull on his pants and methodically fasten them.

He met her gaze with a confident grin. "Good morning, Sarah. Sleep well?"

"I was kept awake nearly all night, and well you should know it."

He came around the bed. Sarah scooted up against the backboard and opened her arms to him. But he threw off the covers, seized her about the waist, and lifted her to her feet.

"I had a merry time in my youth, and I'd probably behave that way again." He gently grazed his thumb across her lips. "But I've found true happiness at last. Are you sure you've totally forgiven me?"

"Do you doubt me after last night?"

"No. I just wanted to hear you say you love me."

Sarah smiled and, tilting her head, kissed his throat. "You know I do." Then, ducking past him, she darted to the foot of the bed. "But you might ask me again later just to be sure."

He raked his fingers through his hair and

frowned. "A properly biddable wife reacts appropriately."

Her smile turned mischievous. "But that's where you're mistaken. I'm not properly biddable, your Lordship."

"I daresay you tempt me to blister your feisty little ass," he threatened, his smile glowing with evil intent.

Sarah retreated a step. "You wouldn't dare!"

His eyes widened briefly, then sparked green lights as he started forward. Choking on a gasp, Sarah whirled around, threw open the door, and bounded into the hall. She tore down the stairs, nearly knocking over Mathilda, who bore a tray of food, and sped through the house to the private garden, where she sought haven beside a rose arbor.

She heard Brendan's thumping footsteps before she saw him. The door swung back on its hinges, banging against the wall. Dear God, he hadn't even taken the time to don his shirt. He stalked directly to the arbor. She'd thought to tease him, but it seemed his humor had turned to anger.

Sarah stepped to the side and flattened her back against the house. She should have minded her tongue, she thought. He looked magnificent enraged, a muscle ticking in his jaw, his hands fisted at his sides. He also looked quite capable of following through with his threat. Out of the corner of her eye, she spotted movement and realized Stratford had stuck his head out the open door.

"Is something amiss, Your Grace?"

"Nothing at all, Stratford," Brendan replied. "Sarah and I wanted to admire the roses."

"Very good, sir."

The servant disappeared inside, leaving them alone. Brendan's stance relaxed. He closed the distance between them, bracing a hand on the wall behind her, the other settling at her waist.

"Madam, I swear you'll have my hair gray before my time."

Sarah bit her lip, still unsure of his intentions. Gripping her chin, he forced her to meet his gaze. "I love *you*, Sarah. You have given me a rare gift." His lips touched hers in a kiss as light as a butterfly hovering over a flower.

"And what gift is that?"

"You've brought laughter into my life. More important, you've taught me to laugh at myself. Before I met you I was becoming rather staid."

"Oh? I never would have guessed it of you," she teased him. "It must be in your head. One's mind tends to get a bit fuzzy with the advancement of years."

Gathering her into his arms, he grinned. "It appears you need to be silenced yet again."

"As you wish."

Chapter 19

Gertrude arrived at precisely 3:00 P.M., with Derek in tow. Sarah, who had been attempting to stitch a tiny gown for Rebecca, set aside her sewing at the welcome interruption. She'd stabbed her finger three times already.

Gertrude fairly beamed that day, arousing Sarah's curiosity. Slanting an inquiring look at Derek, she found his expression gave no clue to the reason for his aunt's exceptional mood.

Derek came forward and kissed Sarah's cheek. Though the kiss was brotherly, the glint in his eyes betrayed his wayward intentions. "You're lookin' well," she told him as she stepped on the toe of his shoe.

"I've come to speak with Brendan," Gertrude announced as she dropped her gloves and reticule on a chair. "But first I'll have a word with you, dear. Derek, kindly fetch your brother, and do tell him it's urgent."

Aiming Sarah a resigned look, he faced his aunt and fell into an exaggerated bow. "Your obedient servant, Aunt Gertrude."

Gertrude broke into a wide grin. "If the rascal remains with me much longer, I'll have him as reformed as Brendan.''

Sarah gave Gertrude a dubious smile. Then, frowning, she said, "Forgive me if I don't share your confidence. I doubt he'll ever change."

"Continue to frown so, and you'll soon have wrinkles," Gertrude imparted. "I haven't much time, so I'll come to the point. You disappoint me, my dear. Why, my nephew has abandoned his womanizing ways, and don't think it was easy for him. He's by nature a man of rapacious appetites. He inherited *that* from both his grandfather and father. One would think you'd be grateful he's already sowed his wild oats. I've been told that a reformed rake is the logical choice for a husband. You won't find him taking a mistress, or even flirting behind your back."

"I never doubted he'd be faithful."

"Ha! You take much for granted. He could easily have any woman he desires. However, in case you've not noticed, he has a high sense of honor."

"I've already forgiven him," Sarah imparted quietly.

Gertrude, who had already opened her mouth to render another argument in Brendan's behalf, fell silent. "Well, I'm pleased to hear it. But you might've waited. I had rehearsed my speech all night."

"You should've been a lawyer."

Brendan arrived with Derek at that moment, concern on his face. "Kindly tell me what's so urgent," he said as soon as he had entered the parlor.

Gertrude motioned for Derek to close the doors. She paused, smiling. "Mr. Montand has proposed marriage. I, of course, accepted. He should arrive this evening to ask you for my hand."

"What wonderful news," Sarah said, embracing Gertrude.

Brendan also offered his congratulations. "I presume I've no time to consider Mr. Montand's request."

Gertrude looked aghast. "Indeed not! Refuse him and I'll make your life hell."

Brendan's gaze shifted to Sarah before he said ruefully, "Madam, I prefer to acquiesce to your wishes. I'm fortunate indeed to have found bliss in my union."

Sarah squirmed, aware of three sets of eyes regarding her.

A thunderous bang came from the area of the hall. All four heads turned.

"What was that ungodly noise?" Gertrude demanded.

Brendan and Derek both moved toward the exit, with Brendan saying, "Sounded as if someone broke in the front door."

"Oh, surely not!" Sarah said.

The pocket doors slammed open, revealing three men, one of whom held a long, wicked-looking knife against Stratford's throat.

Gertrude looked aghast. "What's the meaning of this intrusion?"

Brendan held up a hand to stay her. He

glanced at Derek. "LaFleur's cutthroats, I presume?"

Derek nodded with a grimace.

Sarah pressed a hand over her stomach to stem the rise of panic. Gertrude had told her of Derek's trouble, but she'd assured Sarah that Brendan had the situation well under control. The men, dressed in dirty clothes, torn floppy hats, with guns stuffed into their belts, appeared ruthless enough to murder them all.

Stratford's face had drained of blood. He threw Brendan a beseeching look.

"That's him," the one holding the knife said, indicating Derek with a finger. "Other's too big."

Shoving Derek behind him, Brendan assumed an implacable stance. "Gentlemen, you'll have to come past me." He glared at each in turn. "Which of you has the gumption to try?"

Sarah drew in a breath. What chance did Brendan have against these seasoned ruffians? He must have been mad to taunt them.

Sporting wide grins that showed rotten teeth, two of the men appeared ready to accept Brendan's challenge.

Derek, however, leaped out from behind his brother. Holding his fisted hands in front of his face, he announced, "It's my fight."

Brendan grabbed Derek's arm. Inclining his head to Stratford, he said, "I advise caution."

With a lump in her throat, Sarah noted a rivulet of blood running down Stratford's neck, staining the pristine whiteness of his shirt. Terror seized her heart. She shot a glance at Gertrude. The poor woman appeared stricken, as pale as Stratford.

A squeal that reminded Sarah of her father's prize hog jarred Sarah's attention back to the group by the door. Her eyes as wide as saucers, she watched as chaos erupted.

Stratford had locked his fingers on his captor's nose and, holding the bulbous appendage in a vise, jerked the man's head upward. The knife skittered to the floor at the same moment that Brendan and Derek threw themselves at the other two.

Sarah and Gertrude were forced to rush to different corners of the room as the struggling adversaries stumbled into its center.

Brendan and his assailant bumped into a table, making it totter.

Sarah held her breath. Had she won the man of her heart, only to see him die? She quickly searched the room for a weapon and spotted a figurine. But Gertrude dashed forward and snatched it a second before the table crashed to the floor.

Sarah closed her eyes. The deadly scuffles seemed more ominous when she had only hearing by which to judge. The sound of fists meeting flesh caused her to wince. She realized that she couldn't bear not knowing who had struck whom. She opened her eyes in time to see Brendan struck in the eye by his foe, and she gasped.

A second later, Derek took a blow to his stomach, but he got in two of his own before he crashed to the floor, the victim of a beefy fist to the side of his head. He lay dazed, unable to come to Brendan's aid.

Sarah searched the room again and spotted a heavy potted fern, when a clamorous bang brought her gaze to the doorway.

The man who had held Stratford prisoner fell in a limp heap at the manservant's feet. Sarah grinned in amazement. Holding a very large kitchen pan in her hands, Mathilda stood over that unconscious miscreant.

But the fight wasn't over yet. Derek's attacker joined forces with the man who was fighting with Brendan. Outraged by the unsporting tactics of two against one, Sarah didn't take time to think. She sprinted across the room and leaped onto the closest man's back, locking her fingers at his throat. Shouting a vile oath, the man danced about in an attempt to throw her off.

Within moments Sarah's prey managed to shake her nearly senseless, forcing her to unlock her fingers. She slid down his back but landed on her feet in one quick motion. The man spun around. His brown eyes lanced her with murderous intent.

Sarah's heart raced. In her youth she'd often engaged in scuffles with her brothers. While they'd never purposely allowed her to win, they'd never looked at her with such venom, even when they were angry.

"Well, ain't you a sweet little thang," the man said. He wiped his hand across his mouth.

"Hey, Jeb, I got me a wildcat aimin' ta claw me."

Brendan released a growl and tackled his opponent.

Sarah heard their bodies hit the floor. Though she never took her eyes from the smelly man ogling her, she was aware that Brendan was rolling over and over, unmercifully pummeling the other's man's face.

Sarah's opponent, tired of eyeing her, lunged for her. She was faster than he. She awarded his shin a sharp kick, which made him hop just long enough for her to punch his hose. She then brought a knee up to wound him in a vulnerable spot. With a bellow reminiscent of a scalded bull, he sank to his knees, clutching his groin. Determined that he wouldn't come at her again, she bent down and sneaked the gun from his belt. After she had cocked the weapon, she leveled it at his head.

Brendan rolled from his downed prey and sprawled out on the floor.

"Don't move!" Sarah ordered both men. "Gertrude, come here." When Brendan aunt's appeared at her side, Sarah forced the gun into her trembling hands. "Hold the gun even with his head. Shoot if he so much as moves a muscle."

"Oh, dear me," Gertrude said, her voice much higher than normal. "I've never shot a weapon before."

Sarah positioned Gertrude's finger on the trigger. "Just pull this back if they try anything." Passing by the man she'd brought down, Sarah pinned him with her gaze. "I wouldn't even breathe if I were you. She just might blow off your head."

The man started, his mouth gaping open. "I ain't movin', no, sirree."

Checking the doorway, Sarah saw that Stratford had taken possession of the knife and stood like a triumphant gladiator, one foot squarely in the middle of his former attacker's chest. His dignity repaired, he gave the impression he'd have liked nothing better than to use the blade in his hand.

Sarah hurried to Brendan and fell to her knees beside him. She lifted one of his hands, holding it to her chest as she surveyed his injuries. One eye was already swelling shut. Blood trickled from the corner of his mouth from a small cut, his left cheek was bruised, and the skin on his knuckles was broken.

Dear God, those awful men might've killed him, she thought.

Sarah heard Derek moan and swear as he crawled to his knees. Spotting his aunt, he climbed unsteadily to his feet and took the gun from her quaking hands.

"You may have it with my blessings," she told him. Walking a crooked line to the settee, Gertrude collapsed in a faint.

Mathilda gasped loudly and ran to Gertrude's assistance.

"Brendan," Sarah called as she brushed his ruffled hair from his brow. "Please, don't die." Grabbing his shoulders, she shook him hard, banging his head on the floor in the process. "Brendan! Wake up!"

Her hands were suddenly grasped and held against his chest. "Bloody hell, Sarah. My head hurts abominably as it is. Would you put another crack in it?"

"I was tryin' to revive you."

Brendan chuckled, then grimaced. "Such wifely devotion."

She threw herself atop him and began to kiss his wounds. "When I thought they might kill you—"

"You remembered how much you loved me?"

She looked into his hazel eyes and drowned in the emotion he made no attempt to hide. Gently, she caressed his brow. "I'm doomed to love only you."

He angled his head as if to kiss her, but Stratford cleared his throat.

"Sir, this gentleman has awakened, and I believe he objects to my foot on his person. Have I your permission to fillet him, should the need arise?"

Sarah noticed that Stratford's prisoner immediately held his hands in the air.

Brendan grunted as he pushed himself to a sitting position. "I daresay that would create an unsightly mess—blood all over the floor and all. But if you feel you must . . . If he decides to make a confession, naming his employer and such, I think you should reconsider."

Feeling an urge to giggle, Sarah clapped a hand over her mouth. Brendan had sounded so serious that the man's eyes had bulged. Apparently having lost his voice, he nodded emphatically.

After Brendan stood and offered a hand to Sarah, he said to Mathilda, "Have Tibbs summon the authorities at once." Facing Derek, he added, "I believe you'll have no more trouble from LaFleur's brother. When these considerate fellows implicate him in the scheme to do you bodily harm, not to mention taking the law into his own hands, he'll see reason, if not a stretch behind bars."

Gertrude sat up on the settee and surveyed the room. "Thank God it's over."

"You may rest easy, madam," Brendan assured her. Slipping an arm around Sarah's waist, he hauled her tightly against him. "Everything is as it should be."

He regarded Sarah so intently, squinting to see through his puffy eye, that she smiled at the comical image he made.

"No argument, Sarah?"

"No, your Lordship."

He threw back his head and laughed. "I should mark down this occasion, then."

"Why don't you kiss me instead?"

"We've an audience, madam, or haven't you noticed?"

Sarah flung her arms around him, then stood on her toes and tilted her head in invitation.

Brandishing a wide grin, Brendan cupped her chin. To the applause of his family and servants, he gifted her with a long, deeply passionate kiss that would have put Prince Charming himself to shame.

The authorities had come and gone, and the cutthroats were now safely behind bars. Holding Rebecca in her arms, Sarah left the bottom step and paused in the hall outside of Brendan's study, where Stratford stood his post. Smiling, she crept closer.

Stratford immediately tugged on his vest. "Madam instructed me to—"

Sarah held a finger to her mouth and pressed her ear to the door. Masculine voices from inside of the room informed her that Brendan was still closeted with Mr. Montand. "Have they come to an agreement?"

Stratford's brown eyes twinkled. "A few minutes past."

Sarah smiled. "Gertrude will be so happy. Have you relayed the news to her?"

"I was just about—"

"Stratford! What's taking so long?" Gertrude appeared in the hall and joined Sarah and the servant. "I see your problem," she told the man. "When I sent you to eavesdrop I hadn't an inkling that you'd find an accomplice."

"They're toasting your marriage right now," Sarah informed Brendan's aunt. "But of course you knew Brendan wouldn't let you down."

"I knew no such thing. My nephew can be obstinate when he wants."

The front door opened, and Derek stuck his head inside. "I'm already late. If you don't hurry along, I'll be forced to take your rig."

Gertrude whirled around. "You'll do nothing of the kind, young man. I'll not have that Caroline Belmont fouling the inside of it with her noxious perfume."

Brendan and Mr. Montand joined the gathering in the hall. Shaking his head, Brendan remarked, "I presume that once you're safely wed, Aunt Gertrude, you'll contrive to titter outside your husband's door when he's in private conference."

Mr. Montand shook hands with Brendan, then took charge of Gertrude. Whispering in her ear, he escorted her out the front door. Derek made to follow, but Brendan called him back.

"Don't forget our arrangement."

Derek's eyes narrowed on his brother. "I presumed you were jesting."

"I assure you I was not!"

"But I—"

"I regret that you won't have time to . . . visit Caroline tonight, as your ship leaves very early tomorrow."

"But you can't expect me to up and leave so soon. Why, I—"

"Have no worries to hold you here," Brendan finished for him. "When you reach England, your life's your own. But I advise you to have a care. I won't be available to buy you out of trouble."

Derek strode inside, straight up to Sarah. Holding Brendan's gaze, he said, "Since you're determined to ruin my fun, I'll have a token to see me through my voyage."

Before Sarah could realize what he intended to do, Derek had slipped an arm around her shoulders and kissed her soundly. Squeezed in the middle, Rebecca released a howl. After he freed Sarah, Derek gazed at his daughter. "Good-bye, little one. I wish . . . " He didn't finish his sentence; instead he turned on his heel and hurried outside.

Sarah glanced at Brendan. There was sadness in his eyes. Despite all that had passed between them, she realized Brendan would miss his brother. And judging by the misty look in Derek's eyes, he too would miss this family.

Upset, Brendan walked to the door and slammed it shut.

Rebecca cried louder, until Brendan scooped her into his arms. "There now, sweet. Your papa has you."

Sarah held back a sob at the tender scene. Her daughter responded to Brendan's soothing words.

"You have made another conquest, Your Grace," Stratford said before he caught himself. Blanching, he aimed an apologetic look at Sarah. "Begging your pardon," he added.

Sarah reclaimed Rebecca and pressed her into Stratford's arms. "You may gain your pardon by taking our daughter to Marie. It's past Rebecca's bedtime."

Stratford looked at Brendan, his face draining of color.

"You've had your orders, man. But do be careful."

The servant's face paled even more. "But sir . . ."

A ghost of a smile hovered on Brendan's lips. "Best to hurry before Miss Rebecca christens your coat."

Stratford hurried up the stairs.

Alone in the hall, Brendan pulled Sarah against him. "And now, madam, perhaps you'd like to tell me why you allowed my brother to kiss you."

"I didn't allow him. You were here and saw it all."

"I daresay."

"Surely, you don't think I wanted him to kiss me. Why, he's every bit as much a scoundrel as when I first met him!"

Brendan threaded his fingers into Sarah's hair, sending pins flying to the floor. "If my brother ever presumes to sample what's mine again, he'll find himself on a ship to Hades."

Sarah snuggled against his chest. "Were you jealous, your Lordship?"

"Absurd. You're mine, Sarah. Because I love you so much, I have trust in your love."

Sarah gazed fondly at his bruised and battered face, a face she loved desperately. "Have you forgiven Derek for all he's done?"

"I have. But I won't let him know it for at least a year. Because of him, I found you." He kissed her forehead, then her nose. "And I have Rebecca. One day Derek's past will catch up with him. Likely he'll not be as fortunate as I was."

Touching a finger to his swollen eye, Sarah

awarded him a sympathetic look. "You're a silly sight, your Lordship."

A dark brow slanted upward. "You dare mock your lord and master, Sarah?"

"Have you an objection?"

"Not if you intend to humbly apologize and promise to be extremely biddable," he returned.

"When we're upstairs—" Sarah started to say.

Brendan swept Sarah into his arms. "Madam, when we arrive upstairs, you'll be thoroughly occupied."

Sarah's laughter mingled with Brendan's as he carried her up the winding staircase.

Epilogue

Georgia, 1871

Seated beside Sarah in a small rented buggy, with Rebecca perched on his lap, Brendan resisted the urge to scratch his nose. Brushing his hand over Rebecca's curly dark hair had no effect. Strands of the unruly mane continued to fly in the breeze, whipping across his face.

"Sit still, dear," Sarah chastened the little girl. "You're makin' Poppy wrinkle his nose."

Brendan glanced at his wife and saw her lips twitch. "You encourage her."

"I do no such thing," Sarah countered. "Rebecca arrived at the name *Poppy* on her own."

Brendan sighed and looked down the well-used dirt road. According to his estimation, they'd reach the bend Benjamin Stevens had described in his last letter within minutes. He could barely restrain his patience, for he knew the surprise he'd planned for Sarah was sure to leave her speechless.

"You've taken the wrong turnoff."

"Did I?" Brendan asked with an air of innocence.

"This is the way to the ruins of the old

house." She tugged on his coat sleeve, pointing with the other hand. "You should've gone *that* way. Brendan, are you listenin' to me at all?"

"I always listen when you chastise me, love."

Sarah grumbled under her breath.

He met her gaze. "I listen much the same as you."

Her eyes widened. "I beg your pardon."

"I daresay I'm not nearly as dense as you believe, Sarah. You haven't fooled me once in the past year. You meekly agree with me, then do as you wish. You're fortunate you married such a mild-tempered man."

Sarah pressed a hand over her mouth. "Forgive my laughter."

"You disagree with my assessment?"

"Indeed not, your Lordship. Would I presume to disagree with you?"

Brendan released the laugh he'd been determined to master. "Not only do you challenge my authority repeatedly; you keep secrets." He lowered his vision to her stomach, noting that the deep blue afternoon dress fit more snugly than a week ago. "We've nearly arrived. Will you confess now, or do you intend to wait until we're home?"

"You knew?"

"My dear wife, I know every inch of your luscious body. I knew you carried my child within weeks."

She leaned closer, gazing up at him with bright eyes. "Does it please you?"

"Yes, Sarah. It pleases me immensely. Do you think it'll be a boy?"

"I daresay," she said, lowering her voice to imitate him. "That's your preference, isn't it?"

He leaned down and kissed her, prolonging the pleasure for as long as he considered it safe to take his eyes from the road. The front wheel detoured into a rut, tipping the buggy and causing Rebecca to bounce with glee and kick her feet. A sharp pain in a tender area brought Brendan back to his driving.

Brendan muttered beneath his breath. "Our daughter is determined to unman me." Brendan shook the reins with his free hand and maneuvered the wheel back onto the road. " 'Tis lucky the child's already growing. Another kick like that and I'll be ruined."

Sarah giggled, and fussed with the pink bow in Rebecca's hair. "I sincerely doubt that."

They reached the bend, and Brendan sent the buggy hurrying along the road. Several minutes passed before Sarah looked up. Her gasp of astonishment delighted Brendan.

"Glory be!"

"Poppy . . . house!"

Brendan ruffled Rebecca's hair and smiled at Sarah. "My wedding present to you. I've had the most devilish time corresponding with your father, making arrangements, and transferring money without your knowledge. Your father and I have gone into business together."

Tears began streaming down Sarah's face. Fumbling in Brendan's pocket, she stole his handkerchief and wiped her eyes. "You rebuilt Whisperin' Oaks. And it's even more beautiful than before!"

"Are you happy?"

"Yes . . . oh, Brendan, you . . . How can I ever thank you?"

"Give us three years and your father will have recouped all of his former wealth. As of last month, I'm the owner of the Hammond Compress Company, based in St. Louis. Work has already begun on a two-story plant on Park Avenue at the levee. The fifteen acres I've purchased in St. Louis should handle a capacity of one hundred and fifty thousand bales of compressed cotton. With the new hydraulic and steam press I've ordered, I should be able to compress five hundred bales of cotton to a thickness of nine inches, thus reducing shipping costs tremendously."

"My father grew the best cotton."

Brendan laughed. "I'm gambling that he still does."

"Oh, Brendan you've given me the greatest gift. You've restored my family's pride."

Rebecca bounced up and down again, bringing a groan from Brendan. "It's a small token of my undying affection."

Sarah broke into a fresh wave of tears.

Directing his attention ahead, Brendan drove along with a broad smile. His life had changed drastically since that foggy day outside of London when he'd been forced to kill Lord Ashley. Derek now claimed the title of Wicked Warwick, but Brendan didn't care. Having Rebecca call him Poppy was heaven indeed for a man of his former reputation. But having Sarah as his wife, he thought, was more reward than he deserved.

"You're thoroughly wicked to have kept this from me," Sarah said when she spotted her family standing on the verandah of the grand new house.

Brendan's smile slid into a grin.